But fo

But for the Lovers

A NOVEL BY

Wilfrido D. Nolledo

DALKEY ARCHIVE PRESS

First published in 1970 by E. P. Dutton & Co., Inc.

First Dalkey Archive Edition, 1994

Library of Congress Cataloging-in-Publication Data

Nolledo, Wilfrido D.
But for the lovers : a novel / by Wilfrido D. Nolledo ;
foreword by Robert Coover.—1st Dalkey Archive ed.
p. cm.
1. World War, 1939-1945—Philippines—Fiction. I. Title.
PR9550.9.N65B88 1994 823—dc20 94-9184
ISBN 1-56478-067-8

Partially funded by grants from the National Endowment for the Arts
and the Illinois Arts Council.

NATIONAL ENDOWMENT FOR THE ARTS

Dalkey Archive Press
Campus Box 4241
Illinois State University
Normal, IL 61790-4241

Printed on permanent/durable acid-free paper and bound in the United States of America

For Blanca, Natasha, Melissa,
Ruel Antonio and Orlando

Foreword

Robert Coover

"MAGIC REALISM" AS A LITERARY STRATEGY seems to have arisen primarily in societies with a rich indigenous (usually oral) culture but overrun, often cruelly, by successive waves of more powerful foreign invaders (military, religious, economic), each leaving its cultural traces. One thinks of the islands and nations of the Caribbean basin, India, certain parts of Africa, where the cultural overlays are sometimes so improbable as to seem like surreal dreamscapes given body and duration. Traditional narrative techniques prove inadequate to the paradoxical reality of such places: they can describe, comment upon, demystify, interpret, ironize, show the (comic, tragic, etc.) consequences of, suggest ways of living with or of resisting it, but cannot wholly invade the living dream itself. This is given vivid ironic expression in Placido Rey's history lesson near the end of this book: it's like getting shut up in a small neat room with the doors and windows sealed, while outside, in the real world, madness (life as here lived) reigns. "Literature" often seems like that to me: a safe haven for "serious" people for whom the outside world is a bit much.

No safe haven here. Wilfrido Nolledo's *But for the Lovers*, set in an island nation with an exotic indigenous culture, cruelly overrun by successive waves of marauding conquerors, evangelists, and merchants, is a fearless—and fearsome—book, its author's eyes wide open and imagination running at full throttle, a genuine masterpiece, and a close cousin to those great narratives of the Latin American "magic realists" that were appearing around the same time this book was being written.

Which is to say, some time ago: more than a quarter of a century. For *But for the Lovers* also belongs to that rare subcategory, the undiscovered masterpiece. It was written in the late 1960s, published after many delays in 1970, lost to sight almost as soon as it appeared. No one—but for the lovers—knows about this book. It is now yours to discover, as though until now unseen.

Manila, the Philippines, late 1944, early 1945. The Japanese Empire, though still virulently tenacious, is crumbling, the Yanks are liberating the city and nation for the second time in less than half a century (last time it was from the Spaniards, whose priests and teachers still hold their own in the ongoing cultural war) and are doing it in their usual straightforward fashion of bombing the bejesus out of the place. All the complex strands of native Filipino, Chinese, Spanish, Japanese, and American culture are merging in one explosive watershed moment, utterly inevitable and utterly mad.

The literary master who would find the means to capture this moment in all its fullness was, at that moment in Manila in early 1945, just celebrating his own twelfth birthday. The son of a lawyer and a nurse, the young Wilfrido Nolledo had a major reputation around town as a wily street scavenger, part of the pushcart brigade of devil-may-care foodstore looters in the Japanese districts, and after the Liberation a dealer in foodstuffs with the G.I. bases, where he became something of a camp mascot, treated to rations, cigarettes and chocolate bars.

Not surprising, then, that when he felt prepared at last to tell this story a couple of decades later, he should choose as one of his three principal heroes the cunning and infinitely resourceful street urchin, beggar, pickpocket, courier for the underground resistance, survivor and faithful provider Amoran. The other two members of the odd (but allegorically suggestive) trio of room thirteen at the Ojos Verdes boardinghouse are a young girl fleeing from ruthless village suitors (her name, though lost throughout the Occupation, is "Alma") and an old broken-down Spanish actor named Hidalgo, who, like the hidalgos of the seventeenth-century picaresque novels, is clinging desperately to an elegant but elitist past that is no more.

In the cruel, nightmarish present that these three vagabonds share, everything is in violent transition, love a weird kind of constant, but terror the one truth everyone can count on. As in dreams, archetypes arise like mythic ghosts: the crazed prophet Vanoye, the lascivious landlady Tira Colombo, the sadomasochistic Japanese Major Shigura and his vindictive Sergeant Yato, bearer of the samurai past, the downed American pilot Jonas Winters, the revolutionary showboater Deogracias, and all the others who come and go in these vibrant pages. The savage past coexists, convulsively, with the savage present, all of it rising from the page through a rich tropical undergrowth of multilingual language play.

This language play, as Jackson I. Cope noted in *New Letters* at the time of *But for the Lovers*' publication, is not mere surface decoration, but "is part of the ultimate metaphor which is the novel. . . . It is a personal language, and yet one insistent upon encompassing massive segments of past styles, chanting and cataloguing its pedigrees in an act of desertion, obsequies preliminary to a rite of renewal." It is a kind of magical incantation that, miraculously, conjures up the unimaginable real.

But for the Lovers was first published in 1970 by E. P. Dutton & Co. Its editor was the legendary Hal Scharlatt, who died shortly after, not yet forty, on an indoor tennis court. Without Scharlatt, Nolledo had no one in the industry to champion his writing. Thus it was that one of the best books of the decade, abandoned by its own publisher, came and went virtually without notice. A second Nolledo novel, *Cassandra Pickett in the Wings,* accepted by Scharlatt, was never published, and all further submissions were returned unread.

At the time, Nolledo was living in Iowa City, working as Managing Editor and Fiction Editor of the then-new *Iowa Review,* but soon thereafter returned to the Philippines, where he taught, worked as a journalist and magazine editor, scripted a dozen movies, won awards for unpublished work, and somehow, in a vacuum, with the tenacity of Amoran, the longing of Hidalgo, and the passionate commitment of Placido Rey, kept the writing going.

At his son's behest, Nolledo returned to this country a few years ago, around the time of his sixtieth birthday, and now lives with his wife Blanca in the Los Angeles area, near the rest of his family. After four years of editing a Filipino-American newsweekly, he is now working full-time at his writing, completing a new novel and revising two old ones.

But for the Lovers

Prologue

HE WAS BEGINNING TO EAT FLOWERS and the crescent moon was in his eyes when he awoke again. One night long ago when they had intercepted a code from the enemy on the shortwave and had not needed him anymore, they pulled out their tents, mantled him with leaves, and left him. They left him a rifle, a buri basket and a book of psalms, for the Major had decreed in defense of this murder: Let the little legionnaire lie here and die; it is written, it shall be read. But the boy went on sleeping and did not die and when he awakened it was to see (it was to find himself alone) a bird, a white-winged maya dart in from the west, perhaps headed for the monsoon. Steadying the Springfield, he cocked the hammer with a quivering thumb, and waited. It flew away, whatever it was, and now he squinted up and remembered that it was the first time in a long spell he had seen the sky, and he thought: It is longer, lonelier and lovelier than any of my prayers. He sighted the nimbus—an eagle in captivity—and fired.

Lord, he said, I am punching holes in your garret.

Glang-glang-glang

"Is that a guitar somewhere?" he asked aloud.

It was not music he heard, only himself.

Days passed.

When he was hungry, which was always, he drank brook water. When he was not hungry, which was never, he siphoned brook water. Made heron-beaked wind-planes out of old newspapers from his knapsack which also contained: a Ping-Pong ball, a bolo, and a pair of scissors.

It had become his habit to glare back at the sun. As he did, he realized that the solar system had dilating eyes, an endless ego. So now he only stared: at the moon. How whimsical it is, he reflected. And how infinitely tender.

Now recalling.

The fifth columnists devouring goat kidneys in the market. Unholy Moses, the dynamite they planted in a Japanese bower that had eviscerated not the saboteurs but only the Mandarin chef who was boiling asparagus. The aircraft painted with two red ciphers on each wing swoop down gracefully, noiselessly from a blazing easel one morning: to strafe dung gorges in the rice fields and the bees and the butterflies engraved on verdant plains; and even the cabbages, calmly, peacefully (he had watched all this from a veranda, smiling like an idiot). The company sawbones. Who got uproariously drunk. On his nth anniversary. While revamping a corporal lengthwise. With a razor. Attaching a gumamela *to the man's esophagus. Sewing up the mess again with safety pins. The patient, sure enough, had expired swiftly of floral hemorrhage.*

Demented in the marshes in the moonlight, he thought he saw a deer and straddled it. It was a girl wearing an army trenchcoat.

She howled.

He climbed an acacia tree to seek safety from his dreams.

Midnight. He felt her tugging at his shoes.

Centipede! Centipede! she shrieked.

They grappled with a beastie. Pulling out the bolo from the knapsack, he started to slash, slash, slash in the thicket. Chuckling, he dropped the blade and examined: the bulk of a man. An arm lay unsocketed. He grabbed it and flogged the perforated body: the solar plexus, the vertebra, the collarbone.

Wake up! he ordered.

No comment.

He towed it to the river, genuflected, and commended it to the brine.

In the morning, while he was watching the girl disrobe, the corpse swam to the surface like a crocodile. He hauled it in and kindled a fire around it.

You can get up now, he said cheerfully.

Still the carcass demurred.

Burrowing a hole in the mud near his sentinel site, he crammed this amoeba in. He noticed the length of its remaining arm and dug another pit. The wrist stuck out. He chopped it off with the bolo and deposited it in another, smaller hole.

But he was disconsolate: You never actually bury a volcano. There's always a resurrection.

At dusk, the girl, refreshed, spoke to the acacia.

"What are you guarding?"

"The ammunition," he replied.

"Of course," she said, scanning his camp area and its surrounding hilly terrain, a burnt, blistered patch of land in the foliage heat. Cinder at noon. A strip of dewy sand clamped tight in the evening cold.

"I am guarding the ammunition," he repeated, letting her come closer.

Though neither camp nor ammunition could be discerned from the bivouac, she did not laugh. One did not doubt one's armor. And besides, what could one do with a night that had subtracted the United States from the realm of possibility?

"Four times five equals twenty," the boy was muttering. "Five times five equals twenty-five. I am going to Guadalupe. They have guns in Guadalupe."

That night, he was more coherent.

"What year is it?"

"Nine-teen-for-ty-two," she answered loftily.

"Then we are at war. . . ."

War hissed grotesquely in the stratosphere, rumbled in the creeping gullets; not the burp of infiltrators, nor thunder (The Bomb would be heard later), neither lightning: but the crackling of the bush, the cackling in the canyons, and the Apocalypse coming into its houri. Beating on the drum, the fierce love of the cicadas broke wind, undid the peace.

Chanting she was.

Eagerly he picked up the tune so that for a moment they sang together. It was her hint. She advanced to touch his cheek, to trust the bleary, abstract eyes. Then she took his hand.

It was truce. It was armistice.

For two weeks they drifted around like sleepwalkers, splitting cherries and praising each other. One night, she confided in him. She was Alma, yes, Alma, she said. Over fifteen. A runaway from a plantation and three jealous suitors who always violated her in whispers and immortalized her bosom on alley-wall surrealism in town. She told him about the guitar that followed her forever. The boy recollected: his name was Aron. American. Born in Los Angeles. Zodiac Aries. A raw recruit in the U.S. peacetime army. Yes, yes, he would be her beau—bona fide and brave. She promised to teach him her dialect, diphthongs par excellence.

And so they made a pact.

They unlaced their shoes; waded in the pond.

"Do you know what they did to Pearl Harbor?" he asked.

"St. Peter died that day," she answered dreamily.

"My Commander says a bearded colonel herded all the blond people on a tramp steamer called the Red Cross *till only the wahines who danced the hula remained."*

"When he was alive," said Alma, "my father told me of a hermit who gathered lions, antelopes and gazelles on a raft."

He caught her staring at him and hid his head under an arm in a dizzy, delectable shyness, his eyes narrowing to slits. She blew at them in joyous alarm.

Eureka!

"In Indiana," he said, "everybody is called 'thee.'"

A boat drifted in. They regarded it without interest. At night she complained that her ankles were frozen; he pulled out some grass and covered them.

"Where is the North Star?" she asked.

He produced the scissors. Grinning foolishly, he clipped a lock of her hair.

She blushingly removed her hairpins.

Always at dusk there was a rustling in the hills: perhaps silk hanging out to dry, and in the children a pain near joy seized them with trembling. The girl seemed to turn more Quaker than the grandmother he remembered; the boy became more concerned over the bare feet he knew grew colder in the dew and he shielded them with more grass. She unclasped her hands and received his own, both of them joining fingers fervently, reverently, as though some pearl lay trapped inside their moist palms. They leaned slowly forward, and awkwardly, quite awkwardly, pressed their lips nervously together, frightened and ecstatic, pale but very deep.

"We are terrible," she gasped.

He could not look at her.

One evening while listening to the croaking of frogs, they heard the moans of another voice. It was Alma who inspected and immediately reported that a Japanese sailor was bleeding in a culvert. They found a canteen of alcohol in his overseas kit and drained it on his shoulder. His sword they buried under a heap of wet cuttings; then prayed wordlessly over his wound.

At dawn the relief workers saw how very young their captive was. Who bowed profusely and made it known to his captors that he was a deserter from the Imperial Japanese Navy, bound for Manila Bay. By way of introduction, he was, he said—all the while displaying courtly manners that charmed his juvenile audience no end—Quasimoto. Alas, there was no letter "q" in his native alphabet, he explained despondently (bowing from the waist down, it seemed, with every syllable), but his forebears were something of rascals, and thus, he, Quasimoto IV, was born out of wedlock and had deservedly been doomed to a name that, in an obsolete (though not quite extinct) but still very powerful Nipponese caste, signified an extreme loss of face.

"But I think Quasimoto IV is such a distinguished title," said Alma as her elbow nudged into her beau's side for corroboration.

The boy, not yet thoroughly grounded on his duties as consort, stiffened into attention. With a start, and remembering their pledge by the pond, catching his perjury in her sharp glance, he nodded dumbly, even returning and improving upon one of the sailor's princely bows.

Quasimoto seemed pleased.

"Arigato," *he said in turn; his tone, not military now, gentling in his language. "In my country" (bowing once more) "that means thank you."*

As if a second elbow and another sharp glance had been fired at him, the boy, minus coaching, extended a hand. When he spoke now, his usually off-key tenor assumed a twangy, mannered accent.

"Salamat din," *he enunciated with difficulty, rolling the two words on his tongue like a carpet.*

"That means thank you, too—in my country," Alma translated proudly, her arms relaxed now.

"You have a boat," observed Quasimoto.

"What shall we do with it?" asked Alma, bending grimly for the hem of her dress. But intercepting the wanton spirit in the men's stance, interpreting there the chambers of the sea, a tremulous vignette of rig, rudder and motor churning, cruising the Everglades for swans, palm fronds and Madagascar junk, dredging from that haunted look the fathoms of the Indian Ocean, the volcanic ashes of tropical empires, the sunken treasures ferried from the leagues of storied lagoons: the cataracts of adventure, and perhaps, too, the size and quality of mollusks fished off Tortuga Bay, even the exotic essence of netted spices corsairs liberated from their rum which wafted the aroma of the Spice Islands, (Oh, the Enchanted Isle of Moluccas!) she inquired no more, for even as she stood there envying them, marooned with a tribal pact on a reef, she sensed where it was they were ultimately going.

"I am going with you," she rallied, entranced, lifting her face to incline in the small hale of the breeze. Radiant and windborne from the travel in their eyes, she pranced nimbly, ecstatically on the snowy sand, traipsing on moss, scuffling at pebbles, damp, a little mad, lamenting the solitude of Asia.

Witnessing this gypsy side of her, the boy pivoted to Quasimoto for guidance.

"Are we sailing? Are we sailing?" he asked timidly.

Quasimoto smiled enigmatically.

"All those in favor," said he, "say aye."
"Aye!" all three of them cried.

AND WHEN THE OMENS FAVORED they sailed. The sailor was unanimously elected commodore. Quasimoto, beaming at his promotion, informed his shipmates that their compass was set for the atolls of the Adriatic. During torrential rains, he wrapped his army jacket around Alma, who wore it regally, like a cloak. They bobbed along the river with an incantation of psalms and Quasimoto's fables of dragons; they clung happily to each other, stammering out tales of fairies and habaneras of home.

"Ay," Alma would say ruefully, "I have this vision of suitors inciting a witch hunt under my porch over an old barrio guitar. They are the slothful males who seduce the virgins of the countryside. They never speak delicately of a woman."

The boy inserted a finger into the trigger guard and shifted the stock of the rifle. "Is that what the guitar says?" he asked in a voice heavy with ammunition.

"The guitar?" rasped Quasimoto.

"It will not let me go," Alma said guiltily.

"Where?" asked Quasimoto.

"Everywhere!"

"We will camp here tonight. Aron, fire two warning shots in the air when the guitar comes."

Aron saluted smartly. "It shall be done, my Captain."

Bedded down comfortably, Quasimoto blessed them both, before plopping down on a mattress of soft twigs and his woolen scarf that Alma had squeezed under him in a round cushion.

During every rest period, in every nap, at each interval between land and water, they would dream of food and parents; and when everything seemed serene, they heard the guitar playing dolefully somewhere in the mountains.

"Is that the one?" Quasimoto would ask, rubbing his eyes sleepily.

"Yes," Alma would answer very quietly, scarcely finding the courage to speak.

After a while, the music in the mountains would fade away and they would sleep, hanging breathlessly on the last lilting chords of the vagabond guitar.

In cold weather, the boys warmed Alma between them. She would cough uncontrollably and murmur about ripening maize, about caresses in the crib. To Aron they would croon; Aron, who was still defending apple pie and Coca-Cola against invaders while raving about winter and wisteria. After presiding over their separate religions, Quasimoto confessed to his allies that he was the worst sinner of them all. For he was, he declared with mock solemnity, a traitor.

"I have committed treason," he sighed, never neglecting to cast a troubled glance at the clouds whenever he resorted to this throat-catching word that weighed most on his mind.

"What is treason?" asked the girl.

"Nothing but the width of the universe," groaned Quasimoto. "Nothing but the wrath of man."

"How lovely it is," Alma raved, swaying to Quasimoto's litany.

"Hai," *agreed Quasimoto, "indeed . . ."*

"How lonely it is."

"It is . . ."

They navigated from day to daydream, unwilling to linger in one place. Occasionally, they detected luminous movements in the haystacks, perhaps an ember.

"Cannibals," warned Alma.

"They are just insects—like us," soothed the boy.

"No," she corrected hastily. "It is the guitar, my guitar. . . ."

"No," put in Quasimoto. "It is the wind. . . ."

Suddenly, rain. Bubbles began to spurt through the boards of the boat's belly; and they anchored. Their holiday on shore was balmy and hungry for they only had one sweet potato. Alma peeled it; Quasimoto whittled a wooden fork. When the roast was sizzling over Aron's improvised grille the Japanese made a ritual offering.

Alma shook her head stubbornly.

"Please, please, eat it," begged the Captain, kneeling before her.

Aron: "Please, please!"

Quasimoto pleaded.

"It is the only thing I can give you!"

"No, no," she said.

"Please," chorused commodore and private.

As she licked the sweet potato with disdain, they saw tears on her cheeks.

AND THE RIVER CALMED.

They resumed the journey with a melange of guavas and baked lizards. A python had coiled at their feet in an arbor and Quasimoto killed it with a single swipe of the bolo. Twice Alma boggled at a minaret swinging like a pendulum. They diverted her from wheezing showers, whooshing reeds, mildewed clotheslines with withering scarecrows, preening skulls and Halloween papayas. From a grotto, they espied a balloon in the clouds and below it was another boat, and they all knew that her suitors were not far behind. Invoking the prophets at that critical juncture and calling to the patron saint of navigation, Quasimoto steered away and the boat accosted a rainbow and they went loafing-loving-longing on the crest. They outwitted a flood to ransack an empty farmhouse where posters embossed in magenta proclaimed: "THE JAPANESE ARE COMING!" *They also unearthed New Year hats, buntings, billfolds and tinfoil from a hope chest. Aron flung the Springfield away, drowned the toy forever in a well. Alma idled behind charred sugar cane and spidery stalks as the boy began to tell her she was beautiful. By sunup, they were blue and bold and blighted: they all had insomnia. They made a palatable salad but dared not eat it lest the sound of loud lettuce unleash the hounds of war. They bound their boat to bougainvillea vines. When the boy sneezed, they lost it.*

At sunrise, the drip-drip-dripping in the living room had deepened into a lake; the skeleton of the farmhouse caved in. They fastened themselves to the roof. Which they rode like a ferry in a kingdom burning with water. They scuttled a prairie church; they rang its dented Moroccan bell. The alien boat was not in periscope distance now.

Their provisions consisted of one headless chick, several edible ferns, broiled tomatoes, a radish, six eggs laid in a cookie jar, four grasshoppers, half an onion, and a Portuguese Gramophone. Aron and Quasimoto hooted in the wilderness, challenging each other to a marathon while Alma aspersed lotuses along their dwindling pueblo.

"Yahoooo!"

"Banzai!"

"Arriba!"

Aron, the Olympian, the Gladiator, traversed mania and mileage and raced home to the finish line; Quasimoto, commodore aboard but a turtle on land, panted in to congratulate the victor.

"To the ship's mascot," bequeathed Quasimoto, "my Nagasaki, my Hiroshima!"

They wrapped their remains in heated banana leaves and reposed on a pile of hay. To see: scorpions, vultures, hyenas, tracers in kaleidoscope. Then, in limbo: antiaircraft mushrooms scowl—yonder. Quasimoto had been a voracious reader in Japan and he rhapsodized to them now with rambling monologues. About feudal estates unvanquished in the world's musty libraries. About the portal of scholars in Okinawa and the smoldering Gaelic-heraldic bas reliefs in Kyoto that he adored. He spoke of Osaka, of blossoms, of his meditations on the vertiginous scaffold at the foot of the inconsolable Buddha.

"I miss the pigeons in the park," mumbled Aron.

"Orion," Quasimoto pointed, "The Hunter."

"The Hunter Orion?" mused Alma.

Quasimoto spat into their campfire. "We must leave at once. If we lose them here, they will never find us again."

"Oh let us stay here a little while more," Alma entreated. "I think the war is over."

While her men slept, she etched their eyes in charcoal on trash paper. Alma eyes were almond eyes. Captain Quasimoto? Like needles. But the boy's own were blue. As terrible and American as the flag they buried in a bamboo grove one afternoon. Now she heard her uncle: furtive footsteps on the moon. In their sleep, she saw a purplish glint in the clearing and when she wandered by, suddenly there was her face. It was a mirror. She did not question its presence; instead absorbed her beauty, only braided the ribbon in her hair. No. That color was not twilight at all. Why, that radiance was not heaven's but hers. She hailed the shoes of her nemesis hanging on the branches like star apples and she knew she must wake the others that they may search for a manger again. Yet she could not speak. Could not move. Just went on staring at her face.

Someone touched her shoulder.

Quasimoto IV.

Again it was sunrise. Even when she heard them tiptoe around the meadow closer than ever, she was undaunted. Because she knew she was going to rise, to climb, to leap from Mayon Volcano. Where she would be High Priestess and punish the China Sea.

In their sleep, the boy rose. To walk without them. To smoothen out a trail in the cogonal. It was a bed of threshed rice under an ilang-ilang tree and it could have been the pasture where a shepherd might found his Eden. Finding three lanterns flickering above his head, the boy did not question nature but nestled beneath them. He shed his clothes, shook the ilang-ilang tree and lay down: to let white petals sprinkle his face and body. And once more, he was eating flowers. Naked in the moonnest he waited and Alma was rocking, ruminating. Some dark stranger blew at the lanterns and they died, one by one. The boy allowed them, whoever they were. Now he sucked in the nectar of flora, the wind wailing with fireflies, the guitar string curving cautiously above him. He did not resist (never). But let them (whoever they were) do it, whatever it was. Someone snuffed out the last night so that the boy would understand it all. They wished him no harm, and they killed him, gently.

When they came out, there were four of them. And the guitar.

"It was you," Alma said.

They wore funeral clothes and were armed with rifles.

Quasimoto wielded a stick like a sword.

The old man in the center, a cripple, pinioned Alma's arms behind her.

"Which one is he?" he bellowed though now there were only two of them left when there had been an army.

Quasimoto raised his hand.

"For that you left me," growled one of the three young men.

A breeze came. All six of them glanced at the paddle floating away, and at the boy tied to the roof like a mast. Seeing his mascot, Quasimoto dashed toward him. They shot the Japanese as he ran and shot him again when he stumbled and shot him once more till he ululated in the water, red into green unto purple with a moan like a sigh.

"Where is my family?" Alma whined, sinking down on her knees.

"Your aunt is dead, waiting for you," grunted the old man. "Your aunt is dead."

When finally they rested around a fire to eat canned cherries, Alma lifted a rifle from its nook where they had put it, and pulled the trigger. She saw her venom stab into their abdomens as they crashed against soil, splashed water in a whirling, wrenching pantomime. The youngest, who owned a cow and who had serenaded her for years, rushed screaming to her but when he reached within arm's length, she only laughed, only shot him twice; when he groveled at her feet with the graveyard in his eyes, she shot him again: once more, in the heart. But one of them was unscathed. Now she aimed her passion at all things: to shoot at the leeches in the trees, the larva on the branches, the lynx in the sky. Above all, the sky. She had been angry for three centuries, and she threw the gun as far as she could throw it into limbo where she wished so wildly it would go home, to the Pacific.

Dawn it was when the guitar returned, wearing an aureole of weeds. Alma squatted on a tree stump, singing a lullaby. She did not seem to be aware of the intense young man in front of her. Sweetly, imperceptibly, a tender drawl parted the fireflies: "Capitulate, my Alma, capitulate." The girl did not move, did not acknowledge the disturbance in the wind. She wheeled to the west to catch a dragonfly. Soon the music subsided, was snoring. Walking casually away, tall and tanned and timorous in the trenchcoat, she bore her casualties away.

The young man awoke with the high tide and chased the phantom talking the moon away. It was too late, too late for the likes of him for the river carried her deeper into an elliptical sea, beyond vaporous terraces, nearer belfries, within all birdcalls. The roof rammed a flagpole and stopped, an ugly bloom worshiping its pollen. The man with the guitar sang a corrido: "I give up gambling, I swear!" He called her Perla when the current changed and her nose crinkled; Mutya because his love was deep and St. Christopher dangling from a necklace around his neck could never be cross and would save them both from the grave. And then he called her Silahis.

"Gone Guadalupe," she crooned.

She curled in the helm, cut the dead mast down and tucked in her Japanese brother on her lap. Now the guitar related its odyssey, but the girl did not heed the many endearing names or the feverish strumming of the troubador. Soon she was far away and from the East she heard him call: "Paalam, Dalagita ko!" *The banana leaves fallen into the river burst with foam, sprouting open, its particles of food scattering like leis from the Persian Gulf to the English Chan-*

nel, because now the infanta of the forest had eaten and there was nothing left to guard and no history on earth could write the memory nor light up this night without gods. Down the river the man (the lone brave lover) saw her floating on a piece of house in a dream of life, her hair as long as sunrise. And she also wept, she also sang

*"O Quasimoto-San, I long for your treason.**. . .

* See Chapter Four, page 57.

[1]

"ANDA ANDA," rasped the old man to his dressing-room mirror. Only it wasn't a dressing room. What it was, according to the, ugh, house plan, was a *cuarto* for costumes. *Sí,* a closet, if you were going to be nasty about it. The mirror was a shaft of glass some stagehand had appropriated from where, maybe a bombed-out building.

Off came the rubber nose.

Manila trembled in his old Spanish bones. An air raid, he reflected bitterly, snatching up tissue paper from a box. Actually, it wasn't tissue either. More like sandpaper that'd been dipped in a pan of boiling olive oil.

"Hurry up in there, Hidalgo!"

If they had any breeding at all, they'd knock on the door. *Qué barbaridad,* they preferred hollering for him like a coolie. Hey, rickshaw boy . . . run for your supper! Mustn't be touchy, though. The poorhouse was full of proud Castilians who'd talked back to their bosses.

"What are you doing in there?"

Nursing his blasted tantrum, naturally. The Spaniard two-fingered a toffee-tinted cream from a jar, rubbed chin and forehead with vigorous strokes. Why was it getting harder and harder to declown himself? For his five-, ten-minute skit, it took just a few blinks to construct that Halloween plastic; what proved frustrating was liberating oneself from the iron mask after the performance.

Ponk!

Dropped the eyebrush there. With spine-creaking effort he stooped down to pick it up; when he straightened up again, half his face leered at him from the mirror. Santa Maria, how ancient he was!

For relief, he elbowed open the single shutter. One advantage this room had: everything about it was portable . . . *el mundo corto.* Everything necessary was within arm's length; you could do your ablutions without budging an inch. Lean forward, *ojo,* there was the essential city rushing into your palm with its imperative rhythms.

Always, the painted teardrops were the hardest to subdue. Shaped like inverted teaspoons under both his eyes, they seemed, were they verbal jokes, superfluous on what was already and had been for many years a pathological clown face. Some abrasive chemical in his tinctures gave these teardrops a waxy flavor that resisted cotton and alcohol. The hours he'd spent ragging and raging over them! This Saturday afternoon, in desperation, he attacked the red-bloomed stragglers with his special teardrop cloth. There'd been days when he simply couldn't cope with them, so that he'd been obliged to walk the streets with micro-sunsets encrusted on either side of his nose. In terms of complexion—and about this he could be hypersensitive to the point of gluttony—it was bad enough. But the jibes of his acquaintances accentuated the injury while those damned teardrops dilated an acre per blush for all to see. ("Hoy, Hidalgo, want some tea to go with your teaspoons, ho-ho-ho!") With mounting distaste he lanced at them with scalpel-like tweezers which, for lack of anything better, had provided him with Dorian Gray streaks in his makeup kit. Before him the darkening shaft of glass flaunted his blazing heavenly bodies, teartip-diminished, yes, but proclaiming their circularity. Like enamel, sharp-edged particles peeled off, leaving behind ruby dots of prickly itch which gradually splotched blood to replace the purple halves. Even his agonizing surgical operations canceled but centimeters off the half-moons, and cursing through his pancake, he flung down the tweezers.

. . . *Cuatro, cinco, seis, siete, ocho* . . . that orange concave of a mouth deposited its perpetually hideous smile onto the embroidery of his lace handkerchief. Clown lips, he'd often observed, were the least stubborn. They went as bade, scrubbed to extinction by scarves, neckties, napkins, toilet paper, what not, such erasers to be forsaken unwashed or garbaged forever in cans heaped with last week's rotting glossary of clown grins and grimaces.

On that backless stool he'd sat, humped with last-night mascara and memories. Eyebrow pencil in hand, he'd etched from hairline to wherever whimsy dictated, such outrageous curlicues, what mountebank grotesqueries. This Saturday afternoon was a duplicate of earlier zeal when he'd been inspired and effective. No more. His main concern at present was to clean up . . . what a fiasco his introductory number was a while ago. Instead of appreciative children Tomodachi Toni had promised would be in attendance for her (and his) TONITE ONLY, who should show up but the bar's nightly roughnecks who'd intentionally miscalculated their arrival. The striptease was hours away. Misinformation had matured into menace, a beehive of it. They'd chattered and cackled throughout the proceedings, spitting, crackling peanut shells, hee-hawing over every lame joke. *Sans* dialogue, the old man had accelerated his act in four minutes flat and stomped away, their jeers propelling him all the way to this torture chamber where, like a twilight torero gored by a blind bull, he'd sworn to cut off his pigtail. And that was how matters stood as he sat there, manfully struggling with his Phantom-of-the-Opera face.

Arriba!

Flicked off, the false eyelashes.

Darker still grew the dressing room; louder their summons for the stripper.

HIDALGO!

On the *entablado* the trio that'd drowsed through a *pasodoble* was this very second playing a Japanese march tune. Such felicitous timing, for, *ayan na,* the door swung open, revealing the tic-some countenance of Tomodachi Toni.

"Sergeant Yato," tic, "and Corporal Ito are," tic, "out there," she began somewhat prudently.

"*¿A dónde?*" scoffed the old man, patting a towel on his half-moons.

"Don't you Spanish me you," tic, "Spanish clown you!" And with that she flashed him, tic-tic-tic, one of her famous trade stares, signifying: compliance, or else. . . .

"No, *señora.* I am afraid I cannot oblige. You see," a flicker of world-weariness here, "this is my last season."

Tomodachi Toni reddened, though she was not altogether sure the remark had been fired to that effect. Her thumb hacked at the robe, nearly pulled off a button. "What? What?" Abruptly she swished away, slammed the door, and the mirror fell at the clown's sandals. Below him the old man saw on the floor, stewed in scraps and spittle, a face minus eyebrows, with cheeks rouged-derouged to utter colorlessness, lips cracked from having absorbed various unwanted smiles, only to shed them again until there was no longer sweetness or symmetry to its flesh; there were those temples made craggy with impositions and deletions; and then that nose crinkled in stale comedies, tweaked by audiences young and senile. That jagged mirror multiplied each abuse, distorted every feature. "*Caray,*" sighed the old trouper, this would have to be his last season: in time, time that was drying up his veins and filtering light from his eyes, the rest of his body would contract into a gasp of pain, as his face was scraped down closer, ever closer to its skull.

Hidalgo de Anuncio hounded the vaudeville like a lost legacy. A malingerer at theatre lounges, he was the bane of producers casting low-budget revues. Booking offices listed him in several capacities . . . credits endless and unverifiable. What hadn't he done yet? Of course, this was in the days when his legs were supple, when his name alone (DE ANUNCIO TONIGHT!) had stature. Recently, however, the Hidalgo stock was in active decline. And why not? The man had been cranking his apparatus for ages. Nobody could tell with any degree of accuracy just how old he was. Like a trained seal repeating mechanical tricks, he ingratiated himself as the seventh spear in a *zarzuela,* as the basso profundo extra in a gaudy operetta. *Oye,* he was impresario of his own gifts grown sparse as his white hair and as antediluvian as his embossed *tarjeta:* HIDALGO DE ANUNCIO, *pícaro.*

Ah, but once upon a time . . .

Hadn't he been a prewar hero in the provinces of the Philippines? Upon a makeshift platform in the Lingayen outdoors, he'd courted the fine limits of his forte: commedia dell'arte. He had mastered to baffling perfection the logistics of stumbling on a pail of soap suds, toppling into the mouth of the pail in waltz tempo, then with balletic equilibrium geared for horizontal-vertical leverage, upset the prop into his backward-flung hands, and like a gymnast pirouetting into a hoop of knives, pivoted nimbly through a rainbow of bubbles in a simultaneous curtsey to his audience. He'd climaxed this arabesque with a spellbinding cartwheel, a standard feat he artfully promoted into a tour de force: to the thunder of their applause.

Half of Mindoro he'd toured in '43; but in the big city, he could not juggle his sublime Castilian ironies into focus. Only one evening of ovation had he earned in Manila; this he'd parlayed into eulogisms to repeal the thousand other lusterless nights. What hurt him most was their isolation. A melancholia of misinterpretation had seized the populace. There was neither trade nor trance between them, the people and he. No commerce, no contradictions, no attitude or anticipation to which he could repair and thereby redeem himself.

When he could have embellished on an adagio solo, a virtuoso buffoonery, he remained passive and permitted the starring comedian to hog the show. Fame and fortune he could've absconded from unimaginative colleagues, but he'd desisted. By restraining his ecstasies, by effacing himself completely, he somehow prolonged his life-span on the marquee. As consolation prize, he was paid leftover wages which also went to the maintenance of stage pets, or to a wardrobe hussy who was available as a messenger on matinees and as a mistress by moonlight. Therefore his billing in the theatre deteriorated into the category of the second harlequin, the third prompter, the fifth sideman, the substitute buffoon.

He restored the mirror to its nook, former altar of his art with its flowerless vases, script stacks, sepia reproductions of Hollywood idols, circa '41. In the name of the Father (kissing talismanic vestments), and of the Son (blessing a faded photo of Chaplin), and of the Holy Ghost (genuflecting before W. C. Fields' unsmiling visage in a gilded frame), Amen: he'd severed the umbilical.

With sombrero and walking stick he strode out of the dressing room (for the last time, he swore), and quite proudly still, descended upon the riffraff jostling in their rattan chairs. Tomodachi Toni was busy serving two of her favorite customers—Sergeant Yato and Corporal Ito, who'd missed the clown's valedictory and were standing quietly at the counter, empty beer mugs in their hands. *Adiós,* philistines, muttered Hidalgo, pausing in the uproar, a touch more dramatic than he'd intended. *Adiós* to the piggery, also to the squalor of the misbegotten, most especially to the atrocious wallpaper that had rejected his *saetas,* that had consistently denied him *suerte.* Brushing against the boss-woman, he felt himself go rigid in her moist grip.

"What, ha?"

Too long had Hidalgo endured the matriarchy; he was flying the coop. He extricated himself as gently as he could, yet was unable to resist one final encore.

"Señora," the voice modulated for a Black Mass, "to you I bequeath my body."

Style, ample and deliberate—all he had left.

Not for nothing was Tomodachi Toni nicknamed "The Tamaraw." Positive that she'd been slandered, albeit regally, she took a roundhouse swipe at the departing don; she missed. Three more stops did Hidalgo make, all dressing rooms at: the Cine Oro, the Cine Tivoli, the Cine Odeon. From these dark and squalid cubbyholes he plucked down old press clippings accumulated when his star, such as it was, had been on the rise. These yellowed papers choked with superlatives ("The Once and Future *Pícaro*") he shredded in his constitutional . . . confetti, he thought, for the weeping saltimbanques of the Metropolitan Opera House; though rid of these moldy notices, he had the sensation of vomiting, of discharging gut roots of a fabulous career along with his other vanities that the war had decreed uncontainable. While those half-moons clung, clung with the ferocity of leeches.

Came sundown, he was strolling along Dewey Boulevard. And how could he not again? Little else was there for him to do but redress this city's wounds. By refusing to acknowledge its eyesores, *por ejemplo,* those dingy restaurants, their raucous clientele, would he not, perhaps by indirection, retain that part of Manila which he'd help forge out of a pagan wilderness? Now as in the past, he followed an obsessive pattern: lawns, parks, gardens—whatever was green and lonely. Still restive, he ambled down to the Muralla, where as the hour would have it, he ran into his *amigos,* those pastel princelings of the vernacular stage who sat on benches each dusk, waiting for an *oportunidad.* "*Hola,*" he said, his tone matching theirs, their farce a carry-over from the previous meetings. The tropical dust might poison their collapsible lungs, their boasts might be emptier than their bellies, yet this make-believe could never detract from their individual importance, convinced as they were that hunger was nowhere worse than losing the grand gesture. Each groomed according to his ego, there was not between them enough loose change to make up streetcar fare. What they had in abundance: *palabra de honor,* and this was worth its weight in gold fillings. All of them spoke the language of patricians, except Esteban Año, who, being post-Revolution-born, carried no credentials of antiquity or class. With him, quite condescendingly, Hidalgo conversed in Chabakano, which was strictly Cavite tongue, the poor man's Spanish, idiomatic, excitable, full of vulgarizations and the sort of *kanto* eloquence that spelled the distance between gate-crasher and *ilustrado.* Then, ceremoniously, with profuse bows and sundry courtesies: "*Hasta mañana,*" a ritual misnomer since they seldom met in the daytime, for only in the dark could they profile and fabricate in comfort.

Hidalgo had not much use for Avenida Rizal. Mobilization had given it a red and brown martial look: red of the rising sun flagpoled everywhere; khaki of Japanese soldiers tramping on pavements. Here intersected the major arteries of traffic, a rotational flurry of *carretas* and vans of warplane chassis converging from the Escolta down Plaza Miranda, up the Jones Bridge, circuitously past the Ayala bridge with its fortifications of sandbags and barbed wire, thence to Santa Cruz, emerging from side streets to *callejones,* and again from Azcarraga, receiving crosscurrents of carts pulled by little boys from Raon; another entanglement formed at the Binondo, to fall helplessly in line en route to Divisoria. This parade would last until curfew at 11:00 P.M. Anybody caught outdoors a minute past was picked up by a Japanese patrol. Such civil precautions no longer intimidated Hidalgo.

At his age, he'd been classified harmless by the Japanese Military Administration. True, his skin sometimes sent a sentry after his heels; for papers, for identification. After a cursory checkup, the old man was released again. His Spanishness, in tone and stance, somehow defined his politics. Franco and all that.

Intramuros, the Walled City, lay south of Manila. There it was that Hidalgo's wanderings took him, would take him repeatedly, all tingly and perverse, where the climate was suggestive of, say, the Azores in November. His *querencia,* he called these battlements, the smoky, winding streets, the cobblestones, the mosques and cupolas, all of it pulsing and polychromatic. Although there too had encroached those red and brown installations. The American Air Force had sought out the particular landmark to bomb, lingeringly, almost religiously, with precision and contempt. Filipinos would cheer every air-raid siren; they celebrated each bombing as they did the feast days of their saints; not Hidalgo. If this was his last season on the stage, Intramuros was his last sanctuary in this city, perhaps in the whole country. Even this ridiculous war could not take that away from him. *Haber,* why should he choose between the Gringo Roosevelt and the Celestial Hirohito? Both were moths flickering over the Castilian candle. If the *caudillo* opted for that Mad Dog in Berlin, that was his business. Hidalgo was mainstream. History only breathed in the Walled City, and despite its historical brutalization, Intramuros still belonged to the Spain of El Cid. Yet it was eroding, every day it was dying out. All those tanks, those convoys, the insignia of Nippon announcing the changing of the guard . . . they were maiming her forever, his covenant, the last grand gesture in Hispanic Asia.

In the Mehan Garden he sat on a marble cupid and mentally reworked the scenery. Once more, a sense of dislocation, of disenfranchisement was upon him. Retirement! Initially, the enormity of his decision had merely nettled, hadn't really drawn blood. In retrospect, the breadth and depth of it, indeed its hint of total negation began to plague him. Retirement was for grandees with memoirs to write, or for revolutionaries with axes to grind; it wasn't for bedraggled clowns without savings, without apostrophes of continuity. Possibilities droll and unthinkable loomed before him; alternatives that were the sole domain of his *compañeros* who, by rote, had been forced to: *(a)* get a puppy; *(b)* raise poinsettias; *(c)* play solitaire; and *(d)* brood majestically over the Pasig River, compose sonnets, make absurd analogies between Spanish marionettes and water lilies. Maybe not exactly in that order, but perhaps all at once. Alternatives, think of alternatives. He'd weaved in and out of breadlines, eager for exchanges, avid for familiarities; there was none of either. Like his audience, he'd even lost what few natives he'd befriended. Suddenly become *antipático,* he'd been eased out of their secrets and expectations. Well, he could read their treason, though he was no informer. How naked, how rabid, their hunger for *americanos.*

During these crucial months of the Japanese Occupation, rumor had it that Filipinos were still alive in Manila. For corroboration, maybe: vagrants and bootblacks with nondescript bundles, schoolchildren saluting effigies, elevator riders (conspiring): about The Invasion. Downtown, they had almost forfeited The Dream. Kempetai propaganda trucked you away at lunchtime under suspicion; the army executed you at dawn—sedition for breakfast. But then, there was the Leyte Landing, rekindling a forbidden name: General Douglas MacArthur.

Hidalgo rose on his cane.

It was as he tarried at the State lobby later that evening, the alert signal just starting its whine, when he first saw the girl.

Like him, she had been walking aimlessly. Dark-eyed, delicate of bone, a storm had combed her hair. Certainly she had not eaten, for how long, her blank gaze enumerated calendars beyond human reckoning. Every atom of her being conveyed this; a shudder, an animal gesture. Other not so visible marks of strife: the libido of strangers. Poets and pedestrians had perhaps petted her, yet one could easily believe she had never been in congress. Standing there, a seashell pressed to her ear, she appeared ripe for the next disaster. Were it the Holy Trinity that faced her now, she would not know it.

Again, a male's horizon (the guitar again?), interlocutive, inquisitorial. Who was he?

"Who are you?" she asked.

And overhead, the bombers had come again. . . .

Gravely: "I am a clown and I'm going home to die."

. . . All traffic had stopped, they were rushing to shelters. . . .

Holding out her hand: "Are you going to save me?"

. . . The city shook, women screamed. . . .

"I am dying, child," he mumbled.

. . . Lower and lower, the American planes . . .

Because she'd been examined before, she turned, she tangoed and seemed to be telling him, not without malice, her intimate voluptuousness. As she danced for attention, Hidalgo spotted a Japanese officer at the other end of the embankment.

. . . The walls, the walls, they were crumbling.

"Who is that man following you?"

Shaking her head, "I do not know. But I think his name is Shigura."

And that moment, so rare, so regal, like a triptych saved from a burning castle, would never lose intensity or fade in any measure for Hidalgo, who stood frozen remembering citadels lost, honorariums frittered away, as this dark-skinned girl stared bravely back and saw flame trees catch fire in his eyes, even more perhaps, stranded to distraction there in the State lobby, the sky overcast with bombers, the ayalas cleared of folk, each voice silenced save the cannons of the Walled City, then horribly speechless still and most grievously private together in this city deafened by sirens and strafings, they let the moment distill its madness and its bouquet, until at last the stricken Spaniard surrendered to his fantasies, felt her sway to his thinking as though it were music, and only then, his reef-borne mind now petting chihuahuas, grooming poinsettias, flipping over solitaire knights and queens, dragging the Pasig River for pearls, writing ballades with a golden quill, fishing out water lilies to crown abdicated *pícaros* in the tempest of Intramuros, ay, only then could he take her home with him, *anoche.*

[2]

"*WALANG LAMAN WALANG SABAW*," groused Tira Colombo as she rolled out of bed, smoothed down sheets, gulped down stale lemonade straight from the pitcher. So promising he was, too. *Pero hanggang salita lamang, puro laway!* Had nothing in his pants except that droopy kindergartenia: a matchstick in erection. Allowances aplenty she'd given him, plus expertise she had not squandered on the others. Just didn't have it, she guessed. Owed her two months rent, one chupa of rice, more besides. She'd have to evict him pretty soon, what she ought to do.

Heavy with predicament, Tira Colombo padded indolently to her canvas chair, plumped down, sighed anew with misgivings. Quite bright this morning; although normally weather conditions bored her since she was—giggling at her pun—a habitual housewarmer.

Coffee?

The idea of beverages did not appeal to her. It'd been a fruitless dawn; her chest was sore, kinked up, she feared, in another day's dreary malfunctioning. Mainly because she had supervised the loveplay; he'd simply melted away. And you couldn't invent a tiger from gelatine. Not even her.

Aftermaths like this inevitably left her woozy. The waste, the crying waste! Somebody would have to pay. Wrapping the *kamisola* snugly about her, she hobbled over to the door, poked it ajar, cocked an ear for whatever was going on up in room thirteen. She was sure she heard the old Spaniard slip in very late that night with a girl. *Aba,* could hardly pay and . . . !

Yet no adversity was so crippling it could noticeably lay her low. The fact was Tira Colombo had rebounded from more catastrophes than she cared to remember. If flexibility had any rewards in heaven, she'd be a martyr, *isang pitik*—just like that.

Breakfast?

Why not? She set about heating *pan de sal* on the grille, soft-boiling an egg, putting the kettle of *salabat* to simmer on the charcoal burner. A bite here, a sip there, comb plowing through that knotty hair . . . sixty-five percent out of the dumps. Better.

To business then.

Color pencils sharpened, cup of *salabat* (stirred to flakey sweetness with a spatula) on her rectangular abaca table, two slices of *tinapay* in her belly: and Colombo the Executrix was ready to hold court.

Ledger time meant an inventory of her Balance of Dividends. To wit: (1) how many nonpaying tenants were scheduled for appointments in the basement, on which night, at what appointed hour; (2) the number of boarders who'd met their obligations satisfactorily, thereby meriting grace periods; or, in a manner of speaking, stays of execution. A third classification, tentatively underlined, listed those who were in debt for not more than a month's rent and were therefore on probation. All three items were restricted to males; if married, their spouses were automatically conscripted as Colombo Runners: maids without wages, assured of tenancy provided they relinquished all natural claims to their mates. These functionaries did Tira Colombo's marketing, cooking, washing; even drew her bath, clipped her toenails, etc.

The Sperm Count as of this morning was fifty-fifty. Four probables (two bachelors, two common-law husbands) were remaindered for active duty throughout the holidays. Qualitatively, at least one of them possessed physical assets negotiable in A-1 fornication. About the second team, Tira Colombo had her doubts. They were laborers, past their prime in every consideration, saddled with respective broods, she tallied now, numbering two brats apiece. Which would somewhat neutralize the odds: one radiant evening *vs.* three dark horses. Her epigraph: *Santacruzan at Viernes Santo.*

Tossing off another hunk of bread, slurping *salabat,* the landlady encircled the laborers' quota, blotted that out, decided on question marks instead. The bull of the lot she anointed with an exclamation point. Her marginal notations could be translated thus: *niñgas-kugon* for flash-in-the-pan; *hilaw-na-hilaw* was still-wet-behind-the-ears; *barako* meant brute, the ideal category. In the Colombo computations, lovers were graded (handicaps, demerits) according to initiative. A participant might excel in one department, flunk in another. With objective candor the landlady added, subtracted and shaved points, weighing pros and cons in astrological equations that consigned *A* to two stars for effort, crescent moons to *B* for cowardice in the arena. Finally, with something of reverence, she approached a bracketed entry in her book that had the status of a galaxy; dotting that with asterisks, and like needlework, crocheting red comets about it.

HIDALGO*HIDALGO—

No fancy deviation in this musical math could sufficiently equip the landlady for her resident clown—calculus incarnate. *Hala,* so hieratic, such impeccable colorums, the totality of which titillated her down where she lived. But breeding, she philosophized, was no deterrent to sexuality; her bulbous nose could sniff out a man's genitals in a suit of armor. As her twice-widowed grandmother was fond of saying: All stallions could be mounted sooner or later. *Sugod!* Once or twice, the crafty Spaniard had fallen deliciously behind payments. Tira the Collector had accosted him, almost shyly, chirping how she would be needing money for impending taxes; or that an aunt (fictitious) had gotten ill and required immediate hospitalization. On the other hand (here mellowing, batting eyelashes in compassion at his dilemma), if the old gentleman was short on funds, she intimated how a collateral could be mutually agreed upon, without fuss: in her basement. Yet how elusive, how devious he turned out to be, for that same afternoon his *muchacho,* Molave Amoran, was gawking like an idiot at her door—cash in hand. "Want to count it?" he'd purred.

Putragis!

Tira Colombo shut the ledger so violently the abaca table toppled over, clattering spatula, spilling *salabat,* spinning *pan de sal* on the floor. *Kay hirap ng buhay!*

Remembering the Proposition, Hidalgo de Anuncio fidgeted in room thirteen; sleepless though abed for hours, still delirious over that twilight of pandemonium and the strangeling of the State lobby he had brought home now thrashing about in the cot and shrunken in his shirt; while on the phonograph spun Ravel's *Bolero* (a revolutionary interpretation by a Franco-Italo quartet; pizzicato first on the harp, then andantino on the tom-toms, and over again over, suffusing this room with vibrations, each chord denying diarrhea and halitosis and whatall corruptions in the house extending to its alleys, segnos arching everything into high C, into myth perhaps. Antecedents of this scene, memories ago, hammered Hidalgo's pulse: from Santander, Estremadura, Palma del Rias and Jerez de los Caballeros . . . capriccios espagnoles of his youth. Minutely he studied the girl, not knowing if he had acted on the right impulse; and yet, how could it be wrong? What could be righter than bringing a bouquet into this funeral parlor?

Sharing a room with Molave Amoran (grouched the old Spaniard) had to be the last straw in what had been a camel's progress toward sobriety. Theirs was one of thirteen squalid cabanas in this unlicensed *accesoria;* address: Calle Ojos Verdes in northern Manila, or more precisely, the bottom rung of civilization. West of the block flowed two major tributaries of the Pasig Estuary; on its east side was a teeming military base whose inhabitants made nocturnal peregrinations deep in the neighborhood for *puta,* for *tuba.* In universal parlance: bitch and booze. On Ojos Verdes approximately fourteen pimps were on permanent twenty-four-hour floating shifts, six of them carrying redoubtable references as they patrolled nine hundred yards of Christian complex: to hawk burnt-out hostesses, fledgling whores, and for those who liked to mix their genders, farm childlings imported by white slavers from points south.

Disregard its ecological pretensions (Quality Street) and what did you have? A two-story monstrosity pasted together with adobe and aluminum, defying generous concepts of architecture. Smog and relocation had expelled most of its senior citizens. Termite, arson, pestilence: it had more skeletons than closets. Pocked with graffiti, impervious to all imaginable horrors, the property had become the progenitor of a new class culture.

For the record, its landlady had outlived three husbands, brazened out several mortgages. At forty-eight, two hundred pounds flat, she waddled about her protectorate with the subtlety of a hippopotamus, still partial to a phosphorescent paint that made her oval face glitter in the dark. Bachelors, Hidalgo was told (bringing shivers up his spine), sneaked into her basement figuring, well, there were less expensive ways of fulfilling a contract. In her sagging double bed, Tira Colombo was reimbursed; all comers she took on, dispatched with zestful grunts, libated with magnums of lemonade. Scuttlebutt: she'd once entertained a tubercular plumber for two crazy rollicking nights, emerging afterwards with a pair of blood-stained shorts. A mortician, so the story went, had doffed his beret and pep-talked compatriots into a one-minute silent prayer; whereupon the much mourned plumber was interred by proxy. Everybody'd worn black armbands. "He was de-vo-ted!" wailed Pepe Labito, brother of the deceased. With her usual tact, the landlady had picked this happy occasion to serve *dinuguan* in the dining room. To a man the boarders had abstained; they orchestrated forks on their earthen bowls in a resounding indictment of the management. In lieu of harmony, the Waldorf Colombo cancelled its niggardly meals.

In her cot the girl twisted, exhaled, the shirt billowing about her. No name had she given him, no kin, nothing. Hidalgo bristled with anticipation; was suddenly ashamed of his lodgings. Look again, he thought, and stared. . . .

Painted melon-yellow, *número trece* was in that slum humor of osmosis. For appointments, namely: two rattan chairs, a rolltop desk with inkstand, tablets of green-lined paper, a narra settee, a Sears, Roebuck stove, apothecary weights, a purse of doubloons, carbide lamps for electricity, and the vestiges of the De Anuncio library. Privy that it was, no *brocha* or broom or stretch of the imagination could convert it into an atelier. So Hidalgo tidied it up with pasquinades, *con brio*.

And what would she make of these futile deceptions when she

woke up? What baronial bedrooms had she slept in? *Madre mia,* he had rescued an *infanta* from the bombs, only to transport her to this dungeon.

H-i-n-tay ka muna, contested Tira Colombo in her basement. She resented the *castilla*'s general attitude toward her domain. For instance, room thirteen . . .

Granted: mendicants had rented it, leaving behind a trail of aliases and acrimony, the fingerprints of thieves and octogenarians. But in better days room thirteen had rejoiced in the convivial spirits of chemistry teachers, divinity students, laboratory researchers, encyclopedia salesmen and train stewards. Many of them were industrious bundy-clock men with purposeful lives, moderate habits. Neither too crass nor too cold, each one had been communicative and with them the impressionable Tira Colombo was circumspect. Then: no lemonade, no gaucheries. And she had two full breasts. With what sincerity, what deference she'd been treated!

Bienvenido Elan was sincere and deferential.

From the moment he stepped off the *tranvía,* from the minute she saw him on the landing—he was twenty-one, rather bashful, newly arrived from the province; she was seven years his senior, and spastically nervous—she could tell at once with a woman's rueful intuition that something, its density and focus still unspecified, was pushing irrepressibly closer. Two pesos all he had, he confessed (those Commonwealth coins jingling in his left shoe); but, touchingly modest now, he also spoke of his *afición;* and this she accepted unquestioningly as an attribute of God's frail and gifted creatures. The house ached for curtains, the light bill was due; however, Tira Colombo had gained a notoriety of sorts as a curator of transients . . . and what could one do when they came by *tranvía,* deposited their capital in a left moccasin, and looked as lonely, as vulnerable as Bienvenido Elan? She had taken him in. He was grateful—such piercing brown eyes! Yet the liaison (as she naïvely interpreted it to be) seemed to veer from its center, had begun to cool the fever of that April noon. Summer passed without proximity, its intimacy stranded in her bosom. She rarely saw him in her *comedor,* even when she served what she heard was his *favorito:* an omelet of crab and shrimp. An early riser, he was nearly always out; his payments started to come in regularly. She went to the picture show, visited with relatives. Even bought a radio: to listen to music she could not understand. Each time there was a knock on her door, she panicked. One day she took a stroll; standing around in a subdivision, she was attracted to this building splendidly risen from concrete and steel entanglements. Perpendicular glass casements blinded her, or was it only the sun? Its multilingual conception (did not each beam broadcast a recital of its own?) struck her: the blending of grass roots and *capitolio,* a left moccasin's thrust toward minarets, a stutter that had adlibbed another Rome. These eccentricities were personalized by eaves branching out in turrets, shingles preening like spires, a miniature pagoda notched with a weather vane. Around this edifice she walked until she was winded, had to sit down. Then she read the sign—ARCHITECT: BIENVENIDO ELAN. The name didn't register immediately. But she had been thinking about shrimp and crab omelets and the draft in her room. Lately, she had been pacing outside his door, reluctant to wake him, afraid to sleep. Now she cried. Over the Masonic Temple, for that was what it was. Over the long journey from his roots to Manila to her doorstep to the threshold of his *afición,* which was his epiphany. Bienvenido! While she wept, she felt a hand on her shoulder.

He was her first husband.

But only for a year. So sad, so sweet, so swift a year. There had to be an observatory in Esperanza. Of course he had to go there. And of course he had to die. A high wind was blowing; he'd slipped from a girder, had fallen. His broken body was shipped from Esperanza to Manila; then (it was December)—from the moment they stepped off the streetcar, from the minute she saw that pine box on the landing, she knew the center had collapsed, the chill had hardened into icebergs. Shrieking, she smashed the radio, fled from the house. To seek out his signature on *carátulas,* directories. Two days later, she went home and barricaded herself in the cellar. After the obituaries, she outlawed all seafood from the *comedor.* Profound changes were afoot. The lissome Catholic bride of B.E. lapsed into *sentimiento,* into a Protestant wedding as Mrs. Pardo. Second hubby was a lathe operator who could not compete with the Elan Shrine; eventually succumbed to, *hitsang!,* cirrhosis of the liver. Mrs. Pardo became, via civil ceremony, Mrs. Santos. Santos "The Hopia King" dissolved into gossip before he could assume recognizable shape . . . an anecdote was circulated around the outhouses in connection with this, but never mind. Logically, and in keeping with venerable tradition, the landlady would now have to be called the Viuda Santos. For reasons known only to herself, she reverted to her maiden name, Colombo, affixed with the marital title. And who could contest it? It was her right, paid for by overlapping reverses and a teat rotting with unsuckled milk, requiring a pump-out every weekend. As the country's economy was vitiated by fits of depression, the gentry of Ojos Verdes was supplanted by a generation of androgynous longshoremen and mannish seamstresses who descended upon the boardinghouse with unconscionable strength, infecting its rooms with venial passions . . . it was a blight. Three conjugal deaths, two premature babies born dead, and a calcified breast had depleted and fortified Tira Colombo. She cursed, she chased them out. With her tongue that could mete out excoriating penalties. Sued, reviled, vandalized, she bounced right back with punitive reforms, sifted more vermin from the entrails of Manila. Both defendant and accuser, she rolled up her sleeves for mortal collision. The truculent she tossed out; the meek she manhandled. But sometimes in her blooming basement, she dusted a blueprint of his young dream, a belltower drawn up in great shyness by this tender craft the world had not allowed to grow; while she writhed, could not help but keen: *Al-lah-al-lah-ko!* The streetcar bypassed Ojos Verdes, her lonesome music was scuttled irredeemably in that battered radio, the billboards had scratched out his name forever.

Bienvenido Elan, architect.

As if a wreckers' ball had pummeled her where she stood, Tira Colombo sank into her matrimonial bed—*aruy, aruy, aruy!*

Would she rise again? wondered Hidalgo, watching the girl sleep catatonically in the cot. Better than poodles, brighter than poinsettias: this wind-blown child berthed in his silk bolero shirt.

Just then, the boy Amoran entered, dragging food things with him. Curry, leaped the Spaniard's mind, appreciative.

"Oy, Hidalgo . . ."

But was hushed with a wave of that *pícaro* hand.

Solitaire indeed! Oh, he'd teach her, yes, he would, to her resurrect Old World ruins, for his head was an archive, his heart the flamenco, and as though centennial Majorcan tombs were straining open for a final whiff of ambrosia, each falsetto in his ears, every glimmer of his eyes' retreating landscapes bade her hear and see what he was most crucially bequeathing from Saturday's retirement before the grave.

[3]

LIKE CERTAIN SPECIES of extraordinary mammalia, it should probably be observed only from a safe distance. If it were a microbe, mightn't it defy all lenses under the sharpest of microscopes? For how enigmatic, yet how captivating was its almost photogenic decomposition. Narrow the face was, somewhat compressed with features that could be angelic when they were not tense or concentrated on some facial artifice. Lobes of the ears were oily, pointed and punctured for earrings since infancy; uncommonly high were the cheekbones, even for an Oriental, so much so that from an awkward angle they seemed to be crowding out those pellet-sized eyes into the area where the forehead should have been normally. This lent a lopsided, optical effect, as though two disparate negatives had been superimposed on a sepia screen.

Tira Colombo could and did look back.

At the semi-Negroid lips, offset by a single dimple in the right cheek through which protruded widely gapped teeth. A scintilla of saliva hung at the corners of the mouth throughout speech. The nose was broken at the ridge; its piping sniffles seemed synchronized with asthmatic exhalations from the chest.

The boy's legs were beginning to swell with scabs and all manner of impurities. Nonetheless, to the girl that preposterous body carried a litheness, those bruised, restless hands restrained: what candor? what violence? what beauty?

Molave Amoran . . .

Was bred from four generations of squatter-scavengers in Tondo. He surpassed the stigma of his clan, each of whom had either rotted in a hovel or been carted out by the sanitation corps for fumigation. The last Amoran elder was a syphilitic, homicidal undertaker slain at a cockfight. The soberest of the boy's kin had migrated to Davao, ostensibly to farm a jungle. Nothing more was heard about them except that a few had died of malaria. Some had fallen in with bandits who habitually laid siege to isolated *municipios*.

In room thirteen, Ojos Verdes, Amoran invariably cooked for his "patrons" and waited for evening to collect from the city, he assured them, their inalienable rights—from fodder to futility. Like an injured predator, he crawled back into the boardinghouse, dragging his battered guitar. He collapsed on the floor, without mat, pillow or blanket, his head thrust under the girl's cot and the soles of his rubber shoes—if he had not pawned his latest pair—touching the old man's bed. In his long, fitful slumber from morning to noon, he sometimes uttered his name ominously.

"Amor! Amor! Amor!"

Rousing the zombies in the room.

Despite his relatives' streak of bad luck in the city, Amoran loved Manila. It was his territory. Especially at night of full moon and scrawny cats and dogs. These animals' habits he timed to the second, knowing exactly where to locate them at a given hour, how large a group was loose. That his targets were potential germ carriers did not concern him. Meat was the thing and the Chinese cooks who operated Manila's fringe *panciterias* never asked questions. With a piece of tubing and a loop of abaca twine, Amoran pounced on his small game. He was fleet, coldly professional. In the morning he brought a paper bag to the Quinta market for animal leavings; in the afternoon he plotted a course to smelly, dingy restaurants for leftovers. He scooted back to the boardinghouse with grounds of rice coffee, a mug of brown sugar. This was no lighthearted route since a legion of malnourished juveniles was deployed strategically in a phalanx of pushcarts on every sidewalk. Envious competitors considered Amoran the champion assessor of civic functions for he kept a list of barrio christenings, weddings, conferences and inaugurations. There was simply no end to Amoran's audacity. For instance, the legend that . . .

On Christmas eve he staked out a Mah-Jongg club. To brew black coffee and run whimsical errands. He mooched cigarette butts, urinated in a sponge, tickled women's sandaled feet under the table where the gamblers kept him like a dog. It necessitated a week for the losers to recoup, a fortnight for the winners to win again. Amoran marveled at their sagacity. No money was involved at all. Not a centavo. Only metal tokens with no equivalent whatsoever. Yet they haggled over wagers, shouted each other down with staggering capitals. Unemployed musicians, milkless housewives, doughless bakers collided ridiculously in a fanfare of imaginary cash. Skinny fathers and shrewish mothers who were not worth a spoonful of gruel to their marauding broods endorsed fabulous checks, threatened one another with total ruin, bankruptcy. Once, in a flash of temper, there was even a show of knives. But cooler heads intervened, order was established, and the ivories clacked, the bets called. The drinking never stopped. Maintaining his post under the tables, Amoran waited for their final stupor before he rose: to scoop up bread crumbs, to quaff spilt beer-gin-tea; and then, making sure that not a gambler was awake, ran off with brass spoons, forks, copper ashtrays, and the chipped, steamy Mah-Jongg set in a leather case. For a whole month after that he did not dare show his face outside the boardinghouse, tiptoeing, whispering, always peeking through cracks in the wall. On closer inspection, his loot yielded negligible trade value, if any. The cutlery's grease would not come off. Added insult: the Mah-Jongg set was unaccountably malodorous and would not even fetch the price of a dieter's meal. Finally, his business acumen which had abused the law of averages was meaningless against 198,000 pesos in metal tokens and crisp but unnegotiable checks. Not all storytellers, however, accepted this version of "The Mah-Jongg Affair." There were those who claimed that as a result of this grand larceny, the little brigand had come into a fortune of bric-a-bracs, items of which could still be seen in some of Manila's pawnshops. Others contended that the plunder—unparalleled in the annals of scavengery—enabled Amoran to send money orders to his profligate cousins in Davao. Then there was that bullet (?) wound. How did Amoran get it? Again, factions: disciples, detractors. It was actually a boil. No, an anticholera shot. No, just an ant bite. False, false. It *was* a bullet wound. Not really. It was a piece of shrapnel from a bombing. A hallowed scar from a knifing. Not friend, not foe had so much as glimpsed this infinitesimal wound, but it remained as awesome, as Homeric as wonder and woe could make it. Amoran had participated in the looting of Manila in '42 and a trigger-happy nightwatchman in a warehouse had winged him on a shinbone with a lucky shot. Chewing sweet meat, Amoran had ducked inside an aquarium in Chinatown. It was his baptism of fire. First taste of bacon, first bullet wound. Had Amoran's chroniclers learned about the truth, they still would have rejected it. They had no earthly use for verifications, for authenticity. The only acceptable truth lay in their individual biases; and Amoran's idiosyncrasies and imponderables, a thief's *Arabian Nights* which grew darker and darker with each telling, evolved a measure of truth.

Despite embellishments, the boy's reputation was not all fallacy.

A night mammal, Amoran only came out of his hole with the other mice to track down the scent of quarry. At a bus station he made a hasty but accurate inventory of its dispensable articles. While a caretaker staff snored he rolled Good Year tires out of the motor pool and into the black market. His was a graphic memory that could absorb and retain the minutest detail, that sorted out and categorized unrelated matériel at random. But his most frightening faculty was the ability to ferret bits of nebulous information from unsuspecting sources and by shrewd exploitation expand them into physical assets. He loitered around construction projects whose haphazard foundations he cannibalized of their planks and mortar, thence to the cockpits for mangled roosters, to the harvests for tubers and mongo. Outside of his miscalculation with that nightwatchman, he was untouchable, a legendary figure among his ilk. Never caught, never arrested, in *flagrante delicto* never.

Hidalgo had recruited him from the vaudeville back door while the boy was rummaging through garbage cans. He had persuaded this grimy, bedraggled urchin to assist him in the theatre, in exchange for living quarters. According to the terms there would be no salary, perhaps not even tips. No obligations were binding, no contracts forthcoming. This was to be a gentlemen's agreement, explained Hidalgo, to be dissolved whenever the other party was so inclined. All these ethical considerations and refinements impressed the boy. He thrust out a clammy, leprous hand and they shook on it. From that point, Hidalgo bragged to acquaintances that he had a squire in his employ; Amoran was immensely fascinated with the idea of being an "apprentice." Although things did not work according to their designs, this incongruous partnership weathered misunderstandings and petty wranglings, survived a year of friction and harsh discontent.

At first, the boy, who was given to fits of laughter and idiotic babblings, filched whatever caught his fancy in the room. But soon, he redeemed them all, piece by piece; began to cook and clean diligently for the old man. In company, Amoran feigned sobriety when not shaking with moronic laughter. Though guileless in appearance, save for the pimples on his Mongoloid face, the series of warts and abrasions on his ankles, no one trusted him with a pin. Food and drink being his caprices, it was a sorry day indeed when he could not produce a quantity of either for his "dependents." He spoke incoherently, sang a little, and always scratched his private parts while pretending to listen to his superiors. Fragile, yet agile, he was completely unaware of himself and flabbergasted everyone with his resistance to mockery—which was centered on his throbbing Adam's apple, his unfathomable deformities, the guitar slung on his spine that gave him a stunted, freakish posture. This was an error of judgment Tira Colombo was never guilty of. Coax and coddle she might her pallid boarders, she might trick and titillate her succession of bumbling bedmates, but some imperishable cunning had taught her that only a fool would underrate anyone, especially an operator of such proven caliber as Molave Amoran. Both of them were self-made hustlers, and they were indigenous to Ojos Verdes. Less intuitive individuals appreciated this lesson too late. Amoran's diversionary tactics lulled them into a false sense of security. They joshed and ridiculed him. But when the horseplay was over, everyone realized that the court jester had robbed them blind, had utterly divested them of such intimate belongings which could never be replaced again. Amoran stole from everyone, everywhere. Sacristy or precinct, it made no difference. Deprivation he warded off by turning nails, scrap iron, tin sheets, ball bearings and screw drivers into eggplants, margarine and cassava. Hidalgo often took the ruler to him, rapping his knuckles furiously in cadence with the *Act of Sorrows*.

Hidalgo's lecture: "One day soon, my Barabbas, with those itchy claws of yours, you will pick the grass clean from the mound, the honey from the bees, the saints from the Bible. Then where will we be, eh?"

The boy giggled, as always.

"If there is an arbiter in the order of thieves," the old man growled, "you should be canonized!"

"How many hectares did you lose in your country, Hidalgo?"

"Enough to build a penal colony on. That is what is standing on my birthright today."

"Perhaps I can steal it back for you, *viejo?*"

[4]

"SERIOUSLY you can't be serious!" snorted Tira Colombo at the old Spaniard as her wicker chair was set down in room thirteen by three of her runners. Like an Ethiopian High Priestess en route to the temple, the landlady had been borne up the stairs by her attendants ("maids in wailing") who, dusky and stolid, resembled Babylonian slaves ransomed to Imperial Service. Paying tenants peeked out their doors for a glimpse of their mistress (plumped up by feather cushions) from basement landing, eager to know if she was circulating in her official function as revenue collector, and if so, whose pound of flesh was on the block. The third member of her train was out of breath; coughing piteously, she swooned to her knees, and Hidalgo, the tireless cavalier, helped her up, offered a lace handkerchief for her tears. The pyramid was more than she could bear.

Unimpressed, Tira Colombo patted her menial on the head with her flyswatter.

"Tignan mo nga ito! Her man can't even get up a spit in his, ahem, *trabajo,* and here she is with the morning sickness."

The kibitzers roared from their doorways.

Tira Colombo nodded to them in mock horror, the flyswatter pit-patting on her subject's back.

"Nakakapagtaka!" Pause, *swish!* "Husband's in and out of work, mostly out; can't pay a *kusing,* don't eat hardly . . . and what do you know, his wife's expecting again . . . as if five *tulisanes* weren't enough!"

Again, laughter. A bit forced this time.

By its tone and volume the landlady intercepted currents of unease, of uncertainty. If she were to gauge the situation with some assiduity, she was positive less than four of them out there were actually cash customers; the rest were ready for anything. *Miski na,* they were keeping up appearances. Somehow that denoted extra nerve, a style better coined into . . .

"Ilang buwan?" she asked, swatting the thing on the buttocks.

With downcast eyes, it said: "Two months *po."*

"Hah!"

From his chair, Hidalgo surveyed the farce dejectedly.

"You better tell that *tao* of yours to use his head where it counts, or I'll send for the Commandant's bullies."

Forced labor. The thought sliced through their gasps like a bayonet.

"O sigue, takbo na mga retazo!" And she shooed her runners away with the flyswatter. All three left the room, heads bowed.

Settled at the center of things, Tira Colombo looked around. Seemed like a *pabasa:* shawled women bent to prayer books; two capped and gloved mestizos, vis-à-vis—Hidalgo's representatives, marked the landlady; half a dozen scalawags from the Tondo *barriada;* and that *kantor* of wakes, The Puto-Man. Amoran was their leader; he it was who'd announced that The Girl was coming out of her coma and would be telling her story—for the price of a free meal. Like serfs come to pay homage to a long-lost heiress, visitors filled the table with offerings in exchange for—as Amoran phrased it—*isang kuwentong guinto.*

Cheap, revolting, the old Spaniard called it; asserting that since he was the girl's *descubridor,* her fealty was reserved for him alone. He was still arguing on her behalf when they brought in rice pots, *talangka, sineguelas, kutsinta,* and for added inducement: some *lambanog* to drink.

Blasphemy!

Hidalgo had carried on so, carving syllables of disapproval in the air with his fists, reprimanding each boy, collaring Amoran. Who, flushed with high office, set the show in motion as his *discípulos* arrived in that collective reverence of shrine-goers.

For her part, Tira Colombo was morbidly curious. Indeed not much had been happening to her lately . . . ledger-days and lackluster nights. Even that Prime Meat in her book turned out to be a milkwash. So here she was. Waiting for entertainment.

She leveled her gaze on Hidalgo, who averted his eyes.

Two months, her *taning.* Then that pride would evaporate. Jerking at the robe, she managed to expose her neckline, all pulpy and blue-veined. Enough to make him flinch, turn away. Hah! She would retire him all right.

Their *princesa* moved in the sheets. As if synchronized, hands extended in service: to fan her, feel her pulse, wipe moisture from her brow.

Mga sira, fumed Tira Colombo, now concentrating on the stranger in the coverlets. Nothing special there. A cheekful of blemishes for a face, undernourishment masquerading as a figure. *Walang kuwenta . . .*

"*Eto na!*" hailed Amoran. The banquet table he reached in three bounds; was immediately peeling *talangka,* spooning into a plate of rice. Other *busabos* followed the lead—digging, snarling. If Filipino vigils are famous for their profuse tears, they are equally touted for their gluttony. (Bravos feast and mourners fast, each according to appetite.) Hatching presently in room thirteen, its beak sharpening, its plummage spreading, was a sibling of that bird of mourning.

Whiskers soggy with *lambanog,* the Puto-Man, *kantor* supreme of wakes, howled impatiently: "When do I sing, ha?"

The elders lifted their veils, bared toothless gums, and wheezed: Ay! Rain pattered on the roof, the window misted with dew. Ojos Verdes seemed farther away than America the Beautiful.

Hidalgo rose, perched on the girl's cot.

"*Hija,*" his benediction.

Four hundred years of Spanish romance caressed the word; and that whisper softened further into a lover's hand upon Tira Colombo's breast. Self-consciously, she adjusted her bodice beyond reproach . . . oh, but the pain, the pain!

Opening her eyes as though per cue, the girl began to speak; her scratchy voice seemed to be tunneling from the very bowels of the earth.

They fell quiet.

Slowly, sluggishly, with a labor close to pregnancy, the girl talked gibberish the emotionalism of which struck her audience to the quick. Nothing they could do but advance, move nearer to her side and by her feet, as if not to hear her now when she was obviously in a state of grace meant the forfeiture of blessings, the withdrawal of legacies, the sealing of mysteries forever.

"Who are you?" Hidalgo prompted.

"Who are you?" repeated Amoran.

"Who are your people?"

"Who are your people?"

"Where do you come from?"

"Where-do-you-come-from?"

"*Silencio!* Let her speak."

Even Tira Colombo sat rigidly, lips clamped tight.

"*Salidumay,*" muttered the Puto-Man.

Very delicately, as though pronouncing a Romance language, the girl recounted (in the third person) how *she* was a love child, born in—enunciating the word with the fear of God heavy on her tongue—Ro-sa-rio, an obscure town in the coastal plains. There was a wealthy, vindictive uncle; there was a squad of Ifugao warriors.

"Ah," from the black shawls.

Her story . . .

One of her guardians overseered a herd of carabaos and as head after head of it was auctioned, she was educated so, school after school. She'd agonized over those muddy, meatless beasts that had to be trucked to abattoirs because of her. It was, give or take a few sacks of palay, a cattle curriculum, a carabao culture. For the remainder of a Leap Year she stayed in an orphanage run by missionaries. The wards of the state were given twenty centavos a month; at week's end every child was enjoined to contribute five centavos to the alms box in the *capilla.* With her paltry allowance, she usually bought a decal for the bathroom mirror.

Suicide she'd attempted thrice.

"Patawarin, patawarin!" intoned the black shawls.

Each episode was blessed with varying degrees of clumsiness and theatricality. First time out, poison (labeled "Double X") failed, and the house mistress, scandalized by such gall, had promptly evicted her. In her second try, she jumped into the Pasig River—only to be fished out by a stevedore smoking a Fujiyama cigaret. He took his mermaid home, where that evening, seeing her half-naked (she was busy thanking him for his *ensaymadas* to notice anything peculiar), he had simply imposed upon her the primary acts of love. Puberty did not excite her; sex was just another nuisance. Such docility buoyed up the stevedore, who, like a true son of manual labor, believed that manhood was synonymous with sexual proficiency. Ridding her of wet undergarments, he massaged her navel, squeezed those small, firm nipples. Hungrily, urgently, his thick lips grazed a frozen mouth. Kissed brusquely those parts which until then only soap had touched. Ever adventurous, he then solicited her tongue, which he licked and bit. She merely lay there, accessible yet absent in her arid magnanimity. Which was *insulto personal* to any self-respecting stevedore. He slapped her cheeks, punched her thighs. *Wala rin.* She would be ravished but he would never feel it. For a while he considered throwing her back into the river. Much later, his stamina ebbed: he had exhausted his repertoire of pornographic athletics (he was an avid collector of French postcards), and with mewling apologies, now plying her with tamarinds, had escorted her to a bus stop with a freshly starched blouse and a compact full of talcum powder.

"Salamat naman!" Refrain from the acolytes.

Her third suicide attempt was something else again. She had snitched a bottle of barbiturates from a public dispensary; but even after she'd swallowed a mouthful of it, she only awoke to vomit her supper of quail eggs in the morning. *Ta-ran,* the burlesque came to town. A gossipy janitor had chanced upon the inert, unconscious girl; had summoned a policeman, who sent for a doctor, who absentmindedly telephoned the Dental Association, which informed the Gynecologists Confraternity, which alerted the Society for the Preservation of Cultural Artifacts. It was bruited about that an epidemic was sapping the vital juices of Metropolitan Manila, that a scientific phenomenon's molecular chassis was fast deteriorating. A Hindu mystic dropped by with horoscope pronouncements; stroked the girl's clavicle and exited with a psychiatrical diagnosis. The patient, he told newspaper reporters, was already dead, figuratively dead, and could be resuscitated, not by spirits of ammonia, but with a dash of *amor patriae*. This disease, elaborated the mystic, was compounded by a malignant tumor in her subconscious—a posthumous pellagra. Zealots and bystanders fanned the controversy. . . . The Women's Temperance League paused long enough from a massive offensive against Alcoholicland to institute a fund-raising campaign for: "SISTER PELLAGRA, WAIF OF DESTINY." An irascible sportscaster took the provisional government to task for relaxing its "agrarian policies." Well-placed bureaucrats berated sycophants for subscribing to yellow journalism; an impeached senator laid the blame on the Luftwaffe for launching chemical warfare in Bataan. Not to be outdone, a defunct affiliate of the Philippine Constabulary rallied behind its updated spearhead—"Remember Little Pellie!" Which was trebled into a commemorative libretto by an epidermist turned composer who would never again recapture the splendor and poignancy of his *canta para la niña: Lágrimas para Pella.* Owing to an enthusiastic fan mail, it was popularized into a Bicolano verse play translated into Cantonese as a national anthem. Such momentum in a human-interest story (from backpage to banner headline) compelled an invalid philanthropist to commission an unpredictable portrait painter to "elevate this oread in oil where she properly belonged." The finished canvas to be exhibited for the edification of the masses. An estimable challenge, gushed the painter and vowed self-immolation should his palette prove sterile. He needn't have worried. *Pelas Revisited* was a revelation, a crucible of colors which blended inextricably for all time, Goya, Gauguin, Picasso, and—in caret-flourish, crayon-pink on vermilion oil—Yours Truly. It started a vogue, a restoration, a reevaluation of "visual semantics." Behind on points, the medicos were not disposed to issue simplifications, generalizations. No, the girl had to be confined in a TOP SECRET??? with TOP PRIORITY!!! No one had seen fit to examine her thoroughly and she was turning a cadaverous shade; her pectoral girdle was good and stiff from a bone specialist's masturbative exercises. A cardiologist's verdict: "Subject bitten by carnivorous tsetse fly." The infernal insect was tracked down to its agent: a Japanese grenadier in Hirohito's Royal Cannoneers who had been on active reconnaissance in Africa. He was summarily booted out of the Chusingura cruiser snack bar, where he'd seen action as a mess boy; as a coup de grâce, he was deported back to Japan with signal dishonors. With all such impedimenta cleared away, "Operation P" could now be inaugurated. For lack of an ambulance, the girl was strapped like a witch on a fire engine with bells ringing and paraded, driven pell-mell through Azcarraga and Avenida Rizal, whose citizenry waved and made the "V" sign, thinking the U.S. Paratroops had landed. In the emergency ward at San Lazaro Hospital, a platoon of youthful interns—idle since their last spastic colon—gate-crashed into their Hippocratic Oath by: *(a)* pulling out her wisdom tooth; *(b)* resetting her rib cage; and *(c)* removing her appendix. The packed amphitheatre rumbled with accolades. Nurses and chiropractors touched stethoscopes and cheered. "Done!" cried the head physician; and she was pinched, fingerprinted and ushered out once more, a new woman. It was then she decided that perhaps she was not meant to die after all, at least not by her own hand. . . .

The crackling of *talangka* shells stopped; Amoran was not eating now. Tira Colombo stared in wonderment at the scavenger's expression. Very little in life could distract him from the table, she knew. Like the others, Hidalgo seemed hypnotized . . . another cut glass of *lambanog* for the Puto-Man.

Continued . . .

Out in the streets she ate sporadically, was always drowsy. Once, a movie actor had bumped into her in a hardware store (there was a fire sale) and bought her a popsicle. He'd literally swept her off her feet. When he was about to enter his den where he'd deposited her with his monogrammed pajamas, he found she'd slipped down the fire escape, bound, it appeared to him, for this synagogue across the square.

Where with joss sticks a rabbi conducted orisons for the dead. "Shalom!" he greeted. Devout but uncomprehending, she knelt before him as he droned on about his kibbutz, Yom Kippur, the Star of David. The dim chamber and its tangy air was oddly comforting;

it had meaning, mystique . . . the rabbi transcended the mundane. Full of his piety, she was soon running obstacle courses; messages written in indelible ink she carried to a chain-smoking cryptographer who deciphered everything with variations on nursery rhymes. Various assignments took her everywhere. Dockyards filled the lungs with gaseous fumes, but she was handsomely compensated with cookies dispensed like sultry kisses by her contact man. Morgues, with their dank, murky interiors, suffocated her; for reward there were wads of embalmer's cotton which she stuffed into her ears to blot out the strident honking of cars and the shrill dialogues on the streets. The secret society of three accomplished nothing that could possibly abet the war effort, although she had no inkling of this and blissfully ran interference for her rabbi. Her subversive activities were short-lived. One Saturday she reported for duty and found the synagogue deserted, its ill-lit chamber denuded of its pews and quaint ornaments. The holy man had endowed this drafty storeroom with his personal Genesis, and now he had vanished into a pair of oblong cufflinks which lay discarded in a humidor. She tried to trace him again, reconstructing her labyrinthine progress through junkyards, brothels, unventilated hotels. But he was gone, gone. Everywhere she went, she inquired about the Star of David; she couriered alphabetical cryptograms that divulged the darker aspects of Mother Goose. People patted her tolerantly on the back and shook their heads. Their condescension did not bother her. Somehow she knew her holy man was composing reams of codes—incognito. Somewhere their synagogue must still be praying for the dead. Yet it was hopeless. Along with its shadowy instigator, the organization had folded, its bland middlemen and informers erased from a ghostly payroll. When she heard the rumor, she dismissed it. She could not envision her rabbi as a freedom fighter, as part of a motley band of agitators courting extradition. What was the Hagana? Where was Israel?

Shalom . . .

She had been infatuated once, with a boy who sold flowers. Every day she watched him with his multicolored basket in his corner at the entrance of Santo Domingo Church; she was selling candles. Not a stalk did he sell, not even the strings of *sampaguitas* he kept in a special partition. For who was going to buy them? Unless the dead rose, unless the dead were to rise for roses? Seven days a week he stood there—bloodshot eyes and wild flowers. Solemn, seraphic, like a sacristan. A painting by Raphael a teacher had shown her in sixth grade. Her candles sold, she went home to a friend's attic; he stayed at his post—shrunken, starving and savage. On her way to the outdoor Luneta concert one afternoon, she passed by him. He'd had no luck whatsoever; if a bower had grown about his shanks, mantled his body with aspidistras and African lilies, still the world's carnivores would not have favored him with a centavo. It was then she committed her worse offense: she took out a piece of roasted coconut and wagged it imperiously before him. Despite the hatred in his eyes, some predatory instinct propelled his bony hand to reach out and grab; it seemed to rend him. Too late did she realize how viciously one could expose a human being's sacred vulnerability. The humiliation would have been unendurable to any man, and he was what, twelve, thirteen? who ran into a public bathhouse to gorge on the only meal he'd had since . . . here her guilt conveniently snipped off stark images his fragility evoked. The morning after, she confronted him again. Scuffing his wooden clogs, he blanched and sulked under the arch of the Immaculate Conception; he stood patiently there for an hour; finally when people milled out of the church, he charged, pelting them with posies as if they were poison arrows. They chased him around the park, into the cemetery, up the hills. His mad laugh she heard (and its madness bombarded her ear to this telling) while they ran behind him, spitting out a thousand muted blows, trampling bizarre petal patterns on the ground. At the slope skirting the Azalea Memorial Union, a Japanese sentry in an outlandish poncho materialized from a quadrangle of sandbags and aimed what to her looked like a musket. The boy was climbing a *ratilis* tree, no one knew why; his pursuers stared in bewilderment. Helplessly she watched him double up and drop from the branches like a fruit; when that happened, when he fell, she screamed, she went on screaming. His murderers turned, saw her gaping. The sentry marched resolutely forward, and shaking her by the shoulders, ordered her to identify this disturber of the peace. She said he was her husband, she said she was going to bury him with hyacinths. Afterwards she scrawled a cryptic farewell on the *aparador* of her friend, who notified the Lost and Found. Missing, advertised the friend, a candle girl. Identifying mark: a hibiscus in her hair.

Once more severed: all ties, all faiths renounced. She wandered about the countryside, peeking into antique shops, stopping by at rural fairs and carousels, tapping shyly on burlap doors for a morsel or a mat. Summer's gaiety blew her back into the city . . . to be swept out again by typhoon signals named only for women. When Hidalgo de Anuncio found her, a wisp of hibiscus was in her ear (like a bell).

And that, concluded the girl in the cot, was The Story—as told to . . . ? Would the landlady, she asked now, offer sanctuary?

The eyes of room thirteen were upon the seat of power: for the *Permiso*.

Professional tragedians had milked Tira Colombo dry with similar narratives. The Pauper Orthodoxy, she'd gathered, was founded on compulsive storytelling, the legitimacy of which was corroborated by the number of breadlines in Manila. The girl's own version laid no stresses, keynoted nothing, even forsook The Appeal which, as the landlady had experienced, was necessarily the motivation behind all sob stories. Contrary to expectations (and did they not all regard her with bated commiseration?), the *kuwento* had moved Tira Colombo close to tears. Resignedly, she addressed them now; she said, "All right," her glassy eyes citing Hidalgo, "she may stay."

"Aieeee!" screeched the old women, dropping their shawls.

"Ngayon!" blurted the Puto-Man.

Cue for Celebration. Or: *Ang Pagdiwang . . .*

The Colombo runners returned with *palaspas,* their *reina* gesticulating with flyswatter: *"Mga bata!"* But the intoxication of the tale, the impact of *lambanog* on the Puto-Man, the definition of purpose for the *busabos* boys would not cede the moment. Singing with spears in their lungs, they pounced upon the wicker throne, bearing Tira the Terrible aloft, their undershirts sashed about their waists; and like the Black Nazarene in the Night of the Flagellantes, they carried her—Queen of Ethiopia! They harmonized on alley ballades, one argot prevailing: fucksimile of love, *dilim* and dawn, oooohhhh . . .

They sang:

Ipasok mo!
Ilabas mo!
Pasok-labas!
O! O! O!

And the beggars the hags the golems of Ojos Verdes: they danced. Around the throne, around Tira the Tartar *Tigresa,* their saraband snatching up fertility hollers of Bontok tribes, or the fluvial dirges of the Badjaos and the chants of the Muslims . . .

Stunned breathless, Tira Colombo was hallucinating: she was First Female, the Woman of the *Seigneur* (though Hidalgo did not know it), Queen of the Scavengers, *sarap-sarap!* It was ("Tira-Tira!") insult, slander from the bovine horde; but it was also fermata and twinkletoes, *oo,* the landlady snapped fingers to the tempo, hugged the fervor, forgetting that outside waited Jap Army and imminent air raid, flagstone and slag smoke. So they reached the landing, ascending again, the Puto-Man mashing ginger with biceps in his throat. . . .

Singing *contra forma* from the top: Mayon, Taal, volcanoes eruptive of the Philippines cratered in his lips; tear-stained and tenor, unheard-unsung, not even a bathroom *vida,* hot red peppers for tonsils in Colombo's Coronation by her *basalyos,* skimming through reed notes, fluting his husk to lint then piping it to the rockscapes of Pozzorubio, couldn't even remember when, as he strutted before his worshipers thronging and teetering over the brink of sanity, in anguish and abandonment because the hour it had come, the queen was crowned it was Tira their Colombo, so that like the Red Sea they parted for her jesters and fools in colonnade; implacably sang the Puto-Man, to Delphic wayfarers and *kundiman* kings; sang from his manhood that had sired nine children now doomed to parochial schools and country jails. Listen to the crowing of the cocks, but quiet are the hens, how dominant the male . . . then caroming up the landing again, the throne momentarily halted at the foot of the stairway for an eleventh adoration, the scavenger boys howling, hands bleeding with gumamelas; once more the sullen tenor, stepping forth for a final octavo, a *cantilena* for Colombo: while his heralds they boomed: "Tira-Tira-Tira!"

And in the cot, the girl lay, quizzical, hand in Hidalgo's.

"I want to sleep," she said.

[5]

AND SHE DOES.

Until the tug of bed (the cot inhaling her frailness like aphrodisia) so disembodies her Amoran the nightboy must slap her, like a little midwife, back to life. Nameless she comes to them; and now owing perhaps to some mystical attrition, she has been divested of those droll properties of character by which every human traveler, save the truly faceless, is measured and thereby assimilated by society. If indeed she ever had them, her faculties at this point have been considerably slackened . . . for she is worse than blind: she does not, it appears to her hosts, want to see

(1) The boardinghouse: creeping with exotica; its life source delineated by somnambulistic mammalia whose chief accent is the Scream, whose obsession is Survival at any price;

(2) The Ojos Verdes Baedecker: illustrated graphically in its windows redundant with contagion more properly known as tenants

. . . the street discharges whatever slime is already abundant in the house itself; and

(3) Manila beyond? If one were already maimed from this interior, why extend the injury thus . . . to the ambulant war, to the skeletons roaming the sidewalks, dreaming of American Invaders? There, there lies the atlas of Hidalgo's dolor and Amoran's playground: unfolded, unfolding still.

. . . And worse than deaf, for she will not share: *(a)* the secret music *(b)* of her dream . . . both being incommunicable.

Wiser for her to stay where she is; to leave matters as they are. Hidalgo appreciates the wisdom of this choice and does not attempt to wake her. Except to feed her whatever there is to eat, to make her read *his* books. Occupation enough, he believes, while she is conscious—alive?

Whatever logic motivates him, Amoran is quick to counteract these Hispanic tomes with—and in that half-moon mentality, does he somehow intend them as antidotes?—medical books, shoplifted of course from . . . anybody's guess.

Before and after meals, the girl suddenly finds herself with reading chores.

HIDALGO MORNINGS (when the boy is ahunting):

She reads . . .

About camphor and crinolines, about the minstrels of alfalfa along Puerto de Huelva, about the palm yards of Cádiz reverberating from the gambol of Juarez marionettes . . . Celebrate the jug of ambrosia melting in Malaga, enshrine Barcelona, the *tienta,* the patios animated by the cavalry's parade; ah, to cruise the Spanish depths for dolphin and bonito, to dip one's hand in the electric stream for a cluster of sargasso; sip grape wine, eat the bread and cheese and follow the *corrida* . . . Spain in retrospect—a revelry of sculpture wherein the proud profiles and the poor profanes in feverish Aztec reprisal, a resurgence of limericks and locusts rattling in ravines, a century of gypsies scurrying on the roads, cavorting in the cantinas. . . .

AMORAN NIGHTS (when the old Spaniard is retired):

She reads . . .

About Male and Female, about Coitus, about Egg and Sperm, about Embryo and Placenta . . . that foetus floating in the ammoniac sac . . . commencing between Man and Woman, then between ants, between mice, between antelopes, between gazelles . . . gestation, germination, reproduction—BIRTH . . . a leaf fallen on land becomes a sparrow; in the water, a leviathan. The romance of natural sciences: rock into moss, minutes unto mold . . . Details: migrating sea turtles conceiving in the sea and delivering their hundreds of turtle generations in mud, never to see them again; the vagabond salmon shooting the rapids for their season of ova, to swim upstream therein to birth saline kingdoms, eventually to die awash on the shore; and the epical cycle of the kangarooite from the uterus to the mother pouch where it hibernates into fullness into second life. . . .

It is a game played by a boy and an old man; trade books at different hours. One literature is celebrated, ascendant, all manner and alarum; the other, rough on the tongue, somewhat sneaky, arriving at backdoors and terribly BUT terribly crude

Like the boy himself.

"What else *don't* you know?" inquires the Spaniard.

Everything, it seems. Nevertheless, Hidalgo encourages that. Never granting her the prerogatives of daily drudgery. No, she may not cook or sew, she may not go out to market or talk to *strangers*.

"But I am one myself," she protests.

Hidalgo will not hear of it. Try arguing with a grandee. . . .

At this hour of dusk the purlieus of Ojos Verdes take on the verdant hush of a painted hamlet: exultantly bucolic, burnished in copper, flecked with gold; scavengers are livestock, shacks are silos . . . the air itself distills the ripening of *mabolo* and *langka;* she so aches to explore the fields, even if their maize should prove to be a mirage at second glance.

"Not for you," reminds Hidalgo, "consorting with jackals."

Piqued, she asks: "And what am I to do?"

"Nada, señorita," the old man's reply.

He means it, too. For as time passes, the girl is not permitted to do anything in the house. Hidalgo takes home cronies from his vaudeville days—all of them beaten and withering—to amuse her. Like old pensioners they sit rusted around the room, drinking *limonada,* suturing malignant tissue to the Eternal Youth of Yesterday's Marquee. When it is over, Amoran collects Florentine tumblers, washes them, wipes spilt juice off the floor. By then Hidalgo is snoring.

"Amoran?"

She desperately needs to confide to someone—the ghost talkers already having a locus in Hidalgo; and their grammar is exclusively in the past tense. So where does that leave her? . . . In the future, unborn, to be scraped from musks and bargain-basement lampshades.

"Amoran!"

"Ano 'yon?"

"What does he want with me?"

For deep down she feels the old Spaniard does not desire her. If it is her body he lusts for, at least she will know how to behave. She might even give in. It isn't much, really.

"Do you know, Amoran?"

Stroking his palm (his face has no effect on her whatsoever), she intimates what other men must want with her.

The boy snickers. He is always doing that. Maybe he is just crazy, as everybody else says.

Again: "What does he want, with me?"

"Ang kaluluwa mo lang," the boy replies lamely.

Her soul?

She sleeps on this. The landlady she hears thumping downstairs, primping (the boy tattles) for her *novios*. Lovers? The girl lies awake, her mind reordering, fossilizing quivery biological atoms: rock into mold, panic into foetus. Velvet womb and columnar phallus she has scrutinized with grim absorption in stark clinical photos; both organs fascinate her: they are, as Amoran puts it, her mother and father. The building shakes to the rafters, the sky overcasts with bombers—air raid! No shelter in the house; they must hide under the stove.

"What is it?" she asks in the thunder of antiaircraft guns.

"Nada." Hidalgo, without conviction.

The boy grins sweetly.

"Amoran?"

His wink releases a whisper: "Americans!"

Americans?

Then out of the blue, presto chango . . .

Should she in the future grope for clues leading to its root cause, she will come up with bubbles, and not improbably, a certain foolish smile. Conversely, she can name the year (1521) for Magellan's discovery of the Philippines; she can, with vacuous precision, verbalize blood, cite great battles, uncannily disburse historical data without raising her pulse beat—a kindergarten child's ascent into the abyss. Such is Hidalgo de Anuncio's method: inculcating her with facts that, in the indecisiveness of her limbs, senses, and so forth, must substitute as appendages, as an upholstery even for her metabolism.

Yet still another interpreter of her catatonia is Amoran; his showmanship in the old Spaniard's legerdemain is as spontaneous as it is mindless. For example, now: sunset, Hidalgo is out filibustering with his *campesinos,* Tira Colombo and her minions are perversely occupied, while the sun embered indiscriminately upon nipa and metal sheet of Ojos Verdes roofings like shattered tongues of the Sacred Heart burns indelibly in the boy's watery eyes.

She knows Amoran chiefly by his tread, inescapably for his odors; always so giggly and *malikot* is he she cannot associate him with anything more serious than a frown. But this time, something about the set of his shoulders and the dry catch in his throat warns her that, *hoy,* maybe he is dangerous after all.

"What are you doing?" Her question referring to the instrument in his hands—larger than a book and pouring out disquieting sounds.

His response, a shrug. One of many throwaway gestures in that body vocabulary. Intrigued, she crosses to his right whereat the object he is so jealously shielding to his chest gives off the sheen of polished mahogany, solidifies into a heart shape tapering upwards to angularity—an arm reined with silver.

"What is it?"

Grave robbers must react as he does now: the involuntary jerk of total surprise, the secondary instinct to cover up or flee or strike out. Once activated, the sum of one's criminal reflexes smears the face; each pore swells with malignity, every feature issues a concrescent of evil where it was only hinted before. Red corpuscles of the sun burning his cheeks, boring into his skull, the face of Amoran enumerates, even as the girl is transfixed, crimes against her state of mind. Dazzled, distressed, she steps back.

His hands move to caress, plucking at silver things; when she looks again, she sees that they are strings.

"Did you steal that, too?"

Though he remains sulky, she senses that the danger is past.

"Tell me," her hand on his. "Tell me."

Perhaps never again will she come upon him in this manner; never again feel that there is something in this boy besides greed and malice. How altered is he with that piece of wood; she has to ask again what it is.

"Guitarra," and now the hoarseness in his throat seems chambered in that wooden arm.

Yes, she thinks: guitar.

"You've seen one before."

Yes . . .

"But what does it do?"

Slyly: "Talk to me."

"Then speak to me, too—please."

Logos of Ojos Verdes. Dialect she has never heard him use before; certainly not with the Spaniard or with the landlady. Those thieving hands—not unlike the warped fingers of matriarchs at the looms—weave choral tapestries, tremulously, predominantly blue, textured in the gray of ashes: such harrowing litanies, such raging lamentations the lavender sun of room thirteen appears to cauterize the boy, his brains dripping all wormy-pink but paling before the live coals of his eyeballs, his skin drenched, bleeding with his frenzy.

Because she cannot help it, she very timidly goes behind him: to sway, to simulate the élan of ballerinas. Where Amoran does not see (for now on guitar, he is a thousand miles removed), she dances . . . beginning to discover some purpose to her body. Think of *talahib* in the plains, and she is imitating its bend and rise: the entire symmetry of its grace. While Amoran, perhaps suspecting what is transpiring behind him, fills room thirteen with *eskinita* hymns and what secret ballads of the blind?

Dancing, dancing, dancing.

In Hidalgo's absence, in complete rebellion against Ojos Verdes, the guitar pushes her to immodesty. And in that demented minute—it takes only that long—her mind floats back to high seas and Pacific reefs: en route, she recognizes Amoran as an extension of algae and atolls. . . .

Their maniacal game skips along.

Whenever the old Spaniard steps out, the boy turns the other cheek. Whereas before she has not lifted a finger in household activities, now, without fear of repercussions, the boy orders her about: to do everything. She learns how to boil rice, first by getting the proper middle-line measurement of water into the pot with her third finger. Then by gradually desteaming the grains, watching water evaporate slowly until small craters dilate in the white plateau . . . once cooked, it is, she marvels, excellent rice! Viands she discovers, whether fish or vegetable, can be enhanced by garlic and onions. The room itself she begins to rearrange with growing inventiveness. Naturally, upon Hidalgo's arrival, when he sees what has happened, every stick of furniture goes back to its former place; and he canes the boy until he is blistered. Amoran just titters indecently.

At daybreak, without fail, the woman in room twelve opened her window and sang her singular aria: "One Fine Day." Although she was born Miguela Fabian, she liked to be known as "Micaela," and she had been rehearsing—with heroic confidence in her vocal chords—Puccini, Verdi and Wagner since she was nine. That no theatre played opera that year did not daunt her. Micaela was an optimist. Ruthlessly encouraged by some professor's weird musical taste, she was a sibilant, aging prodigy whose divine squeal served as everyone's alarm clock in the morning, notably Tira Colombo, who was partially deaf and required nothing short of a reveille blast to rouse her. Micaela's diabetic grandfather waited gloomily for her finale, always a stentorian chorus from *Carmen;* and when she relented and took up her mending, the old man switched on the radio for the calisthenics in Japanese, certainly the one program on kilocycles formidable enough to combat the devastating diva.

In the boardinghouse they fried their *tinapa,* they waited for the man from Obando who vended *gatas-sariwa* and who, with conspiratorial relish, brought word from The Others. The word was WAIT. Wait for the Lockheeds with the twin bodies. Wait for the midnight submarine from Australia. Wait for dawn, for doughnuts, for retribution. Ultimately, the magic word ceased to be a word; it became their world. If it was only for the load of smoked snails from Laguna or for the *lanzones* from Pakil, they waited, as they waited for the bathroom in the corridor to disgorge its commuters, and for the toilet bowls to clear their putrid throats. Most of the things never arrived; none of the people came. Jobs were scarce, fruit crops were spoilt. Out of their gossamer barricades they ventured to appraise a commotion, to speculate on tedium; hinting at Sunday alliances, Monday enmities. The man from Obando swaggered in their midst like a shorn, simpering Santa Claus, and they all realized it was only for him that they were waiting.

Through the months Hidalgo cradled the girl.

Zealously, she would confess to her master, for days and nights. Not daring the positive word or the voluntary act, she let him dispense with her according to his mood. Hidalgo would bathe and clothe her. When her mouth refused to open, he pried her lips apart to feed her. She would gaze longingly out the window all afternoon and it was left for him to transfer her, like an inanimate object, from chair to cot that she might sleep. For, like an antique vase on the windowsill, she would surely have been stolen where she was. Before breakfast, he washed that face more fragile than china; he smoothed that erratic pulse. To: Ash Wednesday, and he dressed her for church, coaxing a rosary into her palm for a fumbling adjuration. Walking home after another undigested Communion, both in their own power, she would have a relapse; once again he heaved her onto his shoulder, telling himself that her weight in actual pounds was somehow lessened by her lack of any distinguishable emotion. Quite foolishly he even rubbed his own tears under her eyelids when they tripped on a child whose gangrenous legs had been mashed into a pulp at the butcher shop after an air raid. Forthwith Hidalgo saw in her face inflammations of the skin like melted tallows, perhaps her anguish? So assiduous a fabricator was he, so comprehensive a medium that his trance-child mutely reciprocated—his picaroisms could hardly be mistaken for indulgences or impositions. The girl took them for endearments, to be anticipated, to be cherished without reservations. If the old man died, some priest would have to administer Extreme Unction over her too, so much like a communicant's Mass was their rapport.

The girl asked for a glass of water.

[6]

THE SEA, THE SEA.

Each night, and later it was sunrise, the girl asked to be taken to the sea. Coughing under her weight, Hidalgo performed this task almost like a penance. He huffed. He puffed. He grunted. Soon, though he staunchly denied it, his strength failed. The boy volunteered to take over, claiming that all Amoran males were born nimble and strong. And so, with the girl's legs wrapped in the old man's blanket, Amoran carried her in his arms.

Through the quagmire and entanglement of Manila's streets they wobbled. On pavements they stood like lamp posts; by foot through tenements that bisected tenements—and it was only fitting that people should take a second look at the ragged pair, for there was something vital, something urgent about them—by fancy along the warren of hovels that glared back at them with soot and sores. Wherever they went, the two cast their own light. The boy steered: he was her consort. The girl, though she merely followed, nevertheless imposed her own radius. Somehow it seemed blasphemous to even think she was not adequately protected. They could see an army in the boy's eyes. What matter if they were replicas of tattered beggars on the embankments? Manila swarmed with such stillborn creatures. For such a physical time, flesh seemed transparent, flesh was refracted only from watery green iris. Trucks were driven by insomnia, pushcarts trundled by inertia, the black market skulked on spidery limbs, meals bolted by tubercular street sweepers who left cafeterias thinking of food. Those who worked wondered why they did, and their butterfly jobs became what they were—glass eyes and rubber bellies.

Amoran and the girl.

"Where are you taking me?" she would ask, not really caring; and were she told, would she have known it?

So there he took her, wherever it was. To house and park, by streetcar and *calesa:* to watch carpenters wheedle at wood, horsesmiths shoe nags that clopped along the Raon. Finally, to her sea at the Luneta where she sometimes wept soundlessly over beggar children abed on the sea wall, perhaps oblivious that she was both child and beggar too, and that all of Manila's palms were turned upward.

"What are you doing to me?" she would demand when the silence was beyond endurance and the beggar children too much to bear.

Needless to say he did not know, as he never fully understood whatever it was he was doing. They just stood there, watching and gathering reflections of themselves.

Amoran and the girl.

The abrupt shift in carriers seemed to favor the nymph of *cuarto trece.* Color began to return to her cheeks. Now she spoke more often but only of her town, Rosario: *Hail Mary, full of grace, the Lord is with thee. . . .* With the little they ate, despite the various careers of Amoran, it was inevitable that they would look emaciated. Their diet alternated chiefly between fried coconut and boiled *ubod;* or if they had not exhausted their ration cards, baked cassava flakes, a gruel of corn spiced with Amoran's lurid accounts of how he had procured his ingredients. They tasted no pork at all that year. Occasionally, the boy swam private ponds at night to pick a handful of *kangkong* shoots. Or from the *talipapa* he scooted home bearing a bundle of indescribable animal entrails which he noisily plunked in a kettle; with much clucking of tongue, an endless flourish of obscenity and an unbelievable feat with dried garlic, was miraculously transformed into a stew which Hidalgo had to admit was delicious.

Through all this infantile sorcery, the girl could not help but bloom. Even as Amoran cackled over his witch's potions, her dormant comeliness shone in the sun: limpid dark eyes, long black hair. Minor rashes still clung to her cheeks, like subtle erosions on a star-dappled hill; the boy, between sorties to garrison and grocery, came home with a bottle of face lotion. Pouring liberally into his palms, he commenced rubbing her temples with the lotion, mumbling incoherently as though with his feverish massage and idiotic babblings he hoped to diminish her lingering paleness.

On the landing and seemingly into the light-years, Micaela was heard: "One Fine Day."...

These ministrations, accomplished mainly during Hidalgo's brief comebacks on the stage, were as sacred to the boy as the old man's memoirs scribbled in green ink were to the girl. He had been foraging the city from *basura* to building, and when alone at last with the girl, who never denied her two masters the grandeur of their malice, Amoran seemed to blush at her nearness. For alone with her, perhaps when he was most innocent, most vulnerable, he was humble and chaste. Guardedly though his hands touched her, they moved her, too.

If now the ardor of a man were to pass over her body, he would find there the mindless rhythm of the mistress; yet in repose that face belonged to a pious daughter. The old Spaniard was forever asking, Who was her kin? Mightn't she have inherited those tresses from her mother? And that skin, the dikes in his *pueblos* were never as brown. Where was her father? Did they live in a hamlet? She could only remember the fireflies in her *barrio;* Juanito, riding on his uncle's bullock from the other side of the *kaingin* to the *municipio,* to declare his suit. Could she have been beautiful? she asked Hidalgo. For why, why did they persist? Young and hearty, demanding promenades around the fields where they might smell white flowers and hold her hand. She recalled Pagsanjan Falls, a thresher at her side who threatened to join the constabulary if she did not answer him by sunset.

"And what did you say to that?" asked Hidalgo.

Her abstraction pierced him.

"I do not remember. I only know that by sunrise, he was gone."

Perhaps it was snowing in America. Perhaps lotus blossoms bloomed in Tokyo. Perhaps General MacArthur was having Sanka coffee at his HQ. Perhaps Mahatma Gandhi was fasting again by his spinning wheel. But if Ojos Verdes Street was not aware of such fariy tales, the 7,083 islands of the Philippines in the Pacific were ignorant of them, too. Everybody slept in vigil of the horizon. Hidalgo waited for bells that did not toll again. A dedicated strategist from the underground had climbed the carillon one balmy night to ring out a code and from a distance, in deadly synchronization, they dynamited a munitions train. Stimulating a counterclapper from the Occupation Army. Major Shigura's frogmen, trained seals from General Yamashita's battleship fishpond, disconnected the subversive bell—with fitting ceremonies and a fluvial sideshow—and buried it in Manila Bay.

In the suburbs some desiccated old men thought it was the second apocalypse, so quiet was the carillon. Consequently, these patriarchal echoes of the Revolution shambled under Hidalgo's window and the Spaniard had only to peek through the venetian blinds to see them huddled on the pavement below. They cooked their supper there; there they prayed or sang to distraction. Amoran would fling them a crust of brown bread and retreat: their bark could bite. At the inception of this senile symphony, Mrs. Colombo had expressed some interest. Not that the choral vagrants had resonated a chord in that vastly amusical apparatus. The landlady, if the truth were known, was just another busted eardrum; a bovine Buddha whose gargantuan appetite was more normally suited to a philharmonic orchestra. Anyway, reasoned Mrs. Colombo, it would be a pity to waste male potential, no matter how tarnished, what with the war and depopulation thinning out Filipino hormones. In all probability, some unappreciative bastard would complain about the noise and alert the military police. For violation of curfew or something. These pitiable vagabonds would be jostled, trussed up and jailed, after which, if Amoran's information was accurate, they would be eligible for either the officers' dart board (the nose was a bull's-eye) or the enlisted men's quarters. The idea made Mrs. Colombo indignant. Such bestiality! She would not allow it. Not while she had the basement, the one remaining haven for the oppressed. This sentiment wooed an elderly trafficker from Hidalgo's choir. As usual, Mrs. Colombo's hospitality was overwhelming and the recipient, underweight and astigmatic, staggered back to his colleagues as though he had been spat out by a whale.

Together Hidalgo and these elegiac folk sang. With despairing dialectics they flagellated each other as they moved heaven and earth with mordant oratorio. At spirited exchanges, when perjury prevailed over poetry, the girl would lead Hidalgo away and shake her fist at his foes while Amoran, lying on his pushcart outside, applauded heartily. Or they were eloquent and without animosity and the girl herself would encourage them, while the boy clanged tin cans. She watched *noche* defend itself against *día,* and *corazón* win a moot point over *verdad.* For the Spaniard would rhapsodize in jumbled pentameters—

> Philip, Philip, where is your pearl?
> Raped are your rituals
> Ravished even in reverie.
> Rubbled are your rotundas
> Regressed into Revolution.
> What are icons to an *indio?*
> What is splendor to a savage?

While she gazed in a car's rearview mirror (stolen by Amoran from an auto mechanic's garage) whenever she could. Her face, her face. Receptacle that withheld or granted dimensions (dementia?), even if Hidalgo was careful in repulsing its color, its texture, its lineage, dreading as he did that other eyes would define in its languor what he knew was there.

When the boy took the girl to the internment camp at the Universidad de Santo Tomás on Calle España for a visit, she peered blankly through barbed wire, wondering whether she had been brought there to identify the unlabeled specimens in the cages. She was beginning to be adamant, but her fear of lions now became a dread of men, for these were cringing, crumpled mortals beyond her reach, standing in groups, gathered around a harmonica or a banjo. A lad, skinny and white and hungry, would sometimes reach out and touch her. She recoiled as though bitten. Amoran reassured her they were nothing but fugitives, expatriates, deportees, morticians, teachers, derelicts and moonshine dreamers: American prisoners of war. Outside the gates, behind implacable sentries, Filipinos left parcels containing native cigars, *carioca,* bits and pieces of everything. Messages were serenaded by *banduria,* or leaked out in the urinal; bamboo saplings dangled under graying trees with fruits or tobacco tied to their lengths. These tireless hostages paraded around the campus, infusing each other with manic depressions, exchanging pleasantries, omens, threats and warnings, circling the compound on enfeebled feet and upbraiding their stars. They swore and sulked and smoked and stumbled in a delirium never ending under moon, rusty aluminum ceilings and tarpaulin awnings. Yet they seemed perpetually blessed for, after all, they were Americans.

"How are *they* going to save us?" The girl was curious.

"Hush," motioned Amoran, leading her nearer to his phantoms.

At the center of the refugees sat Vanoye, a young man of half a dozen bloods but predominantly English. Attended by haggard women with cropped hair, he presided over the sweltering afternoons in rancor and recitation. He was believed to have been considered "dispensable" in the mammoth evacuation to Australia. After toiling for two months in the British consulate and having been intoxicated the day berths on the submarine were conferred on an élite corps, he awoke one morning just in time to be indicted by the vanguard of the Japanese occupation force, and thence, incarcerated. Today he was writing inflammatory denunciations on his betrayal. Alone one night on the campus, a hissy pack of political prisoners had mauled him with clubs. As a result, he seldom walked the grounds without his wings, six half-breed Dutchmen who were very good with their fists. Vanoye conducted "conscience caucuses" to the accompaniment of boos and hoots; but to Amoran, who always lingered outside the gates, the young man with the hole in his hand was a poet with a golden tongue.

Now Vanoye, as was his wont, surveyed his hostile audience for potential hecklers; saw the girl with Amoran, and spoke.

[7]

"NECROPHILIACS, ALL OF YOU. You love a corpse, make love to a corpse, and hope is dead. Bible-dead. Hell-dead. You were born dead in the image of God, who was always dead, you were loved dead by the dead, all of us are ghouls sucking hope from each other; therefore is death our destiny. But hope is Lazarus everlasting and therein lies the folly."

Amoran pressed the girl closer to the barbed wire. "Listen," he said. "Listen to Vanoye. They hate him. They steal his food and plant horse manure in his feed can, but they listen to him. He talks about everything and won't even touch the *tamales* I steal especially for him so I can hear him talk. He speaks every Sunday. One night, he spoke about Caligula."

"Quiet!" shouted one of the half-dozen half-breed Dutchmen.

Amoran slid obediently down on his knees, cupping his hands on his chin, gesturing to the girl, who had not spoken, not to speak.

Someone wrapped a clean towel about Vanoye's shoulders. He signaled to the people in the back to sit down. There was no grass in that area; they remained standing. The refugees seemed to obey almost every bidding as they turned simultaneously to the young man with one arm. In front, another of the six Draconian Dutchmen blew out the last drag of an Akibono cigarette; its smoke hung before them all like incense.

Vanoye squinted at his empty palm and continued.

"Let me tell you calmly and without beer the story of Maria. Not you, dear one, who sits this war out in remorseful expatriation, but our new friend here come to visit the Magus: you, the fresh face of all these Sundays subsisting on euphoria. For our leading lady who steps out of the marmalade to receive the accolade, this is our treatise on subliminal hypnosis. Like one of those fraudulent religions coiled about the mace in one Fascist embrace, we must go through the Lutheran lexicon. The synagogue of the country lass has been padlocked by the pretender to the altar, and our heiress apparent, with her scarf blowing sad and silken round her throat, runs into an ecclesiastical conclave; and finding therein a provisional shrine, begins her beauty sleep. Henceforth, a hundred armies will stampede on the countryside in search of the blameless, the dove on the alcove—the Virgin. After our first hero has unearthed her—recognize Magellan here?—from the Provençal fodder, he cannot quite wake her up from the mortal coil. Rites, rights, riots and zealots follow like dusk and dawn. Pirates, prelates, magnates, a tile of the Eiffel Tower, the mongrels of a chauvinistic catapult and Coca-Cola confluence bud and bloat upon the fibrous rock. Still she sleeps, as though long acclimatized to the nightmare, she understands its witches, goblins and worms. Like any neo-Western bastard sect that has evaporated like incest into the chalice, she remains impacted, *Semper Fidelis, inamorata* in a crypt. Oh, the gigolos had better love her deeper than the grave for their childish courtships are mere flesh wounds and do not even touch the inscriptions on the tomb! No. Do not waste pity on her. She's not missing anything. For what is there to miss?

"Surely the truth has not been worth telling for the last two thousand years? Moreover, we cannot even lie with flair. We luxuriate in mendacity, that cancerous, usurprous organism we hail as the Superbiology. With mendacity we mollify the masses; with mendacity we pad the hollows in our character. Cretins need mendacity to get over the shock of birth. World War II, the universal; Filipinos, the particular. If we did not have weapons to kill each other with, we would not live. In mendacity's linguistics, truth is the dead language we must not speak again—let sleeping dogs lie. Tenderness and trauma, arson and acrimony, ossification and obstetrics, that's what we are. Total: zero. Just a bottled scream, no more. A genie without Aladdin. Someone, long ago, stuffed in the cork of convention and the atomizer has lost most of its spirit. Detours, yes, diversions, yes, but it will never be the same again as in that dreadfully saccharine time when the only taboo was tedium. Nowadays, Mr. Average runs beserk commuting between rapine and rhetoric. Beyond that, only the shortwave, and perhaps, if we're lucky, the absentee neighbor's *Frau*. Each act is parent to action; and your genes go back to Abel and Attila, to minuets and madness. We must have an American leap year, a British month, a French weekend, a German day, a Chinese night. And if you insist, a Japanese second. Behind the pass-in review, ticking like the Big Ben, always, the Spanish four hundred. Toss a coin. Heads, you go to the guillotine; tails, you listen to Scheherazade. Too many cooks spoil the soup, the stew is burning, the pot is melting. Is there a doctor in the house? Intravenous shots, somebody! Oh, I could go on a rampaging rupture. I could foment a Rabelaisian recall from pomp to circumstance. There is a Parthenon, a Song of Songs in milady. Jose Rizal wrote *Noli Me Tangere* and *El Filibusterismo,* for which he was executed at Bagum-bayan. The Spaniards shot him because he had gotten too close for comfort. For having lifted the veil thus, Rizal was turned into stone—a monument at the Luneta. It is the *noblesse oblige* of galloping Lilliputians to minimize their shortcomings with a tower of visions. And authorities, being with such authority by virtue of vice, cannot abide insights, leading as they often do to insurrections.

"Where is the area of guilt? Judgment Day for the Filipino will be officiated by tourists and Trappist monks with such paeans and pedantry as will swell automats and archives both. So much for perspective. Since we have willfully cultivated our sacred imperfections —which, at the time of my speech still approaches further perfect imperfections—it is foolish to expect Paradise. One revolution has failed, with more to come, more to fail. Hence, the Filipino, like the

American, the French, the English, the German, the Italian, the African, must be judged according to the malleability that informs his failures. Some perspicacious ghost readers, the decoders you might say of the hieroglyphic, must chalk up his innings. Ten points for foreign trade thus, none for diplomatic relations so. But pray, how does one score the spirit? Statistics for nonintangibles? Preposterous! The figure is lined up for surgery; an appendectomy of inclinations. Free will *vs.* free verse. Place your bets, ladies and gentlemen, place your bets. Narrow down the tension of vulnerability; tighten international lung subsidiaries. The operating table stinks with the patient's mendicant generosity. Visitors have their pick of prime duramatter, down payment on discovery. Theme: East meets West, West melts East. *Taran!* With one broad sweep of the scalpel, they have cut out a useless appendage—the rumor of humanity. Ah, but what a load off the tool chest. So, we come to the Basilica. We—they?—have framed lackey as Filipino on an interior-exterior basis. Surely, the X ray must declare a true blue? But we have just torn down the castle, illusion by illusion. We have not elevated the muck to the moon, nor the soul to sea level. Well, that's the real story behind the beanstalk. Whatever it is, pretend you don't hear it. It is a voice from Damascus that forgot to shave. The wind is its enemy because it will carry it away. And what is the wind in our case but vanilla, clam chowder, Babe Ruth, roast beef, Hollywood that you may never see again. . . .

Vanoye cleared his throat; held up his arm as if to punctuate his closing remarks. He said: "In conclusion, I would like to mention that the Man from the Mountain is scheduled to arrive in Manila by June. The Man, as my committee has told you, is in direct transmitter contact with the Task Force at Leyte. It has also come to my attention that a certain belly dancer, a Cebuana, has been entertaining the enemy with her, uh, belly. Well, console yourselves in the thought that she will be dealt with in the extreme—when the time comes."

Vanoye closed his eyes.

"That is all."

"What do you mean that's all? What kind of jazz is that?" exclaimed a former textile salesman.

"Shut up, Henry," said his wife.

To a prisoner, the compound had wanted this one-armed man to extemporize on sardines, meat loaves, raisin bread, Lucky Strike, and

Betty Grable. In his earlier discourses, Vanoye had done just that. How evocative were his reproductions of Coney Island; what an artful contriver he was of dining-table delights. With pincer-like scoops of his scandalously graceful fingers, he would become a freckled vacationist from San Francisco attacking a lobster thermidor (Amoran's favorite act) and his audience would lick their dirty hands and stomp their feet in approval, begging him to order a second helping. After the wine, coffee and cigar, Vanoye would stretch out luxuriously, wipe his lips disdainfully with the napkin—as to the manner born—and nod to the six Dutchmen, who, as erstwhile waiters at the Waldorf-Astoria, then unfurled an imaginary palm tree, whereupon, the scene shifted to Miami Beach for more of gracious living. Ivy-Leagueish in Bermuda shorts, Vanoye now sipped carelessly at his highball, pinched a blonde, cultured his tan. Glaring sun? Before one could say "*Garçon!*" a Dutchman was leaning over from Vanoye's back to cup rimless hands over Vanoye's eyes. A whirring Wall Street call—plugged in by a Dutchman's big toe—was cut short with a nonchalant "Later." Finally bored with swimming pool tête-à-tête ("Cancel my brunette appointment"), Vanoye disengaged himself with some effort from that tentacled blonde (she had halitosis), stood up, winked at a passing redhead Dutchman, who, in his best Garbo husk, said: "*Ja?*" Then hand in hand, the bored broker and his Ninotchka strode away into the Florida sunset. More than anything else, this particular skit, with its devilish nuances, its whacking gusto, disarmed the theatre-goers. Normally, topical issues were treated like the bubonic plague by the audience, and even in the extraneous slush of Vanoye's latest *interludio,* they had somehow expected a restatement of the gourmet theme which would indemnify them from the facts. A humorous deflector, that was the unspoken stipulation, and grievously had Vanoye answered it. But jollity had given way to jeremiads; the buffer was lifted, now they winced at time's daggery truth in their bones. Since the one-armed man's transfer from Fort Santiago, the weekly milieu had not been the same. Lobsters had become lozenges, bitter to the mouth; smorgasbord became diarrhea. Henry Wachek, the more boisterous of the hecklers, would have no truck with any of this and said so now. His ruined palate was soon vindicated by an overlapping vocal discord.

"Trash!"

"Traitor!"

"Pervert!"

"Lynch the bum!"

"We want our cigarette butts back!"

Amoran shook his head in dismay. Beside him, the girl did not move.

"Come back next Sunday," chorused the six Dutchmen.

Before his attendants could conduct him out of his service behind the backs of the sentries who were now pacing the west end of the compound, Vanoye took out a stub of colored pencil, scribbled something on a yellow pad, tore a leaf from the book and threw it over the wire toward the girl. Amoran hastily picked it up, pulling the girl after him. Two blocks away from the university, he brushed it open. It read: "THE KING IS DYING LONG LIVE THE QUEEN!"

He felt her tremble on his arm.

"What does it mean?" she asked.

"And how was Pius X today?" snorted Mrs. Colombo at the glowing pair from her queenly outpost in the small, acrid veranda. Cardboard fan in hand, rump wedged in her wicker chair, the landlady had just finished her manicure and was absently stubbing at her shredded cuticles on the floor.

The boy softened his features; decided to fence with the old hag.

"Eh, Moranito?"

She knew he detested this diminutive.

Grinned Amoran: *Puki mo.*

Mrs. Colombo smiled: *Bayag mo.*

Arrested in midflight, the girl let her feet rest on the doormat while her eyes were riveted to the landlady's powdered thighs, which seemed determined to burst free from that tentlike bathrobe. A male was present.

"High Mass today?" The cardboard fan moved pendulously, as if to cut off the other female from view.

Instinctively, Amoran rearranged his features again. It wouldn't do much harm, he thought, to tickle the big crotch a little.

"Perhaps you would like to come next Sunday? You could go to confession."

"*Anak ng kwago,* yes, I could go to your shaman, pour myself out to him, and he can, ho-ho-ho, pour himself out to me! After all, two sins are better than one—if you know what I mean!" With that, the great whorled head thumped back in a roar; those whalebone arms whacked at bough-thighs in apoplectic merriment. She was still carrying on when the invisible wicker chair capsized on one of its hind legs. Without a break in vibrato, Mrs. Colombo snatched up the broken leg and waved it aloft like a coronary conductor breaking in a new baton.

"Oh, Moranito *mio,* you'll be the death of me yet!"

"Any time at all, Mrs. Colombo," said the boy, winking at the girl.

Coughing, gasping on her grounded vessel, the landlady dropped the broken leg.

"Too much excitement is bad for me, children. My palpitations could deafen a doctor. Come, feel my heart, Moranito."

Too late to escape. Amoran felt himself pulled, dragged. He saw her wigwam swish laterally, a flap open, and now his hand was propelled up to a mesa of flesh, down to a reservoir of fat, onto the bog of that single breast. Once there, the hand was snagged. Roadblocks seemed to crop up everywhere along the landlady's subway. The flap slid into place, the tent closed, and the dead flesh itself seemed to turn adhesive. For a while Amoran fancied going through life with his left hand in Mrs. Colombo's boilerworks. What a freak show they would make in the circus! *Mano a mano.* Cock and bull. *Anak ng puta!* The trap was roaring once more when the girl spoke.

"Let him go."

"Please" was a fundamental conjunctive in her grammar, but she had not used it this time.

The walrus belched, the blubber rolled: out came the boy's hand, limp and suety.

"By the way," blustered Mrs. Colombo, still savoring her canape, "the Cardinal is half out of his mind looking for his sheep."

Upstairs, a shutter banged open.

"*Ladrón!*"

Oy, Hidalgo.

Like a trained puppy, Mrs. Colombo melted into fluttery gestures and wallflower simperings. The master's voice always did unlace her panties—whenever she wore them.

"*Ladrón!* I know you are down there!"

Nursing a sticky hand, inwardly bruised beyond all self-forgiveness, the boy was undecided whether to sulk on the last debacle or to gird himself for the next one upstairs. When the girl pushed him toward the door, he was grateful.

"Come," she said with persuasive gentleness, "Moranito."

The landlady smiled blandly at nobody in particular.

In the backyard Micaela was gamely unfurling her Barnum and Bailey mosquito net up on the clothesline, like a fisherman spreading his net into the sea. "*Kumusta! Kumusta!*" she trilled. A coloratura squall accompanied Amoran and the girl to the landing as Micaela tympanized her voice into the "Triumphal March" from *Aida*.

Hidalgo was furious when they came up. He refused to let Amoran enter the room. Though she knew it was futile, the girl tried to reason with the old man; finally coaxed the key out of his pocket and unlocked the door. In crept the boy. The girl had gone as far as her wits and daring would allow. Now it was up to him.

Victorious over the clotheslines, Micaela stepped back from her undulating mosquito net, did a jig around it, tried her high scales on "La Paloma," and was crestfallen upon realizing that she was familiar only with the tune, not its lyrics. "*Si a tu . . . si a tu . . . ?*"

"He's incorrigible," snarled Hidalgo, advancing with his cane.

Amoran feinted.

"I myself went," the girl said. "Nobody forced me."

Hidalgo did not bite.

"Don't defend that animal."

Amoran eyed the space under the cot: the only logical place.

"*. . . Si a tu ventana . . .*"

"Perhaps he wants to steal from the guardhouse."

Hidalgo raised his cane; Amoran cowered under the cot, realized suddenly that this could be a costly tactical maneuver, and spun out on the other side as the cane went *splaaaaattt!* on the cot's bedding.

"What can you steal from an internment camp except misery?"

Amoran tested the overlong *sawali* broom handle for firmness and bounce, found it suitable to his purpose, measured the distance, backpedaled for momentum, then pole-vaulted over the table, away from the danger zone, then landed on the windowsill with ease. To recover his range, the old man would have to hop about quite a bit. Given this elbow room, also with his self-confidence recharged, the boy knew that he had earned his lodging for the night. Still, that cane was like a spear.

"And that filthy announcer with the hole in his hand!"

Everybody was aware that the tide of battle had changed.

"*. . . Una paloma . . .*"

"He speaks very well," said the girl, sitting down at last.

"I forbid you to see him again!"

"Why?"

Roosting on the ledge, Amoran stuck out his tongue, made horns with his index fingers on his head.

"Because Grandpa *burat* here wants you for himself, that's why!"

"*Brujo!*"

Amoran cocked three fingers into an obscenity. The old man threw the cane at him, which batted his own hat off the wall; it plopped down on the floor.

"*. . . Tratala con cariño que es mi persona!*"

Downstairs, Mrs. Colombo wondered whether she should wash her hair, set it in curlers, or get a professional permanent from the hairdresser in room eleven. She took a quick look at the loan shark in her drawing room who was self-consciously thumbing through a magazine. He had brought her a bag of boiled jackfruit seeds and the latest bulletins—presumably from the shortwave—on the Pacific campaign. The news was almost always exaggerated, but the jackfruit seeds, his trademark by now, were boiled just right and needed no salt. Beneath that businesslike exterior, between those habitually crossed legs, the landlady was positive there dwelt a tiger. Although for the life of her she couldn't understand why the highlights of his visits should be confined to the domino board. Fretting over this sweet predicament, she took another quick look. Why, the man was actually reading! She shook her head in disbelief and bumped back to the mirror. No. A permanent wouldn't help any. If she were to barge out there with a beehive on her crown, that baboon probably wouldn't even notice. Still, there were many wild and wonderful ways to scuttle a shark, seasick or not. Perhaps they could take a shower together? *Lintik,* the day beckoned with possibilities! She undid her hair from its bun and let it fall on her shoulders; she powdered her armpits sparingly, moistened her lips with a curl of tongue, parted her bathrobe strategically, then walked expectantly into the drawing room to her gentleman caller. Even as she started to speak, a jackfruit seed popped out of his mouth, landed on her left black slipper and settled there like a white mole. Mercifully, they would not be playing dominos tonight. He held his breath. Not for the beehive that she wasn't wearing. Not for anything else that he would not have noticed anyway. But for the lopsided bosom that now robbed him of speech. When she spoke to him, it was with a bathroom voice.

"Now, Rubio . . ."

Afternoon went without discourse, without delight in room thirteen.

Night came reverberative with street hawkers to Ojos Verdes.

"Taho!"

"Turon!"

"Rimas!"

"Kundol!"

"Bibingka!"

"Puto seko!"

"Inihaw na mais!"

"Lumpiang sariwa!"

"Ginatang mongo!"

Songs of *bibingkeras* scented the air, cantos from kettles wafted the wind. *Bilao* on head, a sultan's feast on their lips, they sang for centavos for good cheer, these sirens of the stomach. *Probincianos, probincianas,* they stepped lightly by padlocked doors, stopped briefly under barricaded windows. The men, somehow slim and subdued; the women, lumpy and lyrical. All told of their prowess. For they were their own cooks. One heard culinary chants whose lyrics were recipes. One listened to carolers at the top of their lungs, at the peak of their pots. Melodious were the girls, the grandmothers describing their skills. Tall tales from the *mesa corta,* trudging, teasing, trespassing on the curfew. A redolent refrain on the evolution of preparation: the primeness of ingredients, also their place of origin, how long on the stove with what temperature, plus what magical palms had stirred, shaken, patted them into shape.

"Gi-na-tang mong-go!"

"Lum-piang sa-ri-wa!"

"I-ni-haw na ma-izzzz!"

"Pu-to se-ko-o-o-o!"

"Bi-bing-kaaaa!"

"Kun-dol!"

"Ri-maaaassss!"

"Tu-ron!"

"Ta-ho-o-o-o!"

While Manila dreamed. Of beef steaks and Hershey bars.

"Moranito?"

"Sssh."

"It's all right. Hidalgo is asleep."

"Please. Don't call me that. Not you."

"Why do they call you by that first name? Is it really yours?"

"Because my father tied me to a tree when I was six, he left me there."

"How awful."

"There was a flood. The tree was high."

"I was in a flood once, long long ago. I can't remember now."

"It was a river."

"Who found you?"

"The police."

"And they gave you the name. . . ."

"Yes."

". . . Molave."

"Your feet are cold."

"Your blanket is too small."

"Must be the old man's handkerchief."

"Did he hurt you much?"

"I'm used to it."

"Did *she* hurt you?"

"That doesn't bother me either."

"Do I—hurt you?"
"Most of all."
"How?"
"You ask too many questions."
"I don't even know my name."
"You don't need one. But you have."
"What?"
"Can't pronounce it."
"You are joking again."
"Not with you. Only with them."
"Sometimes I think you are very wise."
"Sure, that's why we didn't eat today."
"He gave me something. I saved a piece for you. Here."
"Thank you—*chiquita.*"
"Please don't call me that. Not you. And don't eat so fast."
"It doesn't matter."
"Tell me, why do you fight him?"
"Don't let it worry you."
"He is really very kind."
"Don't lean on my back. It's still sore."
"It was because you took me there."
"Where?"
"You know where."
"He knew I would do that anyhow."
"What is his name again?"
"You know his name."
"Vanoye."
"That's it."
"How did he lose his arm?"
"He didn't tell me."
"Do you see him often?"
"Whenever I can."
"You always take him food."
"Sometimes."
"He is so strange."
"He's in and out of Fort Santiago."
"What do they do there?"
"Nothing much. Just take your arm."

"Was that how he lost it?"
"Maybe."
"I like him."
"Do you?"
"Did you know what he was doing while we were there?"
"Tell me."
"I felt that he was talking to someone I knew."
"I know who."
"Who?"
"Are you still cold?"
"I am warm enough."
"This handkerchief is hot with tears."
"You are beginning to talk like him."
"Who?"
"That man."
"What man?"
"At Santo Tomás."
"How?"
"Tell me first."
"Tell you what?"
"Who he was talking to."
"The old man will beat me."
"No! I won't let him!"
"Ssssh!"
"Please, Moranito."
"I told you not to call me that."
"If you will answer me."
"All right, all right. But we're waking the dead."
"Who then? Vanoye was talking to whom?"

[8]

YOU TELL YOURSELF don't scream, oh damn it, you're not going to scream. But they hear you just the same, they're laughing themselves sick out of their buckteeth. Coming: boots, keys, DOOR. Clank-clank-clank, thump-thump-thump, jangle-jangle-jangle. Not again oh no not again. Will they never stop stomping? never stop the clank-clank-clanking and the thump-thump-thumping? Scalding in here. A furnace. Your stench, God the Son, Your Immaculate stench.

First Day.

Just a can of brackish water, slab of wormy bread, bucket for your natural deposits. Nothing came on the second, third, fourth, fifth, sixth, and on the seventh, God the Father kept jolly the Sabbath Day.

You howl.

Don't come, Boots. Made for kicking. Howl again, louder, batter down steel void. Water! Time and tears; time drips, do you know that? You stop crying. Can empty. Water! You (scream) at last.

You kick at can at walls at anything at God the Holy Ghost. You water the can. Water! Nobody comes. You stoop to the can . . . perhaps? But no. You don't (don't!) do it. Can't? Do? It? Cry, cry. Eyes dry. Fall down on your haunches, thrust can into your face: drink. Hear them gasping so hard are they laughing. But it's so fresh, so invigorating to wet your throat again. You don't care. Now you're really horribly hungry. Kick cobwebs, kick mortar, kick yourself. You see filth in bucket. Yours. But no. Tell yourself you're not going to do it. You'll die instead. Die you don't. Considerate of them to pull out your fingernails so you can't even prick yourself and maybe bleed to death. You're going to live forever, thirst forever, starve forever.

God, You are a swine. (If that were so, you could eat Him.)

Moreover, God is an absent pig. Holy Hog that He is.

Look at your dirt again. No, no, no, no! You cannot. But you will. And you do. Haha, bottoms up! You retch and vomit. You scoop it up again, retch-vomit, repeat, and you keep on doing this until the mess catches on in there and won't come out anymore. Flesh of your flesh, in a manner of puking. Some meal. What kind of restaurant are they running here, no toothpicks! Boots. Clank-clank-clank. Door. They ask you how you enjoyed it. Your mouth smells of the stuff. You lick your hands. Needs a little seasoning, you say. What happens now? Even *that* came from your last human food. If they're to keep on enjoying this pavane they'll have to come again with another chunk of stalagmite pie, another bucket of sawdust. You know how they operate now. Haven't lost that old-time religion: Intelligence. Therefore . . . conjugate the passage of marigolds, count sun, multiply moon, itemize in-betweens. They do not come. THEY. Leggings and stompings. Still tinkering, confabulating over their next offensive. It was funny for a while there; now the bucktoothed laughter has faded and they know they must surface with another brilliant ploy, if they're to keep up with you.

Jesus Christ, aren't Thou the limit?

You've even stopped imagining what the sentries must be eating and drinking. Quit doing that long ago. Did that come with the last supper? When did you last indulge in sexual substitutes? Why care! recollect the beatings: the frequency, the quality of their spikes on your kneecaps. Sulphur in your nose. Sewer in your stomach. Syringe in your rectum. Then mix thoroughly. Daiquiri, *à la* D.O.A.

Water Cure was nothing. That Basketball game was it.

You couldn't wait to make the team. Because Pancho Rivas would surely be there. Pancho Rivas of the Death March from Bataan to Capas. Viva Pancho, who'd give the shirt off his back. P.R. was head and shoulders above that bunch. Your confidant-*cum*-comptroller in all those lucrative rackets at the Universidad de Santo Tomás camp. A scourge at U.S.T. he was, Pancho Rivas. Major Shigura's contingent met you on the half-court. Only one goal for the Olympiad. *Bakero!* Five players *vs.* one! Where was Rivas? you asked the guards in G-strings. Him no play, said they. Okay-okay, five *contra* one. As if there was a choice. You picked up the ball. Hmm, strange, wasn't it, that it would only bounce several inches off the hardwood? Also too big for a basketball. Like a gymnast's health aid. Though you paid no attention to details. The midsection still hurt. Must've left their jungle boots in there. Whistle! You bounced around like an imbecile because that ball it was too heavy to pass, weighed a ton to shoot. You dragged-dribbled. You scored ten field goals with the gymnast ball. Little or no opposition. You were uneasy. You only had one arm with a hole in the palm and still they wouldn't block you. Speedy and shifty you were all right, but you knew you weren't that hot. Five against one. Crazy. No guards guarding you. Flying carpet. Two points. Jumpshot. Two points. Mad, mad, mad. Even when that gymnast ball bounced off the rim and out of the net, *dos puntos*. Guard, center, forward, you could do no wrong. Nobody stood in your way, nothing was held against you. Double dribble, foul, lofting. They didn't care. Let you do all the playing. You left them behind. You faked them out of position . . . think of all the other possible violations, man, you committed them all. Until you'd run up a wild score like a ticker-tape inventory. You panted, you panicked, you collapsed in your stupendous victory. You wanted a drink. Was given, an *arroba* of it. You asked: Can't Pancho Rivas play too? The minute they heard that, they burst out laughing. You shook ye dripping head. Perhaps you'd cracked their skulls with that adding-machine score. Why couldn't he? you insisted, beginning to titter with the skulls. Because, because, oooh because, they said, laughing, because you've been playing with him for the last four quarters—including overtime! Numbskull that you were, you still didn't get it. You traveled illegally with the gymnast ball and ran all the way to Pancho Rivas's cell. He wasn't there. Then it struck you. You ran with the thing again, reached the kitchen, and with Major Shigura's kind permission, you politely borrowed a paring knife and tore into that gymnast ball: an eyeball popped out, then a nose, and all of it. It looked at you happily. Pancho Rivas had died up to his reputation. Only this time he had given more than the shirt off his back. The poor man had always had a temper, a sentry told you later. Pancho Rivas lost his head in the Major's office. You didn't bother asking about his body. The possibilities were limitless. Think of volleyball, badminton, football, tennis, Ping-Pong. Very athletic, Fort Santiago. Nero was born too early. You buried the gymnast ball in the plot outside. They even let you put a marker on it. Pancho Rivas was Catholic. And because he was, they suggested that perhaps you should fast on his behalf, hahaha. Rations cut off, hahaha. Who could've known that these fraternal Asians, soul brothers to the Filipinos, were so inventive? When you couldn't laugh anymore, you sobbed and screeched. You begged, you begged, please, please, for anything. They left you like that for a while until your lungs were torn till the hole was creeping with dried saliva and dead screams, and you could no longer feel your body. They left you this way until it was full moon and moaning and they came to you with a shovel. Go out into the yard, they beckoned, and pointed to the plot with your marker on it, go out into the yard—dinner is waiting. You reeled with the weakness but still you laughed and kept on laughing and they banged the door shut to your whimper and you called them an encyclopedia of names and yet they were nameless and an hour passed and you passed out with it and you regained consciousness and they were still out there and you could not afford another laugh because you knew it would be your last and anyway they did it for you and it was the laughter of the fed not the feeble and you waited some more and forever passed and God kept you alive or whoever it was kept writing Biblical jokes and you prayed and you blasphemed and still you were hungry and it seemed to be summer again by the fullness of the moon and then you died for the first time because now you called out to them and it was your own voice and it said: "Where is that shovel?"

Yet they don't really want to murder you. Won't let you die. They always revive you. Douse you with perfume. When you're conscious, the fragrance has been sponged away. They think of everything. Why not? They're beautiful. Are you going mad? Not yet. Almost. But not quite. You can't even fake it. Remember how you bubbled and berated and jerked spasmodically on the cold ground. You thrashed about and jabbered. They didn't even bother to use their peepholes. You wonder how many prisoners they have. All of them on the rack. Fort Santiago must be full of pus buckets and fulminating maniacs. If you heard another man's pain, that would be all right. You could tell yourself it wasn't happening to you alone. But you don't hear anything. Have they soundproofed the walls? Very likely. The insularity of anguish. Not a sound, Horatio. Not even a leak from a faucet. There is only you festering in your haberdashery. Beard, beard, pull it out! Chew it. String beans. When you had malaria and your nose was clogged, you cleaned it, gulped that down, too. What else? The only thing you can't digest is sand. You already ate the mat and when supper oozed out of you and you ate it, it was difficult to get that spaghetti in again.

You pace, go on thinking.

How long can you keep it up? You can't vomit-urinate forever. When that's gone, what then? Is that their next move? Can you hurdle that one? If you'd accepted the missal from that drudge they took in to fumigate the hotel, you would at least be assured of breakfast. Look through the bars. Sunstroke. Moon-ague. Daytime. Nightfall. What's the difference? Should have taken that missal, that's what you should have done, boy. Mass would make good *merienda.*

Look, look.

U.S. Air Force calling on you. Out there. Up there. Hum in the clouds. Steel in the sky. A glistening. A growling. Lava. Lights. Rising Sun searching for Stars and Stripes. Spermaceti of Yamashita. (So they have heavy guns at Fort Santiago.) Interceptors ascending to the Furies. Tracer tongues. Pillars of fire. Plummeting plumes. A hit? Whose? A miss! Whose? Nothing can shake up that lordly formation. Laying eggs in a nest of hives. Bombardment for the blessed. This must be deliverance, the devastation, hala, the Second Coming! Yet you're still in the dungeon. Unable to signal to your aluminum gods. Cosmic propellers, Mercury's projectiles, splinters from Saipan, Manna from Washington. Regards from Roosevelt. You cheer, cheer, cheer. Hey, Liberator! Look down! Look down! But gods are impervious to inanities. Won't even bend down to hold your nailless paw. Their hairpin acrobatics will not disentangle you from your cesspool exotica. Wingtips. Tails. Turrets. A distortion of bees . . . aren't they lovely though? Such is the kingdom of MacArthur. And while gods and gorillas pummel each other in the searchlight, something incredible happens. Through the bars you see this snow-white horse charge out into the night. A white/horse/with/a/piebald/rider/waving/a/sword. You cannot hear what he's shouting about but he seems nailed to his white mount framed by your bars and both man and animal are rearing at the sky malignant with meteors. There it is, like a slow-motion Cossack, that snowy horse, that gleaming sword under a white sky with its descending white death. You've heard of pink elephants. You've heard about Hemingway's two hundred and twenty-seven wounds at Fosalta. But of all fabrications of the inmate mind, and of all possible wounds inflicted on man by man, none can compare with that white horse that white night raging against the white gods. Your blood is red. Everything else is a white lie.

Time, time.

You spoke to that potbellied guard—when was it? Yesterday, last year, maybe tomorrow. What did he say? What did you say? He said they didn't really want you to talk. You said you thought they said they just wanted you to be . . . who cares? They're going to parlay you into a model. You're Portuguese, so why stick up for the Filipinos? He said you said they said . . . Water! Niagara Falls. Back to bucket. Can't piss. Try screwing your pipeline. Not a leak. You've drained the font. If you were in church now, you would dive into that holy H_2O for sinners. If you got anywhere near the communion rail, you could grab a dozen communion cookies and gorge yourself. The Pope would call that, heh, heh, gluttony.

You speak of love.

They took you to a detention cell unlike yours, unlike the others in the Fort. Five other men were you, and with you five others; if still possible, hungrier, filthier than you. Love was unloaded from a crate. Body of woman. Body because there was no longer any woman there. She'd been dead some two days. Naked, naturally. Advanced state of decomposition. Nude and Dead. But if she-it hadn't been, you and the five others would've plucked the dermis off her-it. Everybody stared at that body. In that nauseous eyeful, all Christendom was horrified. Some of you were married, had children. Body was probably married, had children too. Behind the door they waited at peepholes. Took another day before anyone of you did anything. A glance. A grunt. A grimace. But glands and curiosity were never ideal neighbors. Temptation provided the spine. Tentative touch became lingering caress and that was soon a vigorous probing. More out of bravado than anything else, one of you, the welder to be precise, stopped fooling around, sat on the thing and did the thing. After that, it was follow the leader. The sentries must have ruptured their kidneys laughing as you lined up quite orderly to take turns at the body used as a urinal—a biologically prodigious act, considering that rigor mortis had long set in. Inasmuch as all private heroics had been rendered impotent by the big war, a breach had to be found in the wall and that body was a hole. Everybody had cannonballs that day. In percussive requiem the guards clapped-banged their meat cans with each thrust, each penetration, clap-clap-bang, clap-clap-bang-bang, in and out, out and in, clap-bang-clap-bang. It must have been on the seventh lap when it happened. Perhaps it was ventriloquism but didn't that pyorrheal mouth with its papyrus gums hiss into somebody's salivary kiss so that all you bumbling bravos bashed your craniums trying to get to that bolted door? And didn't the ghouls outside crack their molars over that one? Wasn't that typical of Filipino womanhood to go to such extremes just to show who was wearing the pants? Oh, but that was really below the belt. Quaking, bunched up against the door like that everybody got hiccups. Except that Calabash Road *cajista,* the ousted Jehovah's Witness with the orangutan slouch. Just to prove he wasn't made of the same liver as you, he broke away from the consensus of fear, held up the dummy by its collarbone and rammed his manhood into it. *"Banzai!"* yelled the Nipponese grandstand. He did it again. *"Banzai!"* And again. *"Banzai!"* You lost count of the *banzais*. All you could see was that piston drilling into that scarecrow. Hiccups went full blast like heartbleats egging on that crazy *cajista* with his pneumatic drill. After his coup de grâce ejaculation, his derrick still rooted in that dead gulch, he raised his arms, clasped hands together in the traditional prizefighter salute. It seemed almost out of character that he didn't beat his chest. Not only was he king of the apes; he was king of the orangutans. He was the Penis of the Hour, the New Testicles. Spent at last, he sagged to the dirt floor, anchored down by his iron mermaid. With a mighty heave, he wrenched sideward, yanking the corpse off its praying mantis crouch, its head thumping against the bamboo bench. You nearly swallowed your Adam's apple—the thing wouldn't let the great lover go! The uterus must've jammed or something. He cursed and he pulled and he pulled and he cursed but what the devil had wrought no *cajista* could put asunder. Round and round he went the cell, kicking, thrashing, dragging the carcass on the ground, like those anguished dogs you saw after copulation running reverse-forward. More sport for the hyenas; everybody sniggered, guffawed. It was soooo funny. The *cajista* braked in midgallop and walloped the weight below his waist with bolo punches that would've killed ten live women. He did this for what seemed like hours, to no avail. Before long, all of you had stopped giggling, had put your heads together for some civil service. The old lecher had had enough. Besides, it wasn't funny anymore. Three stalwarts were delegated to the body; and two for the road runner. Now began a tug of war. Heave-ho! The goons cheered both teams. Heave-ho! Heave-ho! It was as hard pulling the jockey out of that womb as his mother must've found pushing him out of hers. You gave up, you slumped to the dirt floor with the others. That last spurt of energy must have cost him something, for that *cajista* let loose a deafening scream that stilled even the carousing guards. It went on and on and on, that caterwauling until sometime in the night the cell door was thrown open and in strode the Commandant. You almost didn't recognize him without his white horse under that white, blazing American sky. While everybody was agog looking at him, and with not a word, the Commandant, like a High Lama in his white sleeping robe with its purple sash, advanced, sword unsheathed. A ray of moonlight glinted from the open door to the blade as he raised it over his head with both hands. Slowly, slowly, as though any hint of intimacy would stain his blinding whiteness, the Commandant inched toward the stricken sinner. You and the congregation fell down sobbing and walked on your knees, supplicants all, with clasped hands begging for mercy, ay, mercy. Rocking, reeling, advancing on your knees, you saw the Host elevated above the Commandant's head and you heard him murmur, with much pain and without accent: *In nomine Patris, et Filii, et Spiritus Sancti.* Amen. You saw moonlight descend, and the lovers halved. Half a man jumped up, ran out the door. You heard the alarm, the volley. He wouldn't have minded so much being shot down without his boots on. But to die without his balls . . . And when you looked at the thing again he left behind, didn't you see a smile on its face?

Yes, speak now of love.

Listen, listen.

Somebody coming, somebody going. No clanking. No boots. Just somebody without footsteps, without keys. Your door is locked until you leave, if you live. What are they thinking about in Manila? Still about Americans? That was your peculiar treason: that you thought: that they heard your thoughts. Ideas will be the bayonet of you yet. Ideas, not action. For that they throw you into the hole. You don't believe in heaven or hell. To haven or to hole from this depth forward. Sanctum sanctorum. Get up, you. Walk around, you. They're looking, they're still interested. You, the Experiment. You, the condiment. Run, run, run, around the magnetic walls of your hole. You feel your next meal coming. Parts of speech erupting. From pit to pendulum. Cornucopia in a vacuum. Can't be much. Already consumed too much. You can't go on irrigating your own vineyard, reproducing your own carbohydrates. If you had a knife, if you had something to file with, something you could sharpen that loose bar with, you could gnaw on it, like a candy bar with rusty sugar. If you could hack off a finger, that would be delicious. There are fifteen of them anyway, including your lower extremities: odds on your side there. Ah . . . they have claret, they have caviar in Monte Carlo!

You take in this bowl. Very much in control you are. Because when you are so hungry that you're not hungry anymore, you're in perfect control. Bowl contains hot dog. So they say. Liberated from sunken U.S. cargo ship. They say. It's roasted, so black. Looks like *longanisa.* Your teeth are sharp, the meat is tough. You clamp on it, your jaw working like a saw. Doesn't taste much like anything. Taste buds gone. But you know what this meat is, and they want you to know. Playing softball this time and you're the underdog as always. Did they for a second think that you can still be shocked? Down it goes, the little black thing, somebody's pipe, probably in another *bartolina* like this, cut off from his natural resources. Are they plotting the same for you? The realization is sudden. That, mister, is the moral behind the meat. Conveyed with asterisks. Benefit from the bologna.

Tenderloin trauma, it tolls for thee. And if you bleed enough, there is a Tiber of your mother's unhomogenized milk for every pewter this side of Dionysian paradise. Encore! A minor scream. Workout for the tonsils. They'll have to build a better mousetrap from their mountain of mistakes. The rat has gobbled up the cat.

Again they s-p-o-k-e to you.

Bright Wednesday morning, they said. As if it mattered. Now they want you to distinguish the day so the dark can devour you. You anticipate that ruse: can't work again. Not so bad now. Harness the hunger, thaw the thirst. Transcend food. Walk on water. Leading to an overwhelming sanity. That which from the nadir grows and in the evening glows. They have duped, debased, decimated the Old Testament, earthling. What remains after osmosis is yours alone: man of your own making, god of your groin; and neither bile nor balm can touch that, Magnificat.

You stroll around a bit. For subjects without rights, a constitutional. Ha, moldier than Yorick's skull, your sense of humor.

A tapping on the door. Note underneath. Ah, they've surrendered. They're returning you to Santo Tomás. From *purgatoria* to pragmatism. From damnation to Dante. Squeal again, blighted angel, squeal again. Blow the bugles, beat the band, bring out the banners.

You rise.

You repeal God.

You've won the charades, Saint Vanoye!

She would punish them, yes, she would punish them.

. . . And who had serenaded her for years rushed screaming to her . . .

"Wake up."

. . . But when he reached within arm's length . . .

"Wake up."

. . . She only laughed, only shot him twice . . .

"Wake up, I say, wake up."

. . . When he groveled at her feet with the graveyard in his eyes . . .

"Please, wake up!"

. . . She shot him again, once more in the heart . . .

"Oh, wake up, please!"

. . . She aimed the gun at all things, to shoot at the trees, the branches, the sky. Above all, the sky. She had been angry for three minutes, and she threw the rifle as far as she could throw it into the river, where she wished so wildly it would go home to the Philippines.

The boy shook the girl by the legs.

She woke up to say: "Why are you stabbing me, Moranito?"

Looking at his hands, Amoran saw that they were covered with blood.

It was her menstrual time.

[9]

A HEMORRHAGE OF HISTORY laid Hidalgo low. His cough-wracked body overflowed the brass bed with billows of blanket, tangles of dressing gown. The girl lay in her cot, small and sensitized to pain. The boy tried to wash her sheets clotting with blood. One was hot with rage; the other, cold with calm. Hunger made Hidalgo raucous, and Amoran spooned scalding gruel into that twisted mouth. Only water would the girl take in, would pay back in blood. Amoran was reduced to a litter carrier drudging for two patients. A nightmare, also a great waste. There were pockets to pick, goods to pilfer: a whole city waited for his cunning. Temporarily put out of commission, he rubbed the old man's back with hot and cold compresses and washed the girl's feet. Once or twice Mrs. Colombo badgered her way into room thirteen to inquire about her ailing tenants. At her raspy voice, Hidalgo hooded himself with the blanket. Miserably: "There's a bat in the room!" Loath as she was to leave, the landlady tsk-tsked this inhospitable reception, begged their forbearance, and like a grumpy grand dame, bounded away. She left behind a plate of rice fried in soy sauce, pork lard. Speared into the greasy sherbet of grain was a popsicle stick; this was ribboned, in what was intended as a petal pattern, with a paper napkin which also bore the Colombo scrawl—in much the same manner a doomed movie heroine might smuggle in arsenic with her fudge to her falsely accused, unjustly condemned sweetheart for a suicide pact. Such were her hopes, her romantic notions that the landlady was beset by modes of communication, refinements of expression. Her penmanship then, along with its inspiration, did precious little to convey the character of her need, so that her note merely wished the Spaniard a speedy recovery. Alas, such grand passion went unreciprocated. Welcome was the rice, which was gone in a matter of minutes; the epistle, never read, soon complemented the rice in the toilet. Not one to bury the hatchet was our Amoran.

He had no right, no right at all to take her there, thought Hidalgo, as he swung at blankets and bat wings. Did Vanoye tell her what? What could she be thinking now? Anxiously to the cot turned Hidalgo; the girl was staring at the ceiling, so pale, perhaps bewitched. Eyes animated by some light. Worried Hidalgo. Did not want her ambulant and asking. Wanted to sing a lullaby, rock her to sleep. Stand he tried but that dressing gown was a leash, the brass bed a kennel. Believe this now: to his ears did lisp a raga—somebody's radio. Into the room next filtered the shivery steel-wire plectrum of, how could it ever be?, a sitar, wherewith Hidalgo saw Amoran seated quite the snake charmer, Bengali pillow before Manila mattings. In his hands, a face mirror; the girl seemed rapt, liable to rise with the raga; and risen to her reflection, did float out of conjury, out of captivity: to follow her lover without a flute.

Comatose, beaded with sweat, Hidalgo was read to by the boy whose medical appraisals were invariably anointed with mentholatum. Insulated from the citizenry, the soldiery, the blackouts, Amoran let Hidalgo extol the years.

Hysteria, Hispania.

Versus Vanoye.

Evoked a solar year when giddy folk through the generosity of patriots and coastline cavaliers annexed Honduras to heaven, when the profligate *pensionado* came posturing in the *azotea* offering the equivalent of nylons to his *querida.* By gaslight: the plum of prodigy was mortgaged to carpetbaggers—the pirate edition of a nonconformist gazette with a phenomenal subscription almost as heretical as the libel laws it flouted. Kept the Guardia Civil busy putting out the fire. No printing press those days, only the stage where a noble exile made his petition, quoted Virgil (really intimating Marlowe), denounced anomalies—a bluff of Hebrew in smug, mellifluous tones. European steeds reared soon enough, what an inundation of academia! Your Latin, your Greek trumpeting quotidian conceits. *Qué barbaridad. . . .*

"How you would have loved the *comedia* then," reveried Hidalgo, and time like blood gushed out of his eyes, ears.

Hombre, there they were, gloved and caped, sipping only brandy (an *arroba* of it!), loathed by the *nativo* as they venerated Cervantes in cafés, infecting garrets with a welter of New World homilies, a decadence waiting for the brush of a Goya. Youth, wringing hands at the prospect of reversals in Paris, took to the galleons with seedlings in their valises. Barcelona-born, surely. Irrevocably attuned to history. A potpourri of saturnine elegance and deplorable manners, these young bucks returned with the seedlings grown to an ordure of vines. And how determined to conduct all concerts, collect all wagers; they gravitated to the theatre box, to the gaming tables, dilating with eminence, provoking duels, dying with honor as the *mayordomos* stood fatalistically on the lawns; and sustaining a wound from an insult, retired to Byzantine villas on the proletarian east of the suburbs. For the mustachioed swains, the air itself seemed politic as they strutted on the rotundas like dancers of the mime, a stupendous procession of inimitable Byrons who, barely ten years later, would constitute the Old Order—contemporaries to the bone, fastidious spenders to the end though subsisting on the last centimo. *Caramba,* but what a season! Hermit consuls divined ivory baths in lavatories and a Rolls-Royce in every outhouse. Aside from seminarians scowling in their cassocks, everybody else fed them chestnuts, toasted them with punch, swathed their path with torches. The unread, the unregenerate flirted under curlicues, curates mated their hounds, apprentice pamphleteers they squeezed every trollop. O the women of salt! Conspirators, quick to fill the scene, quicker on goblet or couplet, danced carefree to fiddlers and rode on ponies headed straight for the novenas. Impudent on polka, on waltz, they paused long enough: for the pious to commend them on Easter, for jasmine tea, for an assessment of the newest gold mine, for a mistress in her crinolines. Woke up in provincial night courts they did, dined on decrees sympathizers sent through channels by courier. Bounteous suppers followed each other in endless epiphanies. Oaths, allegiances, *caudillos,* holidays: capital such as a politico might build a republic on. The angelus would sound the ceremonies for the ferment of protagonists, boots thudding in parlors, potted plants concealing Mausers; changes, reforms, injunctions—tools of hyperbole. Inheritors of French or German letters bewailed the *yanqui* climate. Age swollen with correlatives. Came the nickelodeon, the constabulary retrenching before the insurrection: somebody had to civilize the *indios.* Now an empire saddled on Madrid waited grimly for Aguinaldo from a casement window. Arrived: the automobile. Crashed against *arrabales,* against corrugated iron. *Sitios* throbbed with mercenaries; fortunately, the *gobernadorcillo* was rescued from ignominy when an agnostic declaiming Marqui de Sade emerged from the arson he'd started in Del Pilar's house and waved sackcloth all afternoon. Old Escolta droned on with patriarchs who had stayed for the centenary. Calle Aviles with its neocolonial germination: "POST NO BILLS." Symptomatic of the times, eh? Smell Bay Rum. Hidalgo de Anuncio passed Carriedo, the street named after a don. All patronized the Merfusha, maybe the Torino for cuisine aristocrat. Or soughed or squandered in a chancery, in a conservatory. Envoys in aloha shirts gorged themselves with huge bowls of *mami* on Calle Salazar. Katy de la Cruz began to sing; a pittance for the Chinese between Calle Fernando and Calle Pinpin with their fripperies. But that was running ahead of the clock. What about: the Franciscans fleeing their cloisters? the dandies craving for Lent, mocking in merriment? the doxies jilted for sieges? physicians tracing elopements? Such badinage could not long continue, the brigands knew; the leafy swards were soon to be spurned. Postulants preempted bargain-basement liberalism—weary of cant *y* cult, they trooped to any war available. Somewhere, someone planted Japanese flame trees, and here, Hidalgo tried to put his mind's hands on this heroic identity. Did the trees burn? Yes. How about Calle Real, or was this leaping ahead of *El Comercio?* the allusions to:

Batavia? Del Pilar's poverty in Madrid? the messages of the Sublime Paralytic? Borromeo Lou had smuggled the *vod-a-vil* from Estados Unidos and suffragettes chirped on the Puente Colgante. *Empleomania,* the Zobels, *majas muchas*. Three Europeans recorded impressions of Manila: his father dined with them. Picturesque, that! Creoles in *charro* dress, the intermarriage pupa, a bonanza in the cockpit—*bravisimo!* The mill of the gods turned. Everybody was on the cultural ride. To Binondo, to Arrocerros. Watch: rice loaded on *bancas,* hear: how cigar-factory girls squeal, drink: the sweet milk of Mariquina, cross: the bridge with seven arches, the Puente Grande.

Oh, the *tertulias,* reflected Hidalgo. Let not Vanoye talk the *tertulias* away! Twilight for the *moro-moro;* the *zarzuela* was in flower. Driving to Santo Cristo in victorias. Haha, swam to nautical school. There was that earthquake on the eve of the Corpus Christi and the lone survivor of the buried city was the church of the Augustinians, which only lost a belltower. Never again was Victorian England seen in this country. Everything was in a tourniquet, like two *tamaraos* locked in horns. Strolling in Lardizabal, you took out a cigar; quaffed mineral water and caroused with *cargadores* or underground royalty. In the interior courtyard, a painting of the Ayuntamiento was retouched by a direct descendant of Philip II. The *caída* boasted the statue of Charles IV of Spain. When they wanted moral armament, they munched santol preserves, twitted harlots, repaired to Antipolo. The Voltaire of the masses conjured up witches in apparels of silk and dwelt amorously on frontiers. Judas Iscariot had infiltrated the *conquista* while the Old Guard sobbed piteously. Rust, rust was coming in! Glory was ebbing, the empire crumbling! Wall Street, was that what came next? Did moats still surround the Intramuros? No chronology. Memory stated no order. Only borders. But surely it had happened by then: Taal volcano had erupted, in the Casino Español, one heard the young, irascible Recto speak. Perhaps Christ met the Manila parvenu in the polygenetic ancestry. Lord Hybrid was in focus: though the Palace where Edward Prince of Wales stopped off to play polo changed, there was this thing: the Gardenia District was abolished, the Pasig Estuary flowed through the reformation to baptize upstarts into New Money. From the slaughterhouse to the sewage incinerator, the speeches had acquired a tongue of spice and the first act of the legislature was to lift the ban on the use of the Filipino flag. It was not a world for timid men, only for the *pensionados* from Nozaleda Park. All glory terminated with Charles V.

Sine die. . . .

Amoran poured water in a glass and handed it to the old man.

Between them, the girl lay in imperturbable animation. Three days long since the old man's seizure. For three edifying days he fought the mandrake roots Vanoye had planted in the girl's mind.

"There was no plumbing in those days," resumed Hidalgo. "A flux there was. Everything was running like water with Quezon and Osmena the deep rivers. The Spanish Novel in the Philippines will be commemorated in English. Everything else is posthumous."

The girl smiled at the old man's sagacity, even as the boy snickered. She loved them both; but also worshiped something more in May, the mountains. May was the month you saw what the young men looked like. Hewn from crags, yet gentle as foam, they were lean and dusky; whistling as white folk sang under the windows. Theirs were the votive noons of May. Dancing in the plazas, they waited for the daughters getting water from the wells. May Men she called them, who were tall, tender boys who brought with them, the *harana,* the harvest.

Hidalgo nodded.

"Let me tell you about Belmonte," he said.

And Amoran watched them both, but was only seeing the girl in her menstrual misery.

"Dígame," she whispered to the old Spaniard. *"Dígame, extranjero. . . ."*

[10]

THE JAPANESE PRESENCE in Manila, while conditioning Hidalgo and his claustrophobic ward to a hallucinatory retreat, proved invaluable to Amoran and the other realists. Sleepdancers in the Pacific War, The Spaniard and the girl, recently convalesced, hopscotched down the streets in abortive pursuit of life: it was the boy who came back to room thirteen with scraps for their bellies, news for their sport. During the latter half of 1944 and certainly in the early months of 1945, the city seemed poised for some terrible onslaught. The "Greater East Asia Co-Prosperity Sphere" (translation: togetherness) of Japanese military officers and Filipino administrators was dutifully recorded by journalism, incessantly parroted on the radio. The puppet government strained at the strings, but dolls were made specifically for abuse. President Jose P. Laurel rolled up his trousers to pad barefoot in the rice fields, to plant a sprig, the symbolic sprout of Nipponese-Filipino brotherhood. How could he have known that the symbol would cost more than a case of colds and cramps? that his countrymen's reclusive dislocation would become, in the American future, a bitter documentation, a Magna Carta of denunciation? With each fig leaf of inter-Asian agriculture, the President did not anticipate how tall a tree of treason he was raising, for treason it was later called. Click went the camera, tat-tat-tat went reporters. Each swipe brought the man closer to an immitigable reckoning. No one could deny that innocents were dragged from their sleep nightly for questioning at Fort Santiago. That minor employees were tortured to confess to trumped-up charges the intricacy and nomenclature of which were far beyond their humble hostilities. Ten years later, the nationalists would still be suppressing dossiers of collaboration. Even as now the military occupation pooh-poohed allegations that it had just lost twenty-five aircraft plus an electronic gewgaw in the latest American air strike over Manila. Unsubstantiated too were popular rumors of five hundred casualties in the infantry. Contested: the charge that twenty-six Filipino shipping clerks suspected of harboring a guerrilla chieftain were held without due process of law in a barracks outside Manila. Vehemently denied: that the Japanese Imperial Air Force was stripping its airfields in the suburbs; such equipment to be flown to a beleaguered front. What could not be denied was the undiminishable fact of the underground shortwave transmitter which relayed grievances and received piecemeal vindications.

A frieze of ambiguities was the Japanese Soldier.

Elsewhere, he was Army, Infantry, Navy, Air Force, Paratroops: the Enemy. In Manila, though he came from brass and bottom, he was the Administrator. The Major commanded, the Private was saluted. The Colonel personally decapitated a prisoner; the Corporal assisted an old lady across the street. The General ordered a township sacked; the Sergeant rescued a baby from a burning lean-to. The Lieutenant disemboweled a priest; the General shot the Lieutenant. Collectively, they were to be seen perhaps a division strong; infallible in parades, illustrious in pictures, invincible in newsreels—Japan. Collectively, a hearty group on leave: commandeering civilian vehicles on the avenues, roistering in saloons, bumbling into bazaars. Collectively, too, a squadron bombing the Allied Forces in Saipan.

Pigeon-toed, built like a *sumo* wrestler, the Japanese Soldier was sunlight before smog. He was well bred (Kyoto), rapacious (North Korea?), peasant type (ah, Osaka!)—the ambiguities. If he stole *cavanes* of rice from tenant farmers, why did he share his lunch of meat balls with a leper? Could they ever forget his face after he pistol-whipped a woman heavy with child: somebody else remembered the same face that wept unashamedly because an orphan had spilled his *salabat*. Sta. Cruz he trod in reluctance and elation because he was born on a dirt farm, yet had always hankered for the metropolis. He called on the natives, refusing their generosity and insisted on giving them his meager army rations. No one who witnessed it could doubt his sincerity when a boy had to be sweet-talked into the dentist's chair: soldier was without candy, but his warmth won the day. With some repugnance he stepped into a bar to drink the local brew. He knew no one there; indeed a large number of its patrons he had dispatched to labor camps. Amoran saw him there, and because the boy had the gift for it, the soldier was soon fleeced of his cash. His acquiescence, which was absolute, seemed part of a magisterial apologia but for whose human continuum the Philippine Islands would have been put to the sword. As these were ambiguities in any soldier in any war, time multiplied, time subtracted them into history. And if history was an ambiguity, then what was God?

Away from objectives, pinpointed targets, docked by trawlers, disgorged by amphibious vessels, grounded by troop planes, the Japanese Soldier could usually be found in that most convivial of war theatres—the bar. In downtown Manila where the friendly bar had proliferated like larvae, he was to be seen with all his accouterments—bayonet, footees, meat can and floppy military cap. Like any soldier, he was a lone wolf in combat, but a duality on furlough. All war wounds were personal, unshared even by the thousand wounded; yet no debauchery was ever truly experienced without its composite half: the sharer. No stein of beer could quench without its complement: the mug of camaraderie. Oldest relationship of all: the Buddies. Hans and Klaus, Luigi and Giovanni. Jean-Paul and Jacques, Joe and Bill.

In Tomodachi Toni marched Yato and Ito, sergeant and corporal. Sergeant Yato, as befitted manual rote and the cliché of all sergeants, was chunky, with an overpowering grizzliness to accentuate his combat record of ten American Marines slain, six wounded, two captured. *Sake*-eyed from the magic fountain of his canteen (refilled by mysterious requisitions at almost every stopover depot), he saw himself as the *kamikaze* roughneck of beachhead landings. He was a prodigious hand-to-hand combatant, the churlish picker of souvenirs (among them, an Australian scalp), which he kept in his rucksack for instant reference. Sergeant Yato had run the gauntlet from homicidal traumas to absolute stillness. He'd done everything in this man's army and did it better than any *kimigayo*-singing son of Nippon. To Amoran, the Sergeant was the inexhaustible supplier of raw fish tails and salted squid sauced in KP latrines. Yato the widower had bayoneted babies in Chungking. Yato the vegetarian had eaten a human leg in Manchuria. Yato the rickshaw man in Yokohama had repulsed homosexual commanding officers in Singapore. Yato the madcap Mandarin of Honshu was now longing to be a Wehrmacht warrior so he could fight side by side with Rommel's panzer at Tobruk against the British and the New Zealanders.

None of these biographical statistics were known to Corporal Ito. At age sixteen, the draftee had not quite reached the glamour of battle fatigue. His induction was a romantic error; he toted a sleeping bag on an inner flap of which he had water-colored his fiancée's sleepy violet eyes. From Sergeant Yato, the authentic *tora,* Ito had studiously copied the itchy tic, the *samurai* swagger, the rakish angle of cap, the boot clicking. Ito disliked intoxicating liquors of any kind—his gullet was quivery with baby acids—but he clinked tumblers with his sergeant with equal gusto. They had been together in eleven patrols and sixteen bars. Each time, Corporal Ito had frozen on his trigger finger, had puked out his beer. Tomodachi Toni's was their seventeenth bar; miraculously, Ito was holding up. Easier came his beerish wink; the *samurai* swagger was hipbone perfect. Ito's buttocks pinch on the bar girls also earned him an extra point on Yato's graph of manly arts. This afternoon at Fort Santiago had been rather eventful, what with Ito standing up to the platoon's boorish initiations. Was Sergeant Yato proud of the way his rifle bearer made water on that bully's field glasses. They would know better than to pick on Ito now. Lick Toyoda man to man he could not; he would be no match for Tamura's blabbermouth. Neither could he drink Yatsuro under the *tatami;* but Ito could write *haikus* and call everybody names in them; as a bonus, he was more than competent with a knife. Wasn't a *ronin* in the whole Japanese Army could cross *katanas* with him in a fair fight. Why, the only man who would have the nerve and the skill for such swordplay was Major Shigura himself, a *Meiji* man and a *kendo* expert. Hmm, thought Yato, that one. Well, perhaps he would learn something about their intractable major when the time came. Anyway, it had been a good day for him and Ito. The kid had heard about Maddalena, the belly dancer.

Who, this humid Saturday night, was the main reason why Tomodachi Toni's was bubbling with business. Tomodachi Toni herself (*née* Tomasa Pompeyo) had deserted her *tres-siete* game in the cellar to help out with the service. Her two Ilongot waiters (all her waitresses had been blacklisted by the Resistance for "other services rendered") were unbelievably inept. One was forever smashing crockery; the other always cheating on the rum, overchanging the customers. With her cheap perfume, artificial eyelashes and outsize kimono, Tomodachi Toni was an inhibiting presence that clients, drunk or sober, had to respect. Nights like this, despite the life-giving ring of the cash register, she was tight-lipped and testy. Nights like this, she would unfailingly think of Lucindo Pompeyo, her husband, gone nine months now without a word, and since then not even a postcard. What could have possessed the man? Tomodachi Toni knew, as indeed all her envious neighbors did, that Mr. Pompeyo had everything a husband could possibly ask for. Three healthy, handsome boys in school, money in the safe, a thriving business establishment, and a devoted wife. All these nine months, when her hair had turned gray, her heart heavy, Tomodachi Toni had been paying for pleas in the personal columns of *The Manila Tribune:* "LUCINDO COME BACK." To this she would sometimes add, "FORGIVE ME," or "ALL IS FORGIVEN." Though she did not know exactly what she had done to him, what she was forgiving. She prayed to all the saints in Baclaran, she melted candles she waited she wept. Lucindo Pompeyo did not come back. Only her customers did. For Maddalena, the belly dancer. Instead of Lucindo, at the bar stood Paeng Redoblado, her husband's best friend, who had not quite forgiven her for their mutual loss. Night after night, week after week, month after month, drink after drink, he stood at the bar, morose and menacing. Like the object of his disgust—he could only regard her as a secondhand kimono—he had lost weight, had become sallow with the waiting. To what she owed this almost vociferous hatred, the bone-weary manageress did not know; she only knew that she too had suffered, she too had waited. She also knew that their silence could not go on much longer. The man was deranged and his derangement was on the tip of his tongue. She needed, demanded to hear the words. They would at least concern Lucindo Pompeyo. These sweet nothings she heard one evening. Drunker than usual, Paeng Redoblado accosted her with all his stored-up venom, verbalizing their loss, their lament. Names she had not heard before she heard that night: that silence had held back a razor-tongue and she let it cut her to ribbons, let the words slap and stab her, rejoicing at the convergence of his anger and her acceptance. It was at this juncture that her two obsequious waiters, thinking to avenge their employer, knocked the cad down and kicked him as he rolled on the floor. Just as she had longed for his vilifications, her nemesis demanded penalty for having uttered them as he lay there in what appeared to be paroxysms of joy. The defilement of their animosity irked her. She had trusted his enmity, so fluent, so lyrical in sound as it had been in silence, because it was fang of her anger over those plaster figures and wax candles, neither of which proved saints and tears enough to bring back her husband. All this she could accept—as she accepted the flagrant heathenism of flagellants in the procession of the Quiapo Fiesta—as stations to her own cross. But what was she to make of this man, nearly six feet tall, thrashing joyously on the floor? She had stepped in to save him from the loyalty of her two ruffians. The night after, Paeng Redoblado, bruised and somewhat transfigured, stood at his usual place by the counter. In his eyes was the same mad gleam: another insult beseeching further injury.

"Drink up! Drink up!" rallied the outsize kimono to Saturday night customers. Tomodachi Toni's was in high gear. An eight-door, brick-and-banyan polyglot period piece on Calle Raon, it was the precursor of the split-level in Manila. In chronological order, it was one of the first tourist agencies in the country, a *hopia* retail shop, an opium den for Chinese nationals; and the headquarters of a religious minority whose one and only uprising had been quelled by the Philippine constabulary in fourteen hours. The story was that even before the ink was dry on the bill of sales, overnight the Pompeyos had converted the Raon relic from a businessman's bromide to a businessman's boon. While every merchant with a windfall to spare was caught up in the *bodega* boom, the Pompeyos were digging a well, praying for a gusher. By dint of hammer and hope, nails and nagging, lights and loans, an establishment was born. The Pompeyos were the talk of the town; they had pulled the proverbial rabbit out of a decrepit hat just as they said they would. In prewar days, the rabbit was known as Texas Toni, with a Stetson hat for trademark. After Pearl Harbor, the hare donned a kimono to conceal its color; a mural of Mount Fujiyama replaced the Stetson. Texas Toni, poor critter, bowed to Tomodachi Toni. So long and *Ohayo!* "I shall return!" swore MacArthur. No ideology involved. Just commerce. And it was "business as usual" this Saturday night at Tomodachi Toni's which was still clean and commodious. On its front door outside was the reminder: "MADDALENA TONITE." The outsize kimono's *paroquianos* came. Come to prey and pander were Tomodachi Toni's regulars—eunuchs, satyrs, most of them married and miserable.

[11]

RITUAL FOR MARRIAGE: to offer the virgin of respect to the wear and tear of he and she. Precedent: such respect, which was the primary illusion and the original sin in courtship, and by any definition, the safe conduct and salvation of the male, soon to be pulverized in the mortality of affection. Respect for the husband as provider, as father, as a functional member of the community, and lastly, respect for man as male. Respect was veneer and mainstream. Without it male knees sagged in love, male spine did not rebound from its labor, male mind dreamed no enviable future. Wives made demands from respect. And it was imperative, yet impossible to meet those demands. Wives were questions; husbands were never answers. Better that there had never been such a mask as this, for then the face would not be so hard to live with. Respect was the oldest child in all marriages, though it never left the womb.

Enter Maddalena, Woman.

That these customers were men for whom love had not lasted was quite evident. It was their singular solace now to relish the aftermath of bawling brats, spidery, fortyish wives, termagant in-laws, ramshackle homes. If the health of conformity had once reconciled their masculine cynicism with the cult of responsibility, they were now reinstated to their old prejudices. The bone of contention was marrow again. In the resurgence of masculinity, wives were widowed, not by the death of husbands, but by the demise of illusion. In this tawdry, steaming room with its sixty-watt illumination, a coroner's autopsy could declare its habitués dead, conjugally, filially dead.

Maddalena's thighs.

What would it profit husbands to gainsay the whore and lose their own semen?

"Hubarin mo!"

"Off!"

"Off!"

"Off!"

Surely the dirty dishes in the sink, the soot on the stove, the imminent (unwanted) baby's diaper did not accelerate the splendor of the loins? After the first and second toddler and their initial jubilation, their cheap cigars, what paternal pride could a laborer feel? Flesh dialogues had terminated in a family, mawkish and mandatory, sustenance unknown. Thorny hands of the carpenter made and were capable only of so many *barong-barongs* in Manila. Eyes of the watch repairer screwed ever tighter over the mechanism of silver or gold karat time. Lungs of the millworker congested a cough away from tuberculosis and a charity coffin while the volcanic ballast of his fishwife drove in a premature cross. *Ave Maria, Luis Contreras, sumalangit ngawa ang iyong kaluluwa!*

Their ribaldries now had ended.

The locksmith, Zerrado Susi, smiled broadly (flashed his eroded teeth in sweet complicity), and casually inched his left hand under his belt. Smacking his lips, he eased his legs from the wooden support of the sofa-also-table, the better to catch Maddalena's next circuit. The effort jangled his keys, which were in a threadbare pouch tied to his buckle. Very guiltily he crossed his legs. Between their pillared heat lay his rod. That old India rubber was paying attention all right. Erect and pulsating like a little tin soldier. The national anthem was playing: the flagpole saluted.

Two hours from now his Saturday night probation on good behavior would officially be over and he would have to drag himself home to his two-door two-family apartment where his wife, Martha, was not waiting for him. (Payday was yesterday.) Martha the prolific. Martha, who nearly succumbed to dysentery the year before. God was merciful, damn it to hell! Martha, Martha, *cara y cruz,* seated to her Bingothon with the other fatuous, blessed harridans who would never, never die of dysentery. Martha, whose leech-tongue in those early years (and late nights) in their marriage exquisitely mistook his brick-hard banana for licorice, though she had called it—what was it?—ah, yes, sugar cane. "Come home soon, my sugar cane," she had cooed as he was about to leave their honeymoon *cuarto* during his apprenticeship at his father's flourishing shop. And because she had a semester of college (midwifery), she called him Cain, Ca-in, pronounced with a *k*. Martha, whose ingenious carnality he had somehow polluted into that most unfortunate and inviolable of all female states: Motherhood. So that now, in their eighteenth year (18!) together as man (?) and wife (?) the immensity of her crime against his passion, the gravity of her transgression—and indeed the transgression of all womankind—assailed him. Martha, mother-flabby of late, early to rise for her youngest's bottle, unresponsive, unsympathetic to his moist curtain-raiser caress. "Beast!" she shouted at his nakedness, leaving him dis-organ-ized in his cot. After a dynasty of noisy Susis, Zerrado still yearned to feed his woman but there was no longer any room in her for him. Probe and frolic he could, he did till his twitchy fingers broke, those congealed thighs would not, did not part. Ah, he had lost the key to this special door; the lock had rusted. Nor would all his prodigy or wit pry it loose again. Martha, Martha, a *nanay* now. She who had never needed any vaseline despite her girlish frailness would have to be blown up by howitzers. Well, easy come, easy go. Zerrado Susi went on about his work in the morning until midafternoon, fitting a smelter's variety of keys into storage doors into porch shutters, sculpturing openings for nightwatchmen for housewives who feared robbery and rape. Back home, Zerrado confronted the now scarifying simper of a dependent across the supper table, whose knee refused to ignite at his switch underneath. "Dirty old man!" she railed. The knee approach had never been one of his effective gambits, not even in her heyday, so Zerrado concentrated on his plate of cold cereal with the scrambled egg on top. Topped only by dessert. A leftover *bitsu-bitso* from her mother's kitchenette just a holler away. After that, bed, but to sleep.

Maddalena glided toward his metacarpus, but turned.

The only gratification in bed now was fantasies—if she did not snore too loudly. In the morning, with his packed lunch (no way of avoiding that *bitsu-bitso*), he received her "be good" kiss and hurried off in time not to hear her bark at the littlest Susi, who was unwinding his wet-diaper tantrum. Bereavement in bed meant Zerrado had to wait until everybody in the shop had gone off to lunch so he could retire to the privacy of the toilet, therein to make most of half a love. This remedial effort was impractical for home consumption, what with all their children running in and out of the bathroom. To the lavatories Zerrado Susi took his surplus manhood for its surrogate sex. Like the confessional, the toilet was secret, it brought relief; like communion, his ejaculations were reunited with Martha's combustible ghost. This satiety of last resort cost him a none too pretty conscience. He was fifty-five, looked sixty. Exposure could wreck the business he had so industriously worked for and so gratefully inherited. But some weaknesses die hard in many men and in Zerrado Susi the weakness was in his top physical condition, a reservoir of indestructible orgasm. Leaning ramrod straight on the wall (a toilet tourist was he), he conjured up keyhole memories of the young earthy Martha, and relived their compatible orgies. In the dark outside burlesque emporiums, he spilled facsimiles of himself on slats, on tile floors. Beast, beast, beast, accused his wife from across fathoms of menopause—while he crouched close to hit the center of the toilet bowl. His trembling once caused him to miss it by a good four inches; his juice dribbled off the horseshoe curve of the enamel and bounced onto his Ang Tibay shoe, like a huge glob of wax. He bent down and wiped it off. For a while he looked wonderingly at it, laughing nervously. Perhaps he should put it in a vial, wrap it in cellophane, give it to Martha on their next anniversary. For auld lang syne, he would say.

Ah, Maddalena! Maddalena!

At a particularly agitated performance, his bunch of keys had dropped in the toilet bowl, sticking into a bowel cake whose core he had creamed with a hasty emission. There it was, that porcupine pie (a baker couldn't have done better), with its milky-white polka-dot frosting, like a one-eyed foetus staring balefully at him, father of ten. Flabbergasted and ashudder, he stooped down to retrieve the keys sticky with excreta. Mother of God, what a birthday cake—a caramel Cyclops!

For a long time after that, he refrained, fasted. When Martha turned a waspish forty-nine, he could not eat her pudding. Only made it worse. Who was *she?* Martha grilled, after the children had been inveigled to bed. He buried his head under the pillow. Martha was not easily put off. Who was she! But the honest truth was that he had not gone into another toilet outside the house for weeks. Made up his mind about that. "Who? Who? Who?" she screeched. Asked about names, face, places. What did she look like, huh? He groaned, wishing he were dead. How could he tell Martha that her rival was a fruitcake in a toilet boudoir? His paramour had one gelatinous eye, sticky skin, sepia complexion, taper teeth. One could blow out the candles on that damned birthday pudding but no one could flush down that smirking putty in the cessbowl. He had heard of women who had given birth to malformed babies: two heads, three legs, one arm. Abominations could still be traced to the Almighty. Monsters were delivered by mothers every day. Abnormalities did not frighten him because they still came from some agent in nature, no matter how monstrous. But his own delivery was none of these. Accidents procreated insights and that creation in the toilet bowl was incomprehensible. By some strange alchemy, he had given birth to himself.

"More! More!" exclaimed the *paroquianos*. Maddalena gyrated obligingly.

The locksmith did not consider himself oversexed, just overendowed. Perhaps he would be one of the select, envied and effervescent, a paragon of Freud. Like a Red Cross harbinger, he would jounce down the streets, doling out tokens to charity balls—"Glands, glands, get your glands here!" As the first sperm donor of all time he would see to it that every impotent got his shot of uplift to see him through the night. He would even cross the cold-war barrier into the Arctic zone to give cheer and charisma to frigid petticoats. Martha the Shrew would be lost in the melee, as he, Zerrado Susi, the Grand Potioner, the Exalted Pied Piper of Passion parted the Red Sterility and revolutionized all sexdom.

Long suspicious of his extended baths and lingering toilet, Martha the Spy had baited him with an empty household and an invitingly neat bathroom, bare of its usual wash and pickled squid drying in the saline air. Wily, pernicious mate that she was, he had swallowed the hook: it was unbearably sanitary. Five minutes after his unbuttoning and at the height of his lyrically lurid rehearsals, Martha the Storm Trooper broke the lock and poked a barbed-nail finger in his blush in her most outraged of all Catholic outrages. Caught with the goods he was, with his right hand wrapped most incriminatingly about his genitals. "Haaaagh!" To which he could only respond with a stupid grin. She kept poking that wiggly finger into his face while enunciating the Scriptures. Backed against the wall, unable to speak, he tried to stick in his member, which had by now turned limp and would have gladly made its exit. But Martha the Saint was not about to forfeit this obvious advantage by losing her *corpus delicti,* so she slapped his hand away and pulled the thing out again. When she did this and looked directly into her husband's eyes, she realized that he was crying. The sight of her locksmith whom she had genuinely loved for ten of their eighteen years together, the wretchedness of his position and the tears dripping on his drooping organ—and it seemed cock and bull wept together—tore at her heart. Suddenly she gathered him into her arms: against her marshmallow teats, against her peninsular abdomen, all the while smoothing his balding pate, stroking his repentant tool. The absurdity of the scene was just too much to bear and Zerrado Susi yielded himself to this fat, grouchy woman he had married in Pateros in his uncle's cutaway, hating St. Joseph down to his unbuttoned pants. ("May my father rot in his grave!") A resolution she knew only too well would be broken, just as surely as her absolution would turn to aversion. They were true to their troth. What was worse, six of their seven boys were soon indulging themselves in their father's favorite sport. There they were in the bathroom, lined up against the wall like a firing squad, the older ones showing their kid brothers how papa shot from the hip. Martha the Archangel slapped them down one by one, cried a basinful, quoted lustily from the Bible all night till her eyes blazed like Roman candles. *"Dios ko! Dios ko!"* she wailed. When Zerrado Susi looked at her again, he knew that in her eyes were entombed six of his sons. It was then that he knew he had even lost that last spark of Martha's humanity in the bathroom.

Maddalena rocked, Maddalena rolled her belly to a stupefied combo of flute, saxophone and castanets. Veiled but vibrant, she cruised among tippers and ticklers behind potted palms and terra cotta antiques, crunching peanut shells on a floor linoleumed with squashed flies, essence of mosquitoes and male droppings. Whiff of whiskey and turpentine tanged the dusty air. A limpid teahouse moon hung on a cyclorama while outside the real one was a crescent; the wind carried downtown sheen from España, where a deportee painted jonquils in his sleep, to Chinatown, where everybody dreamed the Year of the Tiger had come. Was it summer again? Could it still be the rainy season? Yesterday was December; was tomorrow April? Time was as veiled as Maddalena, time was Eisenhower in Europe, MacArthur in the Pacific. Maddalena upended a table—her mind was on Isla de Balut, Higante Islands. Two waiters came with napkins. The disenfranchised patron was brushed, advanced to ringside with nearly half a pint of gin on the house. He toasted Maddalena, Tomodachi Toni, the two waiters, the ragtag band, and a whole catalogue of other benefactors, living or dead.

Placido Rey liked to doodle over his whiskey. Married twelve years to a portly Bicolana, he had only lately joined the carousers in the *kanto* bars and roadside saloons. A "social drinker" had not much use for the all-constricting walls of an *accesoria* governed by a retired high-school principal. For that was what Victoria Salinas Rey used to be. Lesson plans and timetables. Homework and recess. This meant that for fourteen-odd hours a day, six days a week, Placido Rey was duty-bound to see to it that he observed the commandments of irreproachable fatherhood. No off-color jokes (culled from fellow workers at the ice-drop plant) could be repeated within earshot of the Rey progeny, now too many and too loud to enumerate. Table etiquette had to be observed at all times—no slurping of the soup, mainly. Loquacious small fry were not to be spanked: they had to be reasoned with. And if there was a juicy tidbit of gossip not fit for minors' ears, that had to wait too for the more opportune moment when Victoria Salinas Rey was tucked in bed with her skullcap, at which hour she would be ready to render the proper judgment to the party or parties concerned. S.O.P. for Placido Rey these twelve strait-laced years. Neither did he resent or question it. It was law, promulgated, passed and perpetuated. How did one contend with Victoria Salinas Rey? Who was ketsup in the kitchen, skipper in the *sala,* doyen in the dining room, *verdugo* in the bedroom. Victoria cooked his meals. Victoria washed-pressed his clothes. Victoria cut his hair, manicured him once a week. Victoria raised their children, who all looked like her. Victoria answered his letters, and their answers were all addressed to her. Victoria took him to the ice-drop plant each morning, fetched him back every afternoon. Punctual, persevering Victoria, whom he honored not so much as a woman, certainly not as a wife, but as an institution that had always been there. Sometimes he suspected that were he to nick himself while shaving, he would bleed Victoria's dandruff.

Then came Maddalena.

Now Placido Rey had had his fair share of sex. Girl watcher and peeping Tom at seventeen, he had gradually worn out the bulge in his pants by the time he was thirty-six—"an honorable age to retire from that particular appetite." Boredom more suffocating than quicksand had driven him, drippy-nosed and colossally constipated, to outer limits—like voyaging to the South Seas for a beachside fling with a *wahine*—until he became just another ogler at Maddalena's "premiere." All those trinkety Mideastern bangles and Kabuki makeup could not inflate her bosom, which was no fuller than a pair of ripe boils. Sensualists asserted, however, that statistically thin women were far sexier than, say, those mammary Bathshebas of Pasay City. Borodin-burlesque or anemic bust, Placido Rey was sold; he made a return trip.

Tomodachi Toni's was smothering, the crowd unruly. Nonetheless, the saloon exerted its own gravitational pull; its very grossness was contagious. Here, Placido Rey could be ebullient, as opposed to his vow of silence with Victoria, The Conjugal Amplifier. Not that he was a raconteur or a particularly engaging conversationalist. What made him interesting was his familiarity with war developments; also, he knew there was everything to know about Deanna Durbin films and the title defenses of Joe Louis. Besides, he was a big spender from Abra. True, he still smarted from those verbal encounters with that pompous ass, that Hidalgo de Something, but he was reasonably intelligent and could tipple with the best of them. *At saka,* didn't he already prove his mettle to the boys when he stopped that brutish Sergeant Yato from beating up one of the waiters? Victoria Salinas Rey would never have believed that one. And that was the square root of Placido Rey's heartache—that the bar was somehow more congenial than the bed. The ultimate dignity of man, surmised Placido Rey, lay in the cold ability to hold his liquor and keep a conversation going. To Placido Rey any universal crisis could be truced away over a friendly drink. In fact, he was lately formulating a final solution to World War II. What if Hitler were to pick up Mussolini and Hirohito, then join up with Roosevelt, Churchill and Stalin for a comradely cocktail somewhere? Over *geishas* and tea, hamburgers and balalaika music, they could iron out their differences and save mankind. All it boiled down to was a convivial glass between six enlightened men. Samoa at last!

She danced, she danced.

To Corporal Ito, Maddalena was the Hanging Gardens. Art was his dominion; Maddalena was isosceles of that dominion with but a single shrapnel to obliterate what she stood for. To harness it he would have to toe the line, and the line, as qualified by the will of his illustrious Emperor, was this totalitarian aggression of the Occidentals in the Pacific. Ito's own body tensed at Maddalena's maneuvers. He was, if not actually above them, in control of his desires. Maddalena was *haiku:* she transcended her animality. All that promiscuity could be synthesized into iambics.

Sergeant Yato did not share this aberration. Even if he could—and being comrade-in-arms did not necessarily mean bestowal of such a gift—his atavism would rescind it anyway. His *esprit de corps* had been nurtured on gallows humor. Sex he'd had a bellyful of; he was immune to it. Art was for bourgeois idealists like Ito, who, hopefully, would soon outgrow it with his first real shave. Yato was an old workhorse. Surely something else was new? And if this half-baked harlot failed to crease the Sergeant's breeches, Tomodachi Toni still could not look at her entertainer, lest she wet her outsize kimono, Zerrado Susi still coveted her whom he had canonized into menopause, Placido Rey still cashed in on the loose change of the dancer, Paeng Redoblado still mourned his Lucindo Pompeyo; and if bombers flew over Manila now, if bombardiers looked down from the moon glare, they would find this saloon with cyclorama a target ineradicable yet most deserving of chaos, for it was there where it all began, when the rib was taken, when Man became Woman.

Now Maddalena shimmied under the August moon.

[12]

OF THIS PRIMA BALLERINA a tangle of tongues had wagged an embroidery of vignettes. Whatever the tale, it soon achieved a distinct coloration, to be measured, denounced or further embellished, depending on the skill of the narrator, the naïveté of the listener. Thrill seekers only spoke of her prowess as a performer, salivated on her sinuous flair. Could anyone deny her charms? She was an alphabet of her body. Since there was no food, she was food for thought. Denigrators, once freed from her spell, were quick to call her a slut: "What else?" Such rash judgment was not shared by a tolerant minority. To them the girl had to be a misguided Pollyanna—a persona, if you please, whose exhibitionism was a form of expiation for some rancid guilt. This assimilated misinformation was nutritious publicity. Desirable or detestable, she was a celebrity in Ojos Verdes and many points east. Her fame or infamy inscribed her in the libido of men and took her to stag parties and after-show "specials." Everywhere she went, contradictions thickened like flies on syrup. Sentiment: she danced bimonthly to support a bed-ridden mother (PS: she brought home all her earnings). Smut: everybody knew she was a nymphomaniac. Sentiment: daughter of a southern *hacendero,* she was stage-struck, was pining for the ballet. Smut: couldn't they see the girl was insane? Who in her right mind would expose herself like that? Sentiment: she hadn't really *stripped* yet!

"Stop it! Stop it!" yelled Hidalgo de Anuncio, breaking away from the backstage huddle.

Stagehands smiled knowingly and let the old man have his say. Which were wrathful interpolations and choleric intakes of breath. He would be damned before he stooped to their level. "Take it easy, easy!" they remonstrated. Blanching and trembling at their contretemps, Hidalgo could take no more. "Barbarians!" He would stomp out and show these louts that not all gentlemen had perished with Raleigh. And he did. Very much a *don* whose chivalry even in these darkest of Stone Ages had to be respected. On his way to the nearest exit, he brushed his shoulders, as if by this self-conscious gesture the canker of men could be dusted off. If they laughed, he did not hear them. Amoran stayed behind, either out of diplomacy or to uphold the verdict of laughter. Which ever way the issue was resolved, it did not matter. Men broke wind and couldn't smell the rose.

Maddalena—favoring dim lights, soft music, jade earrings—filled their clamorous rooms with gauzy invitations, teasing more than she stripped, belonging more to their dreams than to their arms. Purists of the strip protested her violation of the art. She was lily-livered, said they, if she could not fulfill the contract of her body. *Sin vergüenza,* she wasn't that at all, rejoined Hidalgo. She was just a lily. Period. ("Who asked you?")

"MADDALENA TONITE" was the Maddalena of all Saturday nights past. All the more beguiling because of the veil, her eyes obsidian; Moorish the skin, yet *kayumanggi* too as though its final pigmentation was still unresolved. She could have stepped out of a Japanese woodcut or the Algerian casbah, so curiously compounded was her Orientalness with an irrepressible Arabic strain. Face and figure suggested the Caravaggio model: ascetic, asexual. Her movement could be coarse, could be elfin: the erotica of a gypsy whore, a fairy in the woods. Now Circe was in those eyes, Salome in that bosom, Babylon on those hips: through the thighs too slithered a brown Delilah. Male eyes, male minds were glued to that syntax of enticement. For the argot of all lust and anatomy quivered, beckoned in that flesh.

The saxophone had given way to a horn.

Trumpet bravura, castanet clicks, flute beeps. Arch of neck. Flick of hand. Topography of thighs. Maddalena was theirs: the trio possessed their dancer till the grave. The veil was bass. They fought over the mirage—Baghdad! With reeds with woodwind with riffs with rondos. But always The Emancipation belonged to Maddalena, only to Maddalena, to Maddalena alone.

Trumpet belch.

That burp. Those thighs.

They goaded now. Sauerkraut horn, introverted flute. The contortionist heaved backside at their lassitude—anima, bitch, swan. Distending, conciliating, culminating. Swish of satin while trumpet wheedled, out of kilter, yet worshipful. In all perplexity. To consolidate those calves. Flute followed to mollify in spoors of tactile chords. Again trumpet tonic, ruinously rhapsodizing.

Abjectly Maddalena wheeled to patrons jabbering and slopping their low-grade *giñebra*. A dollop of perspiration in a ringlet of smoke. Zinc-luminous ankles. They rinsed cracked lips. Perforated skin puckered even more for connivance. Maddalena skittered to a stool: sepia chrome of dancer's sweat dappled on one of them. He very sociably licked it. Gustavio Morales, lucky dog to be where he was. They would lap this up in the cabaret later. No time for seconds. Gustavio Morales was content. Maddalena's hands stroked that navel, moved down to the tassel below it. Here, the lights went out. A giggle, a rustle. Then with the lights restored, the dancer was gone. Even as the *haiku* in Ito's mind had evaporated.

(Reorganized by Vanoye's Man from the Mountain—"General Wainwright's adjutant at Corregidor"—the council of elders in Ojos Verdes had agreed to meet one night before the curfew. On the agenda: the Maddalena Referendum. No longer could the men endure the spectacle of Maddalena, the free agent. National prestige was at stake. Who could stand by while she danced before the barbarians? Who could watch her coquetry with the enemy and still call himself a Filipino? It was common knowledge among Ojos Verdesians that Maddalena had slept with the enemy. She had consorted, sir, consorted with the oppressors! Who was so uninformed as not to know that yet? And who was so calloused, so lacking in national character as to allow her to continue like this? Observe, gentlemen, that she's not a common whore—she's a slit-eyed monkey's concubine! Ecclesiastical oratory and theological demagoguery held the rostrum. Again it was the priggish Hidalgo de Anuncio who abstained. Leaving again his squire, Amoran, to clarify his stand, if indeed the Spaniard had one. Arguments pro and con buzzed in the backroom of a laundry. Six hours of circumlocution later, the Maddalena Charter was ratified. With the sanction of the Ojos Verdes elders and through the instigation of Vanoye, twelve men and twelve women were delegated to carry out the sentence. *Dayuhan* or *katutubo,* the plebesciters came from a mixed calling: an Arlegui *basurero,* a short-order cook from Calle Castillejos, three Tanduay *tulisanes,* a *matón* quartette from Pinaglabanan, an epidermist from the Caloocan delta, a poacher from Legaspi City, a runaway Ifugao from the rice terraces, six housewives, all Quiapenenses, three *maglalatik* girls from Maypajo, and three shellfish hawkers from Libis Espina. This was the ingathering of *banguera* lookouts and *bukid* activists. On a given date, at a designated locale, each of the twenty-four conscripts was to deposit an object in a *batalan.* This done, they were to proceed posthaste to their usual destinations and take up their everyday occupations, acting as naturally as possible. At the appointed hour, they were to return to the *batalan,* retrieve what they had put there, and regroup inside an abandoned *topada* to be sworn in.)

Saturday Night, 11:12

"Abad, Jose!"

A hand clasping a stone was raised. "Present!"

"Bermudez, Kikay!"

"Present!" A rock.

"Bornales, Benjamin."

"Present!" Stone.

"Concordia, Felipe!"

"Present!" Brick.

"Enriquez, David!"

"Present!" Rock.

Down to the last assassin, to the last weapon. All were present, accounted for.

11:20

Tomodachi Toni, Zerrado Susi, Placido Rey, Gustavio Morales, Paeng Redoblado sneaked in. All five had been disqualified from the *palabas* because of their "vested interests." Others were barred owing to limitations in space.

11:22

A show of arms. They rattled stone, rock and brick against wall and floor, against door, bench and *pasamano*.

11:25

Sudden hush—the elders had arrived. To preside, to mediate, to modulate justice and hysteria.

11:26

A restless thrum. Where was the sacrificial maiden?

11:27

Amoran led the girl in; she was in a white frock with pink frills. Not the right one, they moaned.

11:34

Those of confused faiths and shady backgrounds fell to grumbling. Their sect was Islam or just insanity; but their passion was patriotism. The Tanduay *tulisanes* shucked off their shoes, prostrated themselves before a yellowing Filipino flag. Then the *matón* quartette from Pinaglabanan reclined on the dirty *sahig,* cradled the flag in their arms, and summoned the women to adore it. Who bowed their heads meekly to the tatatatat-tatatatat of the Holy Week clappers, the *matraca.* "Repent!" exhorted the men, "Repent!" Obediently the wretched women fell to weeping, to the chant of the *cenaculo,* to the *oraciones* of the elders. Some of whom had danced before in Obando before St. Clare, in Pateros before St. Martha, in Pakil before the Dolorosa, in Cebu before the Holy Child. And it was in their *pabasa . . .*

11:40

. . . When Maddalena came, in costume. A spotlight isolated her at once, even as the *salubong* of the *maglalatik* virgins of Maypajo called her *cafre, asuang, manananggal, lamang lupa;* and their stones, rocks, bricks rattled again to record this female's terminal indictment. This was what they had been waiting for, their exoneration—the *flagelante.*

11:47

Believing she was there to dance, Maddalena assumed her stance. The first stone was cast; the avalanche began with the second. Twenty-four jurors hurled, retrenched and retrieved, then hurled again, driving the dancer against the wall. The girl beside Amoran had shielded her eyes with the initial stone but the boy slapped the hand down and pushed her forward, forcing her to look. Smoke and *cenaculo* enveloped the *topada;* each blow was elevated by chanting as the flag climbed inch by inch, stone after rock after brick, its pole. Even in the throes of death, Maddalena seemed to dance forever, to ward off hail and hatred, to dodge orisons and *oraciones.* Broken, bleeding, the dancer retreated; keening, killing, they advanced. The magistrates sat stolidly on their bench of honor. Pelted by pebbles, stunned with stones, rapped by rocks—a boulder of blows—Maddalena creaked, crunched, and finally pitched sidewise on her back, rolled in a mire of gushing blood. But it was not over. Oh, it was not over yet. From the surreal throng of executioners, a slack-jawed elder with rimless eyeglasses made his way through an avalanche of arms. He fell upon the fallen dancer, pulled off a diamond ring from a finger of his left hand, then gouged out Maddalena's eyes. As he turned to hold them up, the girl Amoran held fainted; somewhere a man screamed. Now the dancer's veil came off; the hair dropped: it was a wig. Even without eyes, even in all that blood, Tomodachi Toni could recognize that face.

So did Paeng Redoblado, who had whined his way to the arena wall. He knelt before the eyeless, the faceless Lucindo Pompeyo. "I loved him!" He wailed to the elders, to the twenty-four assassins and to the Philippine flag, but the murderers were now slowly filing out of the *topada,* out into the amethyst sunrise of American bombs, to catch midnight Mass.

[13]

AT THE MOUTH OF THE QUIAPO CHURCH was stationed a raggedy agglomeration of professional beggars, aged six to sixty. Three deaf-mutes could hear and speak; four blindmen had perfect visions; two cripples, only one of whom suffered minor limb injuries. Quezon Boulevard exuded their craft of body English from grotto to gutter; by way of professionalism, they gave you, what—mendicants, inc., carrion incarnate: Lon Chaney impersonations, if you like. Not thunder not intimidation could shake a deaf-mute; neither could lightning dazzle the blind; nor could the law nor the threat of physical harm move those strapped to roller-skatered boards. Flavor them Dickensian, or go back to the Black Hole of Calcutta. In Manila, Victor Hugo's volumes lay entombed in the National Library; in Quiapo beggars opened their bodies like the pages of a doctor's manual on diseases, literature enough for the unlettered and the incredulous. Remember their mime show? They lisped-grunted, groped-stumbled, hopped-hobbled their separate ways into five-ten-twenty-centavo consciences. When lucky or inspired, as much as a hundred pesos were made per day by each beggar. An amount usually expended on shopowners whose commercial locations were well worth the cover charge, which varied from pauper to pauper; a generous bribe to patrolmen reminding them not to be so dutiful on their beat; and perhaps, a little something to one of the sacristans (preferably that hallucinated Bulakeño, cousin to an archbishop)—for *suerte?* Then of course, a tidy sum reserved for the "pointer" who made shortcut arrangements, such as district deployment, territorial copyrights—*ganyan lang ang hanap-buhay!* Many belonged formally to a syndicate, paid weekly dues to "fixers." Welchers were permanently expelled from Beggars' Paradise; if they persisted without union sanction, the police found still another dead body in a trash can the following morning. Only the very stubborn and the hopelessly proud were inclined to risk losing a hot meal for scruples that had no peso value. Subservience, loyalty bought security, doled out solvency for all. There was enough Japanese paper money, for all that was worth; and sometimes, even sufficient leftovers, as indigestible as they were. If there was competition, it was consequently settled on the merit system. Who could stink best? look foulest? sink lowest? When it came to this, aha, none could hold a candle to the boy-man Amoran, who could be the deafest, blindest, lamest of them all.

For
With a tic
With a t-w-i-t-c-h
With a slouch
With a stag-gerrrr

He became the composite beggar, the repertory vagrant—a Job for all seasons.

"Arriba, pobrecito!" hailed Hidalgo one balmy day as the boy went through his paces. Actually, the old Spaniard felt a twinge of shame, realizing that this shoddy performance—and may all the illustrious De Anuncios in heaven keep their peace—was the makings of his next meal. *Madrecita!* All the king's nobles and all the *conquista*'s knights must be groaning in their marble stays. Muttering, Hidalgo de Anuncio shuffled along, forward into the future's unex-

pungeable supper, the cannibal of his own past. Came breakfast came lunch with all the trimmings: one afternoon, showing up in different vicinities, the boy was all of three variants: deaf-mute, blindman, cripple. *Bingi-pipi, bulag, lumpo!* Did this without a pointer, without syndicate permission, with no police protection.

"Tomorrow," piped Vanoye to hunched-up Filipino civilians on the east gate of Santo Tomás University, "tomorrow, we shall pull out the spigots, let out the lost vapors of the West! Tomorrow, the blind will see again, the lame will dance, and the deaf-mute sing . . . for tomorrow, brothers, tomorrow we shall witness the descent from the cross!"

"Bandits at four o'clock!"

And Manila Bay was raging full of them. On the wing, from the east-west-south-north—bogeys, baddies, monkeys, Hirohitos, Yamashitas, all raring to go.

Repeat.

"Bandits at four o'clock!"

(Okay Johnny-O, you hotshot you. Man the guns. For that cute trick in Dallas, "Hi, y'all!" Cuss your ass for being here when you could've been bailing hay in some chick's loft, hey ya, gal! Down with the panties, up with the .50's!)

Tat-tat-tat! Tat-tat-tat-tat!

So they came.

(One, two, three, four, five, six, seven—keep score, cowboys! Johnny-O, Asia is lousy with zeroes and they aren't ciphers from where you're sitting. Clouds squirting multicolored pancakes, just like Aunt Constant's sundaes, eh? Ack-ack! Like bicarbonate of soda, like poison ivy, like locusts. Boom! Boom! Penny arcade *vs* godyen, snake-eyes trumping aces in the hole.)

The formation snake-screened into semi-isosceles, rising sun merging with star and bar. Wings sprouted tracers, were swallowed by flame, were sundered—smithereens. Down, downwards, in a smoky zigzag over Manila Bay, the bandit fallen. One down, an empire to go. Now infinitesimal arabesques in red-white-and-blue. Trigger finger blistered with a mirage of targets. Tat-tat-tat-tat-tat! Zoom!

Good morning, goodbye. Pow! Bully for Golfer Stein, ye Jewish goldprick! What a Passover! There would be a complimentary slug of kosher prune juice after dinner at the base canteen. Shoot the G-strings off 'em! Meanwhile, downstairs. Wrenching out of haze and cross fire: the brown race. (Whatchamacall, Pinoys? What they must be thinking!) Le May in the stratosphere. Running in the streets. Kibitzers glued to windowsills. Acrobats transmitting Indian smoke signals from rooftops. Before the onslaught, a spearhead snaking around an alley. Ration line? Scattered by sound by fury. Ernie Kowalski, that peppermint-chewing Dodger rookie ("Sic 'im, Beanhead!") radioed: that ship with the bogus hospital sign was really a tanker, and so: daredeviled down, started a stink.

They saw toffee-tinted men on the docks, jousting, jumping into the bay. At first none of them could figure it out. A tanker was burning, was tipping over, gurgling in the tub. Jute sacks were dropping over her sides. The tide exploded with white, phosphorus white while the Yanks swooped down, nipped the bud as rent sacks flew, just flew over the enemy vessel. What was it? Then somebody cried: Hot tamale, it was rice! The brown men were fishing for r-i-c-e. And it was rice, rice, rice, seamed across the Pacific. Like cotton, jute sacks billowing in slow motion. There was red, too. As the bay turned purple brown burros slashed into its current like sharks tracking down a bouquet of blood.

"Bandits at twelve o'clock."

Blam! Blam! Blam!

"Nice shooting, Johnny baby!"

"On the house, Moondoggie."

Eeeoooow!

"Dick Tracy to Leader, Dick Tracy to Leader. Judo's on my tail. Shake him off for Pete's sake!"

Gzzzzzooooom! Eeeeyam!

"Thanks loads, Daddy! Will send postcard. Collect."

"Mayday to Spy Smasher, Mayday calling Spy Smasher. Got a leak here. Positive. Got a leak here."

"Break for base, Payoff Three, break for base. Then ditch. Over."

"Will do. Ovah ovah out."

"Spoon-Fed calling Snow Job. Spoon-Fed to Snow Job. Ammo low. Ammo low. What now? What now?"

"Okay, Spoon-Fed. Snow Job says break with Mayday, break with Mayday. Me'n' Cisco Kid here will crack the safe for you pronto. Over."

"This is Popeye, Leader dear. This is Popeye. What about me?"

"I read you, Popeye. You owe me a fin. Now get that anchor off'm clouds and let's mosey down and drop some of that spinach. Over and out!"

Eeeeeyaaaaam!

What they did: dragged sea monsters from the depths, man, woman and child. Lilies, weeds and rusty ironworks. Surfaced and sank again, man, woman and child. A youngster with premature gray hair heaved himself up on a plank, his hands heaping with grains; a skull-faced woman (looked like they were brothers) rushed down to him with her own empty palms. As they touched hands, Sergeant Yato fired a round point-blank from his machine gun, her blood splattered out, mixed with his brains, mother to son. The women were widows, the children, orphans; they materialized from nowhere with buckets, basins, pans, to dig for sunken treasure. They were clubbed to bleeding, kicked and drowned in the bay, somehow they regrouped, rushed out again toward the barricades, wave upon wave of protuberant pupils, hollow cheeks, blotchy harelips, black armbands. They were bayoneted en route and gunned down midway to their goal. Rice, rice, rice. White, white, white. Lightning creased the sky, ack-ack spermaceti reached out for Lockheed bodies overhead that zoomed like lustrous butterflies. Still they dove, still danced in the sea. Country of them, peninsula of brown men with scoopfuls with palmfuls of morning gruel with evening porridge. The Japanese were hard put to decide on whom to vent the most of their might, as the sky itself seemed to fortify the salvagers below. The mania grew. Rice rioted in shiny flanks, rice ravaged sightless eyes the pilots could not see. Rice was in the waves, rice rode the tide. Now an old man, pockets loaded down with breakfast, lunch and supper, was fleeing on crutches. Before he could make it to the sea wall, they cut him down; they kept pumping bullets into this convulsive scarecrow so the others could not get to its pockets. For a whole minute it seemed they took out on that hapless marauder what they could not do to the raiders above; and grains jumped out of its pockets; grains bounced, sprinkled its white hair, its ears, its nose; more grains fell into its open mouth and as they shot that body still, some rice was finally drilled into that gaping stomach.

"Hey, get a load of that!"

The Philippines *po.*

(Will you look at that one? Must be no more'n ten years old, down there with the pros, coming up with a tin can of loot, a riceburger for Mommy.)

"Johnny-O, will ya looka dat!"

Captain Jonas Winters did not have to be told. Made a swift, sudden swerve, his P-38 covering the pandemonium below. He saw them and couldn't believe what he was seeing, a whole race gone mad, gone stark.

"Johnny! Johnny!"

"Roger, I spot 'em."

("Yes, I see him! I see him!")

For down there, they saw him too. Saw him spin-tail down for the annunciation. Saw his spit his spite his Lockheed speed. This was what their fathers and their fathers' fathers had told them. Ye dazzling, pirouetting sleekness of a god: P-38.

Lightning.

Vanoye stood enrapt at Fort Santiago.

Amoran stared, was momentarily blinded.

Hidalgo glared, did not believe it.

The girl just looked.

So much beauty could not last.

[14]

JUST LOOK AT THE AMERICANS . . . no, not up there in the sky. Down here on the University of Santo Tomás compound. She did, this time without Amoran. Despite Hidalgo's interdict. Since hardly were there any white faces in the streets, it was to Santo Tomás she went—a reservation for tourists marooned in their complexion.

Something about them. Struck her personally, repeatedly. Whatever food she could scrape together she took there, offered it humbly to those fair-skinned scaries. Asked her name, they did. Always embarrassed, she could only shake her head to which they shook theirs, maybe understanding, more probably not. Didn't they have their own problems? Well, she could see that, sensing it somewhere in her own inadequacy. Even if she was like *that*.

"Y'know," a descriptive finger inevitably making that funny rotational gesture round the temples, "strange in the head." This much she could comprehend, for she wasn't so "unhinged" that references to her "noodles" couldn't send vibrations to a sensitive nerve.

Anyway, she came back, and back again. For what? for whom? For them, naturally. Leaving them leftovers, picking up their idiom. Couldn't have enough of her white phenomena. Names like: Tom, Dick and Harry. Places such as: Buffalo, New York, Hannibal, Missouri, Phoenix, Arizona. And their stories. Mostly about privileges and pleasures past; of goodies gone, of the reindeer that got away. Each rendering calibered with sky-high this and rock-bottom that, whichever, according to the character of loss—in consonance, derivative, whimsical, lamenting. Could tell them none of her own, she couldn't. Which didn't make her less welcome . . . wasn't anybody else took the trouble. Especially when the other "natives" failed to come as expected; and by their inconstancy, couldn't the Filipinos perhaps be implying their disillusionment, therefore their desertion? Could it not also be that for them the grim spectacle of the White Prisoner at Santo Tomás premised the debacle in the American Dream?

Herself she was faithful—after a fashion. A fixture she became. The Japanese guards at first made fun of her; later decided she was too young for what they had in mind. So left her alone. Wasn't a sport with her. Amounting to an obsession, to be exact. Often did Mrs. Colombo tease her: "Hey, girlie, bring me back some roast beef!" With Hidalgo day by day getting quirky and hyper-everything. Couldn't come home without a sermon greeting her at the door. Amoran was no better. Hmm, getting jealous or something, that one. All this being beyond her. For what was she, actually? Nothing less than a pest, an added mouth to feed.

Her prodigalities through the city elicited pursuing shadows. Of that Japanese officer (even pre-Hidalgo, she'd sensed him) she was more or less used to; then recently there'd been a double exposure: outline of a one-armed man, *cuidao,* that Vanoye. Whenever she visited at Santo Tomás, she felt Vanoye's beady eyes on her, though he be hidden in a crowd, bodyguarded by his half-dozen Dutchmen. At least with the Japanese, there was the consolation of distance; whoever he was and whatever he wanted, he never violated what had seemed for some time their pact on, could it be called trajectory? But with that refugee (and not even American), there was this presumption, this obtrusion. Lurky and suggestive—like Tarot cards prognosticating incubi and pitfalls. She couldn't put her finger on it. Only knew it was sort of, *brrrrr!* eerie. For instance: what was she to make of those crumpled notes Vanoye would throw her way on occasion? *Haber,* what was he trying to relay to her? Secret messages, love letters, what?

The last one read: EMERGENCE, THAT IS YOUR NAME

E-mer-gence? Spell it, amplify it: neither exposition had any meaning to her.

She had to look up the word in Hidalgo's *Oxford Dictionary.* The same word had routed the boardinghouse: another De Anuncio tantrum. Tenants had to almost straitjacket the old man, half the Japanese army'd come, suspecting perhaps conspiracy, if not active subversion, the landlady had to throw open her basement, all her lemonade had to be sacrificed to . . . how ridiculous it all had become! "Here, take it back, you and your e-mer-all," the girl had flung at Vanoye during her next call on the inmates. Merely chuckled, the man did. But mercifully threw her no crumpled something that time. She couldn't have coped with still another.

What was happening?

Hysterical, she repaired to the rooftop to see and later in her paranoia thought she saw: that P-38. Hero of herons, precentor of eagles, Star among satellites. Never had she seen anything like it before. Invincible, indeterminate, not like those white strollers on the U.S.T. campus who had the gall to claim the P-38 as *theirs!* And how could it be? It confused her. Light mist had thickened into fog. To make matters worse, Vanoye, when she'd inadvertently mentioned the discrepancy between that *intangible* in the clouds and those insubordinates on the compound, declared that they were vultures of the same feather. Birds? Feathers! Continued her one-armed evaluator: "They are, my dear, one and the same—talons for thee!" What was he talking about talons now? But he was irrepressible: "You were always their prey, didn't you know? If you still don't, then I'm reminding you: you are. Never forget it. Some day that eagle that has so smitten you will swoop down; will roost on you—you are its nest, ha, and nest egg too, double ha." To this she had bristled: "Stop it! You're insane!" Back she went: to Ojos Verdes, to the boardinghouse, to room thirteen, to Hidalgo de Anuncio. Barely articulate, she poured out to her savior and mentor about eagles about nest eggs. Counsel upon courage she desperately needed. Her sanity was close to extinction. A toothache so pained the old Spaniard that he could only yammer, flail out hands in futile indictment: against myths, against pedantic sorcerers. In better health though next day, Hidalgo had lashed out in typical derogatory Castilian: nonsense and blasphemy; that Vanoye was better off dead, would do Las Islas Filipinas a service thus, and so on and so forth. Exclamations, etcetera.

Which was no relief.

She was as nameless as directionless as before. To Manila's deepening shadows she fled, followed by that Japanese Hopalong Cassidy; awaited by a Sitting Bull prophet at Santo Tomás. She asked for Amoran's help. Nothing there. The boy was currently on the scent of something "really big." Even in her state, she could not deny nourishment. But where next? Friends elsewhere she couldn't find; jobs anywhere she couldn't get. Her cot, the only escape. Excuse enough to fantasize; so she dreamed licentiously about her P-38 . . .

Whose pilot, in her dream, was her lover. Who, like another of her suitors from still another dream, was quite blond, quite bashful, quite bold. This new fantasy she replenished with information from the U.S.T. Americanos. Questions, multiple questions she asked. About aces, about Lockheeds, about a million everything else. Shaking their heads, they told her what data they remembered. Which wasn't much indeed. Sufficient, at any rate, to build castles on in her cot. Air raids she waited for, and though they materialized, that lone, mystical, twin-bodied monoplane did not come back. Where was it? Hadn't Vanoye promised it to her, that it came for her?

Bald rider, white horse.

(Behind her.)

"What do you want from me?" she screamed.

(Before her.)

One arm, paper darts.

"Please!"

In the cot: sleek and superior, she magnified *Novio Número Tres* in the triangle. (And how large was her realm?) To this third blur she was naked, she was venerative. They tusseled in the overcast of Manila, entwined, enigmatic, endless. His goggles came off, as did her chemise; both of them burning, both returning: to Manila Bay, bilingual, bilateral, while the old Spaniard threw yet another fit, while Mrs. Colombo, what was she up to now? Dream, dream the girl did. Drums were beating in her pulse, bombers were pounding her cardiac complex, the city encored in flames; she no longer cared whether she was walking around that infernal campus or still webbed within the cot . . . silences emitted baritones, conversations were mute, where to, for whom, because of what and how, then why? Her mind could not match blanks with bullets in the composite picture of the as yet unapprehended, the perpetually unknown Most Public Enemy Barring None: the topography of man.

She tossed on the compound, strolled in the cot. Her name? Why, of course, Eagle! Allusion, not locution. Unlike Hidalgo's moldy grandeur, her neon was nimbus, not marquee. Physical specifics she attended without knowing it; her fantasies were also brushing her teeth, ironing room thirteen's laundry . . . heads or tails, top from bottom.

Clop-clop-clop, that white horse.

"Wake up! Wake up!" cried Vanoye.

Marginal difference between the two, or none at all.

"*Pobrecita,*" soothed Hidalgo from his toothache. Manila they bombed once more forever, her cathedrals falling, everything green into brown and cinder; her cot reran the P-38's finest hour beyond pillows into pirouettes inscribed with moist G.I. kisses. To cast out the devils, she would sing she would sing till her voice was as scratchy as the phonograph needle; still she would croon she would whisper she would bleed her very breathing into mind-song until inferno became incense. . . .

"Wake up!"

"Mister Vanoye, tell me what you want!"

"Not me but the Eagle, child."

"Lockheed?"

"All that glistens . . ."

". . . Is not all aluminum."

Cloppity-cloppity-clop . . .

"And—he?"

"Echoes, just echoes."

Back in her cot: "Speak to me again, Lightning!"

Hidalgo: "I forbid you ever to go back there again!"

Where?

Streets with white horses?

Camps with one-armed divinators?

Or: cots with aluminum angels?

The old Spaniard sank down to his molars most punishing; Mrs. Colombo reappeared with medications, with sundry offerings.

Amoran was inaccessible.

So for the girl, it went on like that, for a thousand and one nightmares. . . .

[15]

GLARING, UNBELIEVING Hidalgo quit the Ojos Verdes premises for more agreeable surroundings. Eraston Valenzona, his dentist of some two decades and a native-fled of Segovia, had a thriving first-rate clinic in a four-story building right over the hubbub of Plaza Goiti. Hidalgo was godfather to Eraston's youngest child and only son, Folimar Antonio. In better days, every Valenzona *ocasión* featured a De Anuncio in a prominent role. On the strength of his father's *dichos,* the young Hidalgo was the favorite De Anuncio (there had been six or seven of them on the islands at the turn of the century) in attendance. Impetuous was Hidalgolito, full of valorous mischief. Between the Valenzonas and Hidalgo was this rapport that sometimes existed only among the genteel. But Eraston the dentist was also a frustrated intellectual. What was worse, he actually identified himself as that superbreed in this southeastern democracy: the Revolutionary; and his compassion went beyond the misery that came with the extraction of teeth. As his avocation was politics, he was tirelessly holding court in his clinic or in cafés, denigrating this or that dictator, chastising this or that monarchy. Power, absolute power, he lectured, should not be restricted to a corruptible few because power on top created a strong bureaucracy but a puerile citizenry; this engendered a quasination. Power, he opined, as interpreted by Machiavelli and all those decadent princes was an elixir in its time; *pero,* other generations were in the mold, other governments were aforging, bastard heirs were sawing away at the foot of the throne, termites would soon tear down that castle in the moat—for another class was rising, the New Class. He said that for power to be just and durable it must emanate from the peon, not the prince; it must come not from whim but work, from industry not incantation; and above all, power must not come from the *seigneur*s or Nietzschean supermen but from the simple soul. Pshaw! chided Hidalgo. Eraston, said he, was a romantic. Eraston flicked this aside. "No, Hidalgolito. *You* are the worst romantic of all; you've never really left the Middle Ages. That is why you side with Franco and his infamous regime!" Always at the mention of the Generalissimo's name, Hidalgo turned livid, for he knew how his *compadre* evaluated the man. "You watch that dentist tongue of yours!" he cried. Once started, Dr. Valenzona could not stop. They fought the Civil War from *siesta* to *merienda:* Loyalists, Falangists, Fascists, Republicans, generals, farmers, ambassadors, charwomen, cannons, Catholics, rifles, reformers, quotations from Lorca, refutations by Unamuno. Hidalgo was for the Church; *está bien,* Franco was the Church. *Which* church? challenged Eraston. For Basque priests had been martyred, pious peasants mutilated. Eraston: "If Franco's cause was just, how then do you account for all that intravenous support the Republicans got? And from God-fearing, Mass-hearing entities too!" Hidalgo: "Granted, only, what do you call the Russians after the czars? the French after Charlemagne?" To this Eraston invariably countered: "Since you have opted for a reverse inquest, I might also ask, what about Mussolini? What about your Hitler, his Condor Legion?" This was always the last straw, with the crotchety Hidalgo stomping away. The Valenzonas were not sure when Hidalgo stopped coming to their house and to Eraston's clinic. After Pearl Harbor, probably. Now at loggerheads with his erstwhile star performer and

Folimar Antonio's *ninong,* Eraston crowned the rift with thorns when he told the old *caballero* one day that his teeth were all decaying, "just like all the De Anuncio beliefs." Drilling into a molar, Eraston had observed, very sadly, that Hidalgo needed false teeth, that Hidalgo now couldn't eat an apple without dicing it. His point: Hidalgo should stop playing Sancho Panza to Franco's windmill. Which really infuriated the old comedian because he swore by Cervantes. Betrayed, Hidalgo ended the professional visit and cried *adiós* to his *compadre,* as the latter taunted him from his clinic door and all the way down the Plaza Goiti traffic: "Your teeth are gone! Your teeth are gone! Go ahead, sing *The Song of Roland;* your grave is waiting for you at the Escorial!" Hidalgo had rushed out of that clinic, rushed out of the Valenzonas' lives forever. Whenever he met one of them afterwards, especially Eraston, Hidalgo hurriedly pulled out his lace handkerchief, turned abruptly around until the person had passed; or he just walked straight ahead without a flicker of recognition in his eyes. For Hidalgo, a social chapter had closed. Very few Valenzonas were left in Manila and there was nowhere one could go to defend the Generalissimo with the vim one accorded a worthy adversary. Sardonic and heretical Eraston Valenzona surely was, but after everything had been said and done, he was still lint on the satin that trailed the saffron robes of Queen Isabella. For he it was that recited in Hidalgo's *siesta*—

Besos de la reina dicen
los morados circos
de sus ojos mustios
dos idilios muertos.

At *merienda* Hidalgo was nettled to find that without his gold fillings he could not taste a morsel. Also, he felt horribly out of place among customers who ate voraciously whatever their slender salaries could buy. Hidalgo and the diners . . . like one big condor without a bill in the middle of a famine. Yet to each his own.

> And if we are unable to love each other, it is only
> because we are unable to remain alone. . . .

Once, Hidalgo had been the welcome guest of many a respectable residence. Charismatic, scintillating, he was the last flamboyant *castilla de entresuelo.* Today his sole anchorage was that sprawling colonial-style building across the street from Carmelo and Baurman's. Older than anything else in *la ciudad,* it'd preserved its ancient appurtenances: an *azotea,* shell windows, carved *rejas,* even its original embankment. Here resided the Del Rosario sisters, who had suffered the encroaching commercialization of their beloved street yet had steadfastly refused to bend to the cooings of merchants. Huge profit forecasts and storm warnings could not induce the Del Rosario sisters to consider leases or alterations. The hermetic pair invited no one inside their domain save a few "blood friends." For decades outsiders were curious about what the interior of the house was like. The original draftsman's plans of this relic had either been lost, burned, or, some believed, locked in the Del Rosario vaults for future perusal. Those who revered the lavish historicity of the house only from nostalgia did not know (or had forgotten with the passing of time) that inside were some twenty-four bedrooms, eroding furniture and life-size images of saints. Nor would strangers recollect that the Del Rosario sisters were the last of their line; they had no heirs but, according to popular legend again, had adopted some children. (And wasn't one of them a *negrito?*) The years had gravely altered the street, the city, the neighbors around them . . . *que va,* the Del Rosario sisters remained unchanged with their house. Their withered palm branches at the eternally shut windows turned green again in honor of the seasons.

Nobody knew them anymore; nobody remembered them today. Except Hidalgo, who was the only one allowed beyond those forbidding doors, to wander around the musty sitting room with a cup of hot cocoa. At the sound of the air-raid alert, the Del Rosario sisters, like sardine nuns, retreated to their rooms for their beads and light repast, leaving the old gentleman alone to do as he pleased in the *sala* or wherever it was he preferred to wait out this "horrible hour." Hidalgo bowed them away, always regretting the loss of their company, for when the sisters had withdrawn, they were practically buried. Never any new conversations in this house, just reverberations. Hidalgo didn't need croaking voices: the old piping sopranos were best. *Salud!*

Today Hidalgo had chosen the main *sala.* It was a commodious, handsome room extending some sixty feet or so to the far wall; a portion of the floor was set with octagonal tiles. A farther wall was recessed for teak mantel shelves laden with such *objêts d'art* as sticks of Renaissance woodwork, Mexican pottery, jars carved from jade and agate. A drum table contained a rectangular vase with a sprig of greens; a ceramic frame of woven white metal held etchings of hibernias, blue bells, holly leaves. Hanging on the brick and flint wall facing a crenel-like window broken by a run of chipped masonry was an eiderdown; on a rug below lay an ascot. Elsewhere in the *sala* Hidalgo's roving eye caught a frieze of flamingo-shaped claywork, the Infant Jesus in sepia tint, parchments in Gothic script, white chalcedony, Coromandel screens, a golden cedar strip, porcelain-mounted figurines, a lithograph of Picasso's *Guernica,* wrought-iron balustrades glumly transfixed under a slate roof. What Hidalgo favored most of all were the Majolica dishes stacked front-up in a cupboard; and very especially, the triptych of the Madonna and Child. The room was contiguous to its owners' name and source—a hive of heirlooms. Interior decorators would make short shrift of its redundant decor, but no matter; it breathed no Quinta Market offal; it exhaled no eczema that afflicted the Ojos Verdes pauperdom. Where all the rooms in Hidalgo's life had been infected by the avuncular hands of an Amoran, a Colombo, this one, with its patina of Druidic melancholy, renewed it. Veneer was vital. How it galled the old Spaniard to see tartar and carious teeth; to hear nothing but this continuous make-believe of *La Liberación.* He had felt constrained to listen and abide. Little else was there to do. But not here, where he endured no curtailment. No one, least of all those devout sisters, would dare invalidate the past. Here, the galleons could sail again; the past was present, permanent, almost palpable. Here, even the servants were acquiescent and hung on his every word while he dallied over his lukewarm cocoa, apothegmatizing or civilly discussing the weather. What miserable company he had been keeping lately, and in such vapid atmosphere. Pedigree, pedigree! Manila was losing her pedigree!

Las doñas couldn't agree more.

"Don't brood, Hidalgolito. It's a phase."

"Ay, madness will never pass, *hija mia!*"

"And what did you think of Eraston's funeral, *caro?*"

"The Valenzonas were not obliged to notify me."

"Ah yes, a dreary affair, one must say. Times are so hard."

"Hidalgolito, do have another *empanada.* They are so delicious. One wonders how our poor Sotero manages on our finances. But he always has an extra cup, a second helping for a guest. Isn't he marvelous?"

"That he is, *hermana.* However, we should not tempt Hidalgolito unnecessarily. Poor man, what ever will you do without Eraston?"

"And what has happened to that dear little clinic, the one we used to like so much? Has Folimar Antonio mended his ways?"

"*Señoras,* the clinic has been rented by a taxidermist; and I'm afraid my godson has eloped with a maid."

"Poor suffering family! What will become of them now?"

"Don't worry about the Valenzonas, *hija.* They can eat apples without dicing them!"

Hidalgo chattered on, in response to topics the Del Rosario sisters had broached long before. They had already spoken, perhaps would never speak again. They had retired, they had retreated. Just beads, not hands. Just essence, not life. Not wind, but air. Not flood, but dew. Only images, only rituals now. This was, in compassionate reckoning, the congenital invoice of colonial inbreeding: pulse over blood, aura over presence. Hidalgo, sipping cold cocoa, was satisfied.

Came the bombers, fell the bombs. As Manila shook.

Go ahead, *gringos diablos,* dared Hidalgo. Bomb the remembering and the dead. However hard they tried, they could not devastate his *ciudad* of churches and theatres. Intact and inviolate Manila would stay in his mind—a plume in the Castilian archives.

Abrazo, hijos!

Streets with posthumous intimacies!

Calle Yriz, Calle Oroquieta, Bilibid Viejo, Aviles, Morayta, Trabajo, Tuberias, Alejandro VI. . . .

Hasta la vista!

Gums of gentility!

R. Hidalgo: quality address of the Carmelos, the De los Reyeses, the Padillas and the Arces, Centro Escolar de Señoritas with her *internas,* the streetcar line to San Juan and Saturday night at the San Juan Cabaret, *zarzuela* at the *teatros* Zorilla *y* Libertad, Tondo's nobles: the Palmas, the Nolascos, the Sunicos, the De Santoses, the Jacintos, the Jovellanos hegemony, the Escuela Normal. . . .

Avante!

Parocco, subdeacon, *sobresaliente:* commemorate Padre Faura during its ordination, with miter and staff. Imbibe English from Jesuit primates, *kundiman* trousers for the plebian *arrabal,* celebrate pontifical Mass, the *cura* of Tondo does not hear the bombs amidst the religious war of the Catholics and the Aglipayans. *Tirador* and *champorrado, cocido español* at the Letran. All savoir faire. . . .

"Fuego!"

And the bombs did fall.

Over the dead, over the majestic fallen, over *los grandes.*

"Oye!" boomed Hidalgo, hoisting his empty cocoa cup at the raiders who did not hear him. A coronet of blue had risen over Manila; in the Del Rosario house, with its defiant silence, he stood erect, listening but not hearing. The Commonwealth was gone—banished to the New World with its calcifying customs. But in his Spaniard mind resounded revelry: toward the end of January, the gayest season of the east end of Azcarraga, they flocked without fail to the rear patio of San Sebastian when that church and the Centro celebrated their respective fiestas simultaneously and the Centro *señoritas,* in pink *ternos,* marched in the procession of *La Virgen del Carmen.* The *caracol* procession still bore the Santo Niño in a pagoda along the bay; as Manila mothers would forever carry their infants in pilgrimage to the Feast of the Candelaria.

¡Carambola!

But that was not the apex.

Hidalgo, along with Don Tomás Morado, had often been invited to share Don Manuel Quezon's five-o'clock coffee at the Palace. Hidalgo had been one of those in tight-lipped commiseration when Don Manuel and his wife had lost a son. Hidalgo had wept in utter helplessness and disbelief when the despairing parents issued orders to demolish that part of their house where the child had died. Still hovering in the background was he when during early afternoons in 1926, Don Manuel drove his wife along the old road to Marikina Valley. It was there when this magnificent couple stood admiring Mount Banahaw, the chief landscape of the Quezon's native province of Tayabas. Manolito had bought this for his wife: so that she, Aurora, would see another dawn. His gift became the Barranca, the

Quezon hacienda in Arayat. And when she bore him another son, the proud father said: "Now, we have an *insurrecto!*"

El Señor Presidente. . . .

Astarte at four o'clock.

A clock chimed; bells rang, tolled by shrapnels. Choral music in the Basilica: they had struck a church. Yes, bomb the peerage—all are in abeyance. Bomb the inured and enduring, bomb the specious and the shrine. Bomb, bomb, bomb. Even as you do, goblets rise, ghosts march the ramparts. Chaos can only be made intelligible by remorse.

Venga!

Hidalgo stalked in his borrowed sanctuary.

Amoran pointed gleefully at a B-29 from the Colombo rooftop.

The girl waited submissively in their room.

Their landlady was in congress.

Placido Rey comforted his Victoria: "The Americans will never lose!"

Zerrado Susi had been locked in his toilet.

Paeng Redoblado was gawking in the street.

Sergeant Yato was manning a machine gun at the Luneta Park.

Corporal Ito was watching his sergeant.

Tomodachi Toni was in bed with a bad cold.

Major Shigura knelt before his Buddha.

Vanoye was deep in a seance.

Christ in asphalt, Manila in distemper, rattle of gongs, hiss of howitzers, swish of bamboo, cacophony of cocks, cantabiles. . . .

Fray Diego Cera ran for cover. No time to lose; his parish was undefended, though the echoes seemed destined for higher destruction. The friar gathered his cassock about him, dusted his sandals, raced for the woodshed. His helpers had deserted. The sound of muskets must have frightened them, thought Fray Cera. And what was all that musketry about? Perhaps they were cannons. Was the flotilla being attacked by a foreign fleet? Had Mongolian pirates taken Manila Bay? There had been rumors. Letters from the capital bore ill tidings: war was in the offing.

Quickly the friar waded through the muddy clump surrounding the shed. A wooden splinter ripped his cassock; he crossed himself, and at last, on his hands and knees, reached his bamboo pile. He went from one place to another, panting, touching, gasping, inspecting. They were of different sizes, with varying width, span, surface roundness. He had buried them in seasand for a year. It was only that morning that he and his *campesinos* had dug them out. Some came out long and glistening and unspoilt, despite long internment—survivors of rot and weevil. Merciful God, he was right; this project would succeed. For with these Fray Cera hoped to build a bamboo organ that would echo with his Mass, that would later be sent to the throne in Madrid as a tribute; and perhaps, centuries hence, would still play even as Chinese mercenaries shelled Manila Bay. There would never be: another organ like this, five and a half meters high, four and a half meters wide; with five complete scales from *do* to *do,* with twenty-three registers; with a body of nine hundred fifty-three tubes, eight hundred forty-three of which would be bamboo, and two hundred twelve of metal; of such special register that when a little water was poured into it it would produce a sound very much like the twittering of birds. Half a decade later, it would be—and it was—built.

Fray Cera could not contain his pride. Whatever else man committed out of spite, the good Lord still provided this year of 1816 in Las Piñas, Rizal, Philippines.

[16]

TOMORROW Placido Rey will hold *The Manila Tribune,* unable to advance from the front page, where, in violation of all tabloid formats, a photograph will occupy four columns, with substantiating text dangling on three lopsided angles. Japanese authorities will dictate that the picture will be boxed; this will naturally result in a slapdash layout of news items which will be condensed and encapsulated every which way to give prominence to the picture. Which will subordinate the *montada* of the newspaper, editorial policy be hanged. However, since nobody can contradict or counteract this ludicrous dark-room offensive, the picture will have to get printed, unretouched, unrelieved by the propriety, the journalistic know-how it sorely requires so that parlor patriots—of whom Placido Rey must lead the parade—can pore over it and profit in the parable. As per design, the picture's effect will be tremendous. Placido Rey will be impressed by its textual message: the slant-eyed St. George has indeed slain the magic dragon, a U.S. Lockheed P-38, twin-bodied monoplane. Placido Rey, like the others who will be clustered around the paper at his table, will see a frightening demonstration of Japanese might and a disillusioning fact about American invincibility. The P-38 is in flames, is going down in a swath of smoke. Other Filipinos with similar disloyal sentiments will behold it. Everywhere in Manila, in many parts of the country, this will be cause for national mourning. On top of that, not only the newspapers will underline the American fiasco; the radio too will monitor it until one American plane becomes the entire U.S. Air Force. The picture will be so stultifying, so final. Grounds enough for a blow-up. Each minuscule defeat will stoke up an enlargement.

Fortunately, unlike his cronies who can be very defeatist about their war, Placido Rey will not fall prey to exaggeration that easily. He will surmise, and wisely too, that this is an isolated fact. Just a wisp of the whale. He will tell himself that this photo is not the picture. The P-38 fireballing down somewhere in Manila: that can only be a misrepresentation. The implication that this lone casualty is indicative of a wholesale debacle is untenable! Do the Japanese think they are dealing with nincompoops? What about the others? The unaccounted-for P-38's and B-17's and B-29's? When will they print *that* picture? Although one must admit that this photo is sufficiently depressing. From the enemy's point of view, it will have its logistical aesthetics. Consider that meteorite tinder, that rainbowish trail of smoke wrapped inextricably about those twin silver bodies: like a boa constrictor in the cumulus.

Given this, it will still be inconclusive to Placido Rey. Even the most damning click of photography will not deceive him. For instance, what is that white spot on the extreme left of the burning plane? Retouchers, prodded by the military, will not be able to erase or camouflage it completely. Placido Rey will dwell on this: white spot, white spot. Why, of course, he will say, eureka-like. That's a parachute! The pilot is alive! Placido Rey will turn knowingly to his companions but will keep quiet. He will not give tongue to his illusions. But it cannot be denied, the white spot is there, for Placido Rey and for others like him who will have reservations. The photograph then will be a failure. It will not nullify a superstition made irreducible by some forty-odd years of Fil-American cohesion whose racial ambivalences can only be further muddled or finally illuminated out of historical context.

Owing to foresight, Placido Rey will smile most privately and order another round of black coffee for the boys. He will go home to his Victoria and be more attentive to her than usual. Their marriage will undergo a transfusion from that white spot. He will brood about it, toss in bed on it. In a more partisan frame of mind he will deduce somehow that the Japanese have not captured his white spot or there would have been another blow-up, of the American parachutist this time. Adhering to this amorphous rationalization, a secret army of optimists will grow, related to but remote from Placido Rey. In like hope, in like manner, they will congeal in subversive brotherhood, they will celebrate the retouchers' botched job: they will canonize a white pupil gouged out from their eyes.

Tomorrow . . .

Yesterday

Captain Jonas Winters saw rice grains dissolve in the green bay. Out of the blue sky he streaked, downwards, downwards, so close he could see the squirming brown puppies recoil from his rage as he dove and ascended and descended once more for the whitish dissolving grains. For a while it seemed that not only water washed them below but bullets too as more uniformed figures tracked down the little brown men from ships and motorboats and the divers disappeared not in a blue-green bay but into a red of death. All around him were cylindrical patterns of powderish ack-ack and he knew he had to pull a fast one as he zoomed straightway for the ships and the motorboats, his hand clamped on the button-trigger. Captain Jonas Winters felt his body go rigid as horsepower not volition hurtled him beyond vortex into void.

A-tat-tat! A-tat-tat-tat-tat!

Blue, green, red, haywire splotches on a canvas, an easel recharging battery from a peacock. An interceptor caught Winters' blast and bumped engine-stuttery on its right, then tail-tottered over on the other side, and was going down with the swimmers among eel-like sentries, busted valves and strafed septic tanks. He had broken formation, was going back, was arcing crazily for momentum. A flora of flak waxed the floor level of the sky, so soft and sudsy at a distance, so cotton-candy-like in appearance it did not seem possible that it could rend a steel fuselage and reach the god in the leather jacket. On the intercom: the squadron leader's bark to pull out. Torpedo planes had exhausted their hatch; running low on fuel. Giddap! On the double! Even had Johnny Winters correctly sized up the situation, he did not understand the order; he would not have heeded it anyway for he himself had given it. Three! He had bagged three Zeroes; his blood was tingling, and beneath flowing incandescent grass shimmered, showered all liquid fire, all molten embers, like electric loam, like stalagmite lava amidst squirming swimmers in streaming rice.

"Pull out! Pull out!"

Too late, too late.

Fever of pistons. Pumping into his veins. As if the P-38 sensed that from this hour on there could never be another will but its own, it spun vertically, each screw, every cog of its sleek, sun-elongated metal torsos in pleasurable ricochet with that human body at the controls. Pulse sang with propellers. Mind tuned to every dial, every gadget in the cockpit. Exulted Johnny: the Japanese Zero is a pushover in that sardine can, the German Stukka is little more than a hunchback with its V-flaps and landing gears, the British Mosquito is nothing more than a flying coffin with that plywood job, but my P-38 is as tough as Fort Knox and faster than spit!

The madness of abandon lent ace lent plane a blinding, swirling grace that could only terrify those below. Another bogey bumbled in the line of fire and caromed, exploded from the twin bodies' fusillade. It would later be said that every single enemy gun, from poom-poom to revolver, was aimed at that elusive eagle. Even the swimmers seemed arrested, were torn from their pillage of the bay, paralyzed with awe at the lethalness, at the majesty of this forked lightning skimming the waters. The rice had been forgotten, the sentries ignored. For now there was only this divine madman in the aluminum chariot. So tall, so terrible was he that half the city watched in stupefaction. A few miles north just outside Manila, three men on carabaos gazed at the smoky adagios spun through a watercolor cloud; they gazed while double lightning swam a firecracker wind, they gazed as this mad starfish of Manila Bay's roseburst arena dipped its dorsal fins, daring those fishermen below to catch it. The three riders, eyes fixed on their star, coaxed and nagged their beasts into a trot; they knew what was going to happen—and they'd found what they had been looking for. Finally, unable to restrain themselves anymore, the swimmers applauded the bronco rider in the vaporous sky. Who returned. To blast another bogey, to stampede a squad of orderlies on the harbor, to scuttle a speedboat. Now they were waving and yelling up to him in voices he was close enough to hear in a language he did not know but in such frenzy that he could grasp. "Break out the jug, boys!" he shouted from a nose dive. He could see their round brown faces, wet from sea and tears. The shaking, dripping delirium that shackled them gripped him too. One of them, a boy with the most remarkably ugly face he had ever seen, held up a fistful of rice to him. Johnny let go of the stick and waved back. He was out of everything, gas, ammunition, target. The squadron was gone. He was alone over the bay with its blue-green-red waters. Nothing left to shoot, nothing to shoot with. The fever had evaporated; the base a million miles away.

And then they got him.

The official photographer of Fort Santiago was on the battlements with his equipment just waiting for some kind of stasis so he could get a bearing on that P-38. When the antiaircraft guns at the Legarda garrison found their mark at last, the photographer craned neck and gear at the off-center missile and took his picture. Shards of lead shattered Captain Jonas Winters' cockpit and goggles. It wasn't a direct hit: the underbelly of one of the twin bodies had sustained half of the shell. By some quirk of the elements, the P-38 was being borne by a high wind away from the bay, away from the city itself. Captain Jonas Winters had no recollection of fastening on his parachute buckles, or of disengaging himself from the shambled clutter of his apparatus, or of climbing out of the cockpit and bailing out. He was aware that instead of the buildings he expected, there were only trees. He was dimly conscious of thanking his lucky stars that wherever he was going, it wasn't into the arms of the Japanese. He felt himself jerking frantically at the cord, and a vacuum of silk spreading above him. Then he drifted, drifted, drifted in the sky, thinking how very close holocaust was to heaven, thinking how very far one had to travel to reach a Calvinist God.

[17]

STANDING ROOM ONLY was the latest mummery of the Japanese Gestapo at Fort Santiago. A guardhouse novelty: the Mummy Box, constructed and outfitted principally for Vanoye. At five feet eleven inches, he could barely squeeze himself into this metal Egyptian crypt, which at most measured five four in height and just roomy enough to accommodate a bantamweight. Apertures the size of a wink were punctured into the *azero* lid just sufficient to limit oxygen. To breathe at all, one had to press close against the cage lid and exhale into the pinholes whose diametrical ingenuity only bounced the body exhaust back into the lungs again. A vizored peephole was screwed about six inches below the line of vision, functioning as a feeder; one had to stoop, vertical-accordion fashion, so a guard could open the hatch and shove a slab of bread into the prisoner's mouth. For water, a hose was inserted into the feeder and turned full blast until the interior of the box was flooded, creating a pool of urine and excreta up to the knees.

Four days, four nights Vanoye stayed hunched almost in two, ankles bathed in his own dirt. The watch being fickle, sometimes the feeder didn't open until midnight . . . and then, maybe for a change of pace, live squirming worms were funneled into the prisoner's throat. Vanoye ate every single one of them with relish.

Legendary was his adaptability.

What else could they do?

Their resourcefulness was less than illimitable.

Bakero! This one-armed foreigner was tough.

Didn't he enjoy their dragonfly *sopas?*

Cockroaches, on second thought, were the best.

Next course!

Survival, speculated Vanoye, hinged on the art of absolute suspension. True guile soldered into calm grit could nullify the spherical jointures of time. To yield a second was to squander the future. By this Vanoyean theory of elasticity—and given these beyond-the-pale circumstances, could there be another?—the minute had to be the moment; and by extension, only from such moment could evolve the years. For Vanoye this meant an all-out buffering . . . all sensations neutral, each tense perfectly flaccid. Willing pain as the norm, as the sole occupant of his body, he'd negated the pain of torture, thereby annihilating the general concept of pain as the great diminisher. Encrypted unto rheumatism, perhaps close to catalepsy, tortured short of extirpation but probably closer to ecstasy, what sacred salts bejeweled those lips? what extraterrestrial music unwaxed those ears? In this drift of sunless nights and moonless days, vestigially multiplying, down to the dross but still daring, pain became secular. The smudges on his skin belied the iconography of the heart; he'd censored gall, he'd chaliced the mimosa.

They kicked the Mummy Box to toughen their tendons; they rattled chains on it. A guard (the one with hair lice) lit a fire around it . . . cough! cough! A *sumo*-type pair belly-butted down the crypt, rolled it around on the ground for a chortle or two, heave-*ho-tai!* When again they opened the feeder, what did they see but that cruel mouth contorted in a smile? Why didn't they just kill him and get it over with? Improbable but practical. His prospectus at Santo Tomás was almost finished. He had their ear, their soul . . . there was

Amoran and the Connection. The girl? Even her he was reaching, slowly. And the Mountain had been alerted.

Perhaps because nothing more could be done short of execution (and that would be anticlimactic indeed!), the guards decided to leave him alone for the time being. There was still no food, although that didn't really count any more. As long as they came up with those occasional gourmet dishes, he was all right. Later, the familiar guard masks disappeared one by one; to be replaced by—and Vanoye could not believe this—the Major's cherubic moon face. There he sat on a stool, petting his sword . . . in his loincloth, too. At first he would not speak; was content to sit there, more likely in stage lighting: began to laugh soundlessly as if at some irresistible nonoral joke. Vanoye kept up a steady stream of conversation, addressing the loincloth, marking that sword.

"Major?"

Who smiled blandly, raising his *katana* as though to accentuate Vanoye's every sentence.

So accustomed was Vanoye to this one-sided dialogue that the counterpoint, when it came, made him jump in the box, *bonk!* hitting his head on the steel ceiling.

"Vanoye . . ."

Very gentle; *sotto voce* of a priest.

"Yes?"

"I know what you are doing."

Psychic, no less.

"You are trans-pa-rent."

And he'd been gloating about his opaqueness, too.

"Narcissus drowned, remember?"

No comment, Your Honor.

He'd forgotten how light the man's tread could be, and presto, the feeder clanked open before Vanoye heard anything. The sword darted in, probed minutely, found V's mouth dead center, dipped in, made an incision, blood spurted out of the lips, the sword flashed out again like an extinguished matchstick. In a matter of seconds. Vanoye licked his lower lip; the flow wouldn't stop; he felt his already rigid body get colder still with the bleeding.

"You already got my right arm. Now you must be working up to my tongue."

This time he actually heard the phantom swordsman retreat to the stool; from the pinholes he saw that *katana* gleam once, twice, before it faded away.

"Why don't you just take *all* of me, Major? No extra charge."

Ho-ho-ho-ho.

"You're so pretty when you laugh, did you know that?"

"Vanoye?"

"Yes, ma'am."

"I know what you are doing."

"Back to that, are we?"

"Myself I have been following her around the city."

The girl?

"Do tell, Major. You're full of surprises."

"Lovely, lovely." The sword scraped against the stool.

Nth.

"Is that what this is all about then? You want me to pimp for you? Really, Major! You can do better than that . . . than her."

Scrape, scrape.

Couldn't follow the punctuations now. Man out there must be a poor speller.

"It won't work, you know."

"What won't?"

"What you are planning."

"I'm open to suggestions."

"These people deal in actualities . . . stomach realities . . . rice-and-fish facts, Vanoye. Your Trojan horse is beyond them, believe me."

At last, some particulars. If he could just file them in systematics; if he could metaphrase a thesis there somewhere.

"Why not just pick her up and take her to bed, Major? Isn't that reality enough for you?"

Brrrrssss-brrrrssss! Must be using his can opener as a backscratcher.

"They cannot stand second levels, Vanoye . . . too complex . . . they are not built for complexity. Too much trouble, too laborious, too precious . . . takes too much time."

"You're straining, Major; you're projecting."

"Am I?"

Whzzzzh! Must've racked up a fly there.

"What would be the point?"

"Arrival."

"Where? From what?"

"Identity?"

Riddles yet.

"You've heard the trumpet then."

"I had that violinist executed. He got in the way."

(Goodbye, Vienna!)

Was it possible the Major knew what was happening? That the jig was up? But how? And if he did, why didn't he act?

"Because I'm enjoying the denouement too much. I am curious about your so-called Second Coming."

Bonk! and *owwww!*

Must send word, warn the others. Get Amoran, stop those couriers, get something to Deogracias fast.

"What do you intend to do about it, Major?"

Scrape, scrape.

"*Wa-lah.*"

"Nothing?"

"Precisely."

"What does that mean—precisely?"

Hu-tak! Sword in field of fire . . . more flies, probably.

"It means that war, this war of ours, is just an inanity."

"Sure. Everybody's so indifferent on their way to the guillotine."

"Means nothing to me whatsoever."

"You're just passing through."

"Crudely put, but accurate."

Shigura, Major of the Seven Veils.

"It will be the firing squad for you should Yamashita find out."

Hutakkkk!

"Find out what?"

"Your, uh, dereliction of, uh, duty."

"There is no dereliction, Vanoye."

"Sure. As long as dead bodies pile up in Manila, you're very much in command. Doesn't matter that there's no ideology behind it . . . just avarice."

The stool moved. A hand crept out of that night corner.

"You're quite inconclusive, Major."

"While you are so well defined, Vanoye. That is your flaw."

"Flaw?"

Yes, Vanoye, flaw. Nothing is more transparent than ideology.

"Is your smoke screen all that impenetrable? Sooner or later one of your equally bloody superiors will discover that their Man in Fort Santiago has no politics. How will that sit with your warlords in Tokyo, huh? How will you explain your themeless behavior? Your Yamashita may be just as big a ghoul as you, but at least he's an ideological ghoul. I mean, he believes in all that rot about country and code and Bushido and what have you . . . you, my dear inglorious Major, can't even boast of a half-baked Buddha. You incinerate concepts for the sake of, what, ashes? Are you just an old-fashioned sadist?"

Whzzzzh!

"Getting warm, aren't I?"

"Just what do you think will culminate from your cult, Vano-he-he?"

Knee bends: one-two, three-four, five-six . . .

"Oh, I don't know. A butterfly?"

"The girl . . ."

"I told you . . . if you want her, go get her. No problems."

"No. That would be too easy."

"So sorry."

Somewhere in Vanoye's mind went, *pangggg!* a tinge of fear. Something about this whole situation: the darkness, the stool, the sword, the buzzing flies, this directionless conversation. . . . A focus had come, only where? What was the Major up to? If the Cabal had been discovered, then where was the explosion?

Cannibalism . . .

Picking his brains.

Was that what the Major was experimenting on now?

"She *is* beautiful, Vanoye. I watch her every day . . . and every day she is de-ve-lo-ping."

Circles, cycles.

"And," whispered the Major, "should one caponize her, it will not end there; no, it will not. There's an infinity of style about her . . . I know her down to her last instinct, Vanoye . . . she's an agent, not only of yours but of everyone else. She's the carrier of a plague—it's slow maturing into the endemic, her rare disease . . . you are cultivating same, and you anticipate that soon you will contaminate the grassroots . . . you expect that invaders will catch what she so virulently possesses. Oh yes, I see this. I am not blind, you know."

For once, the suffocation was getting to Vanoye.

Hu-tak-tak!

"Why don't you just go out and have your porkies tear the city apart?"

Ho-ho.

"Wouldn't do, Mister High Priest of the Metaphor. I don't want to spoil the virtuosities—yours and hers and *his*."

His?

"You know, the Second Coming?"

"What about the Spaniard, Hidalgo?"

"We both know he is irrelevant."

"And just what do you want, Major?"

"Nothing, One-Arm, nothing."

Nothing adding to so much, nothing and the *Hapon* knew everything that had been happening and what was supposed to happen—tomorrow. Nothing and the Major sat there sword in lap, batting away bugs, crippling causes, mutilating mosaics, everything. This new game was obviously working. Built the Great Wall, the Chinese did . . . but Shigura, he was the original termite.

Scrape, scrape.

"You go back to Santo Tomás soon, Vanoye. But just for a while. Must give you enough rope, he-he-ho-ho!"

The crypt was fumigated; the mummy degauzed, disbanded back to Calle España. Quite a letdown, this, since it meant ceding immortality for the dysgenics and the dying of U.S.T. The repatriated prophet was allowed his old routines—his "soporifics from the Portuguese"; he was fed intravenously on account of a clogged esophagus which couldn't take in nourishment, solid or liquid. Here and there, a few less than subtle changes. The camp hummed with excitement. Whereas before the POWs had been stupefied to the point of sterility, now they were pronouncedly agitated. Vanoye had planted a poppy in their minds when last he left; upon his return the seed had sown sharecroppers whose bruised lips were reconstructed in musical codes.

THEIR CHANT:

Trein-ta'y o-cho pe-se-tas!
Pe-se-tas trein-ta'y o-cho!

A double take for Vanoye.
(P-38?)
Where did they get that Arkansas Spanish?
Hidalgo!
Ingrate, infidel, informer.

CHORUS:

The Eagle is in the Mountain!
The Mountain is the Eeee-gle!
Hip-hip-hooray! Hip-hip-hooray!

Amoran attended a community sing; at his side, *semper fidelis,* the amnesiac of Ojos Verdes. Like an armband. Warnings, warnings all Vanoye could impart. The boy quitted the compound with messages; the girl, who'd stared luminous questions during all this, left in her wake a vapor of expectations.

[18]

TODAY he knew what'd happened yesterday. Today he saw his obits in the paper. His bodies going down like that. Shot, smashed out of the sky.

Voices, voices.

Faces, faces.

Hands, hands.

"Where am I?"

So they spoke to him and he didn't hear. So they touched him and he didn't feel. So they watched him and he couldn't see.

"We better take it out."

Take *what* out?

Faces, hands, voices.

"You're wounded, *americano*."

Don't touch me, you creep!

Voices, faces.

His corpse in the dailies. All bloated up with ack-ack. They'd see it back home. There goes nothin', they'd say. Hell, but higher'n a kite for a while there. Like a millionaire on a yacht just coasting along, not a care in the world. That's the way to play, high up there, bright and free. No mush. A man's got to have that zing once in a while, you know, like you're shooting snookers with a magic stick, like eating free steaks at the Hiltons', like when you pick the time, the place and the broad; nothing goes wrong. Because you got it made.

He raised his head: "Stop givin' me the feel! Who's the big fairy?"

Whispers, withdrawals.

"He's delirious."

Sez who?

"We have to watch that fever."

You just better watch it too, busters. This ain't no community swim.

Again they came, to whisper in his ear.

Jonas Winters had a shrapnel in his gut. *They* were going to take it out.

What about a jigger, fellas? Don't they always give a shot of good old Irish whiskey to a guy who's gonna get sliced up? In the movies. Do it all the time.

Patted him manly-like, they did. A snifter was produced. Not good old Irish whiskey though.

Jonas Winters howled as the knife bored into his wound. Jesus Christ, they were worse than Japs. Butchers, these characters, butchers. Mutilators of Government Issue. Boiled herbs lacerated his brow; the drink was gone. He asked for a refill; it was given, was drunk. Then he saw his body again over Manila Bay, he heard the ovation, he saw rice spilling, like his guts, pouring from his mouth and nose and ears. . . .

"They are coming out, boy, they are coming out."

Yeah, take them out, all that crap. Jesus, snakebite, tomato juice, ketchup in the flicks. . . .

"Easy now, easy. . . ."

Had to come out.

So Jonas Winters spoke.

"My father he owns Al Capone's souvenir baseball bat, my grandfather is just a bat. I come home one day, my brother is born in the bathtub 'cause Mom's so stoned out of her curlers puke's comin' out of her hair. I can't bury my sainted brother in the goddam bowl, the garbage cans are full. My old man says: 'So whyn't you take him to Arlington for chrissake and have a ball?' Rufus Winters, my father. I take the bat off the hook and go for the big slob, my grandfather keels over before I can kill my father. It stands to reason I'm bats, my brains come outa wallpaper and dribble down the slime in the faggot can. It's summer, nobody's wearin' a necktie, the neighbors come to squeak, the cops barge in, the mice they're jumping out of foxholes, they're raiding the icebox. Meanwhile my head is spinning like a top, Mom's tryin' on her fucking girdle, there are flies on Grandpa's crotch. I still wanna bury my blob brother in the ooze of Bedford-Stuyvesant. My kid brother, St. Frankfurter the Foetus. And what you want to live for, you punk? You'll suck the old crow's sewer milk and get scurvy and rickets is all. You'll grow up fast like sin and I'll clobber you when I come home from the parkin' lot, twenty-five stinking bucks a week. You'll grease your stupid mop, snitch hobo butts, drink up a vomit, cuss like the Irish. You'll date and snag a hag, you'll neck and get hitched, you'll live in a cold-water flat and die the rest of your unnatural life, so help me. You'll roll winos in flophouses, you'll cheat on your woman, your balls will become brats, your take-home pay will go down the kitchen sink, your penny-ante gang will get booked. You'll get fat, you'll get thin, you'll get a bonus, you'll get canned, you're in stir, you're on parole, you're rakin' it in, you're on relief—what's the difference? My kid brother, the blob. Oh, you sons of bitches, now hear this! I'll tame me a mustang and ride 'im pronto into the White House on my G.I. Bill. I'll date Betty Grable and make a plaster cast of her zillion-dollar you know what. I'll cut out my CO's gizzards and mail 'em to his Third Mistake. I'll drop the biggest, stinkiest bomb on Tokyo and get some fruit salad for my chest. I'll look up all the Dear John sisters and piss into their puckered Revlon mouths. I'll accept all the keys to the cities of America and open up all the mayors' wives. Then I'll return a bloody hero to my own ever-lovin' jerkwater town, I'll bring nasturtiums to my father's grave, I'll dig up his sad, evil bones, I'll go to the fleabag Y and drop them into the incinerator. My kid brother, the blob. . . ."

Moist hands sutured the wound.

Their faces had voices now. Or voices, faces.

"My name is Jonas Winters," the Captain said. "They call me Johnny."

[19]

BOWED BEDEVILLED BESEECHFUL she knelt on the cold cement floor at an alcove where stood towering in his marble raiment the intumescent mask of St. Anthony. Being a gloomy Tuesday, more rain in the weather forecast, an afternoon of slippery streets from the morning downpour, San Sebastian Church was desolate in the courtyard; emptier, lonelier inside with its pews stretched out like fallen pylons varnished by dolorous residue. From each candlelit nook stared in stony despair one after another saint, regal and rueful: proffering forgiveness, peace, *a todo*. After their Masses after their strolls, the priests withdrew to their cells, themselves praying who knew for whatever? They were not the harried, loosely-habited fathers of Quiapo Church who galumphed through a market atmosphere that mixed fish with Vespers; rather, San Sebastian's patristic flock was as antiseptic and withdrawn as its parish. Here no hawkers tarried for very long; nor were there beggars billeted, nor such other strays.

Something about its locality, its mien of not-altogether-hereness dissuaded affinity with the low-lifes. Come for his Compurgator of the Cross, the Catholic hobo would have to parley with: stained-glass windows, intradoses of Byzantine arches, loral tableaux of cupids and Gabrielites. Less ammoniacal, more alfresco was Quiapo's catholicism, as opposed to San Sebastian's *ex cathedra* formalism. The latter's wafers melted in the mouth, leaving not the slightest impression of even a symbolic Christ—so Latinized was its love, so linear its laity. This was not to say its spiritual crew was not as industrious, not as compassionate as their brethren elsewhere in Manila's churches. For did not their hands labor as much if not more? Did not their tears flow no less quicker? Ah, they would be loved, too; they would inspire trust and faith from those they served—if only they had not raised Manner over Mania. Somehow people resented a church not of their own substance; a church so rarefied it permitted no intimacy, no human folly. The holy house of San Sebastian did not confer, did not cater, did not, ultimately, correspond. And what sinner most contrite could long endure Stage Presence when he came for Sweat and Passion? Folk sorrow demanded more than essences. So carrying their discomfiture over the nervous undertones of sacrilege, some parishioners even suggested that in time the priests of San Sebastian, at the rate of such concrete performances, would replace those benign marble saints stage-bound forever in sabbatical monologues.

She could hardly be blamed for talking to statues, for prostrating herself before marmoreal eyes and lips that could not see that could not speak. Hadn't she addressed herself to those soft-treading, softer-speaking fathers? Obliquely, in voices heavy with liturgy, in gestures pregnant with doom, they'd asked her: her name, her sin. Nameless, she invented a calendarful; guilty by default, she could only adopt the sins of others, so numerous and so vile even her walking statues betrayed, did it come off as shock?

But they said: "Pray for forgiveness, child. Our Lord understands the gravity of each transgression . . . for penance, say five 'Our Fathers' five 'Hail Marys' . . . we are none of us so evil that He will leave us alone in darkness. Pray, child, pray again."

All along she'd wanted to say: My sin is loss. I've lost something or somebody. Day each day I am losing, what is it, my name? Certainly, my future.

Her plea she took to Saint Anthony.

Who'd been, for years, standing before an entablature of tapers, bland in longanimity, in whose fructuous gaze—amid this entrepôt of renitent *santos*—she saw how easily he could repristinate her to beginnings most dear and deeply mourned. Yes, she'd trusted him at once. To him she could unburden herself. Told him stories: snatches, glimpses. Maybe backward: with a raging China Sea; or forward: with a half-man, half-bird. St. Anthony listened indulgently. What did he think of Vanoye's predictions? Marmoreal responses: Perseverance, child, perseverance. . . .

Hidalgo de Anuncio berated her. How incorrigible! Thinking she'd been to Santo Tomás. While in reality she'd just come from San Sebastian, from Saint Anthony.

Saw him smile once. A marmoreal smile.

Made her day.

Pursued this the following evening.

No, said she to her silent saint, we are not alone. We know our loss. What if your keepers will not speak to me? You do, with echoes.

San Antonio?

He seemed to favor the vernacular.

Did he nod?

You'll turn back the China Sea.

Resembled Moses in this light, minus beard.

Yes, you will. For me.

And what would the tide bring her?

Half-man, half-bird.

From the clouds . . .

. . . To Ojos Verdes. More profanity fom Hidalgo. She did not care. Tomorrow's rain came, as forecast. San Sebastian was her ark: with *him,* there was warmth. *Mucho.* They went over it again.

"Patrón," she started blushingly.

. . . In my pillow, my pillow like a crystal ball, I see a face. Someone is buried there, not dead though will be dying if you do not save him soon. I knew him saw him only once . . . he rode an aluminum horse . . . he drove the Japanese crazy . . . they say he's blond that he's brave, that he wants me? Vanoye says, how now? What else? My bird it will fly home, my man will arrive some day, I'm happy yet afraid . . . I lost him along the Coral Sea, long before Hidalgo fished me out . . . but he's coming back, this much I know . . . he is tongue of Vanoye's wild stories, this man who is blond who is calling for me . . . he was just a boy when he left me, so painfully gentle I was always safe with him . . . I lost him anyway, somewhere, they killed him, now he is back—in my cot my cemetery, Hidalgo would bury him forever, why? And what is my name, dear San Antonio? Is it, like the bird, engraved on my pillow? How did I lose it? They will not tell me, no one will . . . yet it's on the tip of my tongue . . . Amoran spoke it once, late at night, before the old man took the cane to him . . . again I lost it, the name from Amoran's lips . . . they say I must be forgiven . . . but forgiven for what? What did I do? Or am not doing? The *americanos* at Santo Tomás, they cannot help . . . they've lost something, too . . . I search their faces, each and every one of them . . . and it's true what Vanoye fears: in those U.S. postcards I am buried individually, as though parts of my body were confetti in their mouths, their ears, their noses . . . I look at them and there I am reflections I am mirages—*Panginoon ko,* what is it! Like your priests, San Antonio, they will not talk to me. I can shout I do scream I can strike I do hit them, yet they will not ever answer! Why am I so evil? What is my sentence? I remember only the river, the river only, it runs in my veins, my hemorrhage is the China Sea . . . that pillow is a marsh . . . there I was drowned, there I am floating forever, I am in the cross currents: Hidalgo, Amoran, Vanoye, that white stallion on the avenues that follows me like a caisson . . . speak, speak, I beg of you . . . while their conspiracy goes on, yes, it goes on like the silence of this church . . . I ask for voices, they give me bells . . . Mrs. Colombo, my precious Saint Anthony, why does she wish me dead? For, *siempre,* I am an epitaph in her eyes . . . after you, there is no one, nothing . . . I go to my cot as to my confessor . . . hooves and wings, stables in the sky . . . an eagle, San Antonio, with Vanoye's dread of talons . . . then a mountain, then a leader, then everything else . . . oh, it will not stop, through the washing through the weeping through the wandering with Amoran through this impossible life with all of them . . . or can it be that I'm really mad, that all this is happening tomorrow to my daughter, and that I am mother of our times? Am I as sick as those American refugees say I am? Is my madness terminal? Tell me, my San Antonio of the marble robes, tell me. . . .

The Saint regarded her with compunctious eyes.

Yes, you do understand.

Solaced thus, she went home again, where neither Hidalgo nor Mrs. Colombo could shatter her absolution.

Amoran sang: "*Loca* has a lover, *loca* has a lover!"

She kept her peace.

San Antonio, Patron of the Lost, had promised her a bird. Everyday she looked out the window. When, when would it come?

[20]

STILL TODAY they were washing his feet, cologning his face, massaging his heart. He sniffed. Was that punch? Rabbit stew? Weak, woozy but patched up, he was in a litter. The pain had subsided. Numbed all over. Limbs seemed to be in traction. Where'd they get him? Twice he cried out. Everything was a blur. A soothing voice (a woman's?) told him it was part of his injury—the gauze over his eyes. Where was this? He guessed somewhere in the Himalayas—the high Arctic wind. Campfire. Somebody roasting on spits. Smelled good. Probably wild pig or something. Living high on the hog they were. Man, he could eat a horse. "What's for dinner?" he asked, hoping the thickness of his drawl would establish that he was out of his cotton-pickin' mind with hunger. For answer a *binatillo* in a poncho went into a garbled description of what was cooking. The poncho explained that the cook, who had the rank of Honorary Dispatcher in the outfit, was in the process of deep-frying. Earlier that afternoon the KP Action had received a suckling pig from loyal civilians in a nearby village. The pig had been cut up by a former butcher (rank undisclosed), the meat was in turn sliced into tenderloin strips for next day's lunch by a former nutritionist (oh yes, the outfit boasted of at least twenty practical occupations), the fat had been scraped clean off the skin, and this was now simmering in the *kawa,* to be made into *sitsaron.* To make *sitsaron,* one had to dump the pork rinds into the *kawa;* all it really entailed was to wait until all the fat had been seeped out of the rinds. When that was done, you got this brown, crispy *pulutan,* a side dish that swallowed well with beer or hard liquor. That was what the poncho said. "Musta had some of these in a delicatessen once," said Jonas Winters, wondering how come the horse he was so keen on eating didn't seem like much now.

They made him sit up in the litter; what felt like cellophane bags were propped under his shoulders. They gave him a drink. First draught he spat out. "Rice wine," somebody said tonelessly. With a nod Jonas Winters made it known that he'd take another crack at it: "Been boozing since I was knee-high to a barstool." A coconut-shell cutlet was pressed to his parched lips. He gulped down the liquid. Had a kick to it. Kinda nice. Was that what was so strong in the air? Yup. They were fermenting rice grains. Something like moonshine. Anyway, he wasn't griping; asked for seconds. After this, declined the *sitsaron,* but was ready for the roast. It was sourish-sweet, fighting tough. Dipped in vinegar, garlic and red-hot peppers, the meat came on Mexican-spicy, good and gamy. Before him, probably beside the fire, a woman was patting *tortillas.* Like in Mexico, he thought. Weren't Filipinos half-Spanish? When he had bolted down his supper, he heard a rustle of—tinfoil? They stuck one of his cigarettes between his lips. "Have one," he said. The pack was passed around; the bandage taken off his eyes. Not much improvement. Again exploratory hands stroked his forehead, kneaded his muscles. They told him not to worry. It was only temporary, this partial blindness. He would regain sight. Very soon. The woman kept patting her *tortillas,* fire logs crackled, mountain air brushed hair onto the bridge of his nose. Now he could make out their rifles slung carelessly on their shoulders with criss-crossed bandoliers.

"Everything's okay, sir." That particular somebody.

"Are you soldiers?" the white man asked.

"No."

Bandits?

"We're guerrillas."

Captain Jonas Winters took a deep drag on his cigarette. Great. If they were guerrillas, he was home free. They would take good care of him, maybe even slip him out of the Philippines and into a neutral country. How far was Switzerland? This was the Orient, so there wasn't much chance in that. Hell, service was tops, the fire was cozy, and he wasn't a prisoner of war—yet.

The dressing continued.

A toothless sarong scrubbed his back, shampooed his matted hair. With a hand towel, she started manhandling his face; tweaked his nose, swabbed his throat—grinning, showing her own decaying gums—and lathered his stubble. A man with a handkerchief swathed about his forehead held up a wicked-looking razor . . . what were barbers coming to? There were pouches under the aviator's eyes which Toothless, a whole seraglio in that sarong, massaged rhythmically, rapturously. Old tootsie had the touch. Meanwhile his lower extremities were receiving loving nursely pet-pats from a bevy of gushing skirts. "Ride 'em, doughboy!" Captain Jonas Winters squealed as he sat up; they pushed him down again. Ticklish he was. Razor clipped his cuticles, gave him a rubdown (nope, pushups too ambitious); armpits powdered. Steaming, grainy coffee was poured into his mouth. Made him think of the time he went couple rounds with this has-been middleweight in Frisco. Just for laughs. Flabby, punchy, the prelim palooka still had enough moxie to slug the bejesus out of him. When the bath was over, they put his uniform back on him. Smelled of brook water, village soap, sunflowers. *Gesundheit!* Before they tucked in his khaki shirt, they wound a red sash round his waist. What the fuck for? he sizzled. To reset the curvature between his spine and hipbone, they answered. Sure enough the Captain felt himself snap back into place. Yikes, a corset yet . . . hurt like blazes! Came his dogtags, all polished and shining. A *bandolero* wedged a compact mirror right smack between his interlocked calves (in Yogaish anti-ejaculation lotus) so he could see himself. No dice. Visibility zero. That didn't faze his vague, muttery beauticians who, after their long cosmetic labors, gathered around or stood back to assess their handiwork. They liked what they saw: a genuine clean-shaven, properly groomed American liberator. Height: six feet three in his socks; weight: one hundred eighty-five pounds, stripped, a natural light-heavy; distinguishing features: indigo-blue eyes, bushy blond hair, scar on left eyebrow, pearly white teeth (not a single cavity). A sunny, mobile face that ladies would droolingly christen "goo'-looking." That was it. In a bombshell. "*Mabuhay!*" they saluted. A regular cheering squad, these jokers. Another bottle of rice wine passed around; Boy Scout fire, barbecued hunter's meat.

Captain Jonas Winters glowered at his shadow in the compact: "Mirror-smirror on my balls, tell them who's the hairiest of us all!" Saw there his length and width. Took him back when he was fifteen or so at Grauman's Chinese Theatre slavering over those cement footprints of the stars. Him and Andy Hardy.

Heard them speak again. Clearly this time.

"Does he look all right now, *jefe?*"

"*Oo, pero kaunting* shoe polish *pa at arreglado na.* And his cheeks could stand just a little more red, eh?"

"What about his hair?"

"*Maari na.*"

"Are his eyes blue enough for you? *Azul na azul na ba?*"

"They're fine. Anything else besides his compass, maps and liquor flask?"

"I saved his other pack of Camels. It wouldn't be right if they saw him smoking *our* brand in Manila."

"Any chocolate bars?"

"Just three."

"Maybe we could cut them up into several pieces."

"What for?"

"You're missing the point here. Chocolate bars in the bellies of our men have no trade value whatsoever. Down there they would fetch a premium. You see, we are building a symbol, not saliva!"

They walked toward the litter with its white man whose mind was arrested over Manila Bay, whose body was still going down in flames.

"Bandits at four o'clock!"

Over the lofty Japanese castle of the Ocampos on Mendoza. Over crummy tenements on Azcarraga, one town house of gentlefolk. Over the Nakpil house on Barbosa. Over the river-end's commercial section.

Over the gloss-gloom of alley masters and mendicants: jewelers, silver- and goldsmiths, icon makers.

Over Villalobos' slipper and textile mart.

Over Plaza Miranda's Spanish *ultramar* stores with its European wines, cheeses, olive oil, grapes, sweetmeats and tinned fish.

Over Legarda, Plaza Miranda, twice-told.

Over R. Hidalgo, realm of the rich: over the Aranetas, the Paternos, the Legardas.

Over the *barriada popular.* Over Bilibid Viejo and its nipa huts clustered around a chapel of Saint Roch.

Over Arlegui to Castillejos and their joining side streets—*mestizo* redoubt.

"Over and out!"

Even Hidalgo de Anuncio had been ineluctably attracted by the commotion outside; had peered out a window for that penumbral P-38 with its double bodies, circling the bay, as the Philippines mind-stretched for the Eucharist (Open, Sesame!), open-mouthed—*Agape!*

[21]

ROASTED PEANUTS, BOILED SABA AND *PUTO-SECO* Amoran was gulping down alternately, his hand plowing through a two-tiered paper sack; his eyes following the projector's fairyland wherein a muscle-toned Tom Tyler alias Captain Marvel a week previous had been routing the riffs in the Sahara. Amoran's fly was unbuttoned, his candy bar being *el notario público*'s mouthpiece, *sub rosa.* Covering the boy's navel down to his feet was the lawyer's *tolda* of a raincoat It was the last day for chapters nine to ten of the magnificent Republic serial and all the Cine Tivoli patrons were waiting for episodes eleven and twelve the next morning. Vacuum ideal for sharks, for submarines.

On the screen the Scorpion's antics had C.M. pretty busy; on his knees, the hooded legal counsel was muzzled . . . molten rock from the Scorpion's ultra-lensed apparatus drove T.T. deeper into the tunnel . . . Amoran's own lava resisted *el notario público*'s lubrications

. . . aha, C.M. had spotted an opening above inside the tunnel; executed a stuntman's leap . . . *bagyo!* the raincoat collapsed, revealing the blow torch as a quavering old toad underneath . . . *Shazam!* Amoran kicked the Bar Sinister over, reached down, felt in that mound of Dead *Seco* Shells the handle of the man's portfolio, and, zigzagging, obstacle-coursing, was running faster than Billy Batson out of Submarine Bay. . . .

"Fine leather there, see?" he pointed to his Villalobos fence, *Intsik Beho,* a Chinaman who'd peddled prewar taho but was at present operating a shoeshine stand as a front to his other, less legitimate businesses. Smelled of *pancit,* he did, and good *guinataan.*

"Where you get this, ha?" Wa-wa-waing as his manicured fingers smoothed the leather case, straps to buckles, exterior-posterior.

Amoran brushed out a banana peel from his pocket. "Never mind, Mister Wa-wa. If you don't want it, I know somebody else . . ." Making preparatory motions as though to leave.

Wa-wa-wa, "You hait ha?"

"*Ah, walang hintay-hintay.*"

Around them a platoon of prowlers waited for audience: with conked-out radios, flat tires, legless chairs and fried-out spatulas. For junk, it was a year of plenty. It'd been showering two days out of three, though now the sun zirconed past cloud banks to smelt a drizzle of silver and gold upon pedestrians, into puddles. Light enough to see all the secondhand dealers clanking around with whatever their quick hands had lifted off hooks, detached from clippers, unhinged from shelves. And for those who hadn't seen everything, there was always Calle Corazón and its Army of Dispensables. . . .

Drenched slowly drying, parked then honking, put-upon now pushing—a traffic vehicular and ambulatory revved up and stepped forward, mortally obeying green lights and jaded instincts: for the mythical fat on Manila's bones that maybe awaited every fanatic around the corner: *inakupo,* what glorious self-deceptions? what debilitating basement deals? Zippered up or vested with newspapers (for such were the armors of the skin), down-to-the-last-cigarette-butt, hands-in-pockets for what small change wasn't there anymore—they prevailed. Feel the lumps, count the creases; their faces, living testimonials to tar-paper shacks, condemned colonies of also-runs, the burnt-homeless, the *asin*-diets just a stringbean above starvation.

These men, these women . . . so frail a breeze could knock them down, yet so stubborn they wouldn't die, continuing a senseless slavery to survival . . . dried saliva on their lips like word crusts . . . some unnameable disease in their lungs. Labor was represented by welders, mechanics, electricians, stage grips: each aching muscle unionized by atrophy. What did they all want that no season of utter, castrating hardship could not once and for all devour them, wipe them off the slum-hives of the earth? Caps jammed down heads, unlit cigars clenched between unbrushed teeth, thinning collars thrust up against the chill: they huddled on their street while home-bound citizens hurried past with not a glance to betray that *they* were there. These were Amoran's kinsmen, his brothers in the trade of scratch, nail-sore to a fist until that pauper's funeral spiked them into a loamy pit where all scavengers and praying mantis go. Survivors, imperishable through laws and rainstorms, held on, just held on, no matter what, because something would surely come up—tomorrow. Bonito Razón, senile-sedentary at thirty-nine, punched blind and aphasic in the prize ring, fiddled-fiddled away on his untuned violin. Strauss waltzes, the Vienna woods: chamberpot music for *los pobres*. Sometimes the blind fiddler was joined by a tall, taciturn Mexicanish horn player . . . *aba, si taas at si kuba nagkasalubong sa gitna!* What a twosome they made. Mister Trompeta: sprouted like a papaya tree in the barrenness of Calle Corazón; Don Violinista: shrinking by the note down into his canvas trousers. At best tolerant of one another's presence, *dos musikeros* had nothing but loathing for each other's renditions. Whatever wistful waltzes issued from the fiddle received contemptuous contrapuntals from the trumpet. Their score: Vendetta *vs.* Vienna, *Sabungero vs.* Strauss. The dueling pair attracted the curious, a number of whom dropped paper money into the ex-pug's tin cup; the Tall One was cupless: he asked for nothing. Soon the waltzes got to be repetitious, boring. The trumpet was somehow more mysterious and inviting: it itemized mutual grievances; it promised: "A SECOND COMING." The horn's many harangues lasted a week; then the Tall One was gone, street lore said, to the mountains where he'd come from. Audienceless and alone was Bonito Razón, groping for his Vienna, crying in his gray Danube. One day, he too disappeared.

From the shoeshine enclosure two blocks away was a sidewalk market where small profits were soon to turn into cabbages, tomatoes and brown flour. Farther down Calle Corazón began Manila's thoroughfares: address for higher enterprise wherein the Chinaman's customers had a slim chance of flourishing. Japanese flags blew in the wind; Sergeant Yato's patrol drove by every hour on the hour . . . *Kaunting ingat, kapatid, ayan na ang mga palaka!* Intsik Beho's shoeshine boys, some fifteen strong, swung their brushes along two lines of footwear whose owners sat as if temporarily paralyzed on wooden stools. Wa-wa-wa, went the fence, his ten fingers now firmly planted on the portfolio. Never could he decide in quick time. Always he had to use both his knobby hands . . . wa-wa-wa, stroke-stroke-stroke. Which was also his way of psychologizing his clientele. They being all thieves, figured the Chinaman, there was no harm in stalling, while: the military police buzzed by, while irate owners of stolen property lurked maybe just a couple of yards away . . . stroke-wa-stroke-wa, very clever, very inexpensive. Worked fiendishly well, you bet; and that scrofulous *Taho*-Man, fugitive from Nanking, wa-waed and whittled down prices, he did, very smart, very cheap. Only with the boy here, this Amoran, ah, so very ugly indeed and quite smelly, the little trick had never applied. Had no nerves, this one. Raised in jail. He could break every finger on his hands, he could lose his voice permanently wa-waing like that, *Intsik Beho* would never get that price slashed.

Comforting to know that behind Amoran stood a long queue of less intimidating scavengers. Would be no business at all if all of them were like this, ugh, ugly smartie. Two army trucks had rumbled down their street; at least four Japanese policemen had passed by —Ugly One had not batted an eyelash. Maybe him come from Nanking too, thought *Intsik Beho* morosely, dropping his hands on his sides, ah, very sorry no can do.

"Okay, okay."

So gave the boy what he asked for.

"Where you steal it this time, ha?"

Counted bills . . . forty, fifty, seventy, eighty . . .

"Who chasing you now, *pañgit?*"

. . . Hundred, hundred fifty, three hundred . . .

"You take that girl out, ha?"

. . . Four hundred.

"What you do with all your money now, haw?"

"Baka bilihin ko ang tindahan mo, Beho."

Hohoho, "You maybe buy my shoeshine store, ha?"

Amoran slipped the bills into his shirt.

Wa-wa-wa, "You very smart boy, very, haha?"

Salad, roast fish, *bibingka* for room thirteen.

"Where is she?" asked Amoran, standing over his skillet floating in lard.

Hidalgo shrugged. "Where do you think? Out there, talking to your one-armed prophet or lighting candles to San Antonio."

And she was . . .

"Eat, old man," said Amoran as he laid out his table.

There was, thought the old Spaniard, another wretch somewhere in Manila filling out forms at the police station, going around in circles half out of his mind, looking for what had now become Amoran's supper. Ay, ay, ay!

But: "Eat!"

In Tagalog, the order was difficult to swallow: *"Lamon!"*

Meekly, Hidalgo sat down in his chair; picked up his handkerchief for serviette, and as always, was inwardly delighted with the Amoran feast. Himself he could not bring home such fare. Who wanted comedy nowadays? Clowns were starving, sir, starving because they stupidly insisted on their art, their integrity. Lesson there, *viejo;* moral enough to discontinue dreams of renaissance. The *bangus* had been marinated in peppered vinegar, some oil before it had been roasted. A delicacy.

"Who was it this time?" Hidalgo's fork flashed; a morsel lingered aromatically on his lips.

The boy seemed preoccupied.

That bundle under the girl's cot.

"What's that, *muchacho?"*

Over by the window: "None of your business."

Back then, oh then, he would have taken the whip to any menial who so much as . . . but now, the roast, the salad, this everyday dependence, total and throttling. One was a prisoner of need. The shame of all those fine families here as elsewhere living on the charity of their devoted but presumptuous help!

Evening came without rain. Bearable enough, with a cool breeze, no air raid, no sign that life was being wasted. Listen to the leaves.

Hidalgo leaned back contentedly, forgetting status, war, and Mrs. Tira Colombo, who seemed oddly quiet tonight. This could be a *residencia* in Madrid, so hushed was everything. It was good, it was very good, just to sit thus and not remember all that was really happening. When one could not see the physical state of the boarding-house, could not hear the cries and the complaints—how rare! War had its lapses, too.

Manila, Manila.

So shielded to the rest of the world it was criminal. Amoran squatted down on the floor and started rummaging through his bundle. Dimly Hidalgo saw: bootees, vestments, kitchenware. "What have you got there?" he asked, knowing no truth would ever come from such meddling. The girl was late; Amoran was listless. And just what could be happening between these two? There were strange books in the house. Much whispering behind his back. Horrible, horrible thought! "Amoran?" The boy gave him his "none of your business" look. So: "Did you see that American plane yesterday with the two bodies?" At once the boy's eyes registered, what cunning for? Plans were aforming, Hidalgo could see, in that abnormal head. Plans excluding him, plans outrageous and obscene. "Boy!" Those grotesque hands closed the bundle, which was slipped under the cot again. Hidalgo's after-dinner serenity could not last long: "Hi-dal-goooo!" Downstairs, she'd begun padding around once more. "She wants you," sneered the boy. Would never give up, that Colombo woman.

And where was *she?*

His turn to tease.

"Just can't get your mind off her, can you?"

"She's late." Interesting to see the boy jealous. It somehow equalized everything. His manners, his unforgivable efficiency, his . . .

"She's with him, you know."

"With whom?" Anger there. More delicious than his cooking.

"Your one-arm . . ."

"Shut up, you old beggar!"

"Why don't you go and fetch her then? If you are so worried. Go ahead, boy. Maybe that white horse has . . ."

"You shut up!"

Ah, now he was having dessert: Amoran's helplessness.

Having stolen, having cooked, there was nothing left to do; Amoran took out his guitar. When first he'd brought it home, the thing had no strings, not a one. Only last month did it have two; then now, noted Hidalgo, there were four.

"Hi-dal-go-o-o-oh!"

Amoran's turn.

"Why don't you go down before *she* fetches you?"

Their merry-go-round, as it had been night after night. They would quarrel, they would nearly come to blows; then the boy played his guitar. *Recuerdo* meant "respite." For Amoran seemed to learn new songs for his four strings; newer each time because room thirteen was mired in its ancient bickerings and hatreds and inundations of hybrid smell. Sometimes Amoran took out a Japanese cigarette and smoked with the playing; the room caught his exhalations, choked Hidalgo. And the guitar, the guitar—*indulto* to them both, language to them all in this house. Post-supper *harana* was about tall Mexicans and mountains, about *segundos* and comings. Catching unease of suspicion in the old man's stare, the boy abruptly, slyly shifted melodies. Themes of his brigandage leaked out of that wood, until Hidalgo was pacified, until Mrs. Colombo stopped her own serenade, until the girl, by a miracle, perhaps by invocation, returned, the scent of candles on her.

As she did now.

"Where have you been?"

The old Spaniard had risen, visibly angry.

How could the boy carry on like that in her absence and be so calm upon her return? Always happened that way. Was it a game they were playing?

"There's food," Amoran said, not looking up from his music.

And she: "I heard you playing; and I came home."

All the way from Santo Tomás? San Sebastian?

"Eat," all that Amoran would say.

Brooded the old Spaniard: and what were *segundos?* what were comings?

[22]

NIGHTMARISH IT WAS.

Amoran would come home to find the girl in her cot, in a deep trance, it seemed no earthly noise could rouse her. Though he shook her so, himself quaking, for it was indeed unsettling: how she could stay thus in perfect stillness when the whole block was astir with Nipponese army and moving with American bombs? They could descend on her with voodoo drums and cannonades: she would not yield that infuriating personal peace. Somber, sealed with private gods, she lay there; and her eyes refracted what illumination? what ungodly self-containment? She was, by this posture, beyond the physical obsessions of Ojos Verdes. As if—and this chilled Amoran to the marrow—she was slipping gradually, gratefully into that halo of canonization.

Hidalgo de Anuncio, reversed in another of his endless "comebacks," entered, perceived their mistress so, and only nodded. Then he too climbed into his sheets. Side by side, *katre* and cot, *viejo* and girl could be two undraped cadavers in a morgue.

NO!

Protested Amoran. Even if he could not define his exact sensation at the moment, he felt that something was very wrong here . . . their lying there, inviting perhaps next-of-kin kisses, wreaths and psalms, the entire industry of death. Knelt before them, he thought he could smell incense of the departed; he heard, yes, *siete palabras*. So composed were their features in an expression of surrender one would immediately assume they had expired willingly . . . that this had been, in fact, a suicide of lovers.

[23]

HE DREAMED HE WAS OUT IN BAYOU COUNTRY, fishing. Lickin' good gumbo and fried 'taters under his belt, sycamores and robins above, creek worms at the end of his line. A feller worked his mule regular, set up his traps, cooked his vittles, and minded his own business. Like the Good Book said. Sunday was for prayer meetin' and visiting your kinfolk; in the afternoon, to the fish by golly. By gum that was what you did if you were born and raised in Jawbone Junction. And if you didn't cotton to that, why, you could always lit out and catch the steamboat to Memphis. This Sunday afternoon on a juniper bush and not yet twenty winks gone in his snooze, the line jumped; he reeled in his catch. What it was, a teensy-weensy thing, worse than ground mackerel, more like a squid tanned to the gills by the bayou sun. Red-faced, hollering fire and damnation, he paddled home. Sneaked into the cabin, threw his small fry into a bowl. Seemed fitting too, seeing as how like a goldfish it was. Shucks, Sunday night with the boys and he had the gumption to show with nothing but a fool's summer wind to blow. All of them were there, that was as plain as the cleft on his jaw—all the greasy-snazzy hicks who boasted each Sunday night at the comp'ny store how they'd been to Europe a spell and fished its clear streams with the far-sounding names. Which was a caution, which was just to get his dander up. That night while they sloshed to perdition on Hooker Jones' dandelion wine and skedaddled around to somebody's harmonica, that night they talked weather and whoppers: "Not catfish, son, but bass, marlin and swordfish!" To that, as on all such fruity Sunday evenings, they guzzled the keg dry and the taproom crunched with harsh-moaning peanut shells and sometimes when the whoppers were mighty big and they were all tuckered out, a filly or two played possum on the floor. That night with the dandelion wine swelling his head full of bait and brine and bonitas, that same night he made home lickety-split and all fired-up snatched out his squid from the goldfish bowl—it, all squiggly like a rattlesnake's toe—and *phffft!* swallowed it straight like it was goulash. In the dream he was also dreaming about how he the racoon's Huck Finn and backwoods caddy for all the crackerjack fishermen hotfooted it not to Europe but to the Orient, where bingo! he had a spanking rod and reel like the best of them and was a buccaneer on all those clear streams and treacherous straits of Asia Minor with the far-sounding names 'cause he caught more'n they could shake a stick to, bass, marlin and swordfish! Everywhere he went his catch got bigger than Captain Hook's buried treasure and before you could say hogwash he had gone and done it, which was become king of the fishermen. But he was born jinxed, said the juniper bush, and he woke up again asthmatizin' in his bunk, achokin' in the bayou, his head halfway blowed off from dandelion likker, only he wasn't king of any such thing, his middle all puffed up like a hippo. And it grew and it grew his belly blue day after day and then some more. What was it? they asked over clam chowders at Albatross Shore. Nobody knew. Mr. Sawbones they called, took his blood pressure as told, then ran off, shaking his head, what was ahead? It got so big, that navel it did, he couldn't stomach it, they had to drive him around on a chuck wagon, they did. Came a specialist, scalpeled into that belly balloon, cut out skin grafts, next week reported: "Junior, what you got in your tummy is a whale, no less." Tarnation, a whale!

Don't you fret none, drawled old-timers at the comp'ny store, you just growed some. But how could it be? And what was there to do? they asked the examining dude, who, like the sawbones before him, only shook like a leaf and left. Weeks and months passed, his feed-bag grew and grew why and how nobody knew. They couldn't get him up into the chuck wagon; he was getting too big even for the cabin, which wouldn't stretch with his suspenders. He was big, oh so lonesome big, like a convoy. Yet he was hungry and getting hungrier by the hour he was. Couldn't eat what humans ate. Besides, warned the medical examiner, the fish in his belly could not long live on cold cereal and on dry ground it sure couldn't. The cabin broke down. He was growing fins. The fellows were fit to be tied, Jawbone Junction was in panic, and rightly so. Lordie, Lordie, fetch the preacher! And fetched he was, only to crow, What now? Landsakes, that belly barracuda wouldn't go with no Alka-Seltzers and leastways it couldn't stand nothing Protestant! Call the priest! Who arrived plumb wore out from the prairie with his missal, and over a toothpick cabin and the armada rising out of it did administer Extreme Unction. Passing the stein around, blessed skinners from the comp'ny store made enough to hire a demolition team from upriver. One fine morning, with torches lit, grace said before griddles, and catfish jumping in the lagoon, they hauled him off and his jumbo belly in chains, dragged him where he had caught his teensy-weensy squid that lazy long-ago Sunday afternoon and weeping and mourning a piece, gave him and his belly some rousing Presbyterian eulogies before commending him to the deep. In times past grief, traveling salesmen recited from county to county the "Ballad of Jonas from Jawbone Junction": "David, he slew Goliath, Jack, he climbed the beanstalk, Aladdin, he let out the genie—but our own poor old Jonas he was the one he swallowed a whale!" And on sunlit porches they swung on rocking chairs, sniffing the magnolia air, listening to loons, old-timers of the comp'ny store who slobbered and squabbled and spoke about the clear streams of Europe; but he was one crackerjack fisherman, on this always they agreed. Oh, that he was, the very biggest born and bred in the bayou, for he was bigger than any fish caught in a 'coon's age. And, truth to tell, that wasn't just old fogies' tale, no sirreebob. In the public library by the briar patch, this nursery rhyme young 'uns jawin' jujube did croon as you must have heard it sung as hobos sing it still over their Mulligan stew, about Saint Peter's busboy, who swallowed this Bible of testaments old plus new with Noah with his ark with its animals dear and true, and powerful hungry still swallowed more, your moon, your sun, your stars and everybody's sky too till he was bust clean through hallelujah and now gone is gone, 'ceptin' of course what a body makes out of Hooker Jones' dandelion wine. Great balls of fire!

Captain Jonas Winters woke up in a cold sweat. Phew! That was a lulu! His hand went to his stomach at once. Nope. Still washboard flat. The sun had dipped behind a cliff. The sports commentator, along with his bodyguard, had disappeared. Somnolent, superlunary, the guerrilla redoubt renounced its own purpose and character, as if this time even Johnny Appleseed had overstepped the bounds of fancy and had transplanted the Winters cuttings to Arcadia itself. This was a tropical Camelot where everything had been refined to a rumor, a rustle. The aerial view of a teeming, broiling Manila had been radically replaced by what the American saw now: a coppice of pine trees upon a high spur of stone cottages; a restless green tumbling under acacia chimney stalks. Somewhere behind him lissome girls wtih frangipani garlands were in a tizz (over him?) as a rice pot burbled untended over the fire. A squelch of boots, smell of carbolic soap, boys fiddling with river dross, a guard in a hand-me-down mackintosh, pacing, equestrian showoffs at the arroyo, a distant innuendo of compline in the wind. Slim-hipped Ilocanitas who resembled dairymaids flashed scarves and swayed to fife and drum while riflemen clapped in the campfire. It was not a general merriment; just an impulsive *habanera* lit by fireflies and long native cigars, celebrated with off-shift sentinels who could not sleep and *señoritas* who were wide awake. Had Jonas Winters gone farther down the slope, out of the music, outside the campfire, he would have found among hedges and tall grass the natural horoscope to this hour: men wombed in lust, women waging their most ancient of all wars.

A dairymaid had dropped her scarf and was wagging an admonitory finger. The men hooted and whistled; a bottle changed hands. Then Jonas Winters saw that the coquette was skipping away into the trees, laughing; and that one of the men, perhaps goaded by the others, had risen, was running after a billow of skirts. From his side of the cliff Jonas Winters could not see what the two were doing down there.

But Dark Glasses, who was a myopic lieutenant and in sole command of the unit, was standing guard on a tree and had a rifle roost. His telescopic lens marked *bravo* and girl. Poor Amador, who was next on relief, could be nailed right where he was, if not by snipers, by his own superiors—for dereliction of duty. However, the young lieutenant, nearsighted and unmarried, let it happen. Not out of charity, or curiosity. He would not benefit from it, one way or the other. Yet he watched them. She, because of her primal gaiety perhaps, her candor; he, because it must have been his first time, though his face was bristly with beard; they, because of their rightness: a delicious tension. The man on the tree could not hear them, although he reasoned that at this moment as in all such man-woman moments, dialogue was held to a minimum. In such an exchange what was more important than the given word was its inference, its intonation, the allusion behind it—while the female ached and arbitrated. Coquetry demanded that desire first be disguised with idiom, for the shame of it would come soon enough. If she taunted him this way or that, it could also mean that she was inclined to be teased here and there. Of prime importance was with what tact, grace and haste the male could interpret the symptoms as they came. Even the most brazen women exercised this little ceremony. Even in lust, thought the man on the tree, standard forms prevailed, operative symbols were required. It was up to masculine intuition to read between the lines. Obviously Amador, the derelict guard, could steal eggs from the nest without ruffling the hen. The tree saw his teeth, her tongue, their mouths. Up on the slope where there were only fireflies now, another girl was embellishing on her own invitation for another *bravo*. Jonas Winters swore. What a time to get grounded! The young lieutenant's rifle was aimed at the tryst. He wanted to call out and warn Amador: Big day tomorrow! But he remained still, speechless. The language of the symbol was over. *Muchacha* and marauder were alone at last together. Yet no true lover was as truly alone as he, lieutenant in the underground. Each lover had his focus; as indeed had each artist—the lawyer had his aggrieved to defend, the guilty to convict; the doctor had the cyst, the cure; the painter had his vision, his vista; the writer had his witchcraft, his wormwood; the composer had his ear, his echo; the builder had his designs, their fruition. But the man on the tree had nothing save a country in his mind which he would have to protect against reality, against hypocrisy, against the tyranny of ignorance. Sometimes that country belonged more to Amador and his slut than to him who would forge it, give it historical relevance. A proletarian utopia lay in labor and unborn while menials made their moment. How many more times would he have to condone the appetites of subordinates? Amador was nibbling at her neck; she gave a strangled cry. Then he kissed her savagely and she pulled his head so that it now nestled on her bosom. The man on the tree let Amador peel at her man's shirt until a breast was bare, that both their mouths might close upon the nipple. Her head she threw back, long hair and streaming, her lips rounded to speak but came no sound. Amador raised her skirts well up to the thighs, then hips, before tearing away her panties. From nipple to navel his lips traveled, through thighs, inside them; and instinctively her legs locked about his head: Amador! In short, gasping agitation he would let go and by some male nuance relay to her an animal need. She who had caught him by the neck now released it and her hands went where he wanted them. She had been dying to do it ever since the first long, salivary kiss, yet had refrained lest he thought her too forward, but now timid, trembling hands unbuttoned him and took out his sex. He had to wheel around for her to do what he wanted, what she wanted him to ask her to do. "Have you done this before?" she asked, he said, "No," and she said, "No." No, no, no, while they did it for the first time, for the last time, before the big tomorrow, for El Aviador on the mountaintop aglow with fireflies. No, no, no, and no again for the thousand terrifying terrified others who would ask each other please please to do it, and no, please, no ever and ever again no, for all the rabid roaming lovers waiting for the anguish, for the night, for the fireflies, so they could say no, no, no, upon their self-destructing sex . . . and no, and no, and no again no. . . .

And that was when Deogracias shot and killed them both, yes.

[24]

AND SHE SLEPT through the night. . . .

[25]

FULL MOON when the sleepy cadre moved its abaca-meshed litter with its American passenger. Japanese military roadblocks and reward-gullible civilians made it necessary for the band to venture out only at night and to conceal itself as best it could in the daytime. Precautions had to be taken every step of the way; the whole countryside was murmury with folk propaganda. Currently bruited about was the story that not one but four, five, six, a dozen U.S. fighter-bombers had been shot down in a horrendous air raid over Manila and that no fewer than thirty suicidal American fliers with blazing Thompson submachine guns were at large. To the perspiring, ragamuffin litter carriers who had taken blood oaths to safeguard their burden, the task at hand presaged gigantic proportions. Fetch and carry, hike, hide and hustle they might, but these were occupational hazards. They had been told, and in terms of an orthodoxy they were not expected to comprehend, that the *banig* no longer bore a man, but a mandate—the future of mankind. By some allurement of the guerrilla officialdom, the mystique behind the lame American had been carefully explained to them. The litter was a loadstone that had to succeed inspite or because of its sheer lunacy. He would feed the hungry, cure the sick, reward the faithful, destroy the opposition, punish the collaborator. Nor did the young lieutenant make it any easier for his men. His orders were quite explicit: he was to transport the wounded American pilot from Baguio to Manila. Once in the capitol, he was to contact a courier who would then give him instructions regarding the second and final phase of the mission, billed as the "exploitation of a metaphor" by the Manila high command.

With this in mind the Lieutenant bade his men take the circuitous routes to points of interest along road, pass and mountain trail. The American raised his head groggily: from Pangasinan to Pampanga. That was Mount Arayat, he was told. Then San Fernando highway. He looked back at Pines City; and past Trinidad Valley, where they had left Acop. Between Benguet and Bontoc was timber highland of the Kalinga and Apayao country. Hours ago (days, weeks, months ago?) still smelled the Arctic fog of the Mountain Province. The litter had been spirited past Japanese outposts along Burnham Park, Session Road. Elevation: 4,700 feet from sea level, Baguio, and they descended, or did they rise again? Cliffs, chasms, plateaus, forests, sweet-smelling woods, tropics—a roller-coaster ride with a charlatan. Onward to Sagada with its Sabbath stillness and etiolated stone quarries. That Merlin-Marxist prattled. About elephants. About Hannibal. On the outskirts of town lay burial caves, weird rock formations. Mesmerized, Jonas Winters saw: deep caverns, and felt their almost vibratory chill; saw pinewood coffins perched like scabbards on mortar. *Eeeee!* cried the litter bearers: some coffins had been gnawed open, perhaps by mongrel men? Johnny could not tear his eyes off the rock loom for they were awesome, horripilating in the moonlight. Now must we lock the tomb of the Cid—that sonorous voice. Onto Alab, an Igorot village where it seemed the female was more heavily tattooed than the male; in a hut, a planting ritual: tobacco-chewing men praying for rain. Still Alab with its interposition of large, smooth stones serving as pathways, pigpens, poultry roosts. Shallower, wider pits used as courtyards, as assembly places. Alab huts built close to the ground with totemic roofs of hay, almost no windows, and interiors that exuded a dank smell. Along the way Johnny saw priapic posts like bleached javelins looming before male dormitories. The *ulog,* explained the Lieutenant: a love nest. The point of the pilgrimage, according to the tourist guide, was founded on pragmatic parallels: cultural ingress, cathartic egress. For you see, said Dark Glasses again, the static quality of mountain culture is emphasized in both rice terraces and design of the Igorot dress. Jonas, bear with me; study the intervals in evidence. Neither terrace nor cloth of the Ifugao has changed in aeons. Philippine life—as the Ifugao design would have us believe—has but one movement and that is round and round a vicious circle, even as the Ifugao dance. Terrace and cloth dance, my friend, yet do not move. But that is a myth begun by Spaniards, encouraged by Americans; and the Filipino is past Ifugao, beyond Torquemada, Tojo—and MacArthur. The tabernacle is Filipino . . . tomorrow!

[26]

. . . AND THROUGH THE DAY, she slept. . . .

[27]

THE MISSION COST fourteen days, nine lives.

But thanks to *tuba* and *tapang usa,* the symbol reached "Rendezvous M" in one piece. In Manila leaflets were printed secretly and handed out furtively. Word was passed to Vanoye (at Santo Tomás), who slipped a note to Amoran, who reported back to Hidalgo, who complained to the girl, who told her neighbors. Mrs. Colombo, whose lemonade runneth over, was thrilled witless. A date was set for the unveiling. First, a small gathering, informal, hush-hush. It was a resounding success. More dates were set. The symbol's schedule grew. Funds were raised; hopes were high. Like Christians in Nero's Rome, the secret gatherers chose backrooms, broken-down mills, or cemeteries—the catacombs of Deogracias' underground Manila. For all that occult atmosphere, the communicants came in Mardi Gras spirit. Better than all the movies showing in town (which, after all, were only Zorro swashbucklers or Nelson Eddy–Jeanette MacDonald musicals the puppet government had approved) was this matinee idol in the flesh ("He has blue eyes!") who had shot down oodles of Japanese planes. If he only grew a *bigote,* he would be Robert Taylor! That wasn't so, he looked like Tyrone Power! Birthdays, weddings, baptisms, christenings, all for the secret presence now here, now there, always whisked off one step ahead of the Kempetai. Now turned haberdasher of ceremonies Deogracias signed up the ever-sportive Amoran as sacristan to assist in this the highest of all high-faluting Masses, Bread and Wine for the masses.

To the Consecration.

Ecce homo!

Surrounded by retinue, garbed in parachute silk ribboned with praise, Captain Johnny, late of a Lightning P-38, met his votaries from a horizontal position. He was shaky and still much the worse for fever but his Air Force glamour undiminished by the circumstances was better than all the static about Guadalcanal landings on the underground radio. They swarmed around him with choked hosannas, in mumbled monotones. At his side was Deogracias, whose officious manner kept well-wishers at a distance. Yet this was Mars and Apollo ("He's so dashing!" females trilled) and it would take more than red tape to scare off the adulators. "Johnny! Johnny! Johnny!" they exclaimed as the litter, borne by four dusky youths who acted like pallbearers came close. The Atabrine-yellow captain surveyed all these brown shadows weakly, his lips bitten raw, his blue eyes watery red. "Wave to them, Captain!" whispered Deogracias, Cardinal and comforter, as he received a flask of adulterated wine from Amoran. "Wave to your communicants!" Captain Johnny obeyed, and for a second, something irresistibly boyish was in that freckled Adonis face: *The Son of Superman, The Return of Batman, Captain America Strikes Again!* When in Rome, do as the Romans do, thought the pilot being celebrated with the honorary rank of Christ. Co-pilot and Pontiff Deogracias made the sign of the cross over the doddering old men, the skin-and-bone children, the *kamisola*-clad elder women. *Dominus vobiscum.* A wave of jubilation followed the litter and its pugnacious crew of attendants and bodyguards. Captain Johnny felt like a bench warmer completing a goal-to-goal touchdown. The *bodega* was solemn, expectant. Just like a stadium. Yeah, the Rice Bowl. Though all his muscles rebelled against the effort, he chortled.

His subjects clapped. Holy Moses, what a Square Dance! At Communion the disciples received, instead of unleavened Christ, chopped pieces of Hershey bars and they mooned and masticated over the Host. There was no organ; in its place was an Aztec Gabriel according to Saint Deogracias: Joaquin playing his trumpet, filling that fetid back room with *pasos dobles ("Por el Señor Aviador")* and old revolution feuds unforgotten and unforgiven. The Secretariat had not figured on an *espontaneidad;* the auspices as masterminded by Deogracias did not include an alto solo. *Pero hombre,* that Joaquin, he was born to cremate lost causes and scatter the ashes of rituals as far as the immigrant heart could roam. Captain Johnny raised a limp arm; this was immediately propped up by applause.

That was how it went. Everywhere. Glory be to God.

They could never have enough of him. Even when he retched, vomited. Always: cheers, clapping, emotions taller than the mountains. Goose pimples. Galore. Oh, these faithful Filipinos, rejoiced Captain Johnny. They just gotta be saved, they gotta be liberated. Worth getting shot down for.

As he passed them they showered him with *cadena de amor:* a wizened old woman came forth with a cup of hot tea ("For the liberation, sir!"), a chorister shined his boots, a *mangkukulot* mussed his hair, two artists drew his face on tablet paper. Or they just touched him humbly, with utmost respect. Captain Johnny took it in. It was for him, all of it, for his flyer's wings, for his parachute silk, for his dogtags, for his whiteness. Never before had he encountered such humility, such sincerity. So unused to reverence was he that this, whatever it was that was happening to him now on this foreign soil, hurt somehow. It hurt most especially upon remembering that among his very own how little honest regard for him there was. In his squadron he had earned the respect that went with fear; with his superiors there had only been scorn or tolerance that came from authority. At the base he had experienced camaraderie, true, but that was camaraderie that thrived on wisecracks and horseplay: it had not touched him where he lived as a man. In the cross-chatter and empty beer cans at the PX there would never be any room for what an individual brought to this man's war, for when you came right down to it, everyone was a loner and would always be a loner as long as there was something left to fight for. Come on, come on, he thought. I love you all; I'm tired of playing the hotshot in a barrel of cold fish. And they came, they did, like red ants on the scent of a honey pot. Lord, they were so lovely, these gracious orientals. Come from shantytown and *sari-sari* store. Milling around him, adoring him. They would never believe this back home. Not in the drugstores. Not on his stoop. Not ever. *Ma-bu-hay!* He winked, saluted. Even knelt, some of them.

A senior citizen, male, morose, and leaning on a cane, was at his litterside. Did nothing but scowl and sneer.

"So what can I do for you, Grandpaw?" Captain Johnny asked solicitously.

As if a bullhorn had been blasted into his eardrums, the old gentleman jerked to attention.

"At ease!" said Captain Johnny.

The place fairly shook with peals of laughter.

Eyes blazing, the old man sneezed, causing his chest and middle to sag into their normal S-shaped position. He cleared his throat, righted his shoulders again, cane-tapped away and was lost in the multitude.

"Relative of yours?" Captain Johnny grinned, digging an elbow into Deogracias' groin.

The Lieutenant let that one pass. Let the American have his fun, he thought. He would have his innings later.

Next came a girl with long black hair and a fair-to-pale complexion. Somewhat appealing, somehow pretty, perhaps even beautiful in a remote sort of way, if one's taste leaned towards the opaque. For this one too, like the old gentleman with the cane, was not quite right. First of all, her eyes, dark and full of promise as they were, seemed vacant, as if they were incapable of holding an image; secondly, she seemed more guided than going, as though she were not there on her own power; lastly, unlike the majority of the first Communion-type girls in white frocks, she had nothing at all to offer the American. Not a flower, not a silk handkerchief, not even a crumb of home cooking. Just when Captain Johnny was inwardly decrying the quality of his crop of admirers, the girl unexpectedly, very shyly leaned down and laid dewy lips against his flushed cheek. Now Captain Johnny, who had long prided himself as a woman's man and indeed had been kissed silly by all types and all ages, was startled by this chaste tribute, or whatever it was. His temples burned, his pulse quickened, and his hand quivered as he touched that cheek, all the while wondering how a peck like that could provoke him and bring back his fever when whores from Brooklyn to base had blistered half his body something awful. Stranger still, she had done this as a grieving, reluctant girl would bestow a last, respectful, frightened kiss on the cheek of a departed relative. Perhaps that was what was so unsettling about it all, the fact that this somewhat appealing, somehow pretty girl with the long black hair, fair-to-pale complexion and vacant dark eyes made darker by their abundant promise had kissed him as though he were already in a casket instead of a litter, as though he were dying or about to be killed—had kissed him as though he were dead. Yet as she rose to take leave of him—and once more, she was more led than leaving—in his eyes as in his mind, which had now canceled a treasury of kisses, rejected innumerable whores, she was beautiful. Puzzled and annoyed, Captain Johnny pulled Deogracias to his ear for advice. The rascal, recognizing this as one of *his* innings, told the American nothing of course, except that the show must go on—which it did.

The American's guardian angels circulated him past more brown Adams and Eves.

Captain Johnny's temperature and blood pressure went up and down. But the *glorias* stabilized it.

"Are they always like this?" the Captain asked the Lieutenant, who had remained disturbingly aloof throughout most of the proceedings.

The man smiled enigmatically. "It is not you who is truly sick," he said. "Theirs is the highest fever. . . ."

Captain Johnny squinted up at Deogracias and chewed on this a while.

Why couldn't the man just say what he had on his mind? All this double-talk!

"Come again?"

Again the thunderous applause.

The presents, the supplications, the communal liquor flask: pandemonium. Rendering unto Caesar what was his due.

"I don't get you at all, No Eyes," Captain Johnny shot back. "Not at all."

Deogracias snapped his fingers, paid off his helpers, and disbanded the congregation. The metaphor had been exploited close to saturation, the job was nearly done. Another word would be superfluous.

Like a performing troupe, the cabalists wormed their way to a new address, another back room, where the American was expected for a last supper before he was taken back to the mountains. The underground's bag of tricks became more outlandish with each rendition. Deogracias officiated, Joaquin played his trumpet, the red ants multiplied, the honey pot overflowed, *and,* as claimed by reliable witnesses, a blind man opened his eyes and saw the Son of Jehovah come down to earth on a parachute; a cripple walked a mile for a Camel; and a deaf-mute sang duets with the fatherly American so that everybody joined in to sing "Ghost Riders in the Sky"! In another week, Deogracias had folded his carnival tents and headed back for the Mountain Province. Too busy scanning the skies for bombers, the Japanese missed one rolicking good show when they let that fly buzz in and out of their noses. Lieutenant Deogracias and his men reached their mountain lair with no Manila fatalities except for the loss of the liquor flask. Mission accomplished and awaiting another, they built a campfire and over rice wine toasted and sang to Captain Jonas Winters: "For he's a jolly good fellow, for he's a jolly good fellow, for he's a jolly good fellow, which nobody can deny!"

"Did you like him?"
"Who?"
"You know who."
"I don't know."
"You kissed him."
"Did I really? Was that really a kiss?"
"It wasn't the sign of the cross."
"He seemed frightened."
"He was wounded."
"Can I have some more chocolate?"
"Save some, for the old man."
"You know he has bad teeth. This could kill him."
"He's going to outlive us all if we're not careful."
"Tell me. . . ."
"Tell you what?"
"Why you are doing this."
"What am I doing?"

"Taking me to meet all these—men. First it was . . ."

"What do you think you are? And how do you think we'll live?"

"What do you mean? Tell me. What are you saying?"

"Do you want me to say it? Do you want to hear the word?"

"No!"

"Stop asking questions then."

"Please! You didn't mean that!"

"Let's save some chocolate for the old man."

"Even after he beat you?"

"Because he beat me."

"Does it still hurt?"

"Nothing hurts forever."

"Please. Tell me."

"Tell you what?"

"That you didn't mean it."

"I don't know."

"Let us save some chocolate for the old man."

"You know he's got bad teeth."

"He will outlive us all, if I am not careful."

"Did you like him then?"

"I do not know."

"You kissed him."

"You told me to."

"Because you frightened him."

"He was wounded."

"He'll come back."

"Why did you steal his f——?"

"Maybe somebody will buy it."

"What makes you think he will be back?"

"From the way he looked at you. And because I think he'll return your kiss."

"Listen, the old man is crying. . . ."

[28]

He cerrado mi balcón
porque no quiero oir el llanto,
pero por detrás de los grises muros
no se oye otra casa que el llanto.

Lorca hung over Hidalgo's half-sleep. Each toss in bed tended to unhinge his bones; his lungs he feared were impregnated with toxic gas. The last air raid had so disoriented him that he missed two consecutive performances at the Alegría; and after that revolting *palabas* at the soap factory, he had been unforgivably atrocious in his three appearances at the Rialto. They had hectored him off the stage, demanding their money back. In a cubbyhole of an office an assistant bursar reneged on his contract and swore that from that night on the management would only hire comedians who *knew* their business. No more harlequins, no more *pícaro*—no, sir! Overwrought and supperless, Hidalgo had escaped from that madhouse with its overflow of impresarios and booking agents to the comparative safety of the Colombo caravansary for his bed of thorns. Even there, they hounded him. Not the Alegría, where he could still bluff out a reconciliation on pain of apology. Not the Rialto, whose reputation in entertainment circles was squeezed from soap opera and for whose producers he harbored nothing but contempt. It was that other thing. The American in the cortege, that *demonio* with the dark glasses. One, perfervid; the other, periphrastic. Both haunted him in that travesty of a Mass.

Ars Deo gratias. . . .

In a *capilla* Dark Glasses had expostulated: "The perspiration of kings is just froth of the decanter. But the *pawis* of peasants dries up, becomes lead that weighs them down the ages. The master wears a necktie; the slave, a grindstone. Between them no relationship is possible except that which exists between mill and grist. And what is private property without public toil? Yet the world perpetuates only the pyramids, only their pharaohs. Nobody remembers or even likes to admit that both came into existence only through brawn and blood that issued from millions upon millions of nameless serfs. You weep over sunken armadas but not over their galleon slaves. You weep over fallen crowns, not for those beheaded. This must stop! We shall stop *you!* Labor has a face, labor has a name! You don't romanticize it . . . you feed its belly . . . heal its sores and sons. All written history glorifies the power of men, not the sweat of man. . . . All this feudal nonsense about lilac-strewn palaces and Cleopatra's bath! Well, the new chronicle will smell as the *tao* smells. It shall be carpenter over architect, farmer over agrarianist, citizen over president. . . ."

Dark Glasses had spoken: of the Filipino as embodied in the *tao*—the *tao* as Filipino.

Just how Filipino was the *tao?* What made a brown man both? Hunger? Poverty? Martyrdom? Did this dispensation acquire stature from the ethnology of smallness? Was one *tao* and therefore Filipino because of the gruel he slurped? the rice and fish he slaved for? Was nationalism then to be appraised in terms of rags and roughnecks? What was the common denominator in the chasm left by Fathers Gomez, Burgos and Zamora after the Cavite Mutiny of 1872? Dark Glasses maintained that the generic Filipino was no bastard of the Creole clergy but the legitimate heir of the *indio* commonality—a glaring historical fallacy, deliberated Hidalgo, since that would infer that this country's heroes (who spoke Spanish, some of them educated in Europe, many related to Spaniards, and all bearing Spanish names) were impostors. In Deograciasian apocrypha, only those executed in the past and suffering today could be deemed Filipino. Dark Glasses advocated separatism and championed the thoroughbred Filipino. Was there a pure American? a pure Englishman? a pure Japanese? or even a pure Spaniard?

A fly buzzed in the room, circled, lit on Hidalgo's dome. He swatted at it; missed.

Tao, tao po!

That of course did not include any bureaucrat, not even the most insignificant clerk. No. *Taoism,* as elucidated by Savant Deogracias, was only levied on the pariah: he who starved, he who smiled for centavos, he whose children were born deformed and nurtured in discontent. In short, *taoism* was next to Filipinism, and this nepotism, if one were to extend credibility a gap farther, led to godliness.

The fly buzzed out of the room.

Bombast, generalizations, these were the covenants of a Vanoye, a Deogracias. Who gravitated to a schism and left it bigger than a gravedigger's pit. Just what did Dark Glasses know about people? So platitudinous a one could only be less than human. Already a half-baked cosmopolite posing still as a Messiah with a Marxian manifesto. Dust, capital of the *tao. Tao's Fate,* by Deogracias Malraux. Coadjutor of the Faith indeed! It was Hidalgo's special prejudice that the elevation of the peasantry by its *bakya* from grassroots to the dizzying heights of nationhood was the most injurious form of idealism. For the *tao* could never be more than a topee on the bald pate of the tyrant: it could tickle the brain; it would never transform it. At best, the titular head of the *barrio* would still be an intermediary of the Palace in Manila—no matter what Dark Glasses preached. Nationhood could never be rice; it would always be venison. Unluckily, these insights were lost on Dark Glasses, who was tragically unaware of the magnitude of his undertaking and whose simplistic view of a pluralistic society was inimical to any kind of progress.

And how did he, Hidalgo, the last of the De Anuncios, figure in this comedy of mannerisms? Assuming that there was going to be one, for whom was the Liberation? Certainly not for a Francophile, not for an unleavened *pan* like him. It was for those who at this moldy stage of Philippine evolution still curried priorities, repatriation. It was for the Filipino Family domesticated by the American Dream, fed by the American Menu. The Liberation was for waiters, *cocheros,* shoemakers, sidewalk vendors—all those who prospected not for a private idiom or a pubescent identity but for *medallas* minted in gold dust.

Was he Filipino? Not conqueror and not conquered, what was he? Nowhere in man's commemorations did a daub of ink allude to the clowns and jesters without whom the king's court would have seesawed between boredom and barbarism. No plumes, feathers, suits of mail for the royalty on foot or the blue-blood beggar. Who was the arbiter of all these panegyrisms that could not confer one anecdote, one adjective in passing on the noble calf in this tyranny of brave bulls? Why did they always write history for the enthroned and the embalmed, for the opposed and oppressed? Surely the Cross burned just as lucently in the mind of someone like him; the crown touched his hair, too . . . for Christ and Queen! It was true—memory was narrow-minded. History had taken him here, yet outside its perimeter. So that when he came (he had not arrived), he was just a cuticle on the gauntlet, a personage undeserving of spoils. And when that era was no more, he was left behind with these brown people on their islands. They bore derivative names with their brown skin, and with it, a persevering hatred. Martinets brought him to these shores (he, hiding under the cloak of conquest and conversion); now he had been divested of the glorious little he had. The sun never shone again, night never ended. When he awoke, there he was: skinless, caponized. Tolerated beyond tenderness, honored without homage. He could not go back. Passage home required not only money but meaning. Madrid was matrix, Manila a mothball. Still, Franco's Spain granted no sinecures to peninsular gigolos who had not married into wealth. Having enjoyed no official capacity, Hidalgo could not even be recalled to the mother country along with those amorous friars and venal administrators. So he was stranded, thus he stayed. To scrimp and scheme a home for himself in Manila's outhouses—a hegira decollated. For a time at least it seemed that he could be happy here, that that was how it was fated to be. Curious how a man often calendared his glory and grief with a woman for asterisk.

Por ejemplo, Mariya.

And perhaps all Hidalgo's remorse in history, all his mortifications in life were just wet gunpowder he meant to ignite with the first torrid summer. Now that he was reopening old wounds, he knew that he was not remembering and suffering in remembrance the collective guilt of a conquest he never really shared in, but only remembering Mariya, who had somehow bannered the impacted shame of the conquered.

Hidalgo, Mariya.

He had courted her with an ardor that brought veils and *mantillas* first then banged on doors and tore down curtains next. The pursuit took him around *paseos* on horse-wild carriages, all senses befogged by orgies and jeremiads; to her doorstep with piteous importunings, under her balcony with Dario seduced from his lips, the Inquisition in his heart, a cane in his hand. Never relenting, never relented, that Mariya. Even when her parents had lost their land to debt, when all litigations failed, when all entreaties fell on deaf ears, when a governor-general waived their pleas—even then. She was Mariya. Why did he persist? What was it he saw in this *morena* who was so blind to him? they asked, his countrymen who rankled in their caste. By turns fawning and duplicitous, this disgrace to the name of De Anuncio whimpered around like a whipped dog, tail between legs; or mulled about with artificer eyes. Yet that *morena* pride had eroded in the face of penury. Had defected by default. Her father and mother had given in. As if they had had to chop it off from her arm, the parents came to Hidalgo's residence one evening to offer their daughter's hand. Having suffered loneliness and rejection, the Spaniard made them bleed first. Why not? The corn was on the other foot now. Dowry? *Dinero?* But Don de Anuncio! He sent for her, and when she was there, he dismissed her elders with a flick of his finger. Now was the chatelaine going to pay for the reckless carriage rides, the wretched walks, the balcony roses thrown up with passion and cast down again with aspersions, the endless entreating letters, the gifts tastefully selected and heartlessly returned, the coincidental meetings that somehow degenerated into public executions—the entire chronology of his longing and debasement. He inspected her perfect teeth, examined her flawless body, as a master would his chattel. Was she fertile? Did she snore? How often did she bathe? The girl just stood there, a Sabine to his Caligula. He asked: Had the silly *señorita* been informed that with a De Anuncio's intercession the governor-general would restore the lost land to her parents? To this she nodded. Her pointed breasts he cupped in both hands. She neither cried nor resisted. What continence! "You shall be my trollop," he sneered, and made her feel his scepter. This she neither held nor let go. Her hand was just on it. Like dead weed on driftwood. The next day, they were married in church without banns; the night following, her parents moved back to their land. In the morning, her father dug a hole in the backyard, wedged his head in it and died. Almost immediately, her mother locked herself in the house; never came out for anyone again, not even when Mariya pounded on the door with the deed of ownership in her hand.

And on their wedding night . . .

He came home drunk, swaggering, closing all windows. By her listlessness in church before an absent assembly and by her languor now, he expected a battle. That was only fair. It was June. A lamp burned on a table. She appeared to be standing just where he had left her before going off with well-wishers to carouse. But if she was going to fight, why was she naked? He stalked, stumbled. Toward her. She did not move. Then in the lamplight he saw it. The knife. In her hand. The right. He crimsoned, not with righteousness, only with relief—with redemption. From the very nature of their courtship—if it could be considered that—he had had a premonition that even if he won her in holy wedlock, their first night together would demand nothing less than a sacrifice. His or hers. But this. He had not bargained on anything like this. How dreary and yet how unexpected. To be welcomed by his bride on this their wedding night with the point of her hatred. Advancing deliberately, he made sure there was room to duck in, should she decide to throw it like a spear; made certain there was ample space for mobility to parry, should she elect to stab. Not too confident of his ground, he feinted with his left hand, braved another pace. The knife did not stir. Not so much as an inch. Blade inward. Point downward. Ha, clever strumpet! Beads of perspiration hung on his forehead and cheeks like frosted tears; his silk bolero shirt clung to his skin and it seemed they were both naked now. Each step lifted her lowered head by millimeters, and in their growing closeness, the lamplight magnified her bosom, stretched her already loosened black tresses, demonized her eyes, made riper her hips, tinted that patch between her thighs into auburn grass. No words. Neither spoke. No air. The room was humid; both of them could feel each other's skin, which (he could have sworn) was crackling under the pressure of their nearness. *Uno, dos, tres:* he was there. At that no-distance from where a man could lose his loneliness. When arms and mouths could redeem what had been long tortured nights and dark demented letters. He was hunched a little forward, so he could bend or block with his arms. If she was going to do it, now was the time.

And she did.

But not to him. He should have known by that stance; blade inward, point downward. Her execution, like every move she made, had grace and precision. Not sudden at all, as with madness, but with calculation. Not intended to kill or maim—just to cancel. For without sound, with no apparent heat or hysteria, the knife entered her vagina. Time locked them there. Time that stopped in the lamp, that swooned in the womb. She had gone limp as his hands fell on her shoulders and he was still too stunned to understand what had happened, what it was he did, what she had actually done. Only when his legs entwined with hers and he felt himself damp, only when the lamplight washed all red in his eyes, only then did he speak and that became a scream. Mariya! He ripped his shirt off—and it hurt for it was a layer of his skin—tried to stick pieces of it into her womb. He upended the bed, shook out its sheets and tore and shredded and plugged and tore again and everything was turning a garish amber in the lamplight in their bedroom. She stood there like a brown cupid in a mountain oozing not water but red wine. He gathered her in his arms, collided-wiped against furniture and walls: it would not stop. Mariya in his arms he ran from the bedroom, out of the house; it was dawn or it was the end of God's time; sprinting, sniveling he crawled to the church where just the day before they had been wed; he charged in and out of the Guardia Civil *cuartel,* he ran all over Intramuros with his Mariya dripping, her bosom firm and heaving, her hair long blowing. But though he cursed and called, no doctor came; though he staggered and screamed, no people listened. He doubled back to the house, somehow tipped the lamp off the table; rushed out again with his arms full of Mariya. To bully and beseech some more. He was spitting out blood; she was weeping over him. Then the alarm. They came out in droves. With pails of water. He collapsed with his bride and gaped dumbly at the vorticose fire. It lasted three hours. When they finally put it out, only the stairway and a portion of the balcony were standing. He woke up to find his bride as white as marble, her body encased in sheets. A doctor had come and gone; a friend had left the doctor's message: She was sinking fast. Hopeless, hopeless. Yet she bled slowly on this their second day; on their third day of married life, she fainted and regained consciousness only to console him. She loved him, she said, she most passionately did. Now asking for his forgiveness or for water. Now stroking his grimy face—her own so pale; her hair seined with ashes. *Pero muy cariñosa!* She had seen a priest—the very same who had joined them in holy matrimony just two days ago. Neighbors had sent for her mother. Who never came. But this *morena* loved him, *sí, sí,* that much was certain. On their fourth day together, she asked him to send for his friends. This he did with misgivings. They arrived. Formed a cemeterial vanguard around the half-balcony. An honor guard for her last wish, she smiled, and it was his very first from her—such perfect teeth! What was it? he asked, wishing she had stabbed him instead. She peeled off her bandages. Nauseated, he reeled away. For somehow that wound had climbed and claimed the rest of her; her whole body appeared to be one gaping womb. My last wish, she whispered, is for you to be my husband now. At first he did not understand. The words were gibberish. But that tone, that look! Falsetto and gleam that transported the religious fanatic into the most frightening state of all. Horrified, he sobbed again. No! It was bestial! It was blasphemous! he cried. It was his right, she answered, it was her duty. For she was a good Catholic, baptized by the same quiet priest who had married them. Moreover, she didn't want to die with this conjugal sin hanging like a wreath over all her other sins. Please, *novio mio,* she supplicated, if you honor the dying, if you respect the deathbed, and if you are a true Christian! He turned to his friends for succor. But they were a bastion now. Again: please, *para mo nang awa,* please, if you are truly my Hidalgo! Eyes clenched tight, and with the weight of Pontius Pilate on his shoulders, he weighted her down with their wedding vows; he took out his scepter and dubbed her in ember and blood on that rubbled semi-balcony with its blasted stairway walled by carousers and firefighters. He stabbed through her bandages and blisters, eliciting from that blessed pyre what could not have been ecstasy but exultation, not sex but sainthood, for she was joining not him but a *gringo* God . . . brutal, beatific. A *beata* from a brute. . . .

"A-mo-rannnn!" the old man screamed in his bed.

Coughing and creaking in his joints, he struggled to his feet. The boy was nowhere in sight; the girl was not in her cot. He padded to the door with much difficulty. Hungry, he was insanely hungry.

"Ladrón!"

Downstairs a board squeaked.

"Can I help you-hoo, old man?"

Mrs. Colombo's theme song.

"Not today—Tira!" Hidalgo hollered back. Not today, Mrs. Harpy, he thought as he picked up a tin plate. Of late whenever Hidalgo overslept, either Amoran or the girl left his breakfast in this tin plate. The old man always knew who had prepared the meal. By its quantity and quality. From where the plate had been put. This morning there was no bread, and the tin plate was on the doormat. Amoran, naturally. But why a piece of chocolate? Famished from his mnemonic ordeal in the past, Hidalgo took the plate to bed with him and studied its single content. In his mind faces pranced without trunks, voices chirped without lips, kisses burned and bled; also starring, that ridiculous poseur, Deogracias, his equally ridiculous bugaboo, that golden-haired *americano,* Eraston and his sardonic smile, the banished harlequin of the Alegría, the perjured *pícaro* at the Rialto, the last balcony with his *maja* of the ashes. . . .

The board squeaked again.

"Old man, would you like some *nice* tomatoes?"

She just wouldn't give up.

No, not today, *dulce compañera,* winced Hidalgo. Slowly, eyes closed tight, he thrust the chocolate shrapnel into his mouth, bit into its solid stone sweetness; and almost at once, a great pain shot from his cavities to his brain and now he was thinking: about the serpent, the forbidden fruit, cider, the "*William Tell* Overture," the apple of his eye: *mansanas!*

[29]

FOR TWO WEEKS and for a loaf of bread Amoran picked balls on a Japanese tennis court. He and the girl picketed Bombay bazaars for thread and *retazos*. They pushed the cart into the Tutuban Station and ogled merchandise coming in from the northern provinces, while the daytime Hidalgo, nursing a toothache, some eight or nine hours away from his vaudeville, strolled around in an unpressed gabardine suit, chilblained hand on cane, and a card in his vest pocket attesting that he was an agent for real estate. In the Colombo boardinghouse the trio munched on cassava flakes fried in oil and flour; the boy concocted a brittle, gum-pricking malt nougat out of coconut milk, which Hidalgo of course refused to eat. Underground hotheads acting without system or authority liquidated stray Japanese soldiers at nightfall and when Amoran found the bodies, he stripped them; finding at times brand-new cartridges or a holstered German Luger that the panicky murderers had left behind. Later, after amassing a miniature armory in their room, Amoran traded in the guns and bullets for a small fortune in food. With this they fed the girl anew. Hidalgo had also begun reading aloud his books to her, one after another, without discrimination so that she was one day reciting a line from Góngora and in the next—courtesy of the scavenger—was memorizing stanzas of *Charge of the Light Brigade* behind the Spaniard's back.

Like a guidon Hidalgo introduced her to a Spanish thesaurus. She was taught grammar, syntax, conjugations in the morning; at night she absorbed the adenoidal dialects of a city that Amoran slit open to her like a goiterous throat. Her mornings were mannered and orchidaceous with Hidalgo's invocations of dons and dowagers; her evenings were malodorous, were morbific with Amoran's influx of urchins and lepers. Two heads had her deity. Belonging to both halves, she became quite as elegant as the old man's picture-book empresses and almost as skinny as the boy's *kanto* compatriots. She longed to visit Hidalgo's Alhambra to worship; yet it was to Amoran's coproumbilical alleys that she went, to weep day and night. Hidalgo and Amoran.

She rode the streetcar from Legarda to Singalong and wandered on foot in the suburbs. At the side of the legislative building government employees had tilled the grounds and planted lettuce, cabbage and sweet potato. Hidalgo had paid for a plot on the cooperative plan and this Amoran and the girl planted with tubers. Recently Premier Hideki Tojo had inaugurated the "Agricultural Reclamation Project" by throwing a handful of seeds into the soil while a properly impressed delegation cheered and civic leaders watched at parade-rest against a backdrop of sickly-looking cucumbers and leafless *manunggay* trees. One night, men carrying *buri* baskets uprooted the sweet potato plots and Corporal Ito emptied his rifle, firing at shadows and fertilizer sacks. The dawn-shift sentry tripped on the corporal's body in the horse-manure patch: the poet's throat had been slit from side to side. The girl came home that afternoon with a *haiku* in her workbag.

A man on a white horse followed her all the way to Ojos Verdes.

"That garden must be full of dead poets," she said.

Seated by the window, Hidalgo exchanged furtive glances with the Japanese officer whose white horse had attracted a small crowd. For her swan song of the day, Micaela the unemployed-unemployable diva was clearing her lungs with the *toreador* aria from *Carmen* but everybody only heard the singular refrain below as that white beast, statuesque and splendid, organ cocked in full fortissimo sprayed the asphalt with a yellow streak until it formed a stream that became a bubbly islet around rider and horse. Fanning herself on her porch, Mrs. Colombo looked approvingly and was deeply touched.

Amoran pushed the girl in the cart to the Normal Institute and together they watched scrawny children flying kites, spinning tops, spelling indecipherable nicknames on dry barks with pocketknives. They watched paralytic revolutionaries with brass cups held out for spectral alms; or they queued for rations that always ran out and even then they remained standing where they were for hours, comforted by the stench and the stolidity of those who were hungrier than they. Heat and hunger seemed to arrest them before bakeries and butcher shops. Told that there was no bread, no meat, they went away, grumbling over their useless ration cards, only to form a line again a few blocks away before another shop, another food store. Hours went by. A baby squalled. A mother squealed. It drizzled. The sun came out. The line only got longer. Shaggy veterans still mourned the fall of Singapore. Aging young cadets just recuperating from the March and whose minds had stopped functioning after Corregidor played checkers on chalk lines they had scratched out on the sand or woodcarved into chess and chessmen as they huddled close in conspiratorial tranquillity. Waifs and vagrants recruited to and fugitives from forced-labor gangs mingled with the ration lines all over Manila. Cruising Japanese pickup trucks braked to a halt, weeded out the runaways and herded them off. Not long after, the lines swelled again, with the same faces. Amoran and the girl passed among them as among rapt participants in a procession so anonymous yet so personal. "I wonder what they are eating in America," somebody would say. "Hot dog! Hot dog!" chorused the skinny children. "Are they bombing Tokyo now?" another asked. "Night and day, day and night!" screeched the skinny children. There was much rejoicing.

On his own, Amoran hiked to the Calabash Road pantheon in Balic-Balic to cut some grass, then hiked again as far as Galas to sell his sackful to the stables. He mined brooks for buried nails, dried them, sandpapered off their rust, hammered them straight and vended them by the kilo to the *talliers* in Binondo. A sure way of making quick money was to act as *agente* for the matronly entrepreneurs of jewelry along Divisoria's "Buy and Sell" quadrangle. Repulsive both in appearance and behavior as he was to most customers, the sellers with whom he transacted (percentage business) soon learned to value his judgment: he had an eye that knew instinctively what was genuine and what was glass; and an ear for the fluctuations of price. Bright and chatty, the matrons bought and sold, sold and bought again from each other. They dealt strictly in cash, by the thousands in one toss, plying one another with huge *bayongs* heaping with paper money. Twenty-five thousand pesos for a *diamante,* cheap; 7,000 pesos for a flawed *brilliante* pendant, a bargain! An astigmatic matron who couldn't even see the sparklers on her four ruby-encrusted rings added three more diamond necklaces to her show chest, and it took two men pushing two carts to pay for the purchase. Inhaling dramatically, eyes averted, the matron-seller bussed Amoran happily on the cheek, shoved a wad of bills into his shirt pocket, and cooed goodbye as she was borne away on one of her money carts like a dead Viking sailing to Valhalla; while the matron-buyer glittered among other glittering matron-buyers in Divisoria's diamond mine ("Come again, *kumare!*"). Clutching currency that would only buy him two very light meals, Amoran wondered how it was possible to have more money than meat, more rubies than rice.

Manila listened to the war broadcasts.

The American fleet, reported the Japanese commentator, had been scattered on the Pacific, and more American airmen were every day being mowed down in one-sided dogfights by the Imperial Japanese Air Force. The U.S.S. Flagship Something had been sighted and sunk in a day; the General was losing the Battle of the Beach, *Banzai!* However, on Placido Rey's shortwave radio with its reconditioned wavelengths, the news was rewound like a film clip in reverse. So: the Flagship surfaced again and torpedo-sank the *Japanese* flagship; the General about-faced and swamped the Battle of the Beach; American airmen rose from the fiery pit and bamboozled the Impotent Japanese Air Force. "Victory Joe!" Amoran took out a map and indicated to the girl seemingly tangential American courses in the Pacific Theater that actually spelled I-S-H-A-L-L-R-E-T-U-R-N! As fast as the shortwave sank the Japanese cruiser and shot down the

Japanese zero, the bigger became the expenditures of the Imperial Navy and the Imperial Air Force. A new phenomenon was also reported: the *kamikaze,* "divine wind." Short-range bombs disguised as planes and piloted by ancestor-bound fanatics on sugar-cane petrol were seeking out and smashing into American flattops. Tokyo Rose, that Devil Flower of the airwaves, was now gloating: "And how do you like them apples, baby?"

"But why do we speak of the war?" Hidalgo sighed. "Let us eat."

"There is nothing to eat," Amoran said. "It's the inflation."

"In the old days," said Hidalgo, "they kept a regular booth for me at the Hotel de Francia. And there I would dine sumptuously on a peso."

They argued the war again.

It would provide them their occupation for the week. Sometimes the three of them walked in the park, chewing pieces of ice Mrs. Colombo had spared from her lemonade pitcher. They passed soldiers washing underwear, children articulating *Nipponggo, pensionados* sunning themselves in wheelchairs along the Luneta. It was about this time that Sergeant Yato—who was profoundly shaken by Corporal Ito's murder—began his own reign of terror.

Barracks duty bored him to death; his ineffectual battle station during air raids was the cruelest joke that could ever be played on a dedicated foot soldier. Sergeant Yato was too much of a professional to give in to the domesticity of military routine. Latrine games and mess-hall chitchat proved a strain, made him queasy and irritable. Even those evacuation drills imposed by Major Shigura on his clerical staff and gunnery crew alike failed to excite him. On the contrary, these feverish activities with their clanging uproar only seemed to impound his reflexes, reflexes dependent not on dress rehearsals but on actual combat for sustenance. For one thing, the Sergeant drew his own line between a siege and a confrontation. Experience had impressed upon him that while the first was sometimes held off by sheer stupid endurance from a distance, the second was fought only with singular daring—face to face. There was a world of difference between a group effort and the lone endeavor, the finer shadings of which could only be appreciated by someone of pure warrior stock like Sergeant Yato. Given the quotient from ensemble morale and interpersonal replenishments, the group effort produced a wholesale, an almost sexless phyma of heroism. Not so the lone endeavor which, by its isolation, was more intuitive, self-sustaining, having no mob animus to parasitize, and, activated by its own beast, arrived at heroism the way a saint sometimes attained sainthood—through consistent irrationality. Therefore were the evacuation drills tiresome to the Sergeant. And what could have possessed the commandant, a *samurai* descendant, to encourage this mass therapy?

Now Corporal Ito's killing acted as an alarm clock; it provided Sergeant Yato with the ruthless incentive his soldier's body required to rekindle the flame of action. His decision to break out of the Commandant's coop, to go over the hill, was abetted by events precipitated by Captain Johnny's solo virtuosity over Manila Bay. This period introduced the *sisid* rice to the black market and to the Filipino diet, and in so doing also coined a name for a new threat to Filipino digestion—the *manas*.

Sisid rice, or cargo-ship rice salvaged from Manila Bay after the American sorties, added another staple to the profiteer's cache of stolen goods. Day-old *sisid* rice—rice that had been in the bay at least a day—which had been sunned like *palay* in *bilaos* before being boiled and eaten by consumers, brought no ill effects whatsoever. Week-old *sisid* rice, on the other hand, having been exposed in the water for five days or more and though accorded similar precautionary measures, more often than not caused the *manas,* an instantaneous swelling, a sudden inflammation of certain parts of the body, especially the stomach. With expert handling, the day-olds could hardly be differentiated from the ordinary non-Manila Bay rice and sold at exorbitant prices, just like the *elon elon* variety. With no alchemistic transformations possible on week-olds, their price was understandably much lower. The week-olds then proliferated the *manas*. Suddenly, *manas* people were everywhere: swollen three-year-old boys and girls, grown too heavy to walk and so just sat stricken by the dozen on the sidewalks; housewives with double pregnancies—from human seed and inhuman *sisid;* elders too with no bellies left to inflame but with backs as round as buttocks. Week-olds made them all flabby and lethargic; to press a fully rounded *manas* arm was to squeeze rubber. Nothing inside but dry wind. Day-olds were sold openly enough. But week-olds, because of their self-revealing nature—carried a distinctive aroma—were sold surreptitiously. This made the nabbing of larcenous retailers doubly hard. Stung by the ever-increasing air raids and their bull's-eye bombing, the Japanese authorities had prohibited the sale of *sisid* rice as early as the first cargo-ship casualty. But as the *sisid* business was conducted so craftily, nobody had been apprehended as yet. To the Makapili (left arm of the Japanese Military Police, composed of Filipino collaborators many of whom were practicing sadists) was delegated the task of putting down the "Rice Rebellion." With characteristic ineptitude and intransigence, that organization closed down *panaderías,* hardware stores, barber shops, even circumvented the fruit harvests of six municipalities. There was reason to believe, announced the Makapili Intelligence, that substances other than citric juice were embedded within pomelo rinds and *mabolo* peels. Acting on this brainstorm, a whole trainload of pomelos and *mabolos* was embargoed at the Tutuban Station; a season's crop was sliced open, squeezed out and squashed down. The entire operation yielded not one grain of rice, *sisid* or otherwise. In all this guesswork and waste, no one had pointed out the simple fact that *sisid* rice being the exclusive trademark of Manila Bay, it was inconceivable that anybody with sense would take the trouble of smuggling it out of the city, go through the elaborate declination of camouflage, and sneak it back to Manila in fruit crates. For weeks the railroad tracks were caked with crushed pomelos and *mabolos;* the station itself began to smell like a sour perfume factory. Worse, the mothers of beggar children did not know what to do with their pots and casseroles of juiceless rinds and fruitless peelings—an omelet perhaps? The pomelo-*mabolo* fiasco, however, did not deter the Makapili from its seek-and-stamp-out gambados. Next to be ferreted out were the sparkling madames of Divisoria's Diamond Street. They were thrown ten-deep into a cell until the old Bilibid was suffused with rubies, emeralds and sapphires. Along Death Row these burbly gate-crashers were known as *Alahas ni Elias Malas.* When the assorted jade-heads and stone-chests were released on bail —having been booked on such equivocal charges as "obstruction of gold traffic" and "illegal display of internal revenues"—the push-carts came, certified accountants arrived with ledgers and adding machines, and Japanese reinforcements had to be called in to help count their own worthless paper money—probably the last thing they wanted to do. Coming as it did after a protracted series of gross misinterpretations and misadventures, "The Yen Affair" convinced *sisid*-rice analysts that the Filipino Gestapo was not exactly Scotland Yard. Air raid after air raid Manila Bay was fast becoming a hotbed; and all of Manila was turning into a melting pot of grain barons and swollen bellies. *Sisid* and *manas* ceased being mere words in the vernacular: starvation's multifaceted ironies elevated them to folklore. This was more than the Japanese authorities could bear. Heads rolled; personnel was demoted. The Makapili was taken off the case.

Sergeant Yato stepped in.

Consulting no one, he became, overnight, a one-man vigilante trudging from one *talipapa* to another. He was too rash, too abrasive to match wits with the profiteers; but he was more agile, much stronger than all the consumers put together. For his target was neither the merchant nor his merchandise. He was after big game—the *manas* itself. At first, he ran through the motions of interrogation and apprehension. He spat in sleepy eyes, slapped indifferent cheeks, stomped on wheezy stomachs. But he soon wearied of such appetizers. When next he perceived his quarry from a distance, he gave chase, shrieked *"Dorobo! Dorobo!"* He pulled out his service pistol and shot them where they stood or lay. It didn't matter who. To him all big bellies were *manas* and *manas* was the enemy. He slew it wherever he saw it. Placido Rey told the story of how, when he and Paeng Redoblado were killing time at Tomodachi Toni's, the Sergeant had barged in, espied a *labandera* with an enormous paunch at the bar, and without a minute's hesitation and ever the perfect marksman (six gold medals) brought her down without even aiming. Tomodachi Toni remarked later that the poor woman, who had merely stopped by the counter to break a ten-peso Japanese bill, was *just* pregnant. Actually, Sergeant Yato's superiors, if not the entire Japanese officialdom in the country, owed him a debt. The *sisid* industry suffered a major setback after the eleventh killing or so. Week-olds were removed from invisible bins. Even day-olds, at whatever price, became a rarity. Sergeant Yato was on the warpath twenty-four hours a day. Earned the sobriquet of *Manas Verdugo,* the Slayer of *Sisid.* Other business items not even remotely connected with the condemned rice underwent substantial underpricing.

For, *listo ka,* there was that mad sergeant, pistol ready, searching for *sisid,* and not finding it, building his private cemetery on *manas.*

"Hala sigue, ayan na si Sarhentong Putok!"

"Takbo!"

"Tawas ni Satanas! Mansanas ng manas!"

"Sisid na, eto na si acido!"

And what was the Fourth Estate printing?

The "Agricultural Reclamation Project" was growing, growing. Cherry blossoms from Tokyo, *Ooka* of Asia. Rosebushes and regards, courtesy of Berlin—*Der Pater* of Europe. Emperor Hirohito had a green thumb. Premier Tojo had just planted another sapling. Co-Prosperity Sphere for all! No mention of Captain Johnny's mandrake roots. Not a word about the spirit of *sisid* or the extermination of *manas.* Unsung and uncaring, Sergeant Yato, holy avenger of Corporal Ito, ranted and ruptured what to him had now become the bottomless belly of the Philippines. Running out of bullets once, he whipped out his cord belt, hefted a *sisid* suspect (a ten-month baby), then with one quick, fluid stroke in the air, strung it up.

[30]

AND A BABY'S strangled chords could still be heard in Amoran's knobby hands as he taught the girl how to play the guitar. He was very shy and could only teach her half-songs he had made up from the solfeggios of the streets. She wanted to learn nothing more. He was partial to the fandango, and would ask her: "Do you remember Rosario?" As if that somehow answered everything. He sat on a stool at sundown, waiting for supper to cook; and she, sylphic, hair still wet, not yet in *tirintas* after her bath, knelt sedately by his feet. They were exactly what a man to a child should be: teacher to pupil. He was demanding. She was devoted. Vanoye she had heard, Deogracias she had seen, but it was only Captain Johnny she dreamed about. Hidalgo slept through it all. Through the boy's immodesty, through the girl's infidelity—like a patriot suddenly too drowsy to fire a shot on the eve of revolution.

Amoran played without flourishes; before the instrument, he had been nothing more than a broom the old Spaniard swept the floor with, a *hampas-lupa* from whose daily maneuverability at procurement they were driven to survive. But now without warning, the swarthy prodigy of the black market was guardian to them all. In his hands the guitar became still another boarder; perhaps a third language.

Listening avidly, the girl hummed along with the guitar's latest litany: *Paalam, manasito ko!* Amoran could only guess that his *kuridos* were causing her much pain. It would have been intolerable to interrupt these two in this sundown meeting, for a kinship of such intensity had taken possession of them—they were talking to each other.

"Blessed are the *sisid,*" she said, "for they are in La Loma."

"*La Loma papasok!*" Amoran's refrain.

In his bed, almost an echo, the old man moaned.

"Tell her about the flamenco, *ladrón,*" he spat. "Tell her about Escudero."

The boy only strummed half-songs over the war and the darkening of the day, over the old man, who mumbled about real estate. Amoran sang and strummed. Micaela, silenced by this clawing music, listened. Alone in her basement, Mrs. Colombo heard the boy too. Across the hall on the second floor, the newlyweds had just moved in, were preparing for bed. The hairdresser's daughter, Lourdes, just turned twenty; the *tranvía* conductor, Mang Isagani, fifty-one. Aling Ising, the widowed hairdresser, did not want to see *it* and so had been presented by the bridegroom with the princely sum of 5,000 pesos for a big pork-chop dinner somewhere on the understanding that she would be back only for a *late* breakfast, or even an early lunch. There had been a modest after-Mass feast at the boardinghouse, with cold lemonade and hot *bodigos* for the *mangkukulot* bridesmaids and the *cargador* best man. At the Sampaloc church, nobody had kissed the bride; but Mrs. Colombo, who was the candle sponsor, had given the groom a slurpy minute-long salute full on the mouth. Tonight Aling Ising went clop-clopping on wooden clogs around the city looking determinedly for the juiciest pork chops her son-in-law's *pabaon* could buy. In the meantime, Lourdes lay in her mother's *katre,* newly showered and powdered, waiting for her man, who was taking his own sweet time brushing his set of *postizos* before putting them in a glass of water. Mang Isagani, needless to say, was no longer a schoolboy and was not one to hurry up things. He had given Lourdes free rides on his streetcar route from Bustillos to Taft Avenue (she went to the National Library almost every day) for nine months before he could muster enough nerve to speak to her. As proof of his affection for this bookish, not so pretty but quite strapping girl, he had, after that, also bestowed free rides on Aling Ising, then on Mrs. Colombo, Hidalgo, Amoran and the girl until it seemed the whole boardinghouse was in transit and Mang Isagani had to allot a certain amount for their fares.

Removed from the streetcar and shed of his soiled conductor's uniform, Mang Isagani appeared even shabbier in baggy pajamas. His skin was the color of brown sugar; his massive jowls sagged to his throat as though permanently anchored there—no doubt one of the many physical liabilities acquired in the posture of punching passenger tickets. Each expression on that face seemed to be triggered by a collusion of wrinkles, so that a vacuous "*Kumusta kayo?*" quite shattered those craggy cheeks and that prognathous jaw. Except for a pampered pompadour (and at fifty-one, his hairline had not receded an inch) Mang Isagani cared little for his appearance. Frugal, set in his ways, he was a creature of habit who was not happy unless he was putting something away for the rainy day.

Pag may isinuksok, mayroong bubunutin.

The sum total of his personality elicited no sensations from either girl or woman; his opinions, whenever he voiced them, caused not a ripple in the affairs of men. Yet it was this very innocuousness that made him so effective, for he was, incredibly enough, also one of the more dependable contacts of Deogracias in Greater Manila. By so many frowns, gestures, grimaces and a whole alphabetical catalogue flashed like Morse code through his ordinarily expressionless eyes, Mang Isagani had been able to relay the information that Captain Johnny was in town, that a *despedida* was slated at such and such a place, on such and such a date. Dark Glasses couldn't have found a more saturative advertiser than this wily conductor who, though having very few acquaintances of his own, supplied Captain Johnny with a full house during his Manila engagement. What was also remarkable was the fact that Mang Isagani spread his good word while punching tickets in a streetcar packed with Japanese soldiers and Makapili informers.

Tonight, however, the diffident conductor, feeling silly and older than his age, was in the unenviable position of relaying not information but his manhood to a hairdresser's twenty-year-old daughter. Aling Ising had been a big enough nuisance and without the 5,000-peso insurance Mang Isagani would have had a churlish witness on his hands in the most crucial time of his life. Nightgowned and nervous, Lourdes lay waiting in her mother's bed, fascinated by all this male vanity. *Aba naman,* her husband had had *two* showers, had shaved off his whiskers (!) and swallowed more vitamin pills than she had ever seen in her lifetime, and was now puttering and muttering about the room as if collecting imaginary fares. Was it her place to call him? She heard the guitar across the hall and knew it must be that boy Amoran playing to Hidalgo and the girl whose name nobody seemed to know. Who was her lover? Lourdes wondered. The old man? The boy? Both? Who was making Mrs. Colombo happy now? And what was *it* like really? The idea of the odd pair making love to the nameless girl stimulated her. She could not imagine the old Spaniard mounting that gawky, quiet nobody. Why, if he did, wouldn't he sprain something? And if he kissed her, wouldn't all his awful-looking teeth just fall out? The boy was scarcely an improvement. With that ugly face and smelling as he did, wouldn't the nameless girl just vomit? But how beautifully he played, how cruelly gentle. Perhaps what they looked like and even how they acted or smelled didn't really count—if they could do this; if this was what they told you they really were. Perhaps faces and mannerisms, perhaps all coarseness and vulgarity were just watchdogs guarding an inner core of softness. From across the hall and into this room spanned the guitar's melodic arms. It no longer mattered who was playing and for whom—the lovers of Ojos Verdes lay listening, lay abed armed to the teeth with chromosomal exhaust. Addenda: the Romeos Respiratory, all sputter and sputum; the Rhythm Regulators, orbital, onanistic.

"Sino ang tumutugtog?"

"Sí Amoran, *ho,"* Lourdes answered Mang Isagani, who was with her now.

"May kaluluwa ang batang yoon," he whispered.

"O-po," she said, feeling his hand on her inner thigh.

"At ako naman ay may katawan din. . . ."

Oo! she thought, not believing him at first but now accepting it at last. She would not have to cry to her mother in the morning, the alley boys could jeer this May-and-December marriage as much as they pleased: her conductor's instrument throbbed just as movingly as Amoran's guitar.

"Why do I listen to you every night," Hidalgo grunted, "when I have a sickness here?"

Amoran just whistled, smacking his lips. But his mind was still on that couple across the hall.

When Hidalgo became more temperate, an attitude of simpering obeisance possessed the girl. The reflection of the Spaniard's face in a drinking glass intrigued her; or she rose to follow the sounds he made at night. It was not a dream that made her rise after midnight at the sight of his scarf and cane to follow the man without slippers and without his knowledge out onto the wharf. Later, he had scolded her for this thoughtlessness. What if she had caught a cold? he barked. She might have died of pneumonia, and there was her funeral to consider. Under Hidalgo's tutelage, she had grown addicted to books and was seen riding the streetcar free to the National Library with the child bride of Mang Isagani. Their lives, as always, depended upon Hidalgo's sagacity in the theatre, Amoran's luck in the black market. The girl helped the old man prepare his fabrics for a skit and even indemnified his most brainless pratfalls with a kind of framework and balance. Just where did she get all these fancy notions about style and structure? he asked her. And, pray, could she tell him more? Without blinking, she replied that structure was that which gave body to a work of art or nature, be it the stanza to a poem or the net to a school of fish; style was the personality in the poem, the specialness of the fish. Straight from the mouths of babes! She laughed solemnly at his frenetic rehearsals; he hated her generous mirth because he could not visualize it on the lips of his audience. She would have to learn to laugh like a certain memory before she could sustain and pacify one angry old man. Hidalgo shrugged resignedly and said: "What would happen to young failures like you if it were not for old failures like me? My dear, this useless old world drags on and on because the catafalque of senile cavaliers still clings to the last laurel leaf. Believe me, the trees are bent bare from our centennial sorrows, year after year after year. Ah, wouldn't your Señor Dark Glasses love to hear me speak thus? The senescent omegas despise the budding alphas only because the young carry with them the banner of their ego: youth. One morning I shall wake up to find my trunk cut down, girded into the barks of steamships, discharging all the droolly Ponce de Leones from one fountain spout to another. It is time, you see, time to surrender my nonexistent plunder, lest I forfeit my resting place. *¿Comprende?*"

The girl beamed, "Yes."

Each night Hidalgo returned to room thirteen with the girl there dreaming herself a woman at his nearness, while the Spanish veil fluttered above their heads. How had it gone with him? she'd ask. "*Bien,* this time the audience laughed." Another white lie. He talked, she listened; Tchaikovsky would grate into music, leak out like an ointment from the long day's captivity. At night neighbors heard the grating nonstop ballet inveigle into dance these three tenants; either they moved to Russian music or they sat before each other, numbed and apologetic. Mrs. Colombo always alluded to them as *they*. *They* were at it *again*. Amoran stole ground corn, made coffee to keep the girl awake; with his books Hidalgo fairy-taled her back to sleep. At daybreak, the boy took down the veil to cover the girl from the cold; in the evening, the old man hung it up again. Hidalgo was out of work; she was promised a job; she was well; the old man was recuperating. Ofttimes they were all ill and lay in the room speaking of the American infantry. "We shall be eating sardines and *pan americano* with *real* butter by next month," they would say to each other. Sometimes the boy was alone in the room and played the guitar—now with a fifth string—perhaps like a sorcerer, to bring her back. Or it was she who was alone and took down the instrument: to simulate a friend's footsteps on a piece of wood. The boy would come upon her in this manner, and tiptoeing behind her, would put his hand on the strings. So that it seemed it was she who had brought him back.

"If you can only bring back the Americans the same way," he chuckled.

"Fools!" Hidalgo bellowed from his bed. "Do they need spectacles to see the heart?" A tic, a gasp. "In the Old Country, they had eyes. *Mira!*"

"Why don't you go back?" Amoran asked, reclining against his guitar.

"Play something, Amor," said the girl.

The old man nodded. "Yes, yes. Wash it away."

To her artificer: "Play."

The boy stared at them both, then stroked the keys. For the muezzin call. He enunciated *moro-moro* verses like a *barrio* bard, as though some foolish god had crucified him on a myth. The girl belonged to all this, a partisan ear. Had Amoran rested but one minute in that second year with her, had he refrained from a single serenade, they would have lost her. Though for her he played many songs, all of them seemed the same for each one was just a continuation of the last. Ojos Verdesians only had to hear the boy play the first chords for them to know it was time to bar their doors because the men from the mountains would descend into their *camote* plots and pluck down from their windows bundles of food they had left there. Also time for children to run home from their games. Time for wild boys to come out. Time for herb women to quit their stalls and street corners because *malas* would surely come. It is time, they would say. In their room, lighted with a candle, Hidalgo and Amoran continued their vigil.

"They are all listening here," the girl would remark.

After that brief hour, all cautions spoken, all dangers muffled, they slept; to let the war engulf them. Robbers, psychopaths, secret police, the underground—they took their measures. The boy laid his guitar aside; the old man held up the veil for the night. They bade good night to each other, but the girl wished the guitar would play again. It was an assignation.

Now something must be said about the Colombo clot.

Who (with avarice, by accretion) pulsed this mud-lawned hovel, for over two years of war. Whether by accident or agreement, Tira's temple regionalized itself into: *(a)* ground-floor Southerners; and *(b)* second-story Northerners. With the latter putting on airs by virtue of their altitude. What with clashing religious backgrounds and historical differences, each group became as clannish as the other.

Even debating on their star placements on the *three*-star Filipino flag. A Tagalog would blurt: "Nobody says 'Visayas, Mindanao and Luzon' . . . only 'Luzon, Visayas *and* Mindanao'!" Moot point inadmissible evidence to a Cebuano: "Still, that's one star *over* you—Mindanao being in the South!" Tagalog thrust: "Who were the first Filipino collaborators? The Southerners!" Cebuano counterpunch: "But Lapu-Lapu who killed Magellan was the first Filipino hero!" Filipino clergy came from the North! So what? Christian faith originated in the South! It did not ease bruised prides any that with typical largesse the landlady had tried to mend her domestic fences by locating the communal kitchen and bathroom-*cum*-toilet somewhere between the first and second floors—both security risks being tantalizingly outside the realm of the first-floor Southerners, yet not quite within the jurisdictional radius of the second-story Northerners. It happened that the Southerners, who had set their sights on the kitchen, took forever to cook skimpy meals and defended their outpost sometimes for days. Having coveted bathroom and toilet, the Northerners returned the compliment by individually taking four or five baths, and for whatever purposes except urination-defecation, barricading the toilet till every last mother's son of a Southerner turned a constipated yellow. Mrs. Colombo soon found herself dead center in a holy war; refereeing for what both combatants eulogized as the "Crusade for Conveniences." Slamming one door, rapping conciliatingly on another, the landlady shook her divided house with Colombo backfire. "What are you doing in the kitchen, ha, you have nothing to cook?" "What are you doing in the toilet, *bastos,* you had nothing to eat!" "And you, what are you doing in the bathroom, you have no skin left to scrub!" All of which hit their marks: a hollow clunk in the empty pot; a solid left hook to the empty stomach. Only Hidalgo, acknowledged baron of the bathers, escaped abuse; likewise Amoran, the pathological kitchener whose quick wits and quicker knife gave the opposition something to think about. Things came to a head one morning when the Northerners stormed the kitchen, set arson to six charcoal stoves, uncapped bottles of *bagoong* debauched boiled frogs and other smelly indistinguishable staples. *"Sugod mga kapatid!"* battle-cried the Southerners as they invaded the bathroom to turn on the faucets full blast; as they c-c-crasssshed into the toilet to uproot privy and pipes as far as their underground deposits. A slushy, sludgy epitaph for the Colombo kitchen-bathroom-toilet ("Luzon, Visayas and Mindanao!") whose combined extravaganzas of broiling charcoal stoves, fecal geysers, rocketing singed corn and volcanic lard in torrential faucetiles splashed all over the landing, cascaded down the porch, sinking the new rattan rocking chair where the landlady had been blissfully contemplating her next basement mate over a glass of iced lemonade and a bag of roasted cashew nuts. *"P-p-porbiddda si utin!"* yelped the dethroned Tira, trembling mightily, begrimed in livid starch and black *tae* as though she had just struck oil. Over the mortal remains of the communal kitchen (which was unresurrectable) the feuding clans grudgingly agreed on a temporary truce, while patching up the bathroom and repiping the toilet. *Guerra patani* was over.

Life, however lifeless, still had to be lived. In the Colombo clubhouse, as well as anywhere else. Lodgers desultory and deregionalized flitted in and out. To stay a month, then go. To come again and settle down till death. Bounding in with nothing for rent but promises and tricks: a family of eight; no roots except those in *ubi* plots that bore no fruit. Loping up the stairs with sneak-food. Husband and wife feasting on *kilawen.* Their four daughters slept the sleep of the hungry. Same husband and wife meeting outside for a leg of roast goat. Daughters just dwindled. Fleshless and whimpery till the *kabaong.* One, two, three, four—snap! A tinsmith sleepwalker tripping on cubicle copulations. Shorts and slips converging. Tinsmith floating through it all—a wanton Lourdes, the Colombo cohabitations, Micaela's incestuous affair with Don Giovanni (in variations of her fantasy, she was daughter to all the great baritones and tenors in Metropolitan Opera history), the cot-creaky pair, Luz and Loretta, who did not care who was looking. Odds and ends. Take the auto mechanic, who refused to believe his missing missus was legally dead. Flashlighting up and down among bedded bodies for his Anita (*"Bakit mo ako iniwan, bakit?"*); and slighted, slapped, returned to his own cell to chalk up on his wall another mark against the world: *They are hiding her somewhere, watch out!* He looked for his wife in every woman newly arrived. Suspecting the worse: that she was under a spell, that her face had been altered by a witch. Anita, *ang sakit,* Anita. . . . No telling what he would do next, he was so jealous. Ask the blacksmith who brought pickups home whom the auto mechanic scared away with flashlights and Anitaisms: "You have her eyes, her dimples, her mouth—oh, why did you desert me?" No way of knowing when the *patis-maglalako* would go into his pet fit: "It's the end of the world!" Be wary of the small-time magician; he threatened to make everything disappear. Be kind to the garbage collector—one testicle; two-timing spouse. Pretend with Paco, the sneaky *sabuñgero*. Humor Kulas, the songwriter. Get rid of Illuminada, the streetwalker with venereal d. So-and-so and so forth and so on and vice berserk. A week. Two months. Four years. Permanent. Passing through. Shiftless. Settled. Mrs. Colombo harbored them all. Char, crones, cretins. Think of Santa Claus. Think *'Kano*.

Whenever the boy was away, Hidalgo gave imitations of foliage to the girl. This recital carried him into: alder, myrtle, deodar, linden. He shaped sepal in his hands and spoke of fatal fragrances. On this personal stage the old Spaniard performed with love and variety for he knew his blushing audience would follow him into the restlessness of his art. He had only to mimic the mating call of cauliflowers and she would reward him with unfeigned, even tearful laughter. Posturing on his wriggly cane, he would amble into center light and venture into the delicate rhythm of lichen. In his preludes, he was always gay, flamboyant. To this she curtsied, joining him breathlessly, his father's book of *dichos* in her hand; and together they would take a bow.

Hidalgo wrote her letters too, wrote them in Spanish and left them everywhere in the room. Though she did not understand the language, the girl collected his letters and read them hungrily. Mrs. Colombo often found some and burned them in her stove to cook her meals. She read phrases from these brown papers, pronouncing Hidalgo's lyrics in her heavy Visayan tongue. Soon, the boardinghouse knew of the old man and his long letters written in green ink on brown paper. When this happened, Hidalgo stopped writing abruptly, and the girl's trinket box was minus the codal half of a summer memorabilia. One night, she read the last of them she had saved from their stove. As always it was addressed to her.

Querida:

Al fracasarme, cada noche, [burned] que tu te enflaqueces. Sube tu fiebre; ni puedes levantar la mano. Todo, se debe al [burned] no puedo provocar la risa como medio para mantener decentemente nuestra vida.

> Cada noche me encuentro[?] mi gente [?] desvelo. Ellos solo me cigilan para no llegar en pasadilla [blotched]. Tengo quen hipnotizarles a fin de demonstrar mi aptitud. Pero, aun con mi fuerza de mímica, lo que se me [crossed out] por delante es más cómico que mi espectáculo fútil; ellos, una generación de [blotched] se ilusionan de su destino en lo del actor cómico. Cree me, [crossed out] esto fuora [?] seria [blotched]. Pues cada [?] pacífica [blotched] un historismo maligno. Te digo [?] grito de [?] pacífica [blotched] 'netrar mas profundo [?] cualquier otro. Mi amo [blotched].

?

!

She wrote him back.

Falteringly, desperately.

Reams of Tagalog.

Scraps of Spanish.

Paragraphs in English.

Even a smattering of *katakana.*

When she had pieced them together and Hidalgo finished reading this wild sweet letter, he shook his head and laughed.

"Are you laughing at me?" she asked indignantly, and the old man realized at once that he was treading on soft ground. He very solemnly flung an arm about her neck and made her sit down.

"No, *hermosa,*" he said. "I may cause laughter, and very little of it, even. But I myself cannot laugh. Not at people. Least of all, at you. I must laugh at myself first. We are compatibles, you and I. We are extreme platitudes, the supreme opposites of each other."

"Are we?"

"Yes."

"Why is that so?"

"It is. That is all."

"Everything you say is beautiful, Hidalgo."

"Because everything that is said to me is ugly."

"You have not heard everyone."

He smiled. "Oh yes, ballerina. To me, even one is the universe."

[31]

SHE WAITED ON THE WORLD in a little café owned by Tomodachi Toni's brother, Victor. No questions had been asked; no references needed. The girl was given a number, was assigned to a table. Already skilled in the various intricacies of kitchen and cutlery, she could also knit now, monogram, and throw a bread knife where it would do the most good. She served manners, not people: suspicion over a bowl of *mami*—and she was quick to reprove a doubting customer with: "That is not horse meat, sir!" (it was dog meat)—fingers that itched; loudmouths whose obscenities were stronger than the odor of the commode. But even if most patrons were either fresh or insufferably rude, she was patient. At least a few were students who were always mysteriously disturbed about something and managed to be, in her presence, incoherently *simpático*. They were sarsaparilla and whiffs of vanilla with soulful eyes. She liked to wait on what she told the cook were the "isolates." Luz, the proprietor's mischievous niece, would usher this forlorn family to her section; and Emma, waitress of table five, conspired willingly. The tender seed of business, mused the grateful newcomer, saluting the dissonant thrill: a transient who recited elegies—a fairy tale; a youthful baker who ordered only tea without sugar. She was especially fond of the young whose appraisal did not molest her; who wore hidden crucifixes under patched shirts and whose order issued from the menu with a hint of boyish disdain. She attended the swirl and buffet of their needs like a malicious child under a tree, one hand always extended to catch a falling fruit. After work she strolled through the Mehan Gardens, down to the "Buy and Sell" block, taking off her earrings—Hidalgo's tokens—and dropping them in her handbag, for each stroll the price jeweled matrons sang would rise a little more than she could bear. She counted yellowing shrubs in a fenced-off garden, six and seven and eight and nine and *mariosep,* the earth was full of them. Japanese aircraft flew overhead, gleamed briefly, met a burst of kites and vanished in another sky. Aside from red suns, she noticed they also had Red Cross banners tied about their aluminum bodies. A street photographer in a tangerine shirt snapped her picture once as she lingered by the tenements. She trembled, recollecting how she came out looking quite pale in the faded print. Why did he make her look so sad? When she came back to complain, the tangerine man was no longer there. It was because he did her wrong, she reasoned. Occasionally, she would sneak out a rice pudding and a can of santol preserves from the café and leave them on newspaper-pavements where she knew beggars slept looking at the stars. A jobless *basurero* coughing fitfully caught her one time and when he untied the banana leaves, he sighed: "Daughter was your age too when they took her, *hija.*" Stooped, silhouetted figures regarded her suspiciously as their hunger rummaged into the bundle. She went home, humming, pretending Amoran had suddenly found her and was conducting her home with a *harana.* On the Colombo porch, a *dalagita* in bloomers panted, clutching a green guava. "*They* are in Baguio," Aling Ising imparted deliciously. In bed, the cafeteria relief waitress deliberated on investments, the substance of her trade, the percentage of charm, the economics of imported linen. She detested hoarders and ration chiefs. She tinkled notes on the toy piano Amoran had stolen for her from a bazaar; she cut out rhymes from magazines. Her only faith was gentleness. This year, however, nothing more was born in the likeness of God; not a gesture, not a breath of the illusion she felt was her due. And what about the Americans? Weren't they always coming? For a favorable rumor, one had to pay candy, a leg of chicken, an excursion into a shade with a man's arm round her waist. Still the Invasion was as distant as the moon. If they came in another ten years, she moaned, she would be a century. Never seriously catering to herself, she found it unforgivable that for the living there were no alms. The memory of the guitar came with a drizzle and sunrise was not long for all the sleepers on the pavements and morning would be kind even if the sun remained, burning temples and fevering the mind.

"Go to sleep, Cinderella," said Hidalgo wryly. "For tomorrow we die."

Amoran giggled.

One Friday, the cashier's brother, co-owner of the café, fled his Nipponggo class and raved about salmon and beans in Divisoria. Emma and the girl wrenched him loose from a fire hydrant. Squabbling with the two women tugging at his sleeves, the cashier's brother produced a silver dollar to bribe them.

"You better hide that, *Manong,*" the girl cautioned. "If they see it we shall all be in the Fort."

They hailed a *karomata* and the man whistled the "Stars and Stripes Forever" so dramatically they had to gag his mouth with a bandanna. After delivering him without mishap to the café, the girl went next to the butcher shop and paid Hidalgo's debts. No, she said stiffly. She would not take his pigs' feet on credit and had no taste for beer, thank you. The wide expectant grin disappeared from the butcher's sweating face. "You still owe me for the liver last month!" he called after her, but the door had slammed safely behind her and she could picture him rushing to the slit in the planks of the rear door to watch her round the curb, hoping for a breeze. All the while she was reconstructing the meat loaves, the peppered chops on the counter and on the larder, haughty in a domain all their own and of such tax and tone as to renounce even the promise of her womanhood. If only she had a diamond ring. . . .

On a day off, she and Lourdes, Mang Isagani's woman, tramped along to the National Library. No, they did not take the streetcar;

they would not even let Amoran accompany them. There was this good, solid woman talk to be done, and a third party would spoil it. Girlishly, and yet with a new air of maturity, Lourdes spoke of her man ("*Ang aking tao*") and—here reddening somewhat—of their nights of love. She confided that the prospect of sex at a relatively early age had been rather distressing. However, the idea of having sexual relations with a man old enough to be her father had absolutely mortified her. But, *ang kapalaran nga naman,* she marveled, her conductor proved neither ravenous nor remiss in the marital bed—he was no *galanteng gipit,* but *malakas at mayumi.* Even in her erogenous zones. And there were other things, too; another side to her mild-mannered husband, she gushed. *Maniwala ka o hindi,* great doings! About a Mister Dark Glasses and the underground. About a Second Coming. About Capitán Johnny. About Joaquin, who was supposed to be somewhere in Manila spreading the Word with his trumpet. Having recounted her pleasures and good fortune, Lourdes cheerfully took her leave with a leather-bound copy of *Wuthering Heights.* The girl had been so engrossed in her *amiga*'s hour-long confidences she had forgotten to take out her own *Green Mansions* from the library. Mystified and excited, she was not aware that she was now walking aimlessly among the faceless throng of Plaza Miranda. Her head buzzed with marine echoes, male moans, murmurs of May. Had other men loved her? Men other than Hidalgo and Amoran—taking for granted that what these two felt for her was what the not-really-so-old but actually-so-romantic conductor felt for the hairdresser's daughter. And if indeed these dark demanding men had truly loved her, did their arms wrap her in submission? Had their bodies lain with her in some dark bed, at some urgent hour, upon some mutual need? If in truth they had not—and the loss was unbearable—when would their lips impart a love bite on her own as Mang Isagani had left on the quivering mouth of his Lourdes? And when would she, waitress of table two in Victor's Café, aimlessly walking along Plaza Miranda, passably pretty—as Hidalgo had said—feel the weight of her own *tao?* Bewildered, she stopped by an ice cart, not wanting to go home just yet. Perhaps she could listen to the drum-and-harmonica blindman whose ration coupon was pinned to his collar. She could look for that unemployed actor and beg him to buy her a trinket that glowed in the dark, take her home again. Perhaps she could undress in the moonlight and swim out to the bay, go to him who waited for her in a litter. Kissed him, yes, she did . . . before they took him away again, to the mountains. She'd stopped her pilgrimage to San Sebastian; that San Antonio was an Indian giver . . . took back her eagle. . . .

At the Luneta Park, two artists were painting the waterfront.

The corpulent one who was chewing an unlit cigar drew merry, full-bodied women on the docks and blocked off the sentry box with a steam-whistle pipe; his Japanese soldiers wore leggings and tennis shoes; his fishermen were interchangeable with the soldiers. The other artist worked mainly with decomposing eggplant green, very disciplined pink-orange, unlike his partner, and red-bordering-on-scarlet. Shawled and hipless were his women; he had no fishermen at all but torn sails and ropey fishing nets, *banca* hulks and fractured fishbones. At first glance, the shawled, hipless females looked like serpents menacing unseen seafarers. For his sentry box: pastel-violet kites fencing violently over the waterfront skyline, while a predatory baby suckled green milk from a stunted mother's coconut breast. Convents were shambles, sunset was without sun, birds were wingless in a cramped, scaly Manila.

"Why did you do that?" the girl asked resentfully.

"Because," the thin artist explained proudly, "they don't conjugate. Because to abstract from the divided is to add to the minus. And mostly because the government expires at four o'clock and I have nothing better to do."

The girl flicked off an insect, thinking about the tangerine man and Vanoye both snapping pictures of the dead. A toddler with a balloon posed under a fire-prevention poster. "Smile," coaxed the tangerine man, and the girl slid noiselessly into a passageway, wishing vaguely he would nudge her by the elbow and apologize. The toddler with balloon would not smile and clung furiously to the string. The tangerine man rolled his tongue in his mouth and departed, click-click-click. A horn. She entered a cabaret and was rooted to a rail for there he was, the Gabriel of Dark Glasses—Joaquin. She closed her eyes and the trumpet singed her ears with unknown messages, dirges high and low that were perhaps dedicated to Mang

Isagani, the conductor of Manila's underground orchestra. BEWARE, a sign read. She recoiled, and headed out for the *estero.* "They arrested seventeen Moslems last week," someone said from a doorway. She reached the sidewalk where the Colombo boardinghouse was, her fists clenched in anticipation. But before she could prevent it, she had taken the road leading to the pavement where her *paroquianos* were. They saw her at once. She opened her handbag and slipped out some paper money and three Akibono cigarettes a customer had given her. They scrambled for the cigarettes and when these had been snatched, they fingered the scattered change but seemed reluctant to keep them.

"Nothing new from the shortwave," she said. "But their time will come, just wait."

They gathered around her in plight, with petitions.

"Did they raid the cellar again, the military police?"

"That is right, *kuya.*"

"Is it true, miss, that Mister Trompeta is back and has given a definite date?"

A date?

"You won't let them get me, will you, miss?"

"I am just a waitress, Emmanuel."

"Miss, Tony got a job, here is . . ."

"Tell him not to drink too much."

"Miss, they are sending me to labor camp . . . my lungs!"

"Here are some herbs. Pound them in a pestle, do you hear? And rub the *katas* on your chest before you go to sleep."

"Miss, they dragged Jorge to the Fort last night. He's only fourteen! Do you know my *bayaw* never came back from the Zona?"

"Miss, oh, miss, where are your earrings?"

She did not speak anymore and walked homeward, where she knew a room waited impersonally for her coming as though she did not quite belong to its rickety cot or to its two masters for she had abandoned so many voices in the curfew of the night and now could never answer to all the fathers in this dream. Behind her, a clop of horsehooves, a flash of white: the Japanese officer had picked up her scent again.

She got home to find Amoran missing; to come upon Hidalgo's latest craze—causes and strangers. They plotted in stage whispers the dissolution of the Co-Prosperity Sphere, the purge of the Kempetai, the assassination of the incoming premier.

"Tell David we cannot wait any longer."

"I'll go myself and plant the charges under the sandbags of the Ayala."

"How much do you think the bomb will burn?"

"They keep spare parts of their bombers in the Old Metropolitan."

"Blow up the arsenal, blow up the dam."

"Who knows Fortunato?"

"Yes! It is said that he can raise a hundred men."

"They took a shot at the President again this morning while he was playing golf."

"They had no right," groaned Hidalgo.

Amoran returned a week later, saying only that a whole garrison was after him.

The spiel on arms would last for hours and it made the girl so busy praying for them all. In their rehearsals for sabotage, the principal actors who had been royally snubbed by the active underground formed their own clique, with corresponding organizational code names, titles, ranks—even a highly legalistic charter. They were bespectacled plotters moving around with more gunpowder in their minds than in their hands. They were Lip Incendiaries. The reconnaissance bands of Dark Glasses that weekly penetrated Manila for climactic conferences called these noisy, theoretical saboteurs the "outside-the-*kulambo* patriots." The deflating gibes infuriated the *kulamboristas* no end, but they were vacillating before the knife-wielding, gun-toting cohorts of Dark Glasses and Mang Isagani. Having vocalized their brand of treason at the Colombo boarding-house, having eaten Amoran's tasty cassava fritters between amendments, the *kulamboristas* shamelessly pawed the girl and harangued Hidalgo, their host, who could only wish he were in Jamaica, wherever that was. They branded him *"inútil,"* a crippled comedian who could not serve the country, which was, after all, not his own.

"This objectivity only after you have dined," the old Spaniard said reproachfully.

The girl drove them away.

"Concubine!" they hooted as they slammed the door.

"Money changers!" she cried back.

But in a week they had commissioned Hidalgo to compose inflammatory propaganda against the Imperial Japanese Forces. He wrote slogans and bulletins and caricatured warlords on brown paper. Amoran and the waitress went around in the evening to scatter the old Spaniard's hackwork among the citizens. Whenever the military authorities accosted the boy, he had learned to trip a nimble dance and do one of Hidalgo's impersonations, and as a finale, howl a tremendous word: *"Banzai!"* For her part, the girl tipped favorite customers at the café with a sketch, a handbill. One night, quite sleepy, somewhat absentminded, and because the face before her was pleasantly familiar, the waitress of table two gave a caricature of Emperor Hirohito to the Japanese, who had been her shadow for almost a year and whose white horse now waited outside the café. (Diners gagged on their food; spoons and forks were frozen in midair, Placido Rey related to friends afterward.) Brown paper in hand, eyes eclipsed by slits, the Japanese officer pored over his mortal god drawn in Mephistophelian correlatives: buffalo horns, flashbulb eyes, black-scimitar mustaches, pitchfork tail—plus an elephantine penis. "Ah, so!" the man said and asked for dessert.

This time, he took the girl home on his white horse.

"It's the Lone Ranger!" Amoran screeched.

"It's that hussy with her new *bihag,*" hissed Mrs. Colombo.

"It's the end of us all," Hidalgo wailed.

But the Japanese just dismounted, helped the girl down, tipped his cap, mounted again, and rode off without a word.

Next day, he was back with presents.

"Ay, *porbida gid!*" exclaimed Mrs. Colombo.

He skulked about the house, listening to conversations, trying to pick up a little Ilonggo from the landlady. Then he showed up with two soldiers, one of them carrying his sword. Later, both the soldiers and the sword were left, presumably in the barracks. He spoke passable English; when now and then he used Tagalog words, tenants in the boardinghouse stiffened.

"What is the matter with everybody, please?" he asked politely.

They did not answer.

"But I am a friend," he protested. "To-mo-da-chi!"

"Not in that uniform," countered Hidalgo, knees quaking.

"So desu ka?"

"That is so."
"I am a major, but that doesn't make me your enemy, *ne?*"
The girl's eyes never left Hidalgo's.
"I am Shigura," the Japanese said.

[32]

MAJOR SHIGURA LIVED IN DREAD OF RECOGNITION, but of course his uniform always marked him. Almost shapeless, monkishly balding, he was the compleat recluse whose taciturnity held him like orthopedic braces. He spoke so softly, treaded so lightly that he was in a room before he was heard. Like a neglected urchin, he restricted himself to a corner and appeared to ache privately; seemed like that innocuous enemy doomed to a tinge of sweetness. From infancy he had wanted to reside in the aurora borealis (whatever that might be), but had been a featureless child who in secret was polarized to the mirror: therein to minister collodion all over his cheeks. History to him was fate still to incubate; fate was history in lonely expectation. He rode an Argentinian white horse (saddleless) and Manila gradually grew accustomed to his eternal tension between duty and dawn: his serene summer landscape, his dark cathartic deeds. When he was visiting at the Colombo boardinghouse, there was an unmistakable air of absence in his presence, for people tended to talk around him—though he was usually the subject of it all.

And so it happened that on a Sunday (postlunch or presupper), you saw him there, unruffled, burnished in sunlight like copperware. He was the venerable visitor who sat with his back to the wall; leery of windows, wary of doors. He carried his welcome wherever he went—a *fiambrera* heaping with rice, meatballs and raw mudfish, some canned bean sprouts he himself would not eat. For Hidalgo he brought a bottle of dearomized wine; a box of tamarinds for the girl. By right of repetition, the rattan chair with a motif of *maya* birds threaded with tinted abaca in its core, became his; and no one else, including the old Spaniard, dared use it, even in Shigura's absence. When the subject was eagles (Captain Johnny in particular), when there were enough leftovers to feed the faith, the Shiguraless chair would suddenly proclaim its presence; and the predators would gag, the wings ceased flapping until someone hauled off the vexing apostrophe and put it out on the landing. One day, after such an intrusion and its resultant expulsion, there was a gentle rapping on the door and when the girl opened it, there stood the Japanese officer, the chair of *maya* birds in his arms.

"So sorry."

Shigura dragged in his movable throne, steered it to its rightful place, slumped heavily down into it, and commenced reflexively to talk about *his* Japan and the snow and his beloved ancestral cats, while Hidalgo and the girl sat before him with varying moues of consternation. Shigura ruminated about geology, metempsychosis, spermatogenesis, land reform, the anatomy of conquest. He spoke of the Alps, which his family adored; of the Himalayas, which he abhorred; and of the Ganges, which was only a hallucination. Then without as much as a goodbye or any such propriety, withdrew; rode away on that arachnoidal white horse. Amoran then alit from a roof beam to sleep on the floor.

They found the man everywhere. At the marketplace the girl would bargain for muskmelons; and there *he* was, inspecting a turnip, sniffing a durian. In a bazaar, Hidalgo's wards would pass their hands longingly on merchandise they knew they could not buy, and *he* was there too to pay for their caprice. In a movie house a shadow in civilian clothes rising to offer the girl his seat (she, who had read about Raleigh and Elizabeth), would be, ah yes, their mysterious benefactor late of the bazaar—a brooch, a pendant. They would be strolling around Binondo, Hidalgo and she, and this monk-bald man who looked like he had just pawned his saffron robes and swallowed his begging bowl would hobble out of an alley, nod apologetically, then step aside for them as though this were the fifteenth century and they were royal consorts to Isabella I, Queen of Castile; Hidalgo, who knew his Aragon, waved regally to the wretch. This familiar freak also stood somewhere back in the streetcar with what other imbuements of paltry courtesies? And it must have been he who ate birdlike meals four booths away in the same café. Hidalgo etched this omniscient face one day and tacked his drawing on the wall.

"Why does he follow us?" he asked. "Does he know anything?"

"What is there to know?" replied the girl.

That evening, Shigura came with supper.

"Tell the boy to climb down from the chimney," he said good-naturedly. "I see this little parasite scratching into flour sacks and waiting for our wolverines to doze in the storehouses; I see him fly down from a tree like a bat, clapping his avarice on scraps. Come out, come out, I shall not harm you."

The bat, with apodal fleetness, seemed to detach itself from a branch; and with digital grace, plopped near the cot.

"You won't shoot me?" Amoran asked, inching toward dinner.

"I have no gun," answered the Japanese.

Indeed when all three of them looked, he had no arms.

Their caterer had brought: four halves of roast chicken (breasts and thighs), sour pickles, and Tokyo rice. The three tenants ate ferociously for an hour. Number one, the roast chicken: what the boy did was to shred breast or thigh of its browned skin and white meat, mash these inside a palmful of rice until it became a small pulpy cake—then popped it into his mouth. After each mouthful (and his masticating processes seemed to involve only one short, gnashing chomp instead of a series of bites), he sucked the grease from his fingers and licked the far-in-between grainfalls from his plate so that both were always clean. Whenever someone dropped a morsel, Amoran either speared it with a fork or lifted a corner of the tablecloth so that the particle slid into his hand and from there, bingo, into that grindstone again. Singed to its undersides, the chicken's rib case was crispy enough to eat, which Amoran did as he crunched away on the tiny interlaced membranes and bones. Nothing was left. The Spaniard was naturally appalled by such manners and took occasion to scold or slap the boor down. Yet he too (noted Shigura) must have wished he were capable of such dispatch. Oddly enough (observed Shigura), the boy, animalistic as he was, would force big balls of chickened rice between the girl's lips. Unbelievably modest, she would shake her head in refusal, but, badgered and nudged incessantly under the table, would blushingly consent to half a helping. Number two, the Tokyo rice: when it did not go into Amoran's pies, was spooned adroitly by Hidalgo into his plate, because it happened to be the safest fare on the menu for his dentures. To Shigura, there was not much thrill in watching the old Spaniard dine. Too inhibited, too straitlaced. The kind of diner who *savored* but did not eat. Or that food snob who knew the various wines by their years and why one had to be iced and the other not. Astigmatism, not appetite. Nothing like Amoran for sheer spontaneity and wolfish relish. Number three, the sour pickles: encore for the boy. Being a relatively uncomplicated item, Amoran just tossed it in, cucumber and cauliflower, as if he were munching peanuts; the sauce he used as drinking water. Pickles unfortunately were anathema to Hidalgo's very choosy teeth; he abstained. The girl must have really looked ridiculous in front of her tablemates: she daintily secured a red pepper with a toothpick and gingerly sipped the sauce from a teaspoon! Further theatrics were averted when Amoran picked up the can, slurped down its liquid to the last dreg, and with a jerk of the head, just gobbled up every single pickle in sight. Earning him both a scolding and a slap—which only whetted his appetite as he put away number four, the bean sprouts, with a few obligatory asides to his right. Except for the girl, no one else had bothered to use a napkin. The table couldn't have been neater. Completely wiped out was Shigura's banquet, save for a pair of thigh bones, which, vowed Amoran, would later go into the pot for broth: "Calcium there, you know." "What about the can?" jeered the old Spaniard. Amoran cackled but seemed to have hesitated long enough to consider *that* possibility.

"Wala bang pangmatamis?" he inquired, working his tongue diagonally to get at a sliver of meat stuck in a cavity.

Shigura's Tagalog was just better than nothing, and it had reached that point now: "Pardon?"

Hidalgo was dying of shame. "He wants to know if there's any dessert."

"So sorry!"

"You didn't have anything, Major," said the girl, darting several reprimands to the boy.

"*Hindi bala, tama na,* is all right."

For he had supped well, too. Just by witnessing them. Another refinement to torture was in not seeing prisoners starve but in watching them eat for the first time after a famine. Saints and heroes were the vainest of mortals; they craved for adversity in its cruelest, most demeaning forms. You starved a priest into sainthood and stomped a soldier to heroism. As exercised daily by the Major's junior officers, these methods elicited their desired results: information, confession. Which fell short of the Major's tenets in torture. Better to break a man with bread than to bless him with a beating.

After their digestive tracts had melted down these calories and carbohydrates, Shigura hustled them outdoors to look at a fat moon. In passing he mentioned that early that morning he had been reading about warlocks in a German translation.

"What is it, Shigura?" the old man retorted. "Is it chess, you want to beat me, is that it?"

(. . . pawn to Pearl Harbor four, rook to Rape three, Moon-goddess to Manila zero: checkmate, King of Castile. . . .)

"Is it culture? Art? Poetry? A test of horses? Whatever it is, you've won. I surrender unconditionally."

Grumbled Shigura: "No. I have lost. I ride the white horse that I may be thrown. I read volumes till darkness to go blind; I scout with spyglasses to be spotted and shot by the underground. All to no avail."

"Stay in the moonlight," counseled Hidalgo. "Maybe the moon will turn you into stone."

Amoran chuckled as he wiggled himself between *kulahan* and *kariton;* he doodled on his guitar, winked at the girl, who seemed to be infatuated with their guest.

"I know a train that passes Rosario," crooned the boy.

Major Shigura liked the woods and two days a week found means to play truant from the Fort and the war. On the white horse, he trotted and pranced around *talahib* ground until his loins were sore and the beast was panting. He then dismounted and took out a notebook of rapacious *haikus* that one of his men had authored and read compulsively with the waning of the light; after that, he remembered the pair of binoculars necklaced with worn leather straps dangling on his chest, and with a woeful sigh, trained them hopefully on the moonrise. Long ago, Buson, a Kyoto painter, had burnt a hole in his roof that he may catch a moonlight shaft for his canvas. Mesmerized by his captive, Buson had not anticipated that in his discourse with the muse he would actually burn a quarter of the city. Shigura tittered, and scanned his surroundings. Surely, he thought, such a generous exposure of one Japanese body would invite reciprocal murder? But the Filipino underground, wherever it was, witnessed this weekly romp (fluctuating between sunbathing and moon baiting), and had long decided that the target presented negligible military value. Since Shigura's Fort Santiago indulgences were known only to him (and why had not Vanoye given him away?) he was not considered prime quarry; in fact—and this was the unkindest cut of all—he was not even considered Japanese. His image was too benign for that. Oftentimes he was spared a hothead's bullet because of the mystique that had grown around him. Killing the Major, arbitrated underground leaders, would not cut the head off the snake, for if this surgery were done, the body would only supersede its dimensions and grow heads too contemptible to imagine. Thus it was decided and therefore decreed: allow him this mythical sanctuary; we shall not sanctify him. Let the Major go, they said. Leave the clown alone. . . . Consequently, Shigura exposed himself to the pranks rather than the pillory of a people. This annoyed him considerably, for he was longing to be murdered.

Amoran trailed him to his haunts one afternoon. There, with his usual accouterments, the Japanese lolled in anticipation of some genial killer. His unhooked sword was at his side; his pistol (whenever he bothered to bring it at all) lay at a distance where he could not reach it, should the occasion and his profession require its use. Yet he remained intact—and insulted once more—throughout the evening, and he rode the white horse home, to plan still another dusk of his own murder.

After his abortive sacrifice in the woods, Major Shigura always returned to Hidalgo and the girl. Again he would preempt the rattan chair and together with the old man went from panegyrics to malapropisms. Sometimes he showed up in a tunic and then began to maunder.

"You have not seen Manchuria. You have not seen China—the butchery, the beheadings. Our war goes on like the growing of rice. Rice is at the bottom of everything, from the day we exhale to the night we fail. Already we are losing the borderline, and we came here for bed space. I lived in Kyoto with my father. In a house he built by a pond, Father reads about *ronins* and honor. There he sits in ceremonial plenty, sipping tea from talismanic pewters, talking about the great *samurai* to a roomful of echoes. If for one tiny, inconsequential moment I should lose face in this army, my father will hear of it from his retreat by the pond; and for him it will be quite impossible to look his clan-clenched neighbors in the eye; must therewith censure and confine himself, and in his finest remaining Java silks, laboriously, repentantly write the proper letter to his betters, cut a lock of his hair, and before I can even conceive that salutary act of heroism to wash the honor I have stained, he will do away with himself as quickly, as quietly as tradition can be done. Perhaps they will send me the lock of hair. And it will serve as a chain around my heart.

"Once, in our fetishistic heyday, a student of Buddha burned down one of Gautama's temples. I think it was a deliberate act of absolution through violence. But such an extroverted truth can only be called madness. Yet that curtailer of a cult spoke for us all. Part of every soldier is assassin. Let me remind you that the world has been apportioned into lucres of venalities, that assassins may skulk around like colossi with arms of purification. I, too, am an assassin, *ne?* I would like to purge the army. If only there were a million like myself who could disband that collective strength by sheer ineptness, by absolute abandonment, perhaps the contumely of scapegoats in uniform will lose the war and win a dignity. If some vast protest existed in the navy, in the air force, and in the secret police, perhaps Japan will revivify—glory? But these infiltrations are hornets without sting and the army will never realize until very late that I was its greatest enemy. I, and this monumental disenchantment with what we are fighting for. Therefore it remains your task, you out there in the honeycombed bunkers: to muffle the artillery, outflank the infantry, sink the battleships, shoot down the bombers. I wish all the armies of the world would collide for the last time and quash the dogs of war. After such a tournament, it may be that the citizen long hobbling on the front (and what is this front but only the backdoor of man's intentions?) may come back to a society without government, to a state without statesmen, to a republic without democracy, to a house without lords. Meanwhile, the stupidity goes on that we lovingly call free spirit. Ah, to be free of the human spirit!"

Without having imbibed, the man was unaccountably inebriated. Shigura was. Hands clasped prayerlike on his lap; the head dangling from an angle reminiscent of a Shinto figure in plaster. Cap askew. Eyes blotchy-red. Hemoglobin all scuttled. Tap-tap-tap, Hidalgo's cane on the floor. A royal signal for instantaneous eviction. But, but, blinked an embargo in the girl's wide eyes. Soundly reproved by Amoran. In a wink, they had removed the chair with its occupant—a Tibetan lama stilled by the night's fecundity—and deposited downstairs in the patio.

"The man is insane," Hidalgo flared, limping back into his room.

Hai, agreed the Major, now under sedation in the moonlight.

Haiku, haiku Ito. He'd read a batch of it somewhere—yes, where? Why should he know it, why should he care?

A restive Ito had gone to his mezzanine quarters—to finagle a leave?—had tiptoed behind the jequirity-beaded door, slipped into the inner sanctum where the Major was at the climax of interrogation. Another guerrilla emissary wouldn't talk: the Major hacked off its tongue with an heirloom dagger; wouldn't tremble: the Major skillfully amputated its fingers; wouldn't listen: the Major slashed off its ears. With what ease he executed all this while Corporal Ito gawked unseen. Kept gawking as his commandant whispered to a headless ear (for no one, not even in his beloved Kyoto, had ever truly listened to the young Shigura); kept caressing handless fingers (for nobody had ever touched the maturing Shigura). Ito had only seen that energy in the martial figures of the Keion Scrolls, or in the fabulous stone lions that agitated in the Temple of the T'ang Emperors. The Major's crouch was close to Niten's shrikes; his visage belonged to the Yamato race—all this in the angry reds and greens of the Kano paintings.

This then was what Corporal Ito witnessed: his commandant, whom he had always fancied too complaisant for his job, fondling five fingers, mouthing sweet nothings into an ear. Sergeant Yato's bestiality was, in retrospect, symptomatic of a soldier's creed. If the Sergeant killed, his victims—regardless of how strained and fallacious the Yato logic was—could still be classified as the opponent. Yato's violence was for the Enemy, whoever and wherever it was. From a military standpoint, this animality was as indissoluble as it was indispensable; it wasn't rootless as was the Major's depravity. With Islamic dedication, Sergeant Yato fought and slew to exterminate something; conversely, the Major, essentially a noncombatant, who even in its very commission actually obviated the act of murder, just sponged off the war psyche. Yet between the Sergeant and the Major sparked electrodes of convergence; and perhaps somewhere in that lunar cycle for pathological assassins, in areas unknowable and ungovernable, the two were almost interchangeable.

Corporal Ito did not understand any of it, as he stood there puzzling over his major's regimen of love; Ito even sat down. The metallic clunk of a chair finally detranced Major Shigura, who wheeled so abruptly around that the ear dropped, and the paw seemed to wag. Ito adored the Noh and in that August-Moon light Shigura loomed before him like a tasseled dragon on the backs of mimetic actors: lips pressed in secret whisper against headless ear; cashmere gloves in deadlock handshake with armless hand. For suddenly in a haze, it appeared that the ear had climbed from the boards to keep its ringmaster in lambent connivance. The Major himself didn't seem to recognize the interloper; even smiled. With not a word between them, Ito had upset his chair, bowed mechanically and trudged out of the room. He had brooded back to the barracks; glanced disinterestedly at an album of pornographia some enlisted men had thrust into his hand, nodded dumbly at Sergeant Yato. There was another air raid that night; the Major personally ordered the company to the shelter and had taken one lazy look at the Corporal, who still had the faded erotica in his hands. Next afternoon, Corporal Ito was assigned to night-shift duty at the Agricultural Reclamation Project.

What to make of this? pondered the poet, as he busied himself with a new *haiku* lethargically scribbled, summarily dismissed on another page of his notebook. Should he tell the others what he saw?

tell the Sergeant? Yato would probably be intrigued—this was his cup of *sake*. Hours went by and still no one came to relieve Ito from his post. A quarter-moon peeked out; the trees rustled; Manila was shuddery with portents: evil tidings of guerrilla bands and American bombers. Yet Corporal Ito dreaded none of these; he had learned from Yato the resignation to duty, the acclimatation to enemy. If one was a soldier, this was only right. One had to live with loss, even if that eventually included one's own life. What was more perturbing was that other thing: the glower of the Dark Ages. As long as Fort Santiago was just another torture chamber, there was, perversely or not, still some justification for it. Perhaps the Americans had a surrogate for that too. As the English had their Tower of London. To torture for information was certainly not the norm in war, and there was the Geneva Convention. Yet torture was an accepted fact, nourished by an expedient brutality. But the Shigura Syndrome? Where did it come from? Perhaps the beast harked back to the Six Canons of Hsieh Ho. . . .

It was a full golden moon as Ito the poet deliberated on this; and it was a full six hours without relief before Major Shigura showed up at the desolate grounds Corporal Ito was patrolling so loosely. As before, they did not speak. There was no need to. Ito saw his commandant's sword still sheathed, but he knew at once—as a deathrow convict could sometimes sense that there wasn't going to be another stay of execution—why the man was there, what was supposed to happen next. With rasping grunts, with a few well-chosen gestures, the Fort commandant made it known that this was going to be a duel. Corporal Ito let both hands fall on the ivory handle of his *katana,* loped two steps forward and, holding his breath, marked the distance necessary to negotiate between his hip and the Major's heart.

Feet planted wide apart for better mobility, the Major, like a fugitive fang from Goya's *Tauromachia,* faced the poet.

Tales of the *shogun* raced in Ito's mind. The *kuge* danced attention upon him; a *samisen* tingled his blood. Easterly winds pranced among the ramparts of feudal Nippon, lotus blossoms spun the parasols of *geishas;* the countryside was mantled in mist as accolade upon accolade the *shi, no, ho, sho* came in worshipful attendance. Yedo artisans and the *hatamoto* arrived with banners and would stay there forever . . . *ich, ni, san, si*. How many *ronins* did posterity demand?

How many beheaded barons and burnt villages would appease their ancestors? If archaeologists were to turn the world over, if aeons of ashes were excavated, what final physiognomy would be unearthed? For was not the deliberate rapine of centuries motivated by the greed of order? Conquest had no conscience, pillage had no passion, genocide had no genes—yet it all sifted back to a kind of regeneration. Killing was mindless, just as compassion was not constructive: life just was, would always be. Vanity only embroidered, imposed an esthetic on it.

Ito's sweat made his hands slip from the sword's ivory; the Major's eyes never blinked.

Why did man have to sublimate it? write poems about it? bury it with flowers? When it left, there was nothing. No chronicle for the dead who would not remember their medals and citations. History was for the living.

And now Ito knew what his fatal error was. Even if he were faster than the Major—and he felt he had always been—there was something else that did not quite jell here. As adept as he was, Ito would never cease to be the man behind the sword; the Major (now) was just his sword: the Sword.

Csssssh!

It was a reverse *jigai,* piercing the throat to sever the arteries, not with a dagger but with a *katana.* From *csssssh!* here to *csssssh!* there—Ito's neck went like a chicken's. The Major required no follow-through; the Corporal fell forward in horse manure. So quick had the stroke been there was hardly any blood on Shigura's sword. He sheathed it and kicked away the fallen notebook. Actually, the duel had lasted only eight seconds but Major Shigura had waited an extra five seconds for the Corporal to disabuse his mind of cause-and-effect deliberations, and had finally decided that the poet (who was nothing more than the flowerlike emanation of a Kiyonaga brush) was the more dangerous because he still groped for a rationale in anything at all.

Social life at Fort Santiago was close to nil. At the beginning of the Occupation, there had been tragicomic efforts by management to fraternize with labor; principally in weekly teas between the Fort

Santiago administration and Filipino deputations on a mission of "peace and understanding." These had been droll, good evening–goodbye affairs wherein diluvial quantities of tea could not thaw out tongue-tied civilians. Via lottery and rotation, Major Shigura's subalterns had taken stabs at a position with the glorious misnomer of "social director." The very last one of this denomination had audaciously rescinded the weekly kettle for a monthly waltz—sort of a third cousin to a policeman's ball. Unfortunately, that too was a certified catastrophe. Guttural Bushido manners just did not translate into corporate cohesiveness; it would entail more than a hearty *banzai* to establish a body politic. The first waltz had a turnout of over a hundred males, an admixture of Filipino and Japanese misfits whose mutual interests were soon muzzled by short English and shorter hospitality; and languishing in the midst of abbreviated gaiety, two fortyish women both too hideous to offset the balance. More infamous was the second and last dance (predominantly a fox-trot), which attracted only twenty-two males, almost all of whom were blithering homosexuals. After this *faux pas,* the incumbent social programmer was relieved of his duties, and with at least two stinging rebuffs in the face, a permanent black mark on his hitherto unblemished record, was deracinated and shipped off to the Leyte front along with mice detergents. A direct offshoot of this was the Major's ban on all social functions. Henceforth, Fort Santiago lapsed back into its primordial gloom.

Recently, however, the citizenry was apprised of weird happenings at the old Spanish citadel—*extra muros.* Deranged prostitutes and escaped convicts regaled Manila with anecdotes of primogenial barbarity. Of these the chief bloodcurdler was something that was eventually dubbed *fandagong hilaw;* at Fort Santiago itself, it was more popularly known as the "Troop Ten Tango." According to a barracks legend, the dance had its informal origins in one Kenji Matomoto, a junior officer of the X-T Signal Corps. A Rudolph Valentino admirer, Matomoto sported the longest pair of sideburns in Hirohito's bald and crew-cut army. As motor-pool dullards liked to tell it, the story was: one sweltering noon, Kenji M. was tangoing with a sultry Filipino belle, when quite unexpectedly during a spectacularly prolonged dip (unexpected, because they had just copulated five minutes previous) the slant-eyed Valentino had experienced an orgasm. This had unduly nettled Kenji M. since he had not wanted it just then and was saving up for bed. Besides, he was a lover who dabbled in hygienic discipline; so, summoning all his military will and biological resources, he weaved through a complicated series of frontal and reverse dips, to prove that ejaculation in the true male could and should be voluntary. His woman was sore and was not functional again for another week after that, but the experiment was a qualified success: Kenji M. had proven without a drop of doubt that he was master of his fluids. Now such a knowledge as that was insignificant if it could not be exhibited freely among other fluid masters. Kenji M. decided to convert his seminal savings into yen. He returned posthaste to HQ, and in one of those lingering leisurely dusks when his co-officers had nothing better to do than mope around or swap dirty stories, Kenji M. organized a parlor game with the aid of some late-blooming *babae* from Harrison's fleshpots. Participants were sworn to secrecy; an arena was set up for a home-made orgy. The Game: two rows of dancers faced each other. Seven males, seven females, all nude, were to tango to the strains of "La Cumparsita." There was no exact specification as to how many could participate, for the space dictated the number; although admittedly the more there were the merrier—and there was the question of the pot into which every officer dropped an ante, the amount to be determined by individual rank and solvency prior to the dance. Object: to harness orgasm. The male capable of outlasting the draggle of Valentino dips without ejaculation automatically won the pot. As safeguards (and added incentive), the enterprising Maestro M. also initiated virility tests in the hands of his taxi dancers, whose manipulations, commented an oft-eliminated tangoer, "could squeeze citrus out of a crowbar." Everywhere he toured with his hastily assembled troupe, the side-burned signal corpsman fleeced competitors with his masterful emission-proof erection. Pot after pot he collected. The "Troop Ten Tango" dipped on and on around campsites draining the tightest of pipelines. When it hit Fort Santiago, Kenji M. proceeded to wipe out every back pay within tango range. Seven up, seven around, and seven down, they went. Ace, frogman, provost marshal, legal counselor—Kenji M. beat them all with simulated aridity. Naked and jumpy, fourteen paired-off apaches bowed politely on the chalklines; retreated in quarter time, advanced on a Latin beat, circled each other like *topada* bantams, preened and puckered for contact, snuggled and swiveled, dipped and punctured, parted, paced back, then collided again. Being staples of the gym drill, the fellows eked out some precision unimpeded by grace; on the distaff side, there was even less art, considering that the burden of proof lay heavily between their thighs. They were merely spastic or spasmodic—neither of which was particularly appealing to the eye. Only Kenji M. appreciated and extolled both tempo and tradition of the Valentino tango, with his *torero* hips, tapering build and flashing gaucho eyes. Like a munificent butler leading a bedazzled guest through the interiors of a feudal manor, he steered his *chinita* from the long-bow span of his arms due northeast, then southwest by the subtlest crook of an elbow, braking dramatically in midpivot with upraised left foot scant millimeters off the floor for the duration of a sigh, before letting her (inflamed and importuning) slide down on his calves like an untouchable groveling for her caste. Wardens in G-strings officiated from the sidelines with field glasses: a white neckerchief signified a checkup; a red one was a disqualification. No timeouts were allowed. Because the house desideratum enforced a minimum of four male coital insertions into the female, some terpsichoreans stepped out of competition and forfeited their capital in place of actual fornication. One, two, three, four, five, six dribbled down the way of Niagara Falls: a shower of sperm all over the sawdust, with Kenji M. left alone with his *chinita* to consummate his yen. Of course, immediately after his triumph, the hardy signal corpsman would collar the prettiest of the spoils and, adding insult to injury, would demonstrate to his outclassed colleagues that he had a Yangzte River dammed up in his groin. How Valentino roared!

Ha-ha, but that was not the end of it. With maddening condescension, Kenji M. permitted himself to be wagered into another bout, two evenings later. And that match too, from its initial whistle, seemed headed the route of all his "Troop Ten Tangos." Three, four, five, the Fort Santiago cupids had spurted a mess: down on their shanks, into their women's hairy patches. Sideburns was completing his sixth dry run when he noticed the sixth challenger, a flabby, baldish squirt who had the makings of a first-dip washout. Who was this pathetic chimp? Kenji M. had asked pacifically. Major Shigura, he was told. Ten, eleven, twelve, thirteen. . . . The chimp, when examined by the magistrates, was as sapless as the sideburns. Fourteen, fifteen, sixteen—*kura!* A leak on the boards; then, another! Dip here, dip there; "La Cumparsita" was rewound, played out, rewound again . . . third big blob. Everybody had assumed that the chimp had sprung it, but wait, interceded an umpire. It wasn't the Major's spout, it was—! Good gracious, it was Valentino's! Sideburns had demanded a rewash, squawking that he was drip-dry. But then his own siren, who was indeed split in a million microscopic aches from the waist down, started to giggle as she forefingered her knees: it was Kenji M.'s signature! The game referees swooped upon the signal corpsman and confirmed the findings. It was official; the chimp was champ! Kenji M. couldn't admit this dismal fact and challenged the chimp. A rematch! The chimp consented and laid down his own condition: Kenji M. was to stake all his camp winnings against a Shigura windfall in one big yen pot. *Banzai!* Third night, it was on: just the two of them. Chimp *vs.* Sideburns. Rubber match. Each was provided, *in puris naturalibus,* with the most seductive harlot that could be hired from Harrison's bordellos. "La Cumparsita" scored them anew. Kenji M. was dapper; the Major was distraught. They did ten dpms, the signal corpsman cutting a very stylish figure in the early minutes. At first, the Major seemed clumsy and couldn't locate his coordinates; was even stepping on his partner's toes. But he slowly warmed up to the sinuous turns of the tango and even improvised several suspended spins that took the spectators' breath away. Dip, dip, dip, dip . . . the floor was spotless, the air was humid and droughty, the single bulb in the ceiling hung like a moth. Then on the second hour, after the one hundred sixty-ninth dip, it happened: a trickle issued from somebody's loins: Kenji M.'s. Sideburns glared down in disbelief. A red neckerchief wafted in; landed on his sticky genitals and was stuck there like a fig leaf. Wardens lurched in and hoisted Shigura's hand: the squirt had busted Valentino's balls. . . .

[33]

ON THE LAST NIGHT OF THE BOMBERS, Manilans saw the sky glitter with metal. Every cloud seemed to contain some secret silver, a steel horde that had an unholy hum. Munching fried cassava flakes, Amoran and the girl climbed the attic to watch the silver battle. They saw the horizon blister with attack; a vision of V-shaped kites flew above another group; those in the altitude behaved like shimmery ideas while the ones in the second level below (always the daredevil rung) purported to be the intermediaries between higher and lower destruction. Whenever a machine in the second phalanx was caught in the central arc—a searchlight as blinding as a carnival blaze—there was a wispy explosion, a brittle purr, and someone was hurtling down into the small fire of machine guns. The first-level, four-engined B-17's and B-24's kept their distance, kept laying larvae all over Manila, knowing neither bravado nor Bushido could reach them. Berserk, burned more by Buddha than by unholy oil, the *kamikaze* streaked up to chalk some glory and was, a-tat-tat-ra-tat-tat, going down again. Eee-ha! Eeee-haaaa! cried the roundup ace—for there was a stampede up there, stallions and stallions of it, mustangs, yes siree, them P-51's! Meanwhile, back on the ranch cloud, the cattle barons, them lordly bombers, just readied the branding irons—the Circle S. P-38's rode shotgun, ta-tat, ta-tat . . . *bandidos* at six o'clock vamoosed, went *s-s-splash!* into Manila Bay. In the houses below, glass shattered; roofs tintinnabulated under a firecrackery sky, and dwellers cheered the American Genesis. Once, for a brief while, a cattle baron strayed from its upper circle and made a descent almost parallel to the first wave; and a beacon wooed it into its sphere. There, like a moth, the bomber was held briefly, coaxed and coddled, before a chinchilla puff from the ground came to claim its booty. Heh hey, laughed the bomber, and hopped nimbly back to Mama. A close call, Junior, too close for comfort, scolded the squadron den brother. "Ah, the prima ballerina," moaned Hidalgo downstairs. And the quadrille snapped back into close-order drill. Never again would the tight ensemble play hopscotch within poom-poom range. Thus remaining indivisible and indestructible—beyond bravura and ballistics. Something new had been added too: the Boeing B-29 "Flying Fortress," the Liberator B-24. And on the ground, Hidalgo smiled ruefully. "*Sin vergüenza,*" he said. "They cannot even kill each other."

After the aerial circus Ojos Verdesians scrambled down from their portholes, garrets and rooftops with vivid reconstructions, breathless exaggerations. Very soon the block was astir with the residue of a semi-invasion. To every customer, the man from Obando gave a free commentary, complete with acoustics, gesticulations. Even those that had quaked in their shelters, many of those that had prayed themselves witless inside churches reemerged with a vengeance, speaking of apocalyptic bombs they had only heard or heard about; describing spectacular dogfights they had not seen. But such was the galloping exhilaration, the high morbidity of expectancy that even cowardice—as long as it did not consort with the enemy—was forgivable. After all, there was time for tolerance, there was cause for *caritas* now that the Liberation was in bloom. *Anak ng kuwago,* the Americans were coming. . . .

With the last of the air raids came Deogracias. Amoran took him to the boardinghouse one night and introduced him to the girl. Deogracias claimed he was a distant relative of Mrs. Colombo, but more properly—and in a stage whisper—he said that he was from *up there,* the mountains, come down to solicit funds for the Revolution. He also mentioned keeping a bicycle in the Colombo basement—in case of emergency. Could he stay, hours at a time? Indefinitely? He was organizing.

"What are you organizing?" boarders asked him.

"The Mountains," he dropped casually.

They told him the soldiers in Manila were hardly soldiers any more. Only caricatures, visions, ghosts.

"What these caricatures, visions and ghosts are doing to our patriots at the Fort is real enough," he snapped.

Now a raffish, bearded organizer with lottery numbers in his pockets, Lieutenant Deogracias was the rebel leader subscribing a massive assault from the hills. He had led (he said) a band of cutthroats in Batangas once, which had further depleted an already diminishing Imperial Japanese Army. The time is ripe, he said: "*Horas na natin!*" Stymied, tenants consulted wristwatches, checked the Colombo clock, and looked at each other blankly.

The man would visit the boardinghouse at all hours of the day, to creep between chairs and sit on the floor in Hidalgo's room, there to read the primer of his January Juggernaut. Consequently, the Colombo house had been enlisted and sworn in. Deogracias recruited them all into the movement whose main axis, said he, was retrenching in Baguio. Brochures were produced, messages decoded to vouch for the Deograciasian Articles of War. He showed draftees typewritten, even printed instructions from *them* that he would have, he groaned, to carry under pain of death, if discovered or betrayed. He always carried a German Luger under his jacket. Old men clapped him on the back; old women gave him crucifixes. To converts and contributors, he promised individual dates of liberation. He disported an official map bearing a deceased senator's imprimatur; and when inspired he would encircle a number with red crayon to indicate the payee's own delivery. He always reminded his clients that the movement was still in its infancy, was still shopping for momentum. Besides, not every man in the organization received three hundred grams of rice per day as the ordinary citizen did in the big city. But given enough time . . .

"Remember, thirty thousand of us died in Bataan and Corregidor," he added, waiting for someone to light his cigar.

Soon, many men came to see him. Placido Rey took his cap and passed it around to *paroquianos* who filled it with anything the moment could afford: cash, suggestions, a written dedication, information, names. Deogracias thanked them all. He said Uncle Sam, Mountain and Country were indebted. They did enormous tasks for him. Neighbors cooked and sang; cooing mothers, perhaps indiscreetly, even led their daughters to him on the Hidalgo porch. They paid for their revolution. Doughty women scrubbed military floors in Manila, sold *damo* in the market and stole unpapered tobacco to nourish his steam. In exchange, the man would disappear at the end of the week; and it was taken for granted by the cognoscenti he had driven back to the mountains for fortification.

He returned at midnight, usually on a Monday. Distracted, chewing an unlit cigar, he straddled on Hidalgo's floor, stroking his beard.

"They are flying dangerous cargo a month from tonight," he started, savoring their attention. "I'm setting up flares and petroleum cans for the landing."

"The mountain?" he was asked.

A gentle tapping on the door.

"No, actually it's a hill by the ocean. . . ."

Sheepishly, Placido Rey entered, and headed immediately for the girl.

". . . But it's ours, too. I am very dry from the trip. Give me water, someone."

They made him a cold drink; the girl (who seemed somewhat piqued by Placido Rey's fatherly attentions) rushed to him with a fan. Contemptuously the Spaniard tossed him some paper money he had picked up from the boards of the last theatre.

"Why don't you shave?" he asked the sullen young man.

Deogracias laughed, putting an arm on the girl's shoulder. "How's Aling Victoria?" he flung at Placido Rey, who, barely a minute in the room, could manage nothing more than a pout.

The old man scowled at the boy, who was sitting on the windowsill. "Why do you bring home everything you find in the garbage cans?"

Amoran looked innocently from Deogracias to Hidalgo.

"At least do us the service of hiding your uniform," snarled the Spaniard. "We would all be shot for your translucent khaki."

"Then let us all get shot," the man snorted.

Hidalgo was not intimidated.

"Not only do we have to pay the rent, but for a mountain as well. Sometimes I only pray this hard for the Americans to come, if only to be liberated from your revolution."

"That's treason!" the Lieutenant screeched, pushing the girl away.

"It may well be, Señor Buonaparte."

"For a handful of Mickey Mouse money you squirm and show your natural colors while I give you—Americans!"

"I want to see Americans, yes, but not invaders."

Deogracias threw up his hands in exasperation.

"Ah, he's crazy!"

As the months and the contributions went by, the Colombo boardinghouse found their organizer to be an egoistic, impulsive disparager living on euphoria. He hated desks and sleep, and in his headquarters, as told, all his revolutionaries sat around him in a quadrangle, leaning on submachine guns. Ranting for hours on any subject, he alluded to himself as "tomorrow's Richelieu," and to his *bundok* as the last recourse. Wall Street would finance him all the way, he bragged—give or take a few dividends. Otherwise, the U.S.A. was merely a necessary fulcrum that would be dislodged when neo-nationalism had attained some kind of stability.

The Deogracias career had of course peaked with the Captain Johnny chapter. Now there was an operation guaranteed to make even MacArthur green with envy. The characters, the climate, the circumstances had just been perfect. Out of a lanky *americano* (plus a few tricks) Deogracias had wheedled a Lazarus—and the Manilans had come to life. Too bad he had to lose his grubstake eventually. Somewhere in the Pacific aquarium, a submarine commander had issued a directive ("From upstairs, boy"), reading back to him by transmitter, the official thanks (". . . for a job well done!"). Before sign-off, it was agreed that the commander's sub, *Pickup Charlie*, would fetch Captain Jonas Winters in two weeks' time. Just like that. With no regard for the Deogracias rank and brilliance. Without reference to the labor of love poured into the making of Captain Johnny. As a consolation, Deogracias ("What's the name again, bub?") was to stand by with his group—"for further instructions and developments." And to keep them going, *Pickup Charlie* would try sneaking into Filipino waters and Japanese mines, a cache of small arms, several boxes of Sanka coffee—and ("Get this!") to boost up the morale of the freedom fighters, a pinup magazine.

The message had been cheered by his men and celebrated that night with an old-fashioned *cañao*. But the whole thing was a fluke. Demoted by a twangy transmitter, sidelined to what was equivalent to a janitorial capacity, Deogracias had sulked all the way to the showers. He knew he had lost Captain Johnny, his very own creation. All that trek and ceremony derailed by static. Showered but still sulking, he had walked stiffly to Captain Johnny's litter with a bowl of rice wine and good news. However, the American seemed to be having a relapse. Drooling on his pillow, the flier was muttering nonsensically and would do so for the next three hectic days. He was given a sedative and put on a liquid diet (not rice wine) by the camp medic. The profuse perspiration, the sporadic muttering had not flagged. As far as Deogracias could make out, the soliloquy was about: *Her* (when it was not *She*), Dark Eyes, Long Hair; on the third day (the liquid diet having been augmented with some meat; two slices of mangosteen), it was: the Kiss. At the time, Deogracias and his most trusted staff could not solve the riddle. Only now in the Colombo house did he piece up the puzzle. Yes, *tama*—the Girl, right here (this very moment fanning him) by his side. Vaguely, Deogracias recollected that there was indeed a girl in one of Captain Johnny's premier performances.

"Do you remember Capitán Johnny?"

The fan halted in midair. Dark eyes, long hair. . . .

"Do you?"

Yes, she did. It was in that look.

"You kissed him."

Amoran shushed her.

"Well, he's going. . . ."

Again she raised the fan.

"Gone. . . ."

Or he could still be up there—drooling, muttering, driving the medic crazy and the KP out of business.

If in Ojos Verdes the war was a monopoly, so was this incubus named Deogracias who mimed his Revolution by day, snored it at night. He loved knives, guns, explosives—the overt display of their power. He had killed dispassionately and artfully, he said, but did not believe this to be his true vocation. An inimitable raconteur of the assassinations in history, he would ramble in a farrago of insurrection, redemption; then a dissertation on Havana cigars. Later on, they discovered he had a weakness for narcotics. Sleep he did not seem to have any use for; he held a religious vigil over his one picayune superstition—strangers: he never collected from widows. Also, he brayed, he brought news from the shortwave transmitted to him personally from Guam, or thereabouts.

"Who is winning?" Hidalgo would inquire impishly.

"We destroyed two tanks today," bit Deogracias. "An armored truck, too; and terrorized half a division."

"Even the boy can raise as much in Tondo," taunted the old man.

One evening, the Spaniard pulled the Lieutenant to the porch, where Major Shigura, bald and bemused, was waiting for the moon: "There is the enemy. Why do you not kill him?"

"A visionary," scoffed Deogracias. "That is the least of my worries."

"What can you do then? The boardinghouse is waiting, the whole block is waiting."

Deogracias broke wind. Squatting on the floor just outside the porch, he began to stroke his beard thoughtfully. Major Shigura appeared to be waiting for him too, as well as for the moon.

"Speak up, mountain," chided Hidalgo, standing between the pensive soldier and the grinning guerrilla. The girl was making the bed, listening to them both.

"With one word I can lead the countryside in one day of reverberative revolution," Deogracias hissed.

"Why do you hesitate then?" rebutted Hidalgo, shaping his fingers into a V; shooing the girl back into her blanket. "Is it caution? Is there more contraband coming? Or are you synchronized with the American invasion?"

"I need a light," Deogracias said; and from the porch, the Japanese took out a lighter. But the Lieutenant turned to the Spaniard for a match.

"It is for me to do that for you—someday," the guerrilla flung airily to the officer, who meekly withdrew to the porch and his moon.

"What is your cause doing in the mountains when you are down here, eating peanuts?" inquired Hidalgo.

"I am here for evaluation. The Revolution takes care of itself."

"Every centavo we earn each day goes to the Revolution, and not a shot has been fired. Well, we cannot eat promissory notes."

"Can you storm a citadel?"

"Every man's hunger is a citadel!"

Deogracias ground his cigar under a heel. "You must wait."

"For the mountain to come down to Mohammed? Man, we are all sinking fast and the only thing that has laid the garrisons low for the last two months is chicken pox!"

"Wait," hummed the organizer, staring after that Japanese officer as he cantered away on a white horse, bearing the moon away.

Amoran guitared on his knee, grinning moronically, crooning to the girl, who was stringing up beads.

[34]

PERHAPS IN A HUNDRED SEPARATE PLACES, as in the township of Rosario, revolution—or at the very least, a collective rage—was the only answer. A detachment of General Yamashita's Korean *pistoleros* had hit town at dawn in half a dozen convoy trucks. While a touring vaudeville was pitching its tents near the *aplaya,* the Japanese *zona* of Garrison 133 swooped down on the entertainers, herded all its female performers up against the battered Spanish walls of the *convento* and interrogated them about the Resistance in the hills. No one had talked, naturally, and foot soldiers were called in. Some of them still stank of the Chinese front and had not seen women in over a year. Toward nightfall, the vaudeville heard the screams of its queens and princesses. Spear boys of the *comedia* wanted to scale the garrison walls with kitchen knives to kill, kill, kill, but were restrained by village elders. Around nine o'clock, *barrio bravos* linked arms and marched down as a body; with clenched fists, they wailed and wailed. From undergrowth and by breakwater they came, susurrous or subverbal: to condemn, to calumniate. An asthenic quantum wielded sticks to punctuate their misericords; foursomes threw dust in the air while bolder ones picked up stones and pelted, at first, banana trees, santol trees, mango trees, and then, the gates of the garrison itself. Amoran, who had been conscripted as third guitar in the vaudeville, now espied the town mayor, a portly man with stringy gray hair who looked like a doctor because of a medical bag he carried everywhere. The official seemed to be on the throes of a remonstration as bystanders who had joined the troupe on the grass informed him that Rosario's responsible citizens were all there, presenting a petition.

"What is it? What is it?" prodded the assistant director of the vaudeville.

Numerous young men came with books; were waving them like bolos. The garrison colonel finally stomped out of his billet, just halfway through his supper, hand on sword.

The demonstrators pressed closer, perhaps to verify the authenticity of his uniform. Amoran guessed that most of them were high-school students; the older ones were probably teachers.

"Mga tarantado," a disgruntled member of the vaudeville remarked.

"They are young people," an old man proudly announced. And they stood there, now chanting in the moonlight, their faces effulgent and joyful as though the garrison searchlight and glinting sabers demanded their passion.

His tin plate was on the doormat again. Again with a brown semiglob in its center. They must think I am a chihuahua! fumed Hidalgo, as he glared at his breakfast, torn between hunger and pride. And who was it this time—the boy? the girl? Amoran certainly would; it was his character—and pleasure. But her, his *infanta!* Yet she had changed radically of late. Since that blasphemy with the *inglés*. Always combing her hair now; staring into that mirror until she was cross-eyed. If she could swing her hips that way, if she could make gaga eyes at their resident *bandido* (and even that Placido Rey!), she could certainly put his breakfast on the doormat.

With a moan, and with all his anguish jumping on his back, Hidalgo stooped to . . .

Pick up anyone in Rosario and he'll tell you that Juan Ferrer is the town *enfant terrible.*

Nothing exceptional about Juan, except for the story that once he had dared woo the mayor's daughter, Lucrezia, and been rejected. His father was a blacksmith who could neither read nor write, but from him the son inherited a kind of lunatic strength. Ferrer Junior, gimlet-eyed and gangling, was as voracious a reader as he was an industrious worker (in his father's lean-to) and was usually found, during noon breaks, curled over a borrowed book under a shade tree. This untypical familial trait had led Ferrer Senior to bemoan the fact that he was shoeing a horse with book covers. Aside from Juan's almost merciless self-study (he had read an estimated three hundred fifty-four of the town library's hardcovers), he had no formal education. At sixteen he had joined a rebellious group of vernacular poets and gallivanted with them everywhere. All of them were secretly writing the Great Filipino Epic Poem. Young Ferrer was nearly finished with his, having written in his spare time seventeen scatological stanzas, including an introduction which every reputable mind in Rosario adjudged brutal but brilliant. The garrison's adjunct of the Makapili goose-stepped the plaza at regular intervals, between breakfast and supper—approximately at the time when the vernacular poets, marshaled by Ferrer, were spoiling for a showdown. There had been minor clashes: the poets' heated words; the Makapili's reprimands. Ostensibly, the chief complaint of the radicals was that countless young men from Santa Isabel, the next town, were disappearing one by one, supposedly trucked off for questioning and inevitable torture at Fort Santiago. In what had commenced as a peaceful confrontation, Ferrer, along with his cohorts, discussed the matter over black coffee with some of the more responsible members of the Makapili. Ferrer was articulate, even eloquent, as he made proposals; defined, refined or amended his movement's more inflammatory views. Not a single Japanese representative was there; it was so convivial a meeting the Makapilinistas could not have possibly objected. All Filipinos, they were gathered to exhume a semblance of order, to expunge the threat of hostility. Repression, orated Ferrer—and the assembly sat enthralled by this reincarnated Demosthenes—could only excite the excitable; strictures were but toxic peppermint that would poison free spirit. Since adolescence, Hugo had been Ferrer's particular hero, and *Les Miserables* his adopted Bible. So did he allude to it again, quoting freely from the classic, burrowing into and restating its concept of justice, which, he now said, must be updated. Conviction from a child was astonishing enough, but this dialectical jurisprudence was almost heretical: they gave him a standing ovation. Both parties seemed well on their way to a rapprochement of sorts as they adjourned and moved out to the park, where a monument of Jose Rizal stood. Then suddenly, the news of a poet's disappearance and subsequent death was borne around the grounds like a dead body. The poets' reaction was instantaneous. Someone spat out a cigarette into a box of explosives just outside the garrison gates. The cigarette ignited a thin, running path to the hangar; and there, just as quickly, fizzled out. A sentry had fired above their heads; then, perhaps mistaking a mother's shriek of pain for a signal to battle, machine-gunned into bobbing bodies. More than ten were killed or wounded in the first wave. The garrison commander had loaded two pistols; had cabled Manila. Juan Ferrer climbed Rizal's lofty clay, waved down his poets into grudging silence, and recited Rizalisms while he clung precariously to the monument's arrested arms. Once more the Ferrer voice, the Ferrer anguish unified them. Vernacular poets and random radicals clustered around the shaking statue. "Down with the rising sun!" they rumbled in unison. Incensed by oratory, a splinter group coasted along, absorbed stray dissenters, then with a rallying yell, crossed over to the field and was heading for the stockades.

An old crone had sprung up without warning, and with a snakelike thrust, had leaped up to the miniature flagpole on the front gate and with a knife that glinted in her hatred, slashed the red sun out of the white cloth. Such a scene demanded a high priestess to elevate the masses to the solemnization of revenge; and such a one was this keening, raging apparition and now cheering poets surged forward and hoisted her up on shoulders that had longed for a deliverer—their marauding Madonna.

"They took out the eyes of my only son!"

Vaudeville females fainted.

"Gouge Tokyo out of the map! Gouge Tokyo out of the map! Gouge Tokyo out of the map!" chanted a hundred poets.

And where was their mediator, the Makapili?

"Eisenhower has taken Europe; MacArthur is coming!"

"Co-ming! Co-ming! Co-minnnngggg!"

Juan Ferrer, trim and intrepid by torchlight, hair wafted like weeds, raced through the riot, still working for an armistice. That mother who had cried, pumped her arms up and down, demanding her son's release. Another sentry aimed from a chicken coop. When Juan heard her scream, saw her stagger, felt her fall, he charged through the crowd that immediately broke ranks to give him way. He had grabbed a bolo somebody was holding and was shouting at the top of his lungs when they winged him. As he fell partly inside the gates, he dragged his feet in with him: and they finished him off with a hail of bullets.

Falling, falling, falling. . . .

Pickup Charlie was late, damn it!

Captain Jonas Winters shivered in his tarpaulin. Where the hell was this fucking island anyway? And where the hell was that fucking sub? Was this the China Sea or what? Never should have trusted that Dark Glasses. Him and his fucking peons. He trotted around the beach, counting seconds. If they caught him now after all that, Christ, it would really be beautiful.

So where was Charlie?

. . . surface again, with breakfast.

Hidalgo eyed the chocolate piece with shuddery contempt. Wherever he was, raged the old man quietly, that *inglés* could go jump in the lake; he would not have anything to do with Air Force droppings. Smirking, Hidalgo put the plate down once more.

Picking up victims the Makapili ran interference for the poets and the soldiers. Which was ridiculous, since the radicals were not talking any more and the Japanese were in no mood to listen. Still, the Makapili bullhorned that everything would be explained. Even murder. But the rabble, quadrupled now with strangers from the hills and provoked by Japanese reinforcements, refused to be coddled. They shook in the rain, smoldered in the mud. Inside the barracks the Colonel lectured earnestly to his men with a manual in his hand. Raucous poets, panicky vaudeville troupers and shaken *barrio* elders pressed nearer, passinge corpses over their heads. "*Saklolo! Sak-lo-lo! Sak-lo-loooo!*"

Israel Trinidad was one of the mavericks from the hills. Occupation: photographer. When first he heard the commotion, he had bolted for his rooming house to get his paraphernalia; and scurried back to the plaza in time to see the fourth unit of the garrison infantry disperse the demonstrators with machine-gun bursts. Israel climbed a *capilla* awning; a sentry shot at him and gashed his right cheek. Palpitant and bloodied, Israel snapped pictures everywhere in the poor light without flashbulbs. He did not know if such a distortion of subjects would ever come out of a darkroom, but he clicked away at random objects and fleeting movements, and when in danger, dove instinctively to the ground or ran for cover. People understood at once what he was trying to do and shielded him. One soldier, surmising belatedly that the unarmed Israel was as dangerous as the armed rebels, chased him around alleys and streets; but shuffling figures clawed at the Japanese and Israel had reason to believe they tore him apart with their bare hands. A Hapon in swimming trunks crouched behind a sand barrel in front of the stockade tossed two German grenades on the street. As if struck, Israel stood there, doubled over his camera, his whole body refusing to function. At this very moment, a barefoot boy—he could not have been more than thirteen—stepped out of the bushes, picked up both grenades and pitched them back to the soldier. A severed head landed near the boy's feet; Israel watched him coolly kick it into a brook where another dead soldier was floating. As he shook himself in the smoke, Israel felt that barefoot boy pull him by the shirttails and lead him into a house. Inside, young men were bent low over rifles. The boy grabbed one and immediately started shooting through a rip in the cardboard wall. He seemed more adept, more accurate than the young men in the room and felled a sentry with his first shot. Israel took more pictures. He had lugged several reels of unexposed film with three rolls of Italian strips and he framed each shot according to action: an elder caught between barbed wire as a Japanese soldier, having no weapon, seemed locked in an endless rhythm of gouging out the man's eyes with his thumbs; the Colonel with perhaps twenty to thirty knife wounds through his face and neck, and both arms missing; the poets in one flowing upheaval in the plaza; the vaudevillians in various poses of confusion; and the barefoot boy, who was always present in these pictures, the one consistent image of destruction, shooting, running, screeching: killer too well too often. Perhaps his own mother lay dead somewhere out there in the street as he seesawed between cover and sneak shooting, with abbreviated heroic violence, till no one in the field could determine who was slowly disposing of the enemy, the wild, scattered strangers, the railing, disorganized poets, or that ill-concealed, half-walking, half-running but always killing, wind-blown barefoot boy. Later in the dark, with the remaining Japanese too frightened to turn on their searchlights, Israel discovered that all the snipers in the room were dead, except for the boy, who seemed immortal. Then he saw this barefoot thing crawl up to him on his belly with a bag of biscuits and four full magazines. In another half-hour, Israel had emptied the bag; the boy had used up all the bullets. Finally, out of ammunition, they escaped to the rooftops, where Japanese soldiers lobbed more grenades at them. Israel could not run and felt himself being dragged, dragged all the way. At one point, the boy tied two small cans of gasoline together, ripped his undershirt off and looped both ends to the cans; and scooting to a pistol lying in a ditch, fired and lit the wick, sprinted to the nearest pillbox, and threw. He blew up six pursuers who had stuck to them like leeches. They could not be sure they were soldiers. Israel, still lugging the camera which had been nicked by a splinter, sneaked back into Manila one night on the last train from Rosario with welts all over his body. He forced his way into a friend's house, refused to say anything, and slept for two days. He did not know what had happened to that ugly barefoot boy. Achoo! he had a cold.

Again Hidalgo stooped to pick up the tin plate; this time came up with it; this time did not bend down to put it back again; this time padded back to the bed; this time lifted the brown heart of its chocolate bar to his mouth and sank his teeth into it; and bang, and bang-bang-bang, Jonas Winters saw the red flashes in the dark on the beach as he splashed into the searchlight sea, into the searchlight moon-draped sea; splashing for that sub's rubber raft and the Nip shore patrol firing like crazy, bang, oh bang, Hidalgo bit again, *sí,* the sea was cold, his teeth were chattering, his molars crunched, his boots loamy, his slippers went down the Colombo floor, going down the China Sea was Johnny Winters, yahoo, *caramba,* blood on his gums, by gum, he was flying again, now he was lying down, the pain shooting up into his skull, now the ocean bed all lit, mines, he thought, what if the sub hit his mind full of chocolate bars, or what if there was a Jap destroyer of his teeth, red was his pillow, so was the beach, flaring, but they had him now on the rubber raft, hands pulled him up, he grinned and his molars came out all bloody from the chocolate, let's beat it, you guys, and he just rolled on that bed as the beach shook with shells he took out another tooth, wishing he'd get out of the drink again back into the air he could not breathe in the pillow, the guy oaring had a .45 on his lap, but he laughed even as blood oozed and still he bit into the ammunition, rat-tat-tat, rub-a-dub-dub, how many boobs on a sub, sobbing, sobbing, grinding solid Hershey to the last bitter end, and then he was inside, the coffee was black and bitter, rolling, rolling, more blood on the sheets, shit splashed all over him, the Japs were trying a last salvo, salved by utter pain, he wrapped the pillow round his head, crash-dive, he sank into a swoon, hoping they wouldn't hit the mines, but his mind was on fire now, the tin plate rolled on the floor, full speed ahead!

A head rolled down an esplanade in Rosario. Odds and ends (men and women?) were crawling out of black cogonal, ashen puddles, grenaded patios, contorted metal benches. Japanese flags had been torn and burned; reprisal leaders and their sympathizers were hanging from branches. Pedro Molina, forty-two, truck driver, had been whipped along into the momentum of the uprising. He was a short, chunky Caviteño with a prominent black mole under his lower lip. Apolitical and notoriously domesticated, he was the most distant mutation of the group; but on that afternoon of collision, unarmed and fearing for his family (wife; three kids), he had hidden (and was deeply ashamed of this) inside a large-mouthed *tapayan* and heard the brave rally and die around him. The small-arms fighting had not ceased at sunrise and he saw a man with a barefoot boy hop from rooftop to rooftop like spiders, while a whole enraged battery went *ping! ping! ping!* after them. Ambulances had screeched in for the military dead, but the rebels drove them out again, *ping! ping! ping!* Those who came out on the streets were either dazed or wounded. Both sides seemed to be running low on ammunition. Molina scampered back to his house and: it was no longer there. A mortar shell had smashed it unrecognizably among other nipa huts. Like a big mother animal clawing for her young, Molina dug into cindered asphalt and ashes and broke all his fingernails. After about an hour, he found all four of them, still holding hands, suspended in one agonized mouthless scream. He buried them under a paper cross. In the morning he sped off on his delivery truck to the next town, where he convinced some cockfighters that they could form a militia. He found an alleged general of the underground who claimed to have been in the afternoon rebellion of the poets; and Molina roared back on his truck, with rifles, bolos and bottles of kerosene. When they arrived in the battle zone, Japanese reinforcements had just motored in from Manila. The truck was stopped by machine-gun fire; Molina geared, reversed, geared and pedaled the truck straight into the garrison gates, his teeth crunching in the black beads of his rosary: *"Dios ko!"* And the day was so white, so pearly white so suddenly it seemed for a while that the sky had crashed against the earth.

("Parang hinampas ang lupa!")

Destroyer!
The Spaniard fell on the floor.
"It's spotted us!"
Ay, Tira, Tira. . . .
"Battle stations!"
The Colombo *sahig,* so cold, so cold.
"Engine room, give 'er all she's got!"
Another tooth came loose.
Ooooga-ooooga!
Howled for them again: his *beata,* that idiot boy.

"Cap'n, this guy's hurt bad."
Not really so bad now, but still bleeding.
"Medic!"
Didn't need a doctor; not now.
"That patrol must've caught him napping."
Sleep, *viejo,* sleep. . . .
"Can't move 'im now."
But he did; rolled on the floor he did.
"Ticker's bad, Cap'n."
Corazón, corazón. . . .
"Where's that medic?"
¿A dónde mi señorita?
"Up 'scope!"
Down, down, down, Manila's slime.
Depth charges!
Oh, oh, oh—but the pain of it.
"We'll try to hit 'er when she passes."
That blubber body padding in the basement.
Ooooga-ooooga!
What did the old crow say? Said something, she did.
"Down 'scope."
Rose once more; collapsed again.
"What's he sayin'?"
Perhaps if he could speak to the girl once more.
"Somethin' about a dame, Cap'n."
Where was she?
"Girl back home, probably."
His little *bonita,* gone.
Blam! Blam! Blam!
That blubber in the basement, waiting.
Blam!
Waiting.
"Up 'scope!"
Downstairs, she was—that fat old destroyer.
"There he goes again, Captain."
Where did she go—his *querida?*
"For Pete's sake, quiet there!"
Laughing in the basement, that Colombo coyote.

"Think he's gonna conk off."
He had thought about it; and now it was coming.
"Give 'im somethin', Doc!"
Even if he lived, what could she give him?
"He needs a priest, not a doctor."
Father, hear my confession. . . .
"Don't just stand there; do something!"
If he could only stand, walk to the window. . . .
"There he goes again—about his broad!"
Where did Amoran take her?
"He's talkin' about a virgin, Mary somethin'."
Sí, where was she? So chaste, so virginal.
"He's goin' back to her, he says—after the war."
Air raid over Manila; he could hear the bombers again.
"Flyboy, isn't he?"
And where was that *aviador?*
"It's no use, Cap'n. He's fading fast."
Oh, but time went so slowly, so slowly. . . .
"Fire one!"
Seconds ticked eternally. . . .
"Fire two!"
Three hundred years he was here. . . .
"Fire three!"
Forever it seemed he lay on the floor.
Blam! Blam! Blam!
They hit another gasoline tank; yes, that was it.
"Got 'er!"
¡Viva, 'Pana!
"Touchdown, boys!"
Just to touch her, feel her body warm.
"Captain, our man is going. . . ."
Jesus mio, and that white man of the Mass!
"Can't you do somethin', Doc?"
Too late, too late—Manila.
"Sorry, Captain. He's beyond help."
He wept on the floor, tears and blood.
"He's gone, Captain."
The bombers had left again; Manila was alone again.

"Wonder who he was."

What was his name again? the Spaniard thought.

"Captain Jonas Winters—by his dogtags."

Hidalgo saw the city abloom in fire from the window.

"Wonder who his girl was—I'd kind of like to know."

The all-clear signal blew.

"Seems like some native girl; didn't know her name."

Hidalgo de Anuncio stood up; and there she was, home at last.

Last of the Rosarioans was Iping Cruz, thirty-eight, migratory farmer. A confirmed bachelor, he lived alone; had no kin, no politics. Iping Cruz was away at the time of the afternoon reprisal, but on the way back to his hut on his carabao, a dying Japanese soldier had shot and wounded him critically. On the grass he lay wounded, wondering what it was all about. He watched the army lumber in on convoy cars; then a tank that had been crippled by a gasoline bomb tottered into view like a headless snake; he saw that insane man on a truck loaded with lunatics charge into the barricade, and the final white flash like the sky itself blot out everything in the town. Rising and falling, losing blood rapidly, Iping Cruz willed himself up, went to the molten mosaic of that supernatural truck and pulled out a pair of hands which must have been the madman's. And thus, with these two charred bodiless paws, he crept painfully to the church grounds, dug an ample grave, and there, not knowing what else to do, buried the three of them, himself and the hands—as he died.

[35]

THE STENCH DIDN'T BOTHER HIM any more; nor did the sirens. Bodies were piled beneath and on top of him: from tuberculosis, dysentery, malaria, leprosy, diabetes and gangrene to water cure, guillotine, poison gas, brass knuckles, stilettos, sabers, bayonets, and just plain bare fists. Whatever the cause, they were all rotting fast. The really foul ones were the so-called PP's, or Political Prisoners, whose slow liquidation was infinitely more inventive—thanks to Major Shigura's bottomless imagination. As for the ordinary burglars and petty pickpockets, their disposal was more accidental than anything else. Nobody worth his rank in Fort Santiago was inclined to expend precious hours of scientific torture on leftovers; and so prison guards were left to their own devices. Which weren't all that deficient, give and take a few crudities.

Vanoye's own ploy had worked like a charm. While part of it was Zen mysticism, the rest of the prescription was just homemade voodoo.

Step one: he scraped a coat of arms from a cardiovascular corpse; and like a sculptor, grained and molded the skin to fit his own, then lacing the wrists with mud and lead to cushion his pulsebeats. Step two: long a deep-water swimmer, he faked an epileptic fit by going into a swoon lasting about five minutes, stuffing cotton into his nose to prevent nostril dilation, *and* suggesting cardiac palpitations. Step three: previous to steps one and two, he had also tampered with the fort doctor's only stethoscope while assigned as a janitor in the infirmary. Even when he had been pronounced dead via asphyxiation, Vanoye was still not sure that he wasn't going to be buried alive after all, for there was a communal grave in Fort Santiago. Luckily enough, two outpost guards wanted to get some fresh air and heaved the excess carcasses into a truck for sea burial at the Pasig.

Pleased with himself, the one-armed fugitive held a running discourse with the cargo of cadavers, who could only gape at him with punctured tonsils and busted sockets. Stupid, he chided, just dumb, no brains, all balls, just sitting there on their haunches and letting it happen. Sure, Shigura is good, but not good enough to smell out a really neat trick as this. He's got flair, grant him that; still, his modalities are just spirals of one big ceremony; and ceremony can be licked because it is ordered, oriented, motivated by the right of repetition and that repetition is flawed by its own redundancy; the ceremony lacks that nihilistic spontaneity that can only come from the purest evil, which is resurrection. Silly, sad and stupid, all you putrefying jackasses—victims of your own ignorance. Evil created the cosmos and only evil can recreate it! Not icons, not incense, not idolatry. You don't wait for conscience, you never hope for charity. You shouldn't pray; prayers are for priests who are Cro-Magnon numbskulls cracking on the walls. Look at you! Faces unto feces, specie unto spittle—the supreme ignominy of birth!

Bump-bump-bump went the truck; ha-ha-ha went Vanoye.

After all this, he told the cargo of dead, I'm going to open a brothel to end all blasphemy. Amoran's harlot will be my star performer; Captain Jonas Winters will be my first client; and that pompous ass of a Spaniard will be my guest of honor!

Something was burning. Vanoye wagged a finger at the inmates: No smoking, please! They only lay about him, fixing him with their malignant, wandering albumens.

Speak up, bastards! he harped.

They only crumpled away in their maladroit radius.

Silly, sad and stupid.

From whose semens and wombs? he thought. Out of what incalculable imbecility? Unthinkable and unforgivable that such a race of nincompoops should people a nation. If only one out of thousands and thousands could survive a Shigura, then Filipinos were not much better than dinosaurs. Millions more would be slaughtered by other carnivorous formalists less endowed than the Major to join the stupid extinct. The Philippines would be overridden by third-degree specialists; the whole country would soon be depopulated by the expertise of conceit, by the languor, by the vulnerability of those to the manner born. Nothing would be left on these islands but anthropoids and interpreters—and, yes, Vanoye.

Smoke, fumes.

Burning, the truck was burning!

Now he knew, suddenly realized that the strongest stench in the cargo was not the dead but gasoline; the Japanese had drenched their lone caravan from its canvas roofing to its interior planks. Vanoye elbowed his way through a ton of bodies, but chopped arms held him back; faceless heads laughed him down. He thrashed and kicked, punching a hole through the cave of scabby skins. Just when he could see sunlight—or flames—the tunnel caved in again. And they were tickling him; fingerless hands were gouging at his eyes. He fought back viciously, man to mummy, as the gasoline seeped in, as the fire licked and spread from canvas to corpse, as two drunken Japanese hellions alternating right-left hands on the steering wheel stepped on the gas, as their truck climbed the Montalban mountains. Vanoye winced: somebody in there had bitten him, or was it the fire? He traded blows with his one arm; was dropped, was up again, was almost near the burning flaps of the entrance, his exit. Then those two guffawing devils jumped clear, as their chariot skidded, lurched, leaped, clunked mightily; and burning still with its laughing hyenas, plummeted from a cliff into the gorge below.

Above, always above the V formation of silver had arrived to annex this piece of sky in the Pacific. Manila knew for a fact that this was *it,* the Invasion—although it was not exactly coming from the Mountains, as Deogracias had predicted. Yet it was most certainly here, and the revolutionary auxiliaries of Ojos Verdes cared not a whit, were indifferent, or, if the truth were known, just weren't aware that *La Liberación* was a mathematical prospectus quite divorced from the invocations and Barnum and Bailey demonology of their Lieutenant Dark Glasses. The miracle of Arrival was all that counted, with the hysterical and the unsophisticated crediting such to their beloved *supremo.* What did it matter if he was constantly changing colors and designations? Guerrilla adjutant, commando chieftain, USAFFE spotter—and lately, Hukbalahap pathfinder—he was somehow instrumental in bringing back the White Leghorn. . . .

But Amoran had no such notions. Neither fanatical nor whimsical, he was that highly intuitive creature for whom everyday facts, for whom all fate indeed could only be savored or salvaged according to one's armory of reflexes. Instinct, to him, meant much more than anybody's mountain, which—as far as his fuzzy mental processes could assess it—was too vague, too remote to be measured in terms of animal habits.

Right now, the boy was more concerned with the questionable location of the Colombo boardinghouse; its proximity to a military installation boded ill any way one looked at it. Something told him, compelled him to pack up the girl's meager belongings and his own, then to flee. In what was perhaps their first quarrel, the girl had gone into an amazing series of facial expressions: she pouted, sobbed, giggled, then in girlish glee, chided him for cowardice; now womanly, accused him, of all things, of jealousy. With each trick, with every taunt, Amoran had simply and bravely played deaf and dumb, pulling her by the arm to the stairway. Sensing finally that nothing would dissuade him, that nobody would come to her assistance (tenants and neighbors alike thought the two were eloping), she had dug her fingernails deep into his back and ripped off his one good shirt. Now Amoran had not minded the scratch wounds that much (his whole ungainly body was their natural reservoir anyway), but he had pictured himself welcoming the liberation forces in his sporty ecru-dyed poplin shirt and for a minute he lost all control. Yelping so outrageously that even Mrs. Colombo was obliged to peek out of her basement, he had clouted the girl on the jaw, knocking her down on the floor by the front door, unconscious. After that (she, pining; he, penitent), it wasn't hard to steer her in the streets all over town, dragging their things behind them. She would never forgive him, she said. Especially not about the old dying Spaniard they—he—had abandoned. Oh, she wept—refusing his hand as they crossed an intersection—she had not even bade goodbye to her Hidalgo. He was all alone up there and perhaps lonelier than all the *dichos* he had ever read to her; and alone with Tira Colombo, she wailed as they ducked behind a pillar. But not for long, smiled Amoran to himself; not with that letter he had slipped under the landlady's door—the letter over which he had spent two sleepless nights of arduous forgery along with that message to Sergeant Yato. The landlady could read none too well in any dialect, but since the letter was addressed to her (her name was all that mattered) and signed by Hidalgo (whose own name was like poetry to her), it was language enough. "Forgive me, *señor,* forgive me!" muttered the shaken, grieving girl as Amoran dragged her around the city's dark, expectant streets, searching high and low for the first American liberator.

Last drop of perfume, last pinch of powder.

That notwithstanding, Aling Tira, proprietress of the Colombo Arms, could not cleanse her body of that malingering fetor more usually confined to her cavernous armpits. With monomaniacal abandon, she scrunched the Paris bottle deep down there among her thistles, to squeeze every ounce of magic from her placebo. Downy was her face, puffy her lips; and the vanity corset, which had only been drudged into after much panting and perspiration, actually did not impound her pelvic muscles, had not exacted a semblance of controlled buxomness. Her ever-bounteous frame simply defied marginalia of any kind. More than sheer tonnage, that quivering school of flesh in the floor-length mirror accurately, even maliciously repeated her regressive anthropology. The Madame, captious and absorbent in her toilet, was at a loss as how to quell all that tumescent jelly, that skin spoored with contagion, that octoroon complexion so self-defining, those old-hag bags under the eyes. Try as she would, nothing short of mutilation could circumvent that gelatinous mammalia. All her primping, all her decorative flagellations had always and conclusively led to that harpie in the mirror. Which stared back at the original with waspish relish. The schoolgirl organdy had not canceled half a wrinkle; nor did that expensive rouge conceal a blemish—it was a moot point whether the mascara had not only glorified her native grotesquerie while it was intended to subjugate it. And if her plastic artifacts did not do the rest, the Colombo Neanderthal took over—and of course, owing to her bark, her bulk, her ogreish totality, that always brought down the ape from its tree.

Putang ina! she could do no more, and collapsed into a chair. Of late she had maintained a reclusive life in her basement, spiking her lemonade with *basi* and occasionally even spurning her currently dwindling tribe of late-night callers. Sometimes from the window she watched all that sinful puberty at its best. Dimpled dainties jouncing to their lithe and laconic lovers. What stung most especially was not that fewer and fewer males were willing to be heroic inside the Colombo basement but that they had grown susceptible to juiceless girlhood cavorting in the alleys. Even Zerrado Susi, that well-tempered cock with whom she had spent one unbelievable night, had not shown up in over a fortnight. Either Mrs. Susi, thought Tira, had opened up her canal anew for conjugal trade, or that indefatigable locksmith had at last found the toilet of his dreams.

But that was broth under the pot, grinned the landlady tolerantly, as she made ready to go upstairs. It wasn't too bad, really; that chimp Amoran had, *sa awa ng Dios,* run away with his adopted princess; and: there was the De Anuncio letter. Thinking of this, she brightened at once. The house was quiet; the neighborhood was distracted. Most of her boarders had fled—without paying the rent—at the sound of bombardment; Mang Isagani, the streetcar conductor, had spirited his insatiable Lourdes (and from a splendiferous peephole in one of the Colombo anterooms, what an erotically manipulative, highly combustible couple those two had made!) to some undisclosed address; Micaela, cracked and bogged down, couldn't be nosey; Sergeant Yato (who, in one drunken bout, had given the landlady a whole hour of couldn't-care-less sex) was rumored to be hunting down Major Shigura for some military infraction or other, while Deogracias was reported to be saving a mountain-grown bullet for the Sergeant.

Lintik, pagkakataon yata ito. . . .

The Hidalgo letter was safely tucked away in Mrs. Colombo's drawer, to be answered promptly by special delivery any minute now.

All that brouhaha around her did not bother Mrs. Colombo. To her, the Liberation meant not much more than an extra *chupa* of rice, perhaps some fresh eggs. Politics, government, religion—they were big, fat gobs of one rotten yolk to her. She would benefit not a single *kusing* from a change of venue; she would not profit from a shift of ideology. Acculturation was for those who did not have or did not cherish what they most privately had, which was identity. The landlady, even with half an ear cocked, with but bat eyes in the daylight, had long reached the conclusion that after Bienvenido Elan, her first husband, there could never be any new idea. History would pass (as indeed it had) over Mrs. Colombo like a tractor, and she would not notice, would not care. What she truly, incessantly lamented was the depletion of man, in whatever form or substance. To her way of thinking, war had been cruel only insofar as it had cauterized the vaginal life source, in its unabating diminution of the male. That cities were razed to the ground, that mothers were ravished in dark rooms, that babies perished for lack of milk only signified (to her) that men were killing each other senselessly, selfishly. No sect could be so sublime, no philosophy so enlightening, no administration so just that could ever again remedy the loss of essence. After the demise of Architect Elan (oh, Bienvenido!), her one last link to any branch of formal constructiveness, Mrs. Colombo just retired from ideas.

Upstairs in room thirteen, a bed creaked.

It was time, smiled Mrs. Colombo, extricating herself from the rattan chair, *sugod!* She hesitated before the mirror for last renewals and rearmaments. Seeing her single breast, she flushed, fumed, fretted; then flung open a bureau drawer; tore into a rag pile of lingerie as an Olympic hurdler would an obstacle course; grabbed panties and hosiery alike, palmed them indiscriminately into a ball, and slapped the cone facsimile inside her blouse with that long-suffering, lone-star bust which had waited a decade for a mate.

Then up the stairway.

Hidalgo, Hidalgo—her heart beat.

Just six more steps.

What sign was this month? Ah yes, *febrero se-is:* Aquarius, of course. Why, that was *castilla's* sign too! Mrs. Colombo paid strict attention to the Zodiac. Herself she was Cancer: what was Bienvenido again?

Three steps.

Needn't hurry, she beamed. He would be waiting. And why now? Only now? Maybe he wanted to get rid of that girl first. Nice of her to leave. Amoran certainly deserved some thanks for this. Perhaps a plate of gruel?

Now just one.

Step lightly, she thought, not wanting to alarm the old gentleman. Oh, but she had craved, pined for this—for Aquarius in bed. She would be gentle, yes, as gentle as she must have been once and as he must still be, and as gentle as her Elan.

She was there, at his door. . . .

Closing of the Pasig River due south started January 9, with his army and navy working twenty-four hours a day. The northern part of Manila had been evacuated in order to mobilize a defensive panzer at the mouth of the Luneta. All bridges were to be dynamited before the Americans—a tortured guerrilla pointer had confessed that the frontal assault of the invaders, as transmitted by shortwave radio, would come from the 37th Division and 1st Cavalry Division—could cross the northern banks. The Japanese High Command had unanimously agreed, after much ado, that the district south of the Pasig was to be their bastion. Each *calzada* had been mined, barricaded from their outer reaches; to be defended with antitank artillery and automatic weapons. Key intersections swelled with camouflaged cannons, as did upper stories of buildings. Their main force south of the Pasig was what could be called heterogeneous, consisting of 13,000 naval personnel; 5,000 army troops—all under Admiral Iwobuchi.

Gratefully, Major Shigura had deferred to the Admiral; allowed him to inspect Intramuros from top to bottom; permitted that popinjay to strut around Ermita with his ravenous defenders. The Major even let him have the run of Fort Santiago; but no, smirked the latter, who was in dire need of a shave—he was no butcher; he was a soldier, even if he was in the navy. Apparently, that was all right too: the

Fort commandant didn't care one way or the other. He wanted to see his friends again. Well, not exactly his friends; but they understood him, or appeared to. It would be pleasant to visit the old Spaniard and his wards for the last time.

Today (February 6, 1945), he rode to the mango grove as usual; alit, gave the white horse a whack on the rump—and it cantered away into nocturnal grass, under a parapet of accacia. Shigura unrolled a sleeping bag, unclasped his sword and placed it two yards from his side. The moon had come out; the wind was nippy, and he was thinking about that nameless girl in the Colombo house. Though he had dogged her tracks around the city for a year now, he did not know her; as in fact nobody in her company seemed to. As he lay down, arms akimbo, boots shucked off, her eyes hung like a galactic scintilla in the cloud banks.

She knew about him, that much was certain.

In her protracted walks around Manila she habitually peered over her shoulder, and when he was not quick enough, she caught a glimpse of him. He had not followed her on the horse but always on foot; occasionally in civilian clothes. This little subterfuge proved futile, for she always seemed to detect him, even in a multitude. Their own dance they perpetuated: she, wandering round the streets; he, shadowing her. She never did anything out of the ordinary—except for that time when she had mistakenly handed him a seditionary poster in place of a menu. (What could have possessed her? he ruminated now.) The girl left her lodgings; she roamed avidly (what was she looking for?), sometimes with that ugly scavenger boy (could they be lovers?); oftentimes, alone (and if not the boy, who?). She strolled to a new site each time; sat down for an hour, maybe two, never seeming to have lunch; stood up, roved anew, then went home again. He could tell by these now familiar vagabondisms that she had no real acquaintances; she appeared to favor strangers, beggars, or stray children like herself. Maddeningly casual, with no self-consciousness whatsoever, she reported for work—by which time he would himself be hiking back to the Fort—and after quitting the restaurant (he knew when that was, too) for the night, began the routine once more—with him a hundred or so paces behind. At first she seemed to have minded his presence, his persistence, but after a few more such excursions and realizing perhaps that he meant her no harm, she relaxed again. Once, when he had so clumsily lost her trail and run three blocks in an effort to catch up, she had suddenly reappeared from a side door—and, he could not understand this up to this day—even smiled. Embarrassed, caught off guard, he had mumbled some apology or perhaps just an oath, then red-faced, hurried away. One time guessing that she was hungry, he had mustered enough nerve to buy an ice-cream cone (flavor: artificial vanilla, semi-strawberry) and made its sidewalk vendor deliver it to her. With not a blush (he rather hoped she would), betraying not a trace of suspicion (for this, he was thankful), she smiled wanly (almost perversely, he reflected) in acceptance, knowing instinctively where to look, whom to thank: two blocks away, like Quasimodo tolling his love for Esmeralda, he waved her gratitude away.

Lying there in the cool air, waiting for another moon, Major Shigura supposed that he had always known her, the way bandit lovers memorized the scent and aura of carriage-borne, castle-bound ladies. For it was she—he would stake his campaign ribbons on it—that he espied one evening in a province somewhere north, tapping on a door, presumably for something to eat. He had been out there briefly on one of his pacification sorties. But it was the girl, there was no mistaking that: she who was—Hidalgo's? Since then, he had seen her around Manila—always with the same absent look, that long windswept hair. He was even there when that old Spaniard picked her up at the State lobby on that evening of bombs.

Yes, yes, he had followed her. With such devotion it was unnerving. He did not know what for and to what end. It was simply that he felt the need to.

At the Fort his officers had their women brought in after dark. As he had, too. Only with him it was more of a ruse, a stopgap. He really had no appetite for any of them. Not for the scabrous hulks of half-Chinese, half-Filipino females that latched on to a meat can of an officer and never let go. Not for the skittish *mestizaje* that wantoned the midnights away; and certainly not for the vulpine, dervish-like widows of slain guerrilla leaders that plotted vengeance after fornication. No, Major Shigura had no stomach for such banalities, the bounty of such professional profligates as Sergeant Yato—that slobbery vindicator of military wrongs. After he had bathed his libido in a photomontage of torture within those dim-bulbed subterranean chambers, Major Shigura felt like a revenant and demanded release from the rancid mess halls, the starchy kitchens, the avian badinage of the officers' quarters. For all its bathos and brutishness, the Colombo boardinghouse unfailingly offered—mainly through that nomadic, nameless girl—a fillip of renewal. She was so rare, a curio from some unexcavated gift shop: a hint of madrigals.

And what of the others—the rankling menagerie in Ojos Verdes? At one time or another, Major Shigura had considered raiding the casbah and dragging off its malcontents to the Fort. Doubtless, something there was not quite right which could have long ago been amended, had he only performed his responsibilities to the hilt. Yet, like a fruit fly seduced by a gangrenous cyst, he had been magnetized to this mucus-ridden stronghold—lair of thieves, Shangri-La for sectless shamans—not to probe or purge, but to plumb and ponder. By now the quadrangle of sluicy pottage that quartered its estuary (bleeding like bayoneted jugular veins), by now the doom-drenched nipa that constituted its shack lot, by now the stark, angular faces that purported to be its inhabitants were known to him with such horror and heraldry. Centrifugally, and if bloodhounds were loosed to track down the mother-sty of its abscess, all the *callejones* and *eskinitas* of Ojos Verdes would inescapably point to its logical intaglio: the Colombo boardinghouse. What the firetrap represented to the passerby, Major Shigura could not tell; personally, that foul edifice was the scrotum to which all his toxic faculties properly belonged. Yet in the house, he had been nothing other than gentle—just the kind of contradiction, he presumed, that would outlive all of man's certainties. The criteria for efficient command—equally applicable to good soldiering—was the ability to neutralize compunction, to negate conscience. There had to be an ineradicable automaton in the upper echelons for whom no human quotient was valid if it presented a detergent to expediency. In any chain of command, the quirks and foibles of the underling must, of necessity, be steamrollered into regimentation. No ego could supersede the faceless authority which sustained that vast apparatus. While the Major was an enigma to most of his men, his decisions were never questioned; his orders resolutely carried out. The precious few that had somehow differentiated the bestial from the benign in their commandant's makeup, kept mum, reasoning that they could have done worse and that the Fort was much safer than the front. At Fort Santiago, as in many command structures all over the country, the unwritten law was: Salute and shut up. For what would it profit the private to gain a dubious insight and lose his rations? Professionally, the Major expected no relationships and extended none. This attitude yielded dividends: nobody jeered, everyone jumped. Between transmission and execution, between order and obedience, Major Shigura was confident he was beyond guilt or glory. In the event of an Allied victory—and the handwriting had dripped down on the other side of the wall—the war trials would, with evangelical wrath, pursue the taint of culpability to their visible roots: Tojo, Yamashita, along with all those warlords that had presumed too much in their "war of expansion." As a coup de grâce, the Emperor himself would be stripped of his celestial robes. Yet after all judicial reckonings and moral retributions, that authorial voice, the one that had exhorted, *"Tora! Tora! Tora!"* while its accomplices bombed Pearl Harbor, would go unidentified, unscathed. In Nazi Germany, the identifiable beast was Hitler, whose certified infamy would soon keep historians busy. *Der Führer* would join all the infamous exterminators of czarist and Stalinist Russia; and *Sieg Heil!* he would go down in the final accounting with Nero, Caligula, Attila and Genghis Khan. But Japan's own Sphinx, enlisting, then exhuming its aliases and despoilers, would survive Allied technology, would subvert man's very theology—to reassess, reconstruct, regroup tomorrow's traumas, the future's feudal fangs for a neo-Nipponese rising sun, for a more bountiful harvest moon, and . . .

This very minute, the Sphinx (or the Manila moon?) was transfusing: through an alias—Major Shigura. Where was he? Ah yes, the Colombo house. Who were the dispensables? Ah so, the progenitors of Ojos Verdes. Now he made his canvass.

Hidalgo de Anuncio? Too old, quite ineffectual.

Tira Colombo? What for? She was a harmless chunk of raw meat ideal for the disposal of undesirables.

Paeng Redoblado? Just a sissy. Hopefully, he would cut his throat without help from anybody.

Zerrado Susi—well, there was a deviate for the books. All told, a congenital showoff. Why tamper with nature's most delectable joke?

The hairdresser's daughter, Lourdes, shared some characteristics with the Girl in a tangential sort of way; otherwise, she was just a piquant, male-absorbing female.

Her mate, that Mang Isagani. *Dorobo!* Now there was an anatomical entity that might produce some very exciting results on the rack. Since this subject had already been proven—although only recently—an underground provocateur of burgeoning importance, he would automatically provide a justification for military third degree. Not that justification was required—but in this case, it would be better to have a reason. Mang Isagani's outward forthrightness would just suit the insatiability of torture.

Placido Rey (minus his Victoria, of course) was an unknown factor and deserved some attention. While he was not underground at all, his sympathies, his convictions were just as submerged. Inactive to the point of sterility, the man was not a direct threat now, but could be a voice tomorrow. Tomorrow, on the other hand, held no special significance to the Major, who was positive that only today was his. So Placido Rey was stricken from the realm of possibility.

But that Deogracias, Mr. Dark Glasses himself, had to be dealt with somehow. Even Admiral Iwobuchi, a latecomer to the show, had brought up the particular name. Major Shigura rolled on his other side, mulling over this one. Why had he waited? Surely something must be done about this unabashedly exposed guerrilla lieutenant who made a mockery of infiltrating Manila from his mountain hideout almost every week? Before anything else happened, before Major Shigura's lock of hair reached his father's house, Deogracias must certainly be eliminated in as ostentatious a manner as possible.

Yet of all the Ojos Verdesians, Major Shigura dreaded no one more than that Molave Amoran. This fear the Major could not rightly comprehend, for the source was, in all its physical manifestations at least, nothing but a boy. So ugly it hurt the eyes. So completely insignificant one had to wonder why he was there at all. All through those man-hours that Shigura had followed the girl, he had seen Amoran too. After months of apparently worthless surveillance, Shigura realized that something in fact was coming to focus. Not the girl's face, which he had long suspected could be lovely; but the boy's moronic persuasions with their bits and pieces that were somehow, inevitably, colliding into a whole. And just what was that? Danger, danger of some unobtrusive fiber. The boy contained and sometimes subsumed a natural malice that could lead to—a definition? But of what? What was so disturbing to Major Shigura was this image of idiocy behind the girl's lackadaisical manner. Something there—not in her alone—something there between them, shared and sublimated. Or more exactly, from him to her. As though, in military parlance again, the boy was a gun runner passing her ammunition!

Major Shigura slapped his thighs and sat up.

Something wrong somewhere, between Amoran and the girl. As there had always been a rapport between Hidalgo and her; although that was dying, or dead. What Amoran had and was giving was very much alive; it was tactile, and spreading—like skin disease. Like Vanoye's dream. Ah, poor One-Arm!

Ba-roooom! Ba-roooom!

Artillery.

With a start, Major Shigura crawled for his saber, just when Sergeant Yato fired. One bullet did it, dead center in the officer's forehead. . . .

Lieutenant Deogracias was running for the Colombo house, swinging the Major's sword over his head, gloating over Sergeant Yato's assassination (had he hit two birds with one stone?) when it came, this sixth of February, when they came at last, perhaps from the sky as he had prognosticated: the Americans; and he cried: "Tira! Tira!" as a building fell on him.

MORTE D'ARTHUR
was the last book they were to have read together. Now she was gone. Emboldened, imperiled—*otra vez,* she was gone. Amoran the argonaut had, with improvisatory functionalism, toddled her off.

Where?

Into a flux of conveyor belts: calligraphic stockpiles, schematized dispensations, spurious reallocations.

(*Gracias,* Señor Hidalgo!)

(*De nada, chica. . . .*)

His *faena* was over.

Rachitic yet magisterial in bed, De Anuncio yowled with soundless clenched lips; his vocal cords had been buried by that chocolate explosion, skewering his dentures and sealing his gums with phlegm, saliva and blood until no speech, not even a moan, could leak out. Like a prehistoric mammal trapped under a fallen bark, his mind first growled, later chugged, now chirped uselessly. Laboriously transcribing random objects in the room: pitcher, cot, chair, slippers . . . an act that did not at all mollify him since the pitcher's water dripped, the cot's springs quailed, the chair's legs scraped, the slipper's leather squeaked. Nor was his body adequate for anything: with his jaw, it had just locked its muscles. His optic nerves too had been turned off, as though someone had pulled a switch—retaining vision but nailing down radius. Visually, everything moved in quarter time: he saw that fly in his cell only after it was gone; acoustically, he could no longer distinguish the buzzing of the fly from the whistling of the bombs. Similarly, his respiration had been cut off—like electricity whose bill he had not paid. He did not sweat; neither did he feel cold. There wasn't even any pain. He was—just there. Like a statue. So this was how it was to be a monument. Quite whole, quite solid. Glacial, spatial; having no boundaries, yet occupying space. Perhaps man's perfectability lay not in the Last Sacraments of Holy Writ but in his biological annulment. *Acedia* the Borgian monks called it.

Flying Superfortresses were hovering over Manila; but in De Anuncio's ear it was only that fly buzzing in the stratosphere. Crusty and recumbent, his mind oscillated from vaudeville to virgins, from slate to lichen, from the hefty buttocks of pterodactylous actresses to that undraped gamin in the cot. When was it—his brain refused to clothe it with tenses—that he had come home late, late one night (tripping on a flower vase downstairs) to see the girl sleeping there? And he had sat by her side for hours, just watching her. Something in his long, turgid day (the noonday wine; somebody's distraught concertina onstage) had transmuted flecks of dust into floccus; the dull ocher of the walls seemed to blaze a slew of ecru. Preternaturally, his eyes had recast the tawdry room for his own delectation; the Colombo environs suddenly assumed his patrimony. Paraffin white was the bedroom, stanchioned by terra cotta, merging with lapis lazuli, yet ineluctably henna, metamorphosed into gauze and hazel. He had entered, in his most exquisite harlequinade investing the wall-to-wall squalor with pride and perfume—to come upon an odalisque: *la mujer,* who was now an Iberian figurine. Though that frowzy virago in the basement yelped and slumped, threatening the moment and the night with customary attrition, she in the cot magnified his illusion. With prosthetic abundance, her body bloomed; her bosom peeked out from her crossed arms as her other half lay carapaced in sheets. Unbeknownst to her, she was now his Modigliani maiden, his Barberini faun. He knelt to kiss the soles of her feet, her thighs, while behind her rose a scrim; above them drooped an opalescent ceiling. He stroked her tumbling soft hair; and she purred, as if in postcoital relief. She smiled—now Titian's Diana—and he watched, he waited for more of her infinite varieties. Turning a split second that side (ah, Degas!), actually breathing on his cheek—*hola, guapita!* Inhaling a touch—which to him betokened Scriabin—her lips fell upon his elbow. She turned Delacroix too, and he was, involuntarily, Morpheus descending. Perhaps his mind then had blended with hers, for their bodies merged in such similitude. His, with optimum endeavor; hers, protean, oblatory. As visitant to sleeper, he was the lodestar, the imposer of laws and symmetry; as beneficiary, she was the Eucharist subject to his witchcraft. And from her he parlayed the corpus of a fairy tale. He was Dionysus coming upon Adriadne asleep: Mercury, Argus, Judith, Holofernes. She was the moon goddess Selene . . . he was the rustic Cymon moved and transformed by the sleeping yet awakening beauty of Iphigenia. . . .

Here was the epicenter of it all: in that Sibylline heap so sluggish —if not dead—no siege would rouse. Was she dreaming? Or had he only dreamed her sleeping? For was he not in reality merely the third party in this vigil? Amoran was the Minotaur, not he. Amoran was the final phallus with whom she would beget—what malefactors, what eerie accidents of consciousness? De Anuncio could deflorate her in sleep and she would only waken to spit out his vestigial sperms. For she was Queen of the Hyperborean Empis Flies and would eat him at her marriage feast. Yet he watched her sleep, sleep, sleep. Little else could he do but kneel and prowl, envious of her sleep, jealous of her dreams that he knew most haughtily excluded him from their fierce convoluted rhythms. Eve first came upon Adam in his sleep . . . was she only a dream before? Or had they only imagined Paradise and were really born in Hell? In the cot, she reduced De Anuncio's topography to a silhouette on her brow; all his daylight tutorings had been synthesized into this little speck barely gracing her cheeks. And if he shook her back to earth, would her next fantasy contain his morning homiletics, his pietistic Sundays? Still she had slept, unmarked by his agony. The woman she was in that state was not the girl he knew at breakfast; a morsel of her dream would also be present at the table: in her pensive eyes, and always, on her moist lips—the mole of a demon lover.

"Hussy!" De Anuncio would snarl at her, dropping his fork and spoon.

And if she was truly innocent, if she had not been faithless the other night, why then, in her own defense, did she only smile?

Superfortresses buzzed in the room; the fly bombed Manila. Was it true that the female of the mantids ate the front half of her bridegroom while his hind half stubbornly completed its task of reproduction?

De Anuncio roistered in the monument. Rest was foremost in his mind as he remembered Calderón *(La Vida Es Sueño)* but, gum-choked, only inflected frugally and mentally, Proust.

I found her asleep and did not rouse her. . . . She . . . was to me an undiscovered country. . . .

"Keep 'em flying!"

Waltz me around again, Willie. . . .

FDR had decided not to see the movie; anyhow his Pacific Theatre
Washington had declared war on Spain, and now, lashing farther
was going strong ("Gung-ho!"). Sloshing in rice paddies, fording
out ("Westward ho!"), chartered steamers to ferry General Wesley
by pontoon, doughboys of the crack 37th Division were closing in on
Merritt's volunteer regiments to Manila—the first complement of
Manila; the 1st Cavalry was pushing onward to San Francisco del
American colonizers to sail from San Francisco to "pacify" the Asia-
Norte Bridge, to liberate the Manilans. Burly and tawny, the GIs
tics. Bearded and drawling, the troops were mostly volunteers from
came mostly from the U.S. Eastern-Southern nebulae: New York,
Western states: California, Nebraska, Oregon, Wyoming, Colorado.
Alabama, New Jersey, Kentucky . . . wearing not English Tommy
They wore campaign hats with their khaki and blue uniforms, and
helmets but deep German-type ones with their fatigues, and jungle
"horse-collar packs" rolled on their necks. Against the bolo-and-

boots, musette bags. Against the Springfield-and-artillery Japs, they
musket Filipino insurgents, they were armed with single-shot Krag-
were armed with garands, carbines, *tres* mortars, bazookas, grenades.
Jorgensen rifles, backed in the rear by Gatling guns. Some of them
Some of them still bore the slime and slander of Hell's Kitchen;
still bore the grime and excitement of boomtowns; still others spoke of
others mumbled about Normandy landings where they'd lost buddies,
Klondike gold-rush days when they had holes in their shoes and a
a million dollars' worth of war bonds. Many had never seen the sea
million dollars' worth of dust in their hot little pans. Many had never
before this. . . . Well, this campaign was one way of getting to know
seen the sea. Well, this was as good a way as any of getting intro-
the Florida Everglades: the Convoy was blasting the Nip tubs from
duced to Melville country: Commodore Dewey had just scuttled
Saipan to Kingdom come. . . . Go for broke! So much for the Japa-
Admiral Patricio Montojo's fleet off Cavite. So much for the Spanish
nese Navy. . . .
Armada. . . .

Many of the boys remembered Bataan, would never forget the
Most of them had never heard of the Filipinos or their Philippines
Rock and All That, even before boot camp. Back home, emotions
before signing on to clean up this mess in the Far East. Back home,
ran high, rations were low; anything to keep the March of Dimes
there was a lot of speechifying and carrying on. Leave it to the poli-
going. The politicians were quiet for a change. Aboard the *U.S.S.*
ticians any time. There was this fellow, Reverend J. H. Barrows, who
Arizona, there was this chaplain, Reverend Howell Forgy, who,
said it for every American methodist: "Whenever on pagan shores
helping out with the eight-inch guns, said: "Praise the Lord and pass
the voice of the American missionary is heard, there is fulfilled the
the ammunition!" These words echoed from preacher to Marine,
manifest destiny of the Christian Republic." And if that was good
from the Halls of Montezuma to the shores of Tripoli, from the
enough for Reverend Barrows, it was certainly good enough for the
BBC to the Voice of America and all the freedom megacycles every-
volunteers. "Yea, yea, manifest destiny, yea!" The Pearl of the Orient
where. Oompah-pah, "Praise the Lord!" Oompah-pah, "Pass the
would not forget. . . .

ammo!" Pearl Harbor would remember. . . .
Rallied from behind by McKinley and a host of Methodist slogans,
Rallied from behind by Roosevelt and the Big Three, assured that
assured of sanctification in heaven, the volunteers sallied forth; its
this was a just war, the GIs leapfrogged in the Pacific with amphibi-
cavalries galloping into hostile towns; their consuls in Singapore and
ous force, descended on Europe like the Furies on parachute; their
Hong Kong promising the Filipinos a free government under a pro-
strategists in the Pentagon and Whitehall pulling rabbits out of steel
tectorate. By July 1898, Spain had abandoned the battle for Cuba;
helmets, plucking victories from miniature flags. By January 30, 1945,
America had humbled Puerto Rico. Still, the "gugus" *thought their*
the XI Corps had occupied the towns of Subic-Olongapo and Grande
own army could do it alone. Manila, defended by 13,000 Spaniards
Island; Manila was defended by 13,000 navy men and 5,000 army
was hemmed in by a chain of Filipino trenches. U.S. volunteer spot-
regulars concentrated in Intramuros, with a ring of trenches extending
ters estimated that the natives had a collarhold from the beach south
from Fort Santiago to the Jones Bridge south of the city; while the
of Malate, with a northward curve through Paco to Pandacan to the
1st Cavalry, reinforced by the 44th Tank Battalion, advanced from
Pasig River. This spanned westward from San Juan across fields and
Guimba. Elements of a guerrilla outfit were also moving on the
bamboo groves to La Loma, the zigzagging trenches veering off the
Walled City from Pinaglabanan, Legarda and Balic-Balic in an
shoreline north of Tondo. Because of this rather primitive albeit
effort to link up with the liberation forces at Manila Bay. Shabbily
effective deployment, the gugus *were actually ready to assault the*
uniformed and sometimes armed only with hate, the Filipinos were
Walled City itself. . . .
aching to take a crack at Intramuros themselves. . . .
Which was something the norteamericanos *could not allow—who*
Which was not exactly honky-dory, since the Yanks were not of a
was liberating whom anyway? The Philippine-American War pulled
mind just yet to liberate anyone before the University of Santo Tomás
the trigger on February 4, 1898 in San Miguel. From there it spread
was taken. The Fil-American hookup was geared to this objective.
like a forest fire: Ermita, Malate, Pasay, Pandacan, Caloocan, Laguna

That February: the Presidential Palace at Malacañang was seized;
de Bay, Tirad Pass, Panay, Leyte, Negros, Iloilo, Cebu, Samar, Lipa,
onward, north from Nasugbu, Batangas, to Parañaque, to Nichols
Marinduque, yippeeee! It was boomtown all over again, and in the
Airfield, west to Antipolo; deeper to east Lubao. Yahoooo! It was a
talahib *rush came the XII Corps, the 1st Nebraska Volunteers, the*
turkey shoot again, and in the breach came: the 7th Cavalry Regiment,
Pennsylvania Regiment, the 3rd Artillery, the 1st Montana, the
the 11th Airborne Division, the 12th Cavalry, the 55th Infantry, the
Wheaton Brigade. The brownies had Tinio in the Ilocos, Concepción
188th Parachute Glider Infantry, the 503rd Parachute RCT. General
and Alejandrino in Central Luzon, Cailles and Malvar in the Tagalog
MacArthur's grasshopper staff was almost flawless: Kenney with his
provinces, Lukban in Samar—and who knew how many fifth colum-
5th Air Force, Kinkaid with his Seventh Fleet, Walter Kruger with
nists in the capital? A few miles east of Manila, General Henry
his Sixth Army, Robert Eichelberger with his Eighth Army. The
Laughton (a Civil War hero), who had captured the Apache chief,
General had said: "Get to Manila!" A few blocks from the Manila
Geronimo, clashed with the Filipino Apache, General Licerio Gerón-
Legislative Building, Sergeant First Class Hank Longhorn, a B.A.R.
imo in San Mateo. The brown general's tiradores de la muerte
man and an ex-barbecue grille manufacturer from Buffalo, New
(sharpshooters trained by an English marksman), were under orders
York, led a squad of crack shots outside a park. Sergeant Longhorn
to aim for one target—that totem-tall, beautifully conspicuous Gen-
had spotted this crazy Jap officer swinging his saber, missed him
eral Laughton, who was killed with a bullet in the lungs.
with a round of B.A.R., then bazookaed him off the street after
But this only served as one glorious footnote in the hostilities, for
hitting what looked like a grocery store.
16,000 dead Filipino soldiers, 10,000 American casualties, 20,000
But the fighting had gone on with more grisly footnotes, all the
civilians injured and 600-million-dollars expenditures later, the Fili-
way until March 4, then after that, August 6 and the *U.S.S. Missouri:*
pinos were saluting and singing to the American flag: "Oh, Jose, can
the Filipinos would be saluting and singing again to the Stars and
you see!" . . . and crippled Filipino guerrillas were reading Tom

Stripes: "O-ooh say, can't you see?" . . . And Filipino guerrillas would Sawyer, *patterning their aborted careers after Lincoln, while their* be reading Hemingway, carving papaya stems into MacArthur corncob *liberators swilled and swelled, pinching brown* dalagitas *in* población pipes, while their liberators grinned and gave, pinching washerwomen *and city, for the old mining days were back, yippeeee! Manila was* in alley and on avenue, for the fighting was done, gung-ho! Manila *speaking the English, the government was military, the gringo would* was echoing with "Victory, Joe!" The government was military, the *teach the pygmies a few tricks; so jump, jump, hearty lads, to the* GI would tell the refugees a few bawdies; so skip, skip, little brown *banjo on the knee, to the cannons of Dewey, to the national anthem.* brother, to the ukelele, to the blitz of Nimitz, to "Don't Fence Me *While the volunteers squashed the papaya, squeezed the* suso, *grav-* In" while GIs squandered the parity, squired the *señorita,* groveled *eled the roads, clipped the cogon, burned all bravado, Listerined* at the inroads, clippered above the cogonal, banned all *bravos,* peni- *native sarcasm, bullied the carabao, tilled the fertile, ransacked the* cillined native injuries, castrated the bulls, tilted the landscape, aparador, *educated the* ilustrado, *shelled the* palay, *whipped the* redeemed the cabinet, briefed the caretakers, leveled the promenade, *coolie, roasted the* kayumanggi, *watered the flame trees, peeled the* whipped their cream, basted the *kayumanggi,* hosed down the ashes, *citrus, smothered the rice, paid back with corn.*
tickled the Tagalog, refilled with orange juice, smothered the rice,

Oh the monkeys have no tails in Zamboanga. . . .

repaid with acorns.

There'll be a hot time in the old town tonight. . . .

"You are my sunshine, my only sunshine!"

"Don't fence me in!"

"Kilroy was here!"

"Querido?"

Inside room thirteen, her idiosyncratic lover moaned.

Still gently, Tira Colombo tried the knob; the door grated open.

Ba-roooom!

Outside and above, those flying Superfortresses. . . .

Somewhere in the wings, she was singing still—Micaela. Drummed out of the opera, unstifled by unemployment, blinkered from daytime and moonshine, heckled by the gallery of Ojos Verdes, the disconsolate diva had at last capitulated to the cymbals that were her next-door critics. No longer did she wash her laundry in the backyard but stayed obstinately in her grandfather's room, eating her poor Wagnerian heart out because even that kindly Mang Isagani was gone, who had always complimented her da capos, oratorios and glissandos. And what if the Americans came again? They wouldn't reinstate the smoky salons, the coralline boutiques, the consumptive demimondaines of her spiritual era. No, no, La Tosca knew the Messiah would only clog the air with Berlin and Gershwin. But there was too much Brunhild in Micaela for her to surrender so easily—even if one of her octaves had been scratched by laryngitis, like a broken needle on a sturdy record. With inflamed tonsils and *La Traviata* tears, she would go down triumphantly with all the ill-starred lovers of her repertoire. . . .

As now, not even half-suspecting that the Widow Colombo—Bizet's unimaginable Carmen—was ascending toward her debilitated Don Jose for the first time, Micaela the Magnifical (an orchid in her hair) was similarly climbing the scales as Madame Butterfly. Despite clumsy costuming and uninspired lighting in her boudoir, the soprano had been a tempestuous Medea, a sultry Delilah, yet nowhere in her limited engagement at the Colombo palladium had she been more captivating than in those rare gala occasions when she played Cio-Cio-San (all girlish and fluttery), waiting, wailing for her Pinkerton.

There in a stuffed chair willed to her by a departed bassoon player, squinting and snuffling, sang Micaela: while the stairway creaked with assignation, while Amoran dragged a truant ballerina, while Vanoye's blazing van careened off a highway, while Deogracias was aiming his German Luger, while Sergeant Yato holstered his army revolver, while Major Shigura sank to his knees, while the Americans were advancing from Plaridel, while Hidalgo was fading away, while Placido Rey was comforting his inconsolable Victoria, while Tira Colombo . . .

Whispered once more: "*Querido. . . .*"

She saw that he heard yet did not turn.

What was the first sexual act Bienvenido Elan had brought to her? She racked her brain for subtlety, for lightness, for tenderness.

Slowly, she moved closer; but the boards squeaked under her feet. The man in bed showed no sign of hearing or of seeing. Long, long ago, when this had been Bienvenido waiting in bed for her, what had she done? Did the boards grunt? No, for she was lighter then. Had he turned away? No again, for he had heard and seen, had, yes, after all, sent, then waited for her.

Squeak, squeak.

Look up, *castilla,* my Bienvenido of today, she prayed—but he did not.

Listen, *querido,* listen, she said—but did he?

And the bed groaned from her weight; and he at last turned, his jaws locked tight. Seeing him in pain, she almost swooned. Never, never had she wanted to see him so. She reached out a hand for one of his. Cold, cold he was, But breathing.

Hidalgo! Bienvenido?

His eyes—why were they like that?

She bent down to embrace him. Always still gentle, at least hoping she could be.

Yet those eyes, those eyes!

She cradled him in her arms, then rocked him, not gently now, for she was frightened by that look.

Why, Hidalgo? I was Bienvenido's, the architect.

Once more she looked into those eyes.

And yes, she knew; now she did.

He was screaming, screaming.

No! No! No!

Why now that he was dying should he think of flower vases?

Crawling out of the park, right hand clutching his rent stomach, Sergeant Yato made it to the Jones Bridge. He slumped down on a sand sack at the first steel girder. When he lifted his hand off the hole in his side, something soggy and sausage-like fell out and hung there between beltline and hipbone. Must be something he ate, he laughed, and with his bloodied hand pushed the thing back into the hole again. If only he had a safety pin he could close the gaping flesh and scoot back to the Fort on it. Maybe that sniper used dumdum bullets—the hole was so big a cannonball could slip in it. Once more, the sausage peeped out. He jammed it back in again.

On the other side of the bridge, there wasn't much movement, yet he knew those hazy green spots behind that bush couldn't be anything else but Americans. He grunted. For the first time in his life as a soldier, he had dropped his service revolver in the thick of battle. Very stupid, very unprofessional. Whoever shot him was probably laughing his head off.

Zing!

A bullet ricocheted off the steel railing. Just a few diameters above his head. Those green spots were actually two riflemen (he could tell by the gun flashes) separated perhaps from the main force. Luckily, there wasn't a mortar team nearby.

Ping-oooowwww!

More gunnery practice to keep him respectful, he thought, and waited. One, two, three, four—five uneventful minutes. The green spots had either moved to a vantage point or were radioing for something more effective. Anyhow, they didn't rush him. Good thinking, too. Must have sensed that while he had no rifle or even a side arm, he might just have something that could blow them off the bridge. Had to be infantry, he grinned. That was infantry know-how working over there.

Tong!

Present and accounted for but wide off the mark. Just reminders. He didn't pay much attention.

Ten minutes.

Ito's watch was still working. Ah, Ito, Ito, that sad little innocent. The poet had scrawled down what he had seen inside the Major's quarters. Sergeant Yato didn't care a yen about poetry but Ito's last *haiku* was an eye-opener. With such simplicity and directness, Ito had named his killer the night previous to his murder.

Monk turned Medusa
Arose mourning I knew
He would fell me by nightfall.

That sausage came out; was slapped in again with a backhand.

Should he have risked the bayonet on the Major? No, no. Shigura was much too good a swordsman for that.

He lay down between two sacks and gripped the two grenades in each hand. The nausea was lancing his intestines; he was terribly dizzy. If the green spots kept this up any longer, he would surely pass out before he could get any of them. Blood had caked on his legs; the hole was opening up like old Fuji. Dizzy, dizzy, dizzy. He spat, and it was blood.

Flower vase, flower vase.

Ha! *That* was a good clout. Now he focused on it: Colombo house, evening, room thirteen, woman (dark eyes, long hair) nude in a cot. He had somehow bullied himself into the boardinghouse, had somehow blundered into that room. And there she was, sleeping. Seeing her so vulnerable (those ankles, those thighs, that . . .), he had, without even stopping to think, stripped. As though drugged, he had thrown boots, leggings, trousers, shorts, all around him and was . . . conscious again (he still could not place how much later), naked in the patio, with a smashed flower vase in his lap. Upstairs in the Colombo house, a boy was giggling, somebody was singing; and down on the road came the tap-tap-tapping of a cane. He had had no time to look for his clothes and had slithered away into the night, a cracked pot covering his genitals.

Zing! Tunk! Zing!

They were charging him now. Yes, the green spots had only waited for reinforcements, which this very minute were flanking the original two with rapid fire.

Sergeant Yato gave that sausage a final elbow jab, sprang up, dashed for the squad running toward him from the other side of the bridge, disregarded whatever it was they were yelling to him (who spoke no English), unpinned the grenades with his teeth, never did get to count just how many green spots he got as he exploded at thirty mph, and was now ground into a firecracker stew, splashing down into the eventide of Pasig River without having known who had crowned him with that vase that vile, bare-assed stupid night. . . .

Verdi was too saccharine; Wagner, too savage. It was left to Puccini to oversee and underplay—the overlooked and the unloved.

That throat was itching; the chest was overdrawn. But not yet, not yet. Micaela hurled thunderbolts and tremolos, ceding not a note to a B-29 in the sky or to the Kempetai pounding the streets.

Lei the lovers.

Petal all passion.

Garlanded thus, the world was tolerable.

If she did not sing, sighed Micaela, whose voice weighed more in the heart than in the ear, Cio-Cio-San would not exist in Ojos Verdes. And perhaps all the Pinkertons in the Pacific would never have been born, would never come, even in betrayal.

Seated like Queen Isabella in the stuffed chair, she reigned for a thousand and one scales: dubbing knights out of mourning drunks; siring nobles from bloated bastards; banishing the uncouth, the philistine, the tone-deaf.

All for love of lovers: abandoned, dispossessed, extradited, unrequited; lovers laid low by levity, slighted by negligence, injured by indifference, slain by stupidity. Flies, snails, mosquitoes, termites, roaches and men: bugs, mollusks and mortals—lovers nonetheless. For whom perhaps, because they made noises for attention, Micaela—who revered all forms of life that amplified their lovings—lovingly sang. From the stuffed chair their accumulative antennae reported back to her that they were indeed all the Pinkertons and Cio-Cio-Sans of passacaglia and fact, and that she was, by virtue of a thousand arias rendered above and beyond the call of divas—their valiant *apasionata.*

In the wings, Madame Butterfly flew again. . . .

No!

She knew he said. By his eyes. From the total rejection of his body. Screaming, screaming, screaming he was—all lockjawed and mute but all thunder in the bed.

No!

Tira Colombo pinioned the arms on the chest, wedging her own large hand between his thighs. She had lost all of B.E.'s tenderness now.

Submerged in tears and tetanus, Hidalgo de Anuncio yelled and flailed with neither sound nor motion. The landlady just giggled, just harnessed him there like an idiot.

No!

No time for gentleness, nor for cooings and such. Slavering, gasping, stripped to her panties, dropping her improvised breast, Mrs. Colombo took out his penis.

Boom!

The Americans were coming.

Boom!

Tira tried slapping it alive.

Boom!

Had it in her fist now.

Boom!

Still wouldn't stand.

Boom!

Let it go; licking furiously now.

Boom!

Her tongue couldn't do it either.

Boom!

Neither could her mouth.

Boom!

Those Castillian eyesores: pleading, pleading.

Boom! Boom!

Perhaps a little loving bite?

Boom! Boom! Boom!

The head came off; a ligament stuck in her incisor left.

Whooooooooooooooooooooooooooooooooooooooooooooooooooom!

Went down the Colombo house. Felled by American artillery. Micaela was the last to go but still she frittered, fluttered, sang to distraction. Seven months later, a clean-up detail would comb through the wreckage to unearth: one incredibly intact pair of Spanish *cojones* (as though left in preservatives), a soprano's dehydrated tonsils (to be mistaken for pig's liver), and a woman's bacterial breast (siliconed with worms). . . .

[36]

"THE U.S. DRIVE TOWARD MANILA," lectured Placido Rey in his history class half a year later, "commenced February first with the 37th Division's unopposed pickup of Calumpit . . . it advanced southeast to Malolos. After a minor skirmish, it secured Plaridel and the Angat River site. On February 2, 12:00 P.M., a motorized column of the 37th Division took Malolos via Highway 3; another motorized unit flanked southeast on Highway 5 from Plaridel. Enemy resistance en route was scattered, nominal. By left flank on February first, the 1st Cavalry Division advanced south from Guimba, fording Pampanga River at Cabanatuan. Pincer contact was established by February 2, 12:00 P.M. between the 1st Cavalry Division and the 37th Division at Plaridel, with both outfits moving southeast, eventually taking Santa Maria. . . ."

Manilans stepped out of their houses to look at their burning city. Menfolk scurried from intersection to inferno and back again, rallying then running down each other. They seemed to be chasing after or escaping from, whatever it was, nobody knew, except that it was here, there, everywhere. Carts obstructed the avenues, were milling toward the bridges. It was: *Febrero! Febrero!* chanted rifle-bearing patriots, and MacArthur was coming, coming! Amoran had tied the girl with a sash on his back and found themselves running with the horde. Still inconsolable, she had been overwrought and screeching since deserting her Hidalgo and had thrice been only silenced with blows; afterwards, bound on the boy's spine. Amoran told her that they were out to get meat: and there it was, going down in smoke. Weaponed, khaki-uniformed Filipinos were initiating some sort of *kusina* counteroffensive by lobbing flares into building windows, hollering out lilting melodies and grunty legatos which turned out to be house codes marked for demolition. *"Ho-ho, isa! Ho-ho, ho-ho, dalawa! Ho-ho-ho-ho, tatlo!" Sssshboooom!*

"January thirty-first: To box in the Japanese troops in northern Luzon, the I Corps of the Sixth Army continued toward San Jose, Nueva Ecija, in a linked mass offensive toward the Cabanatuan-Bongabon-Rizal zone. The 20th Infantry of the 6th Division encountered heavy fire at Muñoz and circled northeast along the Guimba–San Jose road, there driving against concentrated enemy resistance in the southern tip of the town where medium tanks were ingeniously dug in as pillboxes, with a support of infantry machine gun and light artillery. Came February 2, 12:00 P.M., and the 20th Infantry had still not gained a foothold in Muñoz. . . ."

A Japanese tank was cranking near a downtown theatre; someone in a corduroy jacket rolled a grenade in its path. Nothing happened. A cocky ex-jockey who seemed to be nursing a truncated mortar fired and the theatre's marquee collapsed, conked out the tank. Two urchins holding cans of floor wax clambered up to the tank turret and waited patiently; nothing came out the lid. A block away, about twenty-five looters were converging on a cold store. A man smoking a pipe fondled the aluminum handle of a refrigerator, tittered, and pulled it open. He was blown up in front of everybody and salady pieces of his body dressed the cold ham heaped inside the freezer. There were twelve other refrigerators aligned on the east wing of the store, but no one came near them now and in a minute they were outside again broadcasting on megaphones a terrible warning to the populace: the Japanese had mined every piece of meat in Manila! Upstreet, they were still shooting it out with side arms, whoever they were, self-appointed policemen with silvery emblems pinned on their lapels, or children and elders with slingshots and sharpened copper spoons. Since this was the northern part of Manila, they met very few Japanese soldiers—if any. Which was quite frustrating, to say the least. A man who had been circling around from street to street and calling out his wife's name blundered into that first cold store, and forgetting about his lost love, suddenly confronted with plenty, started opening refrigerator doors in a wild, gleeful dash. He had reached the fourth door before he exploded.

"After a vicious battle, the 25th Division captured Umigan, then turned southeast toward Lubao, where it was stopped by pockets of resistance on February 2, 12:00 P.M. Meanwhile, the 32nd Division had crossed the Agoo River, occupied Tayug without firing a shot, then secured San Nicolas. Not much later, it had flushed out the Japs from the Natividad–San Nicolas–Tayug triangle, and seized Santa Maria. On the north flank, the army's 43rd Division was rapidly consolidating its positions. . . ."

In the garment factories, looters were scrambling for position. It was in this vicinity that Amoran, with the girl tied screaming to his back, decided to make a stand. A nightwatchman had dug up a cache of coins. A youth who chewed endlessly on bubble gum he had scraped out of a jar from one of the pilfered shops, was scooping up fistfuls of silver; was merrily casting them into a ditch; and it seemed all the city's children and most of its adults fell on their knees to restore their national treasury. Twice, Amoran palmed about six coins but a wave of wretches would ride him piggyback and wrestle him to the cement. The girl lashed out with hands, feet, and bit at scabby faces. But they backhanded and punched her, then choked her from behind the boy's shoulders with yards and yards of imported wool. One particular lad tried to hang her but somehow could not extricate her from Amoran, who, thrown to a corner by the men, saw a length of wood, picked it up and clubbed anyone he saw. They let the back-fighter go and were concentrating anew on Amoran when the girl, still clutching her coins, reared up again from her precarious saddle and pulled at their hair. The armed, uniformed patriots reappeared, lusting for Japanese. Somebody came up with a map of Greater Manila, coupled with specific instructions; the vigilantes roared away; the impromptu police had by this time detoured all the bridges and were agitating for the banks. *Ba-doooommmm!* Another refrigerator door. Amoran dunked two bigger boys into an ash puddle; the girl jabbed her long fingernails into an elder's eyes. A vagrant with a flag, no one could tell whose, hauled off the national cache and vanished inside an alley. It was a full ten minutes before any of them noticed. They ran, ran, ran; spotted him once more. Someone threw a stove at him. But as he sidestepped a fire hydrant, two bearded men struck him down with hunting knives. The children swooped around the ambushers, who stabbed them too; and two, three, four, fell, wounded, dying, dead. Somebody bleeding tumbled out of uncrated cordage, sped to a bridge, then to other bridges, and before the two bearded men could get away, the uniformed patriots showed up again and mowed them down: systematically, without fuss. Temporarily sated, the guns and the uniforms left again, still scouting for Japanese. *Whoom!* one, *whooom!* two, *whoooom!* three moviehouses emitted pulverized celluloid and crystal; streets and mostly stores that were mined were erupting; water was spouting out from everywhere; streetcar rails had been torn up, mangled by explosions; the cache with the Commonwealth coins lay under a Japanese helmet with a handful of silver coins in it, but now all the refrigerator doors had been opened and detonated and the maelstrom was pushing back to the cold stores again. Two policemen now confiscated the remaining coins in a ***buri*** basket; the children were left strangling one another. Downstreet, Filipino and American flags cascaded out of windows; more firing came. The uniforms and the guns still not finding their enemy, liberated a textile store believed to have been a Japanese franchise. As the children looted each other, the policemen had a falling out and broke their cordon. The women, who were more orderly, were trying to put out the smaller fires along the *avenida.* With thirteen silver coins and a battered guitar between them, Amoran (the girl saddled like a papoose on his back) ran up and down the Escolta trying to escape the ambiguous uniforms and the sniper guns, the wild panting men, the strange policemen, the women with the water pails, but mostly, the beehive children. An old woman pushing a cart took out a can of gasoline and lit it, razing a whole block where two military houses stood ransacked from door to door. A platoon of girls squared up against a squad of boys and howled past with a crowbar between them, headed, it seemed, for the toy stores. A collage of guns and uniforms tangled in the street to squeal it out with whoever it was they fought whenever they passed upstreet. In all this time, no one had seen a single American liberator—or even a Japanese defender. If the Japs were defending the south, then where were the invaders? All around and all over it seemed, invisible yet audible. Guerrillas-come-lately and underground registrants of dubious rank and stripe trooped down the Avenida Rizal from Azcarraga to Binondo, and could not find a hook-up; rattling, quaking, burning as it was, Manila appeared to be invaded by civilians.

"January thirtieth: The XI Corps was driving toward Subic, Olongapo, and occupied Grande Island. To narrow down opposition along the Bataan Peninsula, the XI Corps headed east on Highway 7, from there to Dinalupihan, which resulted in the 38th Division's battle for possession of Zig-Zag. All the U.S. timetables were pluperfect, synchronized to the last second—as can be seen by the almost simultaneous spearheads and arrivals. Nowhere is this better proven than by the 1st Cavalry Division's drive toward Santa Maria for the Novaliches watershed area, reaching Grace Park by 6:35 P.M., February third; a mileage effort reading at one hundred in less than three days. And two days later, that Division liberated the University of Santo Tomás. At precisely 8:30 P.M., February third, the Battling Basic, a light tank of the 44th Tank Battalion, rammed down a front gate of the University compound. The place was pitch-dark; Japanese guards were firing from their concealed posts. Behind Battling Basic trooped in an American column, mowing down all but one of sixty-three Japanese soldiers barricaded in the Education Building. In all, 3,521 Allied prisoners and other internees were freed. The previous afternoon, an American Piper Cub had flown low over the prison camp and dropped something. When the internees retrieved the object, it turned out to be a pair of aviator's goggles with a note attached: "Roll out the barrel. Santa Claus will be coming Sunday or Monday." February fourth: The 34th Division captured Bilibid Prison with its 1,024 Allied prisoners. Sunday, 8:30 P.M.—General Douglas MacArthur ambled into the UST compound. . . ."

Finally, Amoran and the girl stumbled into a burning pagoda; flung themselves onto its muddied marble, and for a while, it was difficult to tell who of them was carrying the other for that one bound to the other seemed to feel the weight even more. She clawed at reed, rock and split masonry; and all her fingernails broke as she murmured prayers that sounded like curses so that her tears scratched the earth; even while she looked up again, she blamed Hidalgo and the universe of man with a voice softer than sleep, louder than nightmare before the boy who could not lock his ears, only shut his eyes as she mourned to a burning city.

"Oh, Molave. . . ."

CORPORAL JACK DANIELS (yep; he had often been kidded about the name) was squatting on the grass, oiling his M-1, when this really ugly kid with a six-stringed guitar strapped on his back trotted along ("Victory, Joe!"). Corporal Daniels' outfit had just camped down on Calabash Road smack in a church courtyard. Chow was being served; the last of the refugees had drifted away, thumbing happily through cadged chocolate wrappers and peppermint tinfoil. This boy had lingered, much to the men's distress, with a letter in his hand.

Himself brother to four brats (how he missed them now!), Corporal Daniels had parted gladly with a can of salmon and a wad of gum. In gratitude the boy had left the soldier his crumpled letter, which—because it was hastily scrawled—the Corporal could not make heads or tails of. When he could at last read it in a better light back at the Snack Bar lean-to, Corporal Daniels—and this time having a harder time with its theme than with its penmanship—still could not understand the letter. With a mild oath the GI had repaired to his cot, and by flashlight decided to write his Mom ("Crazy about your fudge . . .") and his girl Irene (". . . so pucker up, honey; will be home before your lipstick is dry!"); but could not sleep a wink all that night. In the morning, he had seen that ugly boy again, pumped him with questions concerning the letter; came away from the interview with a knot of fresh vegetables and the promise of—*sssh!*—a girl somewhere in a *cementerio*.

Still perturbed, and taking out that letter again, Corporal Daniels overcame a long-standing prejudice and had sought out his CO, only to be informed that the man was out on a "social errand." This was how matters stood when Corporal Daniels bumped into the chaplain.

They started with baseball, of course. The chaplain, bespectacled, carrot-skinned, was in the know and traded major-league batting averages as though he had grown up in baseball parks all over the States. Maybe he had too; Corporal Daniels never did find out. Also, Preach was a New Dealer from way back, with quite an updated vocabulary touching on anything Roosevelt. What else? Yes, they'd had a regular bull on: beer (nothing could beat the Milwaukee brand!), trout fishing ("Any big catch's gotta respect you first!"), the miracle of penicillin ("straight from God's dispensary"), Joe Louis ("he's just got to be the greatest ever. . . ."). Jesus Christ the Catholic came later, and then, not directly, but invariably of a warm, somehow detempled variety. They did not talk war at all. On a somewhat curving pitch, Corporal Daniels finally alluded to the letter. The good chaplain exhaled—his companion noted, with relief—and asked what the boy's problem was. All very warm and comradely, naturally. Sharing a lukewarm Coke, they sat down on a tree stump and Corporal Daniels took out the letter and explained its background. Smiling warmly still, the chaplain opened the crumpled paper and read.

> When she makes her Coming-out party at eighty, I'd like to be there. Here she comes, the cocoon of a century: today's butterfly, tomorrow's dragonfly. The gates open wonderingly like a young man's eyes; the flower blooms and they'll have to take out their Tagalog-Made-Easy in seven continents. "How is it that I didn't see you in the army kitchen?" they ask. Do I need a revolution to lure you out of the quonset? But neither Brooklyn's bravado nor the promise of New York

will take you out of the corn fields. If these were the old days they would unroll the carpet under your feet; lave you with laurels. Now, they just whistle at you. Behold, how she unfolds!

Well, at long last, the die is cast; dawn settles on the lawn. Our pawn comes into its own, and in the crowd, suddenly the shroud is lifted. Nobody yawns; there is only this little moan. Suddenly she rises out of her crisis, the brave little bully like a coolie. The blades dare not come on boots and swagger. She walks among them, the pure, prim debutante, crowned princess of the Brown Soiree, the languid Miss Native coming out of the locomotive. Is it sunset? Is it sunrise? What is it, really? But no matter, she has made her move. The backwoods queen has cornered the playboy king and now all the horsemen have been sidetracked into the gulch; all the bishops have been defrocked; all the rookies have been exiled. And now that the daffodil has climbed out to touch the sun, let us kill the weeds in the natural garden!

"What do you make of it, Chaplain?"

"I'm not sure, son."

"Do you think it's some kind of code?"

"Could be. We'll have to get the experts work on it."

"It's funny, is all."

"Did the boy say he wrote it?"

"Nope. Said some guy called . . . now let me get this name right—yeah, some fellow by the name of Bah-noi-heah wrote it."

"Is that Japanese by any chance?"

"Dunno."

"Hmm."

"Think I should turn this over to GHQ?"

"Seems like a good idea."

"Maybe I'm nuts, but it sure sounds fishy to me."

"Well, it could be one of the natives just practicing his English."

"Doesn't sound American at all, that's what I'm saying."

"Yes, we can't be too careful in this war."

"Sure, I figure it's got to be a secret message, you know? Like a password maybe."

"That makes sense."
"You think I should report it then?"
"Play it safe, I always say."
"It's funny, is all."

Epilogue

HE HAD BEGUN TO ACHE FOR HER.

Longed to speak to her, to somehow affix to her woebegone eyes the cicatrix of his own vision. Yet how could it be if one had to address such a class as this? History indeed! Permitting himself the drollery of recitation, he plodded through the miasma and minutiae of assorted facts. What to her had been the magenta skies of indiscriminate shelling, he translated—abetted by ruthless monotones and a firm grasp of diction—into a patchwork of bland reportage. To break the felicity of narrative, to stray one guilty eye on that quite improbable pupil—she of the back-row bougainvillea—was to invite a most unshakable censure.

Typical of man's enduring cannibalism, reflected Placido Rey with mounting queasiness, was to serve homogenized facts to those who had not yet recovered from their own unspoken (unspeakable) black suppers. As this hodgepodge disguised as curriculum led to higher perjury. . . .

Facts webbed in Teacher Rey's mind, though in his inner eye, their color was amber; in there facts roved and raged with the alluvial deposits of the Pasig Estuary: a sputum of citron, burst canisters, shuttled and shambled Intramuros, an ectoplasm of motheroids and childlings, boat prows carrioned with decapitulates, cantilevered corpses plumed with embers, castaways rotting on tripods—a shoal of flesh commingling and corroding, deliverer and dissected intersecting and interminable: all reflected in her eyes, if one gazed long enough into them—as he did, as he always would, now. Being Placido Rey, he could not invert history's prodigality; and yet, like a ventriloquist deprived of a dummy, he could not resist playing the rhetorician.

Facts: she was wounded, scarred by them (he could see); still, he presumed and persevered as he orchestrated deeper into superficiality.

Were a choice open to him, he would close in on this girl who, perhaps because it was not in her nature, did not mock him in her silence.

Facts, facts, facts.

Placido Rey was their natural factotum; with them he was an exquisite arranger, a meticulous portraitist, a nimble deployer. He could assimilate, redeem, categorize and even embellish on them at will.

A gust of wind blew her hair (he saw) and once more he shuddered at her frank look.

Had she eaten today?

Placido Rey slapped his paunch, just three hours old from a breakfast of powdered egg, two slabs of white American *pan,* a helping of sardines—plus strong Virginia tobacco from the quartermaster. Ah, K rations, more facts. The estimable teacher was in good graces with the Legarda Elementary School U.S. encampment and thereby had been presented—subject to his disposal—crates of goodies fresh from the PX. Such bounty, it was casually hinted, to be his weekly emolument as liaison officer between the occupation forces and the citizens of Manila. Other faculty members of the Galas High School had been similarly repatriated. The principal himself (who had always doubted the *americanos* would ever return) was ferreted back and forth in a jeep, chauffered by an affable private from Hoboken, New Jersey. Two male teachers were the paid tourist guides of several WAC lieutenants who were writing a series of articles ("Manila Revisited"), to be illustrated, it was hoped, by a Europe-based Bill Mauldin—all for *Yank* magazine. At least three other degree holders were on the *plantilla* as English teachers. And, Placido Rey heard, four part-time female instructors were stepping out regularly on dates with AFWESPAC colonels.

Grinning, Placido Rey rubbed his middle contentedly. What was for dinner? He would certainly hate missing that Saturday night salami ("And all the powdered juice you can drink!") at the officers' barracks.

"Pay attention now," he barked, and that mask of obedience settled back into place inside the classroom.

She was officially listed in his army notebook—a name probably given her by Molave Amoran. And whose hands touched her now?

Though not yet a woman (as which of these borderline cases was not yet advancing from puberty to lasciviousness?), she was no longer just a girl. That chest had matured into a bosom; those legs that must have been a tomboy's once were full thighs now. Some of her female classmates (and not infrequently, a few boys too) disappeared after recess and, as rumored around the compound, were weaned from arithmetic by smooth white talk and bubble gum. Mothers descended on the principal with complaints ("My Felipa didn't come home last night," or "Teresa came home only this morning!"), before being gently shooed out again with sage counsel. Still another parent would protest: "What's wrong with my Nenita—why *don't* they take her out?"

And who took *her* out?

Private? Corporal? Sergeant? Or would she start at the top?

She had been comely; but she was lovely today. Where she had been pale, a complexion had arrived; once she was almost as grubby as that Molave—no more. She had a Moslem's dark eyes; long hair of an Amorsolo model. To Placido Rey, her beauty had long been a myth: it was a fact now.

And who would she love?

If indeed she was *inamorata* to De Anuncio; *geisha* to Shigura.

Without knowing why, Placido Rey quavered.

Facts, facts, facts.

His pupils listened attentively.

But he found himself studying her now, even more than before. Seeing to it that she was present each day, and missing her mortally if she was not. She flitted in and out of his classroom with customary languidness; never seeming to pay attention, answering obliquely when questioned, sitting there in impenetrable detachment, letting the teacher's lackluster summations pass through her like a lymphatic wind; then rising, deserting him once more with no assurance that she would be back. Placido Rey took his seat five days of every week, mechanically intoning the roll call, daring not to look up from his table lest that one overt act dissolve that particular voice, cancel that special presence. At recess, he was wont to stand by the window, trying to sort her out from that strident group by the fountain. Sometimes, and very much against his will, he would follow her after dismissal: only for a while, though, to reassure himself that she was still there—somewhere. As he did, his head buzzed with reprimands. He was, after all, not the stuff Don Juans were made of. Yet she had become a habit; not in the way a wife became one—but rather in that timorous way one could still indulge in: innocently, with no possessive designs, without even a flicker of lust.

Such remorse, such anguish drove Placido Rey into seclusion. Weeks on end, he would absent himself from class and all his scholarly duties at the Galas High School. Since there were very few qualified instructors to go around—especially one with such formidable connections as Mr. Rey—the board of directors only rewarded this obvious dereliction with a promotion, promise of a retirement pension, a silver plaque (for past services rendered) and a commemorative bust in the Teachers' Memorial Union.

The sirens could have sung themselves hoarse: the unbribable Mr. Rey held his fortress and repulsed all their academic blandishments. Letters of commendation were fired off to the Rey Redoubt like flares; all were extinguished by the Rey Resistance; parleys were dispatched for a Rey Rapprochement, and were spurned by the Rey Reconnaissance. American brass tried a rearguard action (more PX tithes)—with no luck. Schoolchildren, irrepressible and unmusical, scaled his vines and serenaded his window.

"Pla-ci-do! Pla-ci-do! Pla-ci-do!"

Mr. Aloof cut down the beanstalk.

So they left him alone at last—for lost. And perhaps he was. For closeted in his modest library, removed from his own squalling children, a bed away from his ailing Victoria, Placido Rey, in an attempt to exorcise his current fixation, plunged furiously into his journal on Ojos Verdes. On ruled, yellow tablet paper, with a jug of tea and no tobacco, he wrote his blood pressure high and low with all the figures of speech at his command; carving curlicues out of a vernacular that defied his saluations, his emendations, his immolations; recanting, reviling, demythologizing a legato of facts; reconstructing with vicarious military acumen every facet that had engendered and ennobled Intramuros—all with a historian's unjaundiced eye. But after he had sipped his sugarless, creamless cold tea, after he had missed his pipe and its good handout American tobacco, after he had perused his Dickensian notes, he would see there on pages crammed with insipid objectivity and ornate vernacular, the footprint of the marginal one, the dark Moslem eyes of the Girl he had followed in middle-age passion—stuck between columns of verbiage; somehow leaked unobserved in redundant passages about invasions; distilled like a single tear among cremated gazebos; engraved between crevasses of concrete like regrafted plumage from a phoenix regressing into or ripening from ashes. More wounding than finding the girl within the loins of his all-male epic was being accosted by that American Leatherneck at school who had blurted: "Gee, would I like to get that knockout in my bunk . . . y'know, that girlie in your back row—what's-her-name?"

So, Maria. . . .

He did not, could never divulge to that soldier or others like him her name; not a syllable of it, he swore. Perhaps that soldier or others like him would linger for a millennia, to inquire about the same, even give her another. All this was immaterial—incontrovertible?—to Placido Rey, who, in imminent dissipation, was beginning to suspect, with a terror and lucidity reserved sometimes for the criminally insane, that only blasphemy could sanctify in the end. And for whom did she exist, to whom would she belong? Neither a Hidalgo nor a Shigura, given all time and giving back tyranny, would leave one mark on her that she would not somehow shed like a molting skin—being as she was that most irreducible grade of human a snake ever turned into. Thus sultana of and subject to inquisition—her innocence decreed it; her *nom de plume* deflected it—she would hound

Manila, followed by Molave: durable in diminuendo, dispersing, describing her beauty with patronymic hands that still touched the fingertips of gloaming lamented clowns, even if everybody else only spoke, never saw or heard, therefore never understood the loneliness of the cicadas. As long as she was a dryad among demons on pontoon bridges, as long as she was a decibel in the drum roll of the U.S. Cavalry, as long as she was a cricket in the crusts of Intramuros, as long as she was a cedilla in Placido Rey's anguished cantatas—and as long as she was Mandarin eyes and Malayan hair among benzedrine masks and blond cornucopia, he would—hopefully—never again (but never) breathe her name to another living soul.

(Ay, Maria Alma. . . .)